TO LOVE THE DRAGON KING

DRAGONS OF IVRIA
BOOK ONE

ANTONIA AQUILANTE

CHAPTER 1

The high gray stone walls of Castle Grau were bleak against the slate-colored clouds blanketing the sky. Sascha shivered and huddled deeper into his fur-trimmed cloak, despite knowing the reaction hadn't been entirely—or even mostly—caused by the raw chill in the air. His first sight of the place he would live for the next several years made him wish to be anywhere else.

But he couldn't stop staring out the carriage window as they approached the building. He schooled his features carefully into the serene mask he'd practiced for long hours until he could hold onto it even if everything inside him quaked, as it did now. Deliberately forced his breathing to even out. Best to prepare himself when he was alone, Lord Jannik's man of business having chosen to ride up with the driver the whole journey from Sascha's family home where the man had retrieved him and turned over the contractual payment to his parents. It had made for a long and lonely trip—all day yesterday and overnight in the carriage—but Sascha wouldn't have chosen the company of the other man anyway.

He wouldn't have chosen any of the circumstances for this

journey, and the manner in which it was being made—not to mention the sight of its endpoint—was not helping Sascha hold on to any hope that this portion of his life would be good. And hope was something he'd determinedly clung to since his parents had told him of the contract they'd signed, making him Lord Jannik's concubine.

The carriage rattled over the cobblestones of the road leading to the castle's imposing front doors and slowed to a stop behind a second carriage. There was a flurry of activity around it, as servants loaded and secured baggage. Was Lord Jannik leaving with Sascha arriving today?

The door beside him was pulled open abruptly. The stern-faced man of business—what was his name?—stood there, looking particular dour.

"We're here." He didn't offer assistance or wait for Sascha to climb out before walking away. Concubines were supposed to have status and respect on par with that of spouses—both traditionally and contractually. Sascha hadn't been treated that way so far.

He took a long, slow breath, searching for calm despite the sick roiling in his stomach. Then, gathering his cloak and his dignity around him, he stepped down from the carriage. Another couple of servants were coming for his trunk, and he thanked them, receiving nods in return. Moving away from the carriage, he surveyed his surroundings. The castle looked no less forbidding up close, but perhaps the place would be more pleasant in spring. Late winter meant bare trees and no flowers or color anywhere. Even the snow—something Sascha usually saw the beauty in—didn't help.

A young woman about Sascha's age hurried through the castle doors. Her hair shone gold in the weak sunlight before she flipped the hood of her green cloak up to cover it. She was halfway to the carriages before she stopped abruptly, her gaze landing on Sascha. Her rosebud lips turned down in a brief frown. When she moved again, it was in his direction.

He straightened his spine against the fine tremors moving through him and waited, watching her approach.

She flicked her gaze over him briefly once she stopped in front of him. "So you're my father's new concubine?"

"If your father is Lord Jannik, then yes. I'm Sascha of Clan Sapfir."

If anything, she looked more troubled. "I can't say you'll like it here and mean it. I'm grateful my marriage is getting me away, and I have no idea what it will be like. I can only wish you good luck."

Sascha blinked at her, shock robbing him of words.

"Lady Triana." The stern voice had them both looking toward the man of business. "It's time for you to go."

Triana nodded regally, but she turned back to Sascha instead of moving toward her waiting carriage. When she spoke again, her voice was barely a whisper. "My father's man of business is horrible, but the housekeeper and the maids and kitchen staff are all kind and helpful. Take care of yourself."

He took the hand she held out to him, let her squeeze his nerveless fingers. "Thank you. You take care of yourself as well."

With a brisk nod to him, she moved away, sailing past the glowering man of business—Sascha had been told his name, hadn't he?—to the carriage where a footman assisted her inside. The driver got the horses moving immediately, and Triana was on her way to an uncertain future...but one she'd rather confront than the past she'd left here. What was Sascha walking into?

"You need to go inside." The man's clipped tone drew Sascha's attention once more. "You don't want to keep Lord Jannik waiting."

Sascha raised his chin a fraction in an effort to appear calm and dignified. "Of course."

Heart beating wildly, he concentrated on his breathing, on taking measured, graceful steps across the stones and through the open door. His heels clacked loudly on the marble floor, the sound echoing in the large entry hall. He almost flinched at the noise, but servants still hurried around in the wake of his arrival and the departure of the daughter of the house and the stern-faced man had followed him inside—Sascha refused to show such weakness in front of them.

His resolve didn't stop him from jumping when a voice bellowed from deeper in the castle. It didn't stop his hands from trembling when he realized the owner of the bellowing voice was coming closer. And that, from the reaction of the staff, the bellower had to be Lord Jannik. No one had taken Sascha's cloak, so he clenched his gloved hands together beneath it and strove to regain his tattered self-possession as he was left alone in the center of the hall, the servants scattering, the man of business halting several feet away from him.

Sascha's first sight of Jannik did not inspire calm—nor did it inspire feelings like desire or infatuation or even interest, and so he let go of any dream of such things he might've had. No, the man who strode into the hall inspired nothing but fear. Physically, he wasn't imposing. His build was average, and he was older than Sascha's father. Gray streaked his thick blond hair. But an aura of menace surrounded him. His eyes were hard and cold, his lips set in a mean twist. His movements were sharp and authoritative. This man was in complete control of his household, of his affairs, of all he considered his—and his control would not be kind or fair.

Sascha understood Triana's warning now.

His breathing had sped up and he focused once more on slowing it.

Had his parents known what they were sending—selling—Sascha into? They couldn't have. No matter how attractive the contact and connection to a prominent family, they wouldn't have gone through with it if they'd had any idea of the man they were giving him to. Sascha knew well his role in the family—like that of his sisters—was to make the most advantageous match possible, whether as spouse or concubine, and he'd accepted it long ago. But did the match have to be this one?

Lord Jannik stopped in front of Sascha and scrutinized him head to toe from his position a half a head taller. Sascha had never been so glad for the enveloping cover of his cloak as that gaze slithered over him.

"Well," Lord Jannik said finally, "your face is as exquisite as they told me. Let's hope the rest of you is as well."

Sascha's lips parted, but his mind was blank. He could think of nothing to say in response to that greeting.

Lord Jannik didn't seem to expect a reply. He turned to his man of business. "Hannes, I need to see you in my study for a few moments." He directed his next words and his hard gaze back to Sascha. "While I'm in my meeting, you will go upstairs and bathe. No need to dress after. I want a good look at you, and as long as you please me, more than that."

Sascha still couldn't seem to conjure a reply, but he gasped when Lord Jannik reached out and gripped his chin firmly.

"Don't think to keep me waiting, little Sascha. You're mine now to do with as I will, and you won't like the consequences if you disobey." He pressed a hard kiss to Sascha's closed lips, then released him as abruptly as he'd grabbed him. "A maid will show you up."

He turned and strode away. Hannes followed on his heels, not sparing a look for Sascha.

Sascha stood for a moment and trembled, his cheeks burning fiery hot. Waves of alternating fear and dread and embarrassment crashed through him, leaving him hot then cold in succession. He was just supposed to go upstairs and... And Lord Jannik had seen fit to order him to his bed in front of his man of business and several servants, and now all of them knew...

And Sascha was just supposed to go whether he wanted to or not, and let Lord Jannik do as he pleased with him. This wasn't how it was supposed to be. A concubine was supposed to be treated with respect, and the legal standing they deserved. He wasn't supposed to be ordered about and threatened. He wasn't supposed to be a possession.

Apparently, none of that mattered in Lord Jannik's domain.

Inside his head, he was screaming, wailing questions about what his parents knew. Surely they would've looked into anyone making an offer for one of them? Surely they would've cared? What could they have gotten out of this arrangement that was important enough to put Sascha through this? It couldn't have only been the money, could it? What did Lord Jannik have to offer that was so important?

"Sir?"

The quiet voice startled Sascha so much he jumped again, but he didn't have the capacity for more embarrassment. His vision refused to focus, spinning and twisting and blurring, but, as best he could, he brought his attention to the young maid in front of him.

She bobbed a quick curtsy when she had his attention. "Your things are being brought to your bedchamber. I can show you upstairs if you're ready, sir?"

Unspoken was that he'd better be, and her eyes were filled with so much sympathy Sascha wanted to weep.

"Yes, thank you." He didn't manage a smile for her— couldn't—but he refused to be anything but polite to the staff, especially when they were being kind to him.

She turned and made for the sweeping stone staircase at the other end of the room, and Sascha forced himself to move, to follow. He fisted his hands in the folds of his cloak to stop their shaking and willed himself to steadiness as he slowly climbed the stairs behind her. Something pushed him to move faster, cold dread of what could happen if he wasn't exactly where Lord Jannik wanted him when he arrived, but if he moved any faster in his state, he'd tumble down the stairs.

He needed to pull himself together. He was stronger than this.

Wasn't he?

As he took the last step to the landing halfway up, he stopped abruptly and frowned. "Do you hear that?"

"Sir?" The maid stopped and turned back to face him. Worry and impatience lurked in her eyes, but instead of saying anything, she frowned too.

It was wings. The sound of many large wings beating at the air, flying closer. Landing, from the sounds in the courtyard outside. Then shouting.

The doors to the entry hall burst open, and the room was flooded by soldiers wearing the uniform of the king. Someone was shouting orders, more than one someone. Sascha froze for an instant, then grabbed the maid and dragged her down with him. He huddled on the floor with the teary-eyed girl, scared and confused and unable to even speculate as to what was happening now.

LYSANDER STRODE into Jannik's home—his home for the time being, anyway—and surveyed the situation. His soldiers had fanned out at the direction of Alan, Lysander's cousin and commander of the royal forces, who was still issuing orders from the center of the room. The only others present were several servants in the badge of Jannik's household, but none were fighting or seemed inclined to do so.

"Are you certain you should've come inside already, Your Majesty?" came a respectful voice from behind him. "Perhaps you should wait until Jannik and his family are found and the castle is secured?"

Kirill—and Alan too—would've preferred he'd waited at Wyndward for Jannik to be brought to him. Lysander didn't agree. He wanted to be part of this—and he wanted to see the castle that was now his.

Traitors forfeited their property to the crown, after all.

"The commander seems to have the situation well in hand."

Someone sighed softly behind him, the sound almost inaudible—and probably meant to be—among the noise echoing in the room. Likely Kirill, but Romilly was behind him too. Neither was a soldier or fighter, but they were two of his best negotiators and diplomats and they had discovered the treasonous plot that brought them here today. They were also both leaving Ivria soon, and though they would be well placed, he would be sad to lose them here. But he would use their skills and minds for the time they remained in Ivria.

The soldiers were imposing order rapidly, herding frightened but cooperating servants in one direction, coming and going with reports for Alan. Faint sounds of conflict came from somewhere beyond the entry hall, and Alan dispatched more soldiers in that direction before returning to Lysander.

"Your Majesty, if you and Master Kirill and Honorable Romilly would please come with me?" Alan gestured toward the left. "Jannik has been located, but some of his guards are fighting back, and it would be safer for you to not be in the open."

"We're hardly defenseless, Commander." He, Kirill, and

Romilly all had the dragon Talent in sufficient strength to allow them to transform into dragons—which was how they'd all come here.

"I'm aware, Your Majesty, but as the king, you should not take unnecessary risks." Alan stared at him levelly. "Let us do our work."

He'd been king long enough to know there were times when risk was avoidable and times when it wasn't. This situation wasn't one where he had to go charging into battle. His part would come after. "Fine."

He allowed himself be ushered into a small room off the entry, likely where unexpected guests were left to wait, with Kirill and Romilly and two soldiers at the door. He paced to one side of the small, sparely decorated room, then turned to pace back.

Kirill and Romilly remained standing. Neither would sit before he did. "Sit, both of you. Just because I don't want to doesn't mean you have to be uncomfortable."

Romilly was the first to move. They glided over to one of the chairs and sat gracefully, then wrinkled their nose. "It's probably more comfortable to stand, Your Majesty."

Kirill only shook his head.

The wait wasn't long, but Lysander's impatience made it feel like hours. He and Alan had made the decision to bring more soldiers than were most likely necessary for this task, agreeing it was safer. There were laws about how many personal guards anyone in Ivria could have, but with what Jannik had been doing, Lysander could see a distinct possibility he might have broken that law too. He was, perhaps, beyond being surprised after learning the information Kirill and Romilly had brought him.

The interminable wait finally came to an end with Alan striding into the small room. His hair was slightly disheveled, but otherwise, nothing in his appearance indicated there had been any fighting.

"Commander?"

"We have the castle secured and Jannik and everyone else present in custody. We were unable to find his son or daughter."

Lysander frowned. They'd have to speak to everyone in the household, but with Jannik's reputation, it was unlikely he would work with or confide in any of his servants. His family and his man of business were the most likely to potentially be involved or have knowledge of the conspiracy. "Did they escape?"

Alan shook his head. "No, Your Majesty. The housekeeper says his son has been away for two weeks. His daughter left just before we arrived. Jannik arranged a marriage for her, and she was to be conveyed to her future husband today."

"And you trust the housekeeper?"

"She seems truthful. None of the staff, barring Jannik's man of business, seems particularly loyal. No one is holding back when asked questions."

Lysander nodded.

"I had Jannik's concubine separated from the servants and held on his own."

"Jannik has a concubine? How did we miss that?" Lysander didn't like to think of what else they might have missed, if they hadn't known something so important. "I thought our information was the contract with his concubine expired months ago."

"That was the information we were given," Kirill said when Lysander glanced his way. Dismay had settled over his angular features.

"This is a new one," Alan said. "Just arrived today, right before us. I feel a little bad for him. He's shaken."

"Who is he?" Lysander snapped out. Was the concubine or his family involved?

"Sascha of Clan Sapfir."

Romilly let out a little gasp. "I'm sorry, Your Majesty," they said when Lysander raised an eyebrow. "Sascha is my cousin."

He hadn't expected that. "Your cousin?"

Romilly's family was wealthy and well-connected. What reason would they have to contract a son of the clan to someone like Jannik? None of the reasons Lysander could think of were good.

"Well, not a first cousin. The blood relationship is more distant—he wasn't born into the main branch of the clan. His family isn't titled or as wealthy. Sascha just came of age." Romilly frowned. "He and I were always close, and we knew they felt making an advantageous match was his role in helping the family. I just..."

"Wouldn't have thought of Jannik as advantageous?" Kirill offered as a potential end to Romilly's sentence.

They sent a grateful look his way. "Yes, exactly. Now I'm kicking myself for not keeping in touch better."

Lysander thought it unlikely Romilly could've done anything to prevent this situation. If Sascha had just come of age, his parents had likely signed the contract on his behalf before his birthday, and if they were set on the match—if it could be called that—he doubted they would've changed course on Romilly's word. Because to enter into a contract with Jannik, whose reputation was no secret, they would have had to desperately want whatever he offered them, or be in it for some other reason. For instance, sharing Jannik's views on the future of Ivria. Perhaps being part of the plot.

Romilly had obviously come to the same conclusion. "Your Majesty, I had no idea. I haven't seen Sascha's parents in years or heard anything untoward about their views."

He nodded, accepting Romilly's words, for the moment at least. Nothing marked Romilly as untrustworthy. "We'll have to investigate them, of course. If they're part of this, they'll need to be dealt with."

Only a hint of the distress they must have been feeling showed on Romilly's face. "Of course, Your Majesty. I'll tell you everything I know about them. Sascha might know more about the current situation there, but they did try to keep him and his sisters quite sheltered."

From just a few of Romilly's statements, Lysander was already getting a picture of a family that adhered rigorously to the more antiquated ways. He had more sympathy for Sascha now and doubted he was a part of Jannik's schemes, whether his parents were or not.

"Let's talk to Sascha."

Alan's eyebrows climbed toward his hairline. "You want to talk to him before Jannik? Your Majesty."

He let the slip go with only a quirk of a sardonic brow at Alan. "I do. Let Jannik wait."

"It might only give him time to line up excuses," Kirill said tentatively.

"And none of us will believe them. We're going to search this place top to bottom and find every scrap of information here linking him to the conspirators and about their plot. Jannik won't be weaseling his way out of this," Lysander said firmly. "He will be punished for his crimes, and we'll leave here knowing more than we did before. Now, bring Sascha."

He, Romilly, and Kirill waited in the small room while Alan went for Sascha. If he'd thought about it, Lysander would've moved to a more comfortable location for this interview, but he'd been too shocked by the news of Sascha's existence and his relation to Romilly and too busy considering implications to focus on comfort. After they spoke to Sascha, they'd go to Jannik's study. Surely the room would provide more comfort than this one and also potentially contain information they sought.

Alan's sharp knock sounded at the door before it opened. He stepped aside and ushered a younger man into the room.

And everything else faded away.

Objectively, Sascha—for this had to be Sascha—was beautiful. His hair was a rich, deep red and his skin a flawless ivory. Lysander couldn't see much of his body because he was huddled in a white fur-trimmed cloak, but his face... His features were so perfect Lysander couldn't believe it possible, and his large eyes were a blue that brought to mind the finest sapphires. Lysander's first thought was that he wanted to shower Sascha in the gems. His second was that too much fear filled those eyes. Sascha held himself tensely as if he were poised to flee.

The realization acted as an icy douse of water, extinguishing the flame of his wayward desire.

Romilly made a soft noise beside him, and Lysander nodded. They took his cue. "Sascha."

Sascha started and focused on Romilly. "Romilly? What are you doing here? Have you come to take me home?"

They swept across the distance separating them from Sascha and took him into their arms. Sascha continued to hold himself rigidly for a moment, then melted into Romilly's hold. The resemblance between them was stark. They shared the same red hair, the same blue eyes, the same delicacy of features. They might be only distantly related, but the family traits ran strongly in both of them.

Romilly was murmuring to Sascha, perhaps comforting, perhaps explaining the situation. Lysander wasn't certain he wanted that. As much as his instincts told him Sascha was unlikely to be involved, he had to confirm it, and he couldn't have Romilly leading Sascha, even if it was done inadvertently.

Lysander stifled a sigh. "Romilly," he said quietly.

They released Sascha from the embrace but kept close, kept hold of Sascha's arms. Romilly glanced to him and nodded at whatever he found in Lysander's expression.

"Sascha, this is His Majesty King Lysander. Your Majesty, may I present my kinsman Sascha?"

It seemed Romilly's presence had calmed Sascha somewhat, but there was still too much fear in his blue gaze, along with a dazed quality Lysander didn't care for, though he couldn't understand why it mattered so much to him. Nevertheless, Sascha bent into a graceful, utterly correct bow. He'd been taught well in that respect, it seemed, but if his parents had hoped for either a good marriage or concubinage, he would have been rigorously educated in such things. With Sascha's beauty and grace, his parents could've held out for a better match than Jannik. The situation became more suspicious by the moment.

Lysander gave Romilly a significant look as Sascha was straightening. Faint surprise washed through their eyes, but Romilly nodded and turned to their cousin. "Sascha, come sit with me for a little while."

Sascha's gaze darted between Lysander and Romilly, over to Kirill then back to Lysander. "All right."

Lysander's heart clenched at the tremble in his voice. What was Sascha doing to him?

CHAPTER 2

Sascha allowed Romilly to lead him across the room and coax him to sit. The chair was hard and straight backed, not at all comfortable, but the observation was a distant one. Sascha's heart was still galloping in his chest, his hands still shaking no matter what he did. What was going on? Why was Romilly here? Why was *the king* here?

He'd been dragged from the floor with the maid by soldiers and then left alone in a room, then brought here. He'd thought they were bringing him to Lord Jannik and he'd wanted to run, but where was he to go? He was contracted to Lord Jannik, and there were soldiers everywhere.

But Romilly was here and Romilly was his closest friend. Perhaps they might help him, or at least tell him what had happened.

After another quick glance at the king—he'd stepped away to stand with the soldier and the other man in the room, not out of earshot but giving the illusion of privacy—he turned to Romilly who had settled beside him. "What are you doing here, Romilly?"

Romilly smiled softly. "I came with the king. Lord Jannik has been arrested for treason."

Sascha gaped at them. "Treason?"

"You had no idea?"

"How would I? I'd just arrived, and he…" Sascha shuddered. "He said I was as beautiful as he'd been told, and he wanted to see the rest of me. He ordered me upstairs. Told me I wouldn't like the consequences if I didn't do as he said. I hadn't even made it up the stairs when the soldiers burst in."

Romilly's face creased in a frown, and they took Sascha's hands in theirs. Romilly's fingers were hot against Sascha's icy skin. "I'm so sorry that happened to you, Sascha."

"His daughter warned me. Obliquely, but she warned me it wouldn't be good here," he said absently, staring down at their clasped hands. He needed to pull himself together, start thinking, but there was this haze. Romilly was here, and Lord Jannik had been arrested. Surely Sascha would be all right now. If nothing else, he wouldn't have to be Lord Jannik's.

"You knew his daughter?"

He shook his head. "I only saw her for a moment. She left just as I arrived."

"To get married."

"So she said, but I think she was glad to be leaving no matter the reason." He would've been, and he'd only met Lord Jannik for a moment. Sascha knew what being a concubine entailed. He'd known he'd have to go to bed with Lord Jannik—he'd been instructed and admonished to keep himself untouched because of it, as, in the old traditional ways, concubines were required to go to their contracted untouched. And if those traditions had loosened over the years, his parents didn't believe they should've. Sascha had never felt any particular desire to go to bed with anyone he'd ever met, but he'd known what would be expected of him. He just hadn't anticipated someone so vile.

"I can imagine." After a brief pause, Romilly said, "I hadn't heard your parents had contracted for you."

"It happened a few months ago. They'd been looking, of course, and I don't know how long they'd been negotiating with him, but they finalized everything a few months ago." He'd been calm at the time. Why wouldn't he have been? He'd been raised for such a fate.

"I wish I'd been here."

Now he looked up to meet Romilly's gaze, so concerned. He needed to pull himself together, if for no other reason than Romilly shouldn't have to worry about him. "You had important work, and you couldn't have changed their minds. I was always meant for this."

"You weren't meant for him," Romilly spat out vehemently. Then they visibly calmed themself. "What do you know about Lord Jannik? Did your parents say anything before you came here?"

"Just basic things. Where he lived, his clan, his family. Why?" It came to him as soon as the word left his mouth, his thoughts sluggish. He gasped. "He's been arrested for treason."

"Yes."

"They told me almost nothing." The lack of knowledge had made his anxiety worse, but he'd dismissed it, assuming everything was normal, that nerves were normal. When he'd gotten here, though, even before, when Hannes came for him... "Did my parents know?"

"Did they give you any indication they did?"

He didn't want them to have known, didn't want them to be involved. His parents wouldn't have been party to treason... would they? No, he couldn't think such a thing of his own parents.

His horror must have shown on his face because Romilly squeezed his hands. "I know. They're your parents. I don't want to think it either, but we have to consider it."

Sascha's gaze strayed to the three others in the room. He'd almost forgotten their presence for a moment. But they were still there—the king and his soldier and the other man, whoever he was—listening and likely watching too. Were they waiting for Sascha to incriminate his parents?

"Sascha." Romilly squeezed his hands again, drawing his attention. "I know. I do. But this plot, what Jannik is part of... It's bad. And others are involved. Your parents might not be among them, and if not, we need to rule them out too."

Sascha took a deep breath. If one of the others had said the same to him, he wouldn't have trusted it. Perhaps he should have trusted his king—he hadn't heard anything about King Lysander to make him doubt he deserved loyalty—but they were his parents. Even if they had sent him into this situation.

"They never said anything in my hearing, nothing that sounded suspicious," he said finally. "They were quite pleased about Lord Jannik wanting me. I didn't get a say in whether they accepted his offer or what the contract said, but I didn't expect to, so I don't know if that is suspicious. I..."

"You what?" Romilly asked gently when Sascha trailed off.

"I...I started wondering if they knew how he was. If they knew I'd be treated with such disrespect. Threatened and humiliated. I kept trying to convince myself they couldn't have known what he was like or they wouldn't have agreed to it. But if they did...why would they go through with it? Why wouldn't they turn him down? Unless they were getting something big out of it."

And if they were conspirators with Lord Jannik or trying to get his favor in this scheme? How big was the plot anyway? What had Lord Jannik been trying to do?

"I have to admit I wondered the same."

Sascha's heart sank at their words.

"We'll find out the truth," Romilly said finally. "Try not to worry. If they haven't done anything, nothing will happen to them."

"And if they have done something?"

"You must know the punishment for treason." The king answered, not Romilly, his deep voice clearly pronouncing the words into the silence of the room until it seemed they echoed around Sascha from all sides.

Punishment for treason was death.

He drew in a shaky breath. The king might not have meant the statement as a question, but he was the king and Sascha had to answer. He only wished he could manage to put more strength into his voice. "Yes, Your Majesty."

His parents couldn't be involved in treason, could they? What reason would they have to do such a thing? He returned his gaze to Romilly. "Can you tell me what happened? What he did?"

Romilly turned to the king. "May I, Your Majesty?"

King Lysander watched Sascha for what felt like a long time, his mahogany gaze intense. When he turned his attention to Romilly, Sascha nearly sagged, as if he were a puppet with his strings cut. "Tell him, but don't go into too much detail."

"Thank you, Your Majesty."

"You two and Kirill, stay here. The commander and I are going to go question Jannik. I'll call for you when I need you."

The king strode from the room, taking the commander with him. The other man—Kirill—remained behind. He studied Romilly and Sascha for a moment, his green gaze keen, before he spoke. "Would you prefer I left? I can step outside and give you some privacy."

"Yes, thank you, Kirill," Romilly said.

Kirill nodded. "I'll be right outside if you need me."

They waited while Kirill crossed the room and left, closing the door behind himself. Then Romilly turned back to Sascha. "Now, before anything else, tell me if you're all right. Really all right, not what you think I want to hear."

Sascha laughed, but it sounded creaky to his own ears. "I wouldn't, not with you."

They smiled, gently again as if Sascha were breakable—and oh, how Sascha wished breakable wasn't how he felt. "I didn't think you would, but I have a feeling they've been instructing you in proper behavior even more than usual lately."

"They wanted to make sure I was ready, that I wouldn't bring shame on the family."

Romilly frowned. "We'll get back to that in a moment. Are you all right?"

"Yes. But today has been...a lot."

They seemed to relax a fraction. "Jannik didn't hurt you?"

He shook his head. "He grabbed my chin, kissed me. Mostly, he made sure I knew he could do whatever he wanted to me, and I couldn't do a thing about it."

Romilly's frown was back, deeper this time, and their eyes flashed. They pushed a lock of hair behind their ear. It seemed to have escaped from the tie they'd bundled it back with. "I'm going to take a good, long look at that contract."

Sascha didn't argue. He wouldn't mind a glance himself—since his parents had signed it before he'd come of age, they'd dismissed any questions or desire to see it he'd expressed. Romilly would give him the details, at least, if he still couldn't get his hands on the document. Or didn't understand it.

"Will you tell me about the treason now?" he asked, his thoughts bouncing to another topic without his permission.

"All right." Romilly paused for a moment, seeming to sort

out their thoughts—or perhaps just what they believed King Lysander would allow them to tell Sascha. "We have information that a group within Ivria wants us to stop hiding, to stop hiding the dragon Talent."

Sascha's mind went utterly blank for a moment as he stared. They wanted to what? He wasn't sure if there was a law in Ivria that forbid revealing the existence of the dragon Talent and of Ivria itself to anyone outside the kingdom, but if not, it had been a tenet of their society since its birth. Hundreds of years ago, those who possessed the magical Talent allowing them to change themselves into dragons had lived in all the lands of the world. Then the dragon hunts began. People who feared the dragon Talent or wanted to control it hunted down those who had it, trying to kill or capture them. Those possessing the Talent fled with their allies, searching for a place of safety. They found land in the middle of an impassable mountain range—impassable except by flight—and took refuge there. Eventually, Ivria was founded, and their society grew from those beginnings.

Through all the years, even after dragons faded into legend in the outside world, and some Ivrians began venturing out of Ivria to study or find others like them who might have managed to survive there, their one rule was to never tell anyone of the dragon Talent or of Ivria's existence. Everyone knew their safety depended on it. Everyone knew their history.

"But...why?" And if they wanted Ivria to stop being a secret, why plot? Couldn't people talk about it, talk to the king, come to some sort of agreement? Perhaps he was naive to think it, or perhaps the group was conspiring against the king because they knew most Ivrians didn't agree with them.

Romilly bit their lip. "I don't know how much His Majesty considers details I shouldn't tell you... We discovered a plot in which the conspirators wanted not only for us to stop hiding but to also…begin conquering, I suppose. They seem to feel the dragon Talent makes us superior to our neighbors."

Sascha shook his head, disbelief robbing him of his voice once more.

"We managed to stop them from plunging us into war, but the people who were caught weren't the only conspirators, and the plotting went much further. I'm sorry I'm being so vague."

Sascha waved a hand, though his mind still spun. "I understand."

"Thank you. Now you know why we're here. King Lysander must find the rest of the group, and we learned Jannik is a part of it."

"And you're wondering if my parents are part of it."

"I'm hoping they aren't." Romilly sighed. "But we have to consider it because this plot is a danger to King Lysander and Ivria. Everyone Jannik had dealings with is going to be investigated. That includes your parents."

He nodded. "Signing the contract with him makes it more suspicious."

Romilly watched him for a moment. "You think so too."

Sascha sighed and slumped down in the uncomfortable chair. "I don't want to."

"Did you hear anything at home about why they were so pleased with the match?" Romilly pressed gently.

Sascha appreciated the care and hated that he couldn't be helpful. "They didn't talk in front of me, except to tell me it was happening. You know them—they're traditional to the point of being backwards. They have two sons who inherited the dragon Talent whom they treat as important members of the family. My sisters and I didn't, so we're only good for marriage or concubinage, to bring wealth and connections to the family."

"You know that's not true," Romilly said fiercely.

"So you've always told me." Sascha smiled, trying to keep the sadness, the bitterness, from showing. He would've liked his family to see him as Romilly did. He would've liked to have a choice. "But you know what their beliefs mean. The girls and I are practically locked away. We certainly aren't asked for our opinions or given any important information."

Romilly's expression took on a knowing edge. "And that means you never get it?"

Sascha rolled his eyes. "Of course it doesn't. A lot can be learned by walking softly and keeping one's ears open, and talking to the maids."

"But nothing about Jannik," Romilly said slowly.

He frowned. "No. And thinking about it now, that's odd. None of us overheard anything about him, and we did try."

"It sounds as if they were being especially careful when talking about him."

Sascha didn't like the sound of that. "Maybe."

Romilly sighed. "Try not to worry too much. King Lysander is fair. He isn't going to punish them for no reason. They'll be investigated and questioned."

"My siblings too," he said dully.

"Yes. And, like I said, if nothing is found, they'll be exonerated."

He worried about the other possibility, but he nodded.

"All right. Why don't we get you something to eat? Are you hungry?"

"Not really." Sascha twisted his hands in his cloak, then let go and tried to smooth the creases. The material would be ruined at this rate, and it was such a pretty cloak too. He loved pretty things, had been so happy to be given new clothing before he left home. "What will happen to me now? Will I go home?"

"I don't know. Jannik committed treason."

And he would be executed. As horrible as the man was, Sascha still didn't want to think about it.

"Yes."

"Well." Romilly spoke slowly again, as if choosing their words with care. "When someone commits treason, all their wealth and land and possessions become the property of the crown. That includes any contracts or agreements they've entered into. King Lysander holds the contract now, so he'll have to decide what to do about it."

Lysander stared down at Jannik, who knelt in the center of what had once been his study. Something about the room and the way it was decorated gave the impression of cold despite the roaring fire in the hearth, or perhaps it was just the man in front of him.

"Your Majesty, forgive me, but I don't understand what is happening."

Lysander was surprised Jannik didn't choke on the words. "I won't beg forgiveness when I say I seriously doubt that."

Jannik's eyes went wide. "Your Majesty!"

"Spare me your protests. You know exactly why we're here. You and your guards certainly fought hard enough as you tried to escape."

"We didn't know who was attacking! My guards were only trying to defend my home—"

"Soldiers wearing the king's badge? Proclaiming they were here in my name?" Lysander interrupted, gesturing at Alan in his uniform, looming over Jannik. "Don't treat me as if I'm stupid, Jannik. You know exactly what you've done and why we're here."

Jannik said nothing, simply stared back at him. The brazenness of the look did nothing to cool Lysander's ire. Though little could've when he thought of what Jannik and the others had been doing.

"We know, Jannik. The plot you and your fellows set into motion in Tournai, trying to plunge Ivria into war and force us to reveal our Talents, has been discovered and stopped. Two members of your conspiracy died; another is in our custody. We have their papers, which led us to you." Lysander made each statement firmly but emotionlessly. He would not let loose his fury on this man, not unless such a display would help.

Shock flitted across Jannik's face. He hadn't known their plan had fallen apart. Lysander wasn't surprised but was glad to have his assumption confirmed.

"We know you've committed treason, and you won't be talking yourself out of the charge. In fact, the only talking you'll be doing is telling us every detail of your conspiracy. Everyone involved. All your plans."

Jannik's expression settled into defiant lines. "Never."

Lysander let a cold smile spread across his face. "Oh, I think you will. You can do it voluntarily here with us—which will be far more pleasant for you—or you can do it later with someone asking the questions who will be far less kind."

"Are you going to be kind to me, Your Majesty?" Jannik asked with narrowed eyes.

"You're going to be punished for your crimes. How painful everything is leading up to that point is your choice."

"I'll tell you nothing," he spat.

"So be it. I'll find out anyway." He gestured to the soldiers behind Jannik. As they dragged him to his feet, Lysander continued, "And, of course, all your lands, possessions, and wealth are now the property of the Crown."

Jannik sputtered protests as the soldiers dragged him from the room. Lysander doubted his confinement would convince him to talk, but he would find out all Jannik knew one way or another. For now, they would search Grau from top to bottom.

"He seems more upset at the loss of his possessions than at the other consequences of his treason," Alan remarked. "Odd priorities."

"I wonder if he still thinks he can talk himself out of this."

"If he does, he's gone about it in a poor way. He's all but admitted his guilt."

"I know, and I certainly don't plan on letting him get away with it." Lysander shrugged. "Let him think he can. Perhaps his delusions will help us in the long run."

"And in the short run?"

"We tear this place apart. If he's hidden anything, I want to see it."

"Yes, Your Majesty. Would you like me to organize a search or would you prefer to conduct it yourself with Master Kirill and Honorable Romilly?" Alan asked.

"Leave the study and Jannik's bedchamber for us, but task your people with searching the rest of the castle. It will take us long enough with several searching." Lysander rounded the desk. "You still have people questioning the servants?"

"Yes, Your Majesty. So far, no information about treason but plenty about how horrible Jannik is. I'll have a report for you."

Lysander nodded. "Good. I want to talk to his man of business myself, or perhaps have you and Kirill do so. I still believe he's the only one who might have some idea of what Jannik has been up to."

"Do you want him brought up now?"

Hannes was being held in the cellars just as Jannik was. There were far too many small stone-walled rooms with the look of cells down there. Lysander wanted to believe they were storage rooms, but he couldn't help wondering. At least it gave them places to keep Jannik and Hannes.

"Not yet. I want him nervous, and I don't think he's been down there long enough for reality to have set in." He sat in the chair behind the desk. Unlike the miserably hard chairs in the room where he'd left Romilly, Kirill, and Sascha, this one was almost extravagantly luxurious.

"Probably not, Your Majesty. The man is a piece of work from what I've seen. He's a match for Jannik."

He glanced at Alan, who remained standing in front of the desk, back straight, nearly at attention. "We'll get him to talk."

"I don't doubt it."

"Good. I'm going to begin going through Jannik's papers. I could use Kirill and Romilly, if they're finished speaking with their cousin."

"I'll let them know, then check in with my people."

"Thank you, Commander."

Alan bowed and started toward the door, but stopped almost immediately. "If Romilly and their cousin are done, what should I do with Sascha? It seems like cruel punishment to leave him in such an unwelcoming room."

Lysander bit back a curse. He hadn't thought of it. "You're right. Where did you have him before?"

"A small parlor. We separated him from the servants once we realized who he was, and it was the most convenient place at the time."

"See if he's comfortable returning there." Lysander leaned back in the chair. "I don't believe he's involved in this. His parents very well may be."

"For what it's worth, my instincts are telling me the same," Alan said. "His parents obviously adhere to some of the worst of the old ways. Giving him no choice or say in his future. Keeping him sheltered and secluded. My guess is anyone in that family who didn't develop the dragon Talent is good only as a bargaining chip or brood mare."

Lysander sighed. "I think you're right, but I thought we'd progressed past those beliefs. Romilly's branch of the family doesn't hold with those particular traditions, as far as I know."

"There are some people who stubbornly resist all change. It doesn't always matter if another part of the clan, even the clan head, has let those ways go. If Sascha's branch of the family tree is a bit isolated from the rest and headed by one of those stubborn people, I'm not surprised at what they did." Alan shrugged. "I am surprised at their choice of partner for Sascha. Based on his face alone, they could've found a better match—someone more highly placed—or even a good marriage. But they contracted with Jannik."

"He either gave them a sum of money they were desperate to have or they were currying favor with a member of the conspiracy they had joined. Or both." He hadn't wanted to say all of it in front of the young man—who, yes, was exceptionally beautiful—but he'd been thinking it. And they'd certainly implied enough for Sascha to catch on. He seemed quick as well as lovely. "One of the things I'm looking for is the contract Jannik and Sascha's parents signed."

"Probably a good idea." Alan bowed again. "By your leave, Your Majesty?"

"Yes, go on. Find out if you can where the daughter went. There's probably correspondence about the marriage here too. We'll need to speak to her and look into the husband's family as well. Jannik isn't the type to confide in his daughter, but she might know something, and he might be making connections with others who are a part of this."

As he suspected Sascha's parents had.

"Yes, Your Majesty. I'll see if anyone knows where his son is as well."

"We need to retrieve him before he learns of his father's capture and runs."

"If he's innocent or wants to appear so, he might come after his father," Alan suggested.

Lysander frowned. "Possibly. Let's find him anyway. I don't want to take chances."

"Yes, Your Majesty."

CHAPTER 3

Alone, Lysander turned to the desk in front of him. He started with what was out on the surface, though he doubted anything pertaining to treason would be lying about. Jannik did not keep a neat desk. Lysander began sorting what he could see by subject—estate records, correspondence, and so on. All of it would have to be scrutinized, especially the correspondence, but he'd prioritize to start. The center drawer held paper, pens and ink, and wax and seals. He ran his hands along the inside of the drawer searching for anything hidden or secret compartments. Finding nothing, he turned to the drawers on either side.

Kirill came in and bowed as he was tugging on the last of them. Lysander glanced up at him. "These are all locked. I don't suppose you can pick a lock?"

"You need Romilly for that," Kirill said seriously. "They're getting their cousin settled, then they'll be along. In the meantime, I can help you search for a key."

"Check those cabinets, if you can get into them, both for the key and for anything else of interest." Lysander turned back to the desk, this time in search of a key for the locked drawers. Perhaps Jannik had it with him—he'd have to ask Alan what was found when they searched Jannik.

Romilly glided into the study while Lysander was half under the desk, and Kirill was pulling ledgers out of the one cabinet he'd been able to get into. Romilly lifted one slender red brow as they surveyed the scene in front of them.

"Kirill tells me you can pick locks. Get us into these drawers," Lysander snapped out, maybe more sharply than he should have. But Romilly was forgetting themself a little.

"Yes, Your Majesty." They came closer. "If you'll allow me?"

Lysander climbed to his feet and moved away so Romilly could take his place behind the desk. Romilly pulled a hairpin from the simple style they'd confined their red hair into today and knelt. They set to work immediately, an expression of intense concentration on their face.

Lysander watched Romilly. But despite his curiosity about this skill of Romilly's, his mind wandered almost immediately to Sascha. He'd noticed earlier how the cousins resembled one another, but Lysander had never experienced the immediate attraction he'd felt for Sascha in regard to Romilly. He'd certainly noticed Romilly's beauty and would have been tempted by the possibility of an affair with them if they'd expressed any interest, but Romilly hadn't and Lysander himself wasn't interested enough to ask.

Sascha, though... Lysander was only now realizing how strong his desire for Sascha was already. And he shouldn't be. Sascha was confused and upset—in the small amount of time he'd been in contact with Jannik, the man had obviously scared and disturbed him. Then, there was the old-fashioned contract that harkened back to the earliest days of Ivria and the possibility of Sascha's family being involved in treason. The slim possibility Sascha was involved himself should doubly keep Lysander away. Bedding someone with a part in a plot against him was a bad idea.

"Got this one." Romilly's statement interrupted Lysander's thoughts, and when he focused again, Romilly was tugging one of the drawers open. "If you'll let me get the other one on this side, I can move out of your way and work on the others, Your Majesty."

Faint surprise washing through him, Lysander waved at them to finish and went to Kirill, who seemed amused. "Have you found anything?"

"Mostly estate records. I found the contracts for his concubines." Kirill held out a sheaf of paper tied with black string.

"Concubines? More than one?"

"Not at once, Your Majesty, or at least not that I've seen. It seems Jannik has had a series of them over the years."

Lysander flipped through the papers, noting dates. The contracts went back decades. His eyebrows went up. Such a thing wasn't unheard of, but it wasn't common either, especially in these numbers.

"I heard he likes them young," Romilly remarked from their position at the desk. They pulled open another drawer. "Perhaps he discards them when they get too old for him."

Disdain and disgust dripped from every word, and well deserved. "Your cousin's contract is here."

Romilly glanced up as they moved to the drawers on the other side of the desk. "May I look at it, Your Majesty? I told him I would, and I think he'd like to as well. He was never given the opportunity."

Lysander didn't blame Romilly for the anger simmering under the surface of their polite tone—he'd be angry too if Sascha were his family. "I'd like to read through it myself, but you're welcome to study it after. Sascha as well."

"Thank you, Your Majesty." Romilly went quiet again as they fiddled with the next lock. Lysander turned to the contract as Kirill sorted through estate records and began skimming through it, making note of provisions he wanted to study further. When he got to compensation, he began to read more closely. Money or other goods often exchanged hands in marriage and concubinage agreements, often in both directions, these days to make certain the less wealthy spouse or concubine had some measure of independence. While Jannik had given a sum of money to Sascha's parents, Lysander saw no provision for Sascha. His parents might have done so privately, but most wanted everyone's rights in the relationship laid out clearly. The sum itself, while not obscene, wasn't inconsiderable. He still believed Sascha's parents might have been able to find a more attractive offer, but the money could have swayed them, especially if their financial situation was precarious.

Lysander frowned as he read further. It was a five year agreement without an option to continue the arrangement. He flipped to the others in the stack and found the same clauses—he also found the ages of Jannik's prior concubines. Some were only a little younger than Sascha, but some were quite a bit younger, too young for such an arrangement. Romilly had been correct. Jannik liked his concubines young, and he discarded them when they became too old for his tastes.

Forcing down his disgust, Lysander turned to the rest of Sascha's contract. There were no protections for Sascha, even aside from the lack of monetary considerations. While Sascha was here, he had no right to leave, no right to contact anyone outside this castle. No right to do anything without Jannik's permission. It had the worst provisions of the concubinage agreements of long ago, provisions Ivria had rejected. Had such things actually been outlawed? Lysander made a note to look into the matter—such things couldn't be allowed to occur.

Why had Sascha's parents signed a document so lacking in protections for their son? They couldn't believe Jannik was highly placed enough to make up for these terms—if it were Lysander, no amount of money or position could compensate him for subjecting one of his children to this. Sascha's family moved up higher on his list of those potentially involved.

"I have the daughter's betrothal agreement," Kirill said. "Everything here seems to be legitimate, nothing criminal."

"And I have the last of the drawers open." Romilly climbed gracefully to their feet and dusted off the knees of their pants. "Would you like me to search them, Your Majesty?"

"Look at your cousin's contract and then take the left side."

He handed off the pages as Romilly expressed their thanks. "Actually, read through all of them. See if anything jumps out at you, and take note of the names. I don't know how far back this conspiracy goes, but I'm not taking any chances. We'll have to look into everyone."

"Yes, Your Majesty." Romilly took the contracts and retrieved pen and paper from the desk. Then they settled at a small table in the corner, out of Lysander's and Kirill's way, and immediately became absorbed in the documents.

Lysander left them to it and began ransacking the desk drawers Romilly had opened—he wasn't going to ask how Romilly had learned the skill, but he wasn't going to complain either. He set aside more stacks of documents and correspondence, each tied with a different color string, to review later. Several velvet pouches sat in one drawer. He dumped out one after another on the desk and found mostly gold and silver coins, but also some gems, the majority unset with a few pieces of jewelry mixed in. He'd have wondered if the jewelry was meant as gifts for Jannik's daughter for her wedding if she hadn't already left. And from the way Jannik had treated Sascha upon his arrival, Lysander couldn't imagine any of it was meant for him, though the sapphires would suit him. So why were such valuable items here? As payments? For ease of access in case Jannik had to flee? Would they find similar stashes when they searched his bedchamber? Lysander wouldn't be surprised.

In a lower drawer, he came across a wooden box on top of another pile of folded papers. He pulled all of it out and set it on the desk. The little box wasn't locked or secured in any way, so Lysander flipped up the lid and found a set of seals on a bed of black velvet. He took one out and examined it, frowning. Unlike the one he'd found in the unlocked drawer, this seal was not marked with the device of Jannik's title and clan. He'd never seen this symbol before.

"Kirill, take a look at this. Have you ever seen a mark like this?" He handed the seal to Kirill when he came to the desk. Romilly looked up from their work but didn't move.

Kirill studied the seal carefully before passing it to Romilly who gave it the same careful attention.

"Well?" Lysander asked.

"I think I saw it on a note tucked into the back of one of the journals we found," Romilly said. Romilly and Kirill had discovered journals written in code by one of the participants in the treasonous plot. Those journals had led them to Jannik.

Kirill took it back and scrutinized it once more. He shook his head. "I don't remember, but I trust your memory of it."

"We can match it up when we get back," Lysander said, holding out his hand for the seal again. He turned it over in his fingers absently before staring at the symbol again. "I wouldn't be surprised if it's something the conspirators use though. Jannik kept it in a locked drawer. His regular seals aren't under lock and key."

"It does seem suspicious, Your Majesty," Kirill said. "Were those papers with it?"

"Yes." He turned his attention to the pile of papers that had been tucked under the box. When he unfolded the first one, he found what looked to be a letter, but completely incomprehensible. "Written in code. The same one as the journals?"

He handed it across the desk to Romilly, who studied it carefully. "I believe so. I can try to decode it for you. I brought my notes on the code with me."

"Later." Lysander unfolded each sheet in the stack and found more letters written in code. "We need to know what they say, but there's quite a stack here and plenty of work all over to keep us busy."

The task ahead just here, searching Jannik's home and gathering every bit of information from it, was daunting. Never mind everything after. He wished he had brought more people with him, but he was hesitant to trust anyone beyond a select few. Lysander was trying not to wonder what he'd do without Kirill and Romilly when they left Ivria again. He had to determine who else he could trust and soon.

"Of course, Your Majesty. Whenever you like," Romilly replied.

"Finish reviewing those contracts first. We have to search Jannik's bedchamber." Lysander surveyed the wreckage of books and papers and other assorted items they'd created in this room. Should they finish here first, or would it be best to search that room now and look through everything they found at once? He shouldn't be having such trouble making the decision.

"Perhaps you should stop for a meal first, Your Majesty," Alan said from the doorway. Lysander hadn't even heard him open the door—dangerous in an uncertain situation, despite the soldiers stationed outside. "It's been hours."

Now that Alan had brought up food, Lysander's stomach reminded him stridently how hungry he was. He sighed. "Yes, I suppose a meal and a short break would be helpful. Is there food?"

"Yes, Your Majesty, and it's even edible. I've had a meal laid out in the dining room."

"Managing me?" he asked Alan with a raised brow.

Alan's face remained bland. "You need to eat, Your Majesty."

"Yes, fine. Let's all take a break. We can start again after the meal." He wasn't even certain what meal it was meant to be. How long had they been here? He stood and beckoned Romilly and Kirill to accompany him.

"Has Sascha eaten?" Romilly asked Alan.

Alan frowned. "I don't believe so, but I can have food brought to him."

"If Your Majesty would permit me, I should eat with Sascha," Romilly requested. "I don't like leaving him alone for so long. He's had a trying day in ways he never imagined."

"He can eat with us." Lysander started for the door. "Be careful what you say in front of him with regard to our purpose here and what we've found. I don't believe he's involved, but I'd prefer we err on the side of caution."

"I appreciate your allowing him to eat with us, Your Majesty."

Lysander turned to Alan as they left the study . "Do you have keys to the various rooms in the house?"

"At the moment, I believe I'm the only one who does. I personally relieved Jannik and Hannes of their keys. The house-keeper volunteered the other sets." He shook his head before Lysander could say anything. "Of course I know she might not have been truthful. We're watching, but the staff has been nothing but cooperative. Some are understandably afraid, and still they aren't obstructing us."

"All right. Do you have the key for the study?" Lysander accepted the key Alan gave him and locked the door behind them. A soldier remained on guard outside the room, but Lysander felt better with the door locked as well.

"I've secured Jannik's bedchamber," Alan said as he led them to the dining room. "It will be undisturbed until you're ready to see it."

"Good. Romilly, why don't you go get Sascha?"

"Yes, Your Majesty." But Romilly hesitated. "He asked me what was going to happen to him, if he was going to be sent home. I told him it's your decision, Your Majesty, and I didn't know."

"It is my decision, and I don't know what it will be. But he can't go home, not yet."

Would he want to go home, knowing his parents hadn't cared who they were selling him off to?

"Unless we can keep knowledge of Jannik's arrest from filtering outside these walls, they're going to find out," Kirill remarked.

"That's why no one is leaving here yet." It wouldn't be a permanent solution, and if someone came visiting, they would be in trouble, but it was all he had at the moment. They had to move quickly, far more quickly than they were. "Get Sascha. We need to eat so we can go back to work."

SASCHA DIDN'T KNOW what to do with himself.

Romilly had left him in a small sitting room, which was at least comfortable. But he'd been left alone. There was a soldier outside in the corridor—Sascha had no idea if she was there to keep him in or others out or for some unrelated reason. And he didn't plan on asking.

He'd finally taken off his cloak and laid it over one of the room's chairs. Though this room was pleasantly warm with the fire crackling in the hearth, he'd still had to force himself to do it. Curling up inside the cloak—hiding under it—had been comforting. Safe, somehow. But he couldn't stay that way forever. If anything could calm him, it had to be knowing Jannik wouldn't be touching him, ever. And Romilly was here. Romilly wouldn't leave him on his own to flail about in this situation he didn't know how to navigate. He just had to calm down and think.

Sascha began to pace the small room, the low heels of his shoes rapping against the stone floor for a few steps before being muffled by the carpet in the center of the room. He counted his steps as he walked the pattern, onto the carpet and off it again, timing his breathing to his steps. The repetition was soothing. Nothing had prepared him for today. He'd been educated. Not the way Romilly had, of course. Romilly had been sent to school. Sascha had been taught at home to a point and had furthered his education by reading books from the house library or sent to him by Romilly. His parents hadn't cared for it —they believed he and his sisters didn't need much more than social graces, an ability to make polite conversation, and an extensive though theoretical knowledge of what would be expected of them in the bedroom. It was only because of his grandfather that his reading had been allowed. Perhaps if he'd been less isolated...

But, really, how did anyone prepare for walking into an arrest for treason? How did anyone come to terms with his parents potentially committing treason?

Was it selfish to wonder what was going to happen to him?

He stopped in the middle of the room, deliberately slowing his breathing again.

No, no it wasn't. He had to think of himself. No one else would. Romilly would do their best, but they had more important things to worry about. Sascha's parents had certainly been looking out for themselves more than Sascha when they'd sent him here, even if treason hadn't been involved. So he had to look out for himself. Which meant calming down and beginning to deal with this situation as logically as he could.

Sascha wasn't brilliant like Romilly, and he wasn't as educated. But he wasn't stupid, and he did have all those social graces to rely on. Courtly manners and an ability to hide emotions were a start if he could only collect himself. He took slow, deep breaths.

Trivial as it seemed at the moment, the first thing he wanted to know was where his trunk had been taken. A change of clothes would help. He felt grimy after the journey. He'd assumed he would arrive and be able to clean up and change in order to make a good impression—he'd already chosen clothing. Sascha had wanted to make a good impression, to make this arrangement work. He hadn't expected to be ordered...

No, he wouldn't think about it. And he wouldn't allow himself to flinch at the thought of going somewhere in this castle to bathe and change because of the way that vile man had treated him. He could clean up and put on the clothes he'd been planning to wear—clothes that had been given to him for his new life, which should've put him off them except he'd adored them from the beginning—and make it his armor for the next time he saw the king. He would make a good impression on King Lysander to make up for the king's first sight of him.

As he began to calm, embarrassment surged through him. Sascha's face burned as he thought of how the king had first seen him. He'd never imagined he would meet the king at all, and when he actually had, instead of being poised and graceful, he'd been shaking and near tears. A glance in a mirror hanging nearby showed him his appearance now wasn't much better. His clothing was crumpled, though the white and pale blue of his jacket and narrow pants remained pristine. His eyes were still red from battling tears and his face was almost as vibrant a shade as his hair.

He supposed it was possible for him to have made a worse impression on the king—a king who held his future and his family's future in his hands more directly than ever—but he wouldn't want to contemplate how.

Sascha went to the mirror and stared at his reflection. He took deep breaths as he smoothed his clothing as best he could. Once done with that, he turned to his hair. It had fallen to his shoulders in well-ordered waves when he'd left home, but between travel and the chaos since his arrival, it had become disheveled. He frowned. Disheveled? His hair was a rat's nest. How had it gotten so bad and when?

Methodically, he began to comb through the waves with his fingers, wincing every time they caught on knots. He wanted his hairbrush in addition a change of clothing. Could he ask the soldier in the hallway? No. She wouldn't have any idea what had happened to his trunk; she wouldn't care. The king's soldiers had important duties that did not include finding his misplaced belongings. The staff who might know the answer were likely all being questioned, probably not as carefully as he had been. Or maybe they were—he shouldn't assume the king's people would be cruel. They hadn't been when they'd found him and the maid on the stairs.

Was it wrong to hope they were harsh with Jannik and Hannes? Maybe, but he couldn't quite bring himself to care.

"Sascha?"

He whirled from the mirror and pressed a hand to his racing heart when he saw Romilly in the doorway.

Romilly looked contrite. "I'm sorry. I didn't mean to scare you."

"It's all right. I wasn't paying attention." Sascha tried a smile. "Is everything all right?"

"As all right as it can be at the moment," Romilly said. "Are you hungry? We're taking a break for a meal, and we'd like you to join us."

As soon as Romilly mentioned food, Sascha's stomach rumbled, reminding him breakfast had been a very long time ago, but the rest of what Romilly said made him hesitate. "Who would we be eating with?"

Romilly tilted their head to one side inquiringly. "Kirill, the commander, and the king."

Horror washed through Sascha. He couldn't see the king again like this. "The king?"

"Yes. Is there a problem?"

"No. I just..." Sascha looked down at himself. "I had hoped to clean up before I saw the king again. I wasn't exactly at my best when you introduced me to him earlier."

Romilly's expression softened. "I understand how you feel, but we're not formal right now and His Majesty hardly expects you to dress as you normally would for a meal with the king."

"Still." How could he explain how much his clothing was his armor? Like a shield and part of the mask he wore...and all of it felt dented by his earlier outpouring of emotion. He needed to start fresh.

But there was something in Romilly's eyes that said they understood without Sascha explaining. "Unfortunately, we can't keep him waiting. I wouldn't mind a change of clothes too. I dressed in a rather severe way today because it made sense, but it didn't really feel right."

Romilly shrugged slightly, and Sascha felt terrible. He was complaining due to his own vanity; meanwhile, his cousin was having a day when they didn't feel right in their own skin. "I'm sorry. I think I have a couple of ribbons in my pocket. Perhaps we could fix your hair?"

Romilly came over to give him a hug. "Thank you for the thought, but we can't keep the king waiting—couldn't even if there wasn't quite a bit of work waiting for us afterward. We'll both have to make do."

"I understand." He glanced over his shoulder into the mirror. Could have been worse. At least his cheeks were no longer bright red. "Shall we go then?"

Romilly nodded and gestured for him to follow. "We'll find somewhere for you to clean up and change after, if you like. And sleep. As much I would love to get this done in a day, I can't imagine we'll finish."

Sascha didn't like the idea of staying, but he had no choice in the matter. He didn't even know where he would go once he left. "If someone could find my things, I would appreciate it. I know everyone is busy, but I would like my trunk."

"I have no idea where it is, but we'll find it." Romilly held out a hand, inviting Sascha to come with him. "It may have been searched. We're searching the whole castle. I don't think anyone would've made an exception for your trunk, if they even knew it was yours."

He tried not to shudder at the thought of some solider pawing through his clothes with no regard for them, discovering his love of silk and lace and pretty things. Or, frankly, anything else about him. No, he didn't like it one bit. So much about today felt like boundaries being crossed and pushed. "I understand."

Relief colored Romilly's face. "Thank you. I am sorry it had to happen."

"I know."

Romilly embraced him briefly. "Shall we go eat?"

Sascha assented and followed Romilly out into the corridor.

As they walked, he glanced around him. Soldiers were the only people he saw. But he was calm enough now to notice more about the castle. It was...ostentatious, as if decorated by a man enamored of his own sense of importance. If the king hadn't arrived today, if Jannik hadn't committed treason, Sascha would be living here.

He couldn't regret the king's arrival, even if it did bring with it worry for his family.

CHAPTER 4

Romilly ushered him into a dining room with a fire roaring in the massive fireplace and a long table in the center. King Lysander sat at the head of the table in a heavily carved chair that brought to mind a throne. Since Sascha didn't think the king traveled with a throne—he could be wrong, but such a thing would surely provoke talk that even he would've heard—it was likely Jannik's, and Sascha thought himself lucky again for not having to live under the domination of a man who thought himself a king.

The man currently sitting in the chair was, of course, actually the king of Ivria. And Sascha would've known him to be just by his manner. It wasn't the demeanor of someone like Jannik who wielded what power he had by force. Sascha had heard for a long time how good their king was—strong but fair, wanting the best for his people. Now that he thought about it, much of the detail he'd heard, especially of good things, had come from Romilly. But now he wondered what his parents thought of the king. They didn't talk about such things in front of him or his sisters, not the way they did with his older brothers and he couldn't remember overhearing anything.

But the king was in front of Sascha now, and he could form his own impressions. He could wish one of them wasn't how handsome the man was. King Lysander's appearance, the look in his eye, the commanding way he carried himself, affected Sascha in a way he'd never experienced before. He hadn't noticed it when he first saw the king, with panic and fear filling him, but now that he was calmer, looking at the king made something roll through Sascha that he found unnerving.

The king lounged in the throne-like chair, his muscular physique filling out the jacket and pants he wore in oddly distracting ways. The clothing wasn't made for court, but it wasn't made for fighting either, the cut and decoration simple but the fabrics high quality and the shade of blue rich and saturated. His hair was thick and dark, cut well above his shoulders, and his skin was a rich, dark tawny gold. Chiseled features and a closely trimmed beard made up a compelling face, and intense mahogany eyes, he saw when he straightened from his bow, studied Sascha.

A jolt went through his entire body at the attention, but he had no idea what it was...fear, shock... No, it didn't feel as if it were those things. Before he could analyze it, King Lysander turned back to the table and beckoned him and Romilly forward.

"Come and sit so we can eat."

Sascha went with Romilly to the table and took the seat beside the one they chose, which thankfully did not put him next to the king—Romilly had that position with the commander and Kirill across from them. Sascha focused on his plate and tried to be inconspicuous, something he'd learned to do at home, though everything he'd been taught was about how to stand out. The food was simple but hot and filling. Sascha wondered who had prepared it. Had the king brought his own people or were Jannik's staff working again? While his curiosity itched to be assuaged, he ask. He didn't want to be a bother to the others at the table.

The others talked while Sascha ate quietly. Little they said contained any specific information; most of it involved plans for what they would do next in their search of the castle. There seemed to be some debate about whether they should finish reviewing everything they'd found in Jannik's study before searching his bedchamber. Personally, Sascha thought they should search the bedchamber first—what if someone got in and took what they were looking for before they had a chance to find it? But, he said nothing, just continued to attempt to be invisible as he ate his food. He was surprised he had an appetite at all. Apparently, his stomach didn't care about how tense the day was.

Finally, the king made the decision they should search Jannik's bedchamber first. Sascha found himself nodding slightly when the king spoke but stopped himself quickly. He glanced up to determine if anyone had seen his gesture, and his gaze collided with the king's. He froze, unable to look away, kicking himself because he hadn't controlled his reactions better.

But King Lysander said nothing to him, only watched him for a long moment during which his eyes held Sascha captive and unmoving, during which his gaze seemed to bore into Sascha in search of...something. Sascha had no idea what. After what seemed like hours, the king looked away and Sascha drew in a breath, trying to suck in the air he needed as unobtrusively as he could.

"It's time to get back to work," the king said. Romilly, Kirill, and the commander all said some variation of "Yes, Your Majesty" and stood from their seats. Sascha hastened to follow. He assumed he would be going back to the little sitting room he'd been sequestered in, with the hope of being reunited with his trunk at some point in the future.

"Sascha, wait a moment." The king's deep voice froze Sascha once more, before he'd even taken a step away from the table.

"Your Majesty?" Romilly inquired. "I thought I'd escort Sascha back and then have a word with someone about finding his things."

"The commander can ask someone to locate them when they have a moment. Go up and begin searching with Kirill. I want to speak to Sascha, then I'll see he gets back to where he needs to be."

"Yes, Your Majesty," Romilly answered with a bow. They sent a glance Sascha's way, inquiring, concerned. But what could Romilly do in the face of orders from the king? The three others filed out, closing the door behind them, and Sascha was alone with King Lysander.

Lysander sat back in his chair and surveyed the man standing in front of him for a moment. Sascha no longer seemed on the verge of falling apart. Throughout the meal, Lysander had been contemplating the suspiciously striking change and watching Sascha carefully. Now, he caught sight of the slight tremble in Sascha's hands before he clasped them in front of himself. Sascha wasn't as calm as he appeared, which was something of a relief to Lysander. For someone not intended for court life, Sascha was good at masking his emotions. Notwithstanding the events of earlier today, which would've been too much for many of those at court.

And with that measure of calm, Sascha might be even more lovely. If Lysander saw Sascha every day, would it feel less like all the air was being knocked out of him when he gazed at Sascha's face?

He'd removed his cloak finally, and Lysander was able to see the body previously hidden beneath it. Sascha was sleek and slender—elegant. Yes, elegant was a good word. The silk of his long jacket and narrow pants were understandably wrinkled, but the clothing was tailored well to fit his frame and show it off to best advantage. There was a bit of lace at collar and cuff, some delicate embroidery, and his shoes had a bit of a heel. The style wouldn't have looked out of place at court, despite not being the most current fashion. Sascha would certainly garner quite a bit of attention. But Lysander shouldn't be imagining him there.

Throughout Lysander's scrutiny, Sascha stood still and straight, giving every outward appearance of serenity—except for the tension in the grip of his hands. Lysander admired that strength—he admired too many things about Sascha. He couldn't let his attraction color his perceptions; he wasn't going to assume Sascha was part of this treasonous conspiracy without proof, but he wasn't going to be so naive as to discount him entirely because of a pretty face.

More than pretty, and with a form that matched. But, as much as Lysander wanted to make an advance, he was going to hold himself back. Sascha had been through enough in just a few moments with Jannik...and Lysander preferred to trust his lovers. Which was why he'd had so few in recent years. His instincts—and Alan's—told him Sascha wasn't involved, but it would be prudent to wait for confirmation before making decisions.

"Have you been made comfortable, Sascha?" he asked, finally breaking the silence in the room.

"Yes, Your Majesty. Thank you." Sascha's voice was pleasant and smooth. It moved through Lysander, igniting fires inside him. He needed to get away from Sascha before he threw all his lovely logical conclusions and resolutions out of the window.

And yet...

"Would you tell me if you weren't?"

His question startled a smile out of Sascha. Just a small one, but lovely enough for Lysander to conclude a full smile would probably dazzle even the strongest of men.

"I...I'm not certain, Your Majesty," Sascha said. "I wouldn't want to bring trivial complaints to the king, especially after my behavior earlier."

"Your behavior? I don't remember anything objectionable."

"You're kind to say so, Your Majesty, but I know my outburst wasn't appropriate."

Lysander raised an eyebrow. "I think your feelings and behavior were quite understandable given all that had happened to you today."

"Oh. Thank you, Your Majesty."

"That said, are you comfortable where you are?" Lysander pressed. "I don't want to treat you like a prisoner."

"But I can't leave."

"The castle? No, not now. Is there somewhere you'd like to go?"

"I almost said home," Sascha said after a brief hesitation. "But my parents might be traitors to Ivria. I hope they aren't, but they might be. And even if not, they sent me here, to Jannik, with no regard for how he might treat me. Not even a warning. So, I don't know if I want to be there. I suppose here is as good a place as any for the moment. That sitting room is a trifle boring."

Lysander chuckled at Sascha's last statement, as Sascha had perhaps intended—the rest of what he'd said wasn't nearly so amusing, and Lysander was disturbed by how much the restrained pain in Sascha's speech affected him. "I suppose it would be boring. For now, I need you to go back, but I'll have some books brought to you.

"I have a few in my trunk, Your Majesty, if it can be located," Sascha offered.

"We'll find out where it was brought. You may have to make do with books from Jannik's shelves until then." At Sascha's murmured thanks, Lysander continued. "Once I know what rooms have been searched, we'll find a bedchamber for you to use. No reason for you to be up all night just because the rest of us likely will be."

"I'd be happy to help, Your Majesty, if I can," Sascha ventured tentatively.

The offer surprised him, and he wondered for a moment if Sascha had some ulterior motive for wanting to become part of their search. But his large blue eyes were guileless. "Thank you for your offer, Sascha. We'll come for you if we need another pair of hands."

"Of course, Your Majesty." Sascha bowed his head briefly. Did he realize Lysander didn't entirely trust him? For all he was sheltered, Sascha didn't give the impression of being anything other than bright. He had to understand he was under some level of suspicion, watched until Lysander could say for sure Sascha wasn't a part of this mess. But if he knew, he didn't appear bothered.

"I have to go back to work, so let's get you settled."

"Your Majesty?" Sascha asked tentatively as Lysander stood. "Yes?"

"What will happen to me?" Sascha stood straight, his posture not betraying the anxiety he must feel. "I know you hold my contract now, and Romilly said you would decide."

"I do hold your contract now, and I will decide. Romilly is right about that." He came to stand in front of Sascha, looking down into his blue eyes. A vision of Sascha wrapped in nothing but glittering jewels—diamonds, sapphires, rubies as red as his hair—flitted through his mind, tantalizing and not at all appropriate. He wanted to make it happen. "I haven't decided yet, however. You can't go home, not now, even if you wanted to."

"I know, Your Majesty."

"What would they do with you anyway? Find someone else for you?"

"I assume so, Your Majesty. It's what they decided my future would be years ago." He said it with the air of someone who had long accepted something, whether they entirely liked it or not. Lysander was beginning to believe Sascha didn't like it one bit.

"Hmm." He studied Sascha for another moment. "And if your current contract remained in effect?"

Sascha flinched. "I thought... Not with Jannik. Because he can't. He's a traitor."

"No, not with him. Jannik has been stripped of everything, including his rights under any contracts he made. I'm asking what if I took his place?"

Sascha's eyelashes fluttered before his eyes went wide and his lips parted—and even that expression of shock was beautiful. If he wasn't careful, Lysander was going to get himself into so much trouble over a lovely, sheltered young man whose family might be plotting against the throne.

"You... Take his place, Your Majesty?"

"It's well within my rights to do so." He was standing close to Sascha now, closer than he should be, but he couldn't help himself. He wanted to touch Sascha, just a light brush of fingers along his cheek—the skin there would be soft and warm from the flush beginning to spread high on his cheekbones—but he wouldn't. Not without permission, and he'd prefer the permission be an enthusiastic invitation.

Instead, he stepped back. "We'll both have to think about it. I'll escort you back to the sitting room."

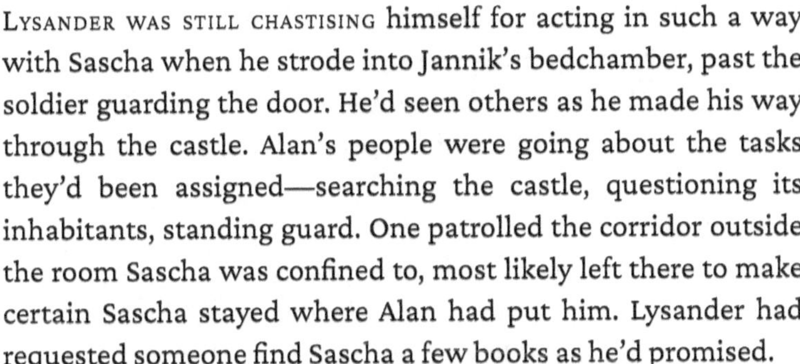

LYSANDER WAS STILL CHASTISING himself for acting in such a way with Sascha when he strode into Jannik's bedchamber, past the soldier guarding the door. He'd seen others as he made his way through the castle. Alan's people were going about the tasks they'd been assigned—searching the castle, questioning its inhabitants, standing guard. One patrolled the corridor outside the room Sascha was confined to, most likely left there to make certain Sascha stayed where Alan had put him. Lysander had requested someone find Sascha a few books as he'd promised.

But now he had to put Sascha out of his mind.

"Have you found anything?" he asked as soon as he entered the room.

Romilly and Kirill were both there, Kirill rifling through a small writing desk while Romilly looked through the drawers in the bedside tables. They both straightened and bowed when he spoke.

"Nothing yet, Your Majesty," Romilly said. "Aside from learning Jannik has particular tastes in erotic art and a rather large collection of it."

"Nothing relevant, then. Unless something is hidden within the collection?" He didn't plan on asking what Jannik's tastes were. He didn't want to know, and from Romilly's face, they wished they didn't.

Romilly shook their head. "I searched through it all, or all I've found, and there's nothing concealed within it that I've been able to find."

"Nothing here either, Your Majesty," Kirill replied when Lysander inquired of him. "So far, I've only found writing supplies in the desk, none of them used, and a few history books in the sitting area."

"Anything in the books?" Lysander asked. Perhaps something had been tucked in the pages or jotted in the margins. Something, anything, that might help them.

"Not that I could see on first glance, Your Majesty, but I set them aside to study more closely." Kirill gestured at the small stack on a table near a plushly upholstered chair. "Especially with the subject matter—the glory of Ivria and the dragon Talent."

He nodded. "What's left to do?"

"We've searched the obvious places in this room, Your Majesty, and some of the not so obvious ones," Romilly said. "There is an argument to be made for tearing through it top to bottom in case Jannik secreted something away in a place we'd never think of."

Kirill added, "From here, we need to move on to the dressing room. There's also a bathing room attached. I can't believe he would hide anything in there, but it's probably best to be safe and search it too."

"Good, do it." He glanced around. They didn't appear to have need of him here, as much as he wanted to do something, to be useful. Sometimes he hated the part of being king that required him to wait around while other people did the work he directed. He missed being able to go out and do things himself —which was why he was here instead of waiting back home for news, that and the need to show these traitors the strength of Ivria's king. "Do you have it handled, or would another pair of hands help?"

Romilly and Kirill glanced at each other, which was telling enough. They didn't need him here looking over their shoulders. Kirill launched into an excellent refusal that did not actually refuse explicitly. Lysander waved a hand to stop him. "Fine, fine. You two keep searching here. I'll go back to the study and those papers we found. Bring anything of interest to the study.

Let's consolidate our findings as much as possible to guard from prying eyes."

"Yes, Your Majesty," Romilly and Kirill answered in unison.

He left them to their work, knowing they would attend to it diligently and scrupulously. They weren't spies but envoys—diplomats, negotiators between clans—and still they'd discovered this plot and brought it to his attention; they would be capable of searching a room, even if they didn't care for the task.

Lysander wound his way through the castle again, back toward the study and the work awaiting him there. He encountered Alan on the stairs, and they continued down together, waiting to speak by mutual and silent agreement. They'd grown up close, Lysander obviously alway destined for the throne and Alan—Lysander's cousin on his mother's side—always planning on his guard. Lysander had felt the distance in their relative positions more since he'd inherited, and he hated it. He trusted few people completely and had exceedingly few friends. Alan was both, and he didn't want to give that up.

A soldier remained vigilant outside the locked study door. Alan had a few words with them, checking in while Lysander unlocked the door. Once he and Alan were inside, he closed the door again to give them privacy. Surveying the study, he frowned. The piles of papers and ledgers looked no less daunting even with the fortification of a meal. Lysander stifled a sigh.

"Did you get Sascha settled again?" Alan asked before Lysander could speak. The question and its tone would have been unacceptable from most, but from Alan they were merely impertinent. Lysander glared at him for form's sake.

"He's back where you put him earlier. I asked for a few books to be brought in, give him something to occupy himself so he doesn't cause trouble."

Alan's stare was knowing. Too bad Kirill and Romilly weren't here so Alan would feel constrained to temper his words and expressions. "I doubt Sascha could cause trouble, not the kind you're referring to. He's beautiful enough his face could probably cause riots, but that's a different issue."

Lysander shot a glare at Alan over his shoulder as he walked to the desk. "Have you spent much time staring at his face?"

"Some," Alan said mildly. "It's difficult not to look at such a face. I'm sure most people would agree."

He wanted to keep glaring, so he forced himself to sit and drag a pile of papers closer.

Alan was undeterred. "You have been doing a lot of staring."

"I haven't."

"You have, and you have too much dignity to allow this conversation to descend into childishness more than it already has."

Lysander's glare had more heat to it this time, and he directed the full force of it at Alan, who had moved to stand in front of the desk.

Alan's gaze remained keen and unwavering, though there was some mischief lurking in the depths of his eyes. "You're going to deny what I can plainly see?"

He glared a moment longer. "Fine. I've been looking at him. As you said, who wouldn't?"

"You don't usually. Not to say you don't find people attractive, but you don't generally look so obviously."

"I was not being obvious about anything."

"Obvious to me. I do know you well."

Lysander nodded, conceding that point. "Is there a reason we're talking about this? Or are you just amusing yourself by harassing me?"

"That is a factor, I won't lie." Alan grinned. "But I am

wondering what's going on. I wouldn't have thought you'd let yourself be distracted now by a pretty face."

"I am not being distracted. I've noticed him. That's all," Lysander said firmly. He could order the discussion ended, but he had just been thinking of how much he liked that Alan was a friend—it seemed wrong to bring his position as king into their conversation.

"Is it? You seem...fascinated by him." Alan shook his head before Lysander could speak. "And I'm not saying you shouldn't be, but have you thought about whether pursuing anything with him is wise while we're embroiled in this mess? That his family might be part of. On the other side."

Giving up, Lysander let out a long breath and rubbed a hand over his face. "I've thought about it, and I know very well it isn't wise to become involved with Sascha. At least until we know what his parents did and whether he's a part of it." Maybe not even then. "And whether his family are traitors or not, they sold him into this arrangement with Jannik. He's had no choice in the matter that I can see. I don't want to be another thing he has no choice about."

Alan nodded. "Sensible. Admirable. But?"

Lysander glowered at him. "But, as you say, I'm fascinated by him. And since I now hold everything of Jannik's, Sascha's contract transferred to me. I've been considering what to do about him, especially if he isn't involved but his family is. And I'm tempted to...keep the contract in place."

Alan's eyebrows lifted. "Really? I had no idea you were thinking of entering into such an arrangement."

"I wasn't." After his father's death, his mother had pushed him to wed, but he'd put her off, with the excuse of potentially having to marry more strategically later on. He'd had children after he was crowned because he needed heirs, and he'd always wanted children anyway. He didn't need to be married to have children eligible to inherit under Ivrian law. Privately, he'd hoped for some kind of connection with a future spouse. A concubine arrangement had never once entered his thoughts. Before.

"But you are now? With Sascha?"

"I am considering it," he said slowly. "And we've probably talked about it enough when there are more pressing matters to attend to."

"Very well. I'm here if you'd like to discuss it further."

"I'm sure you'll let me know if you want to," Lysander said with a sardonic look. "Now, give me an update on the current situation in the castle."

Alan switched topics immediately. "The search is progressing well. It's taking time, of course, because we want to be thorough."

Lysander understood the enormity of the task and only wished they could have brought more people, could've trusted more people, but he couldn't yet. He gestured for Alan to continue.

"One of my people found a cache of coins and jewels behind a panel in a wall. It might mean nothing, or it might mean Jannik was keeping wealth handy. I'll have reports from questioning the staff for you shortly," Alan continued. "Nothing I've heard sounds suspicious. No one has spoken to Hannes yet."

Lysander sat back in his chair. "We're going to have to question him. I'm pondering how long we should let him sit alone before we do."

Perhaps some time to think about the consequences of his actions would make him more amenable to talking, or perhaps he would remain belligerent and uncooperative and utterly loyal to Jannik.

"Are you planning to try Jannik again? Or leave him to be interrogated after we return home?" Alan asked.

Lysander pondered it for a moment. "I think I'm going to leave him where he is for now. When we remove him from the castle, you can have the guards drag him past me. We'll see if he's inclined to talk then."

"Yes, Your Majesty."

They separated after a few more moments of discussion, Alan to check in with the progress his people were making and Lysander to the stacks of documents they'd found earlier. He set aside the encoded papers for Romilly. Romilly was proficient with the code they'd found other conspirators to use, assuming this was the same one. If it wasn't, they'd need the help of someone more skilled in codebreaking. Lysander would deal with that eventuality if it occurred.

He became engrossed in piecing together everything else to get a sense of Jannik's affairs. Some ledgers looked perfectly normal, but he found some odd entries when he looked more closely—amounts that seemed out of place. Lysander frowned as he tried to decipher them. He'd purposely taken up the ledgers because what he'd seen of the concubinage contracts was infuriating. The terms were bad enough; the ages of some of the older man's concubines were worse. Some far below the age for which such a contract should even be allowed. They'd have to look into every person and family mentioned for connections to the plot, but he chose to exercise his prerogative to leave them for Romilly.

A guard interrupted Lysander's work some time later. "Your Majesty, the belongings of Lord Jannik's concubine were found. The trunk is in one of the bedchambers upstairs. Would you like it moved?"

"No, leave it. Unless that room isn't appropriate for him?"

"No, Your Majesty. Shall I escort him up?"

Lysander waved a hand. "No, I'll take care of it. Tell me which bedchamber it is, then return to your work."

As the soldier left, Lysander glanced out of the window and saw just how dark it had become. He'd been working for quite a while—so had Kirill and Romilly, and he'd expected them in the study long before now.

Best to check on them. He'd walk Sascha up and then find Kirill and Romilly.

When he arrived in the small parlor where he'd left Sascha, the room appeared empty. Had Sascha gotten past the guard in the corridor? Then he saw a flash of red. Walking softly, he rounded the corner of a small couch. Sascha lay curled up on it, fiery hair spilling over the cushions like a cascade of rubies. He had taken off his shoes and left them neatly beside the couch but remained dressed otherwise. His eyes were closed in sleep, and he had one hand beneath his cheek in a position that should have looked utterly innocent. Somehow it didn't. Which had to be Lysander's fault.

Sascha should be in a bed, not on too-short couch. Lysander leaned down intending to wake him, but hesitated. Instead, Lysander continued to bend and gently lifted Sascha into his arms. Careful not to jostle him, Lysander straightened, but Sascha didn't stir. He had to be exhausted to fall so deeply asleep.

Lysander cradled Sascha gently and carried him from the room. He wasn't heavy, but Lysander had to admit that even such a light burden as Sascha felt heavier after he'd climbed the steep stairs. He found the bedchamber, and a guard in the corridor, whose eyes widened at the sight of Lysander, opened the door for him. At Lysander's order, she closed the door behind him and left him alone with Sascha. The bedchamber was smaller and far simpler than Jannik's, but Lysander hadn't seen enough of the castle to know if that was typical. Lysander had to assume this was meant to be Sascha's bedchamber as his trunk—sitting at the foot of the bed—had been found here, but he was surprised the chamber wasn't more luxurious.

Lysander laid Sascha carefully on top of the bed, then straightened and contemplated the young man. Sascha would likely be uncomfortable sleeping in his clothing, but Lysander wouldn't presume to undress him. If Romilly felt Sascha wouldn't mind them doing it, he'd leave Romilly to take care of Sascha.

He turned from the bed, and a section of the wall swung open with a bang.

CHAPTER 5

Sascha gasped and sat bolt upright. He flailed for a moment, sinking into the soft mattress beneath him. Wait...mattress? He looked around. He was on a bed in an unfamiliar bedchamber without his shoes. The king was standing over him, and Romilly and Kirill were spilling into the room through an opening in a wall. What was happening? Was he dreaming? He'd curled up on a couch earlier...

"What?" Sascha rubbed his eyes, trying to clear the fuzziness of sleep from his mind. "What is going on?"

"That's an excellent question," the king said as he stared at Romilly and Kirill. "Do you two have an answer for us?"

Sascha was certainly eager to know why Romilly and Kirill were walking around in the walls, but his question also referred to how he'd gotten here. He doubted Romilly and Kirill were the ones who could answer that part of it—he also wasn't certain he could bring himself to ask King Lysander for the information.

Romilly and Kirill stared at them, eyes wide, for a moment, before snapping out of their own shock and answering.

"Your Majesty, our apologies for the intrusion," Kirill said.

"While searching Jannik's dressing room, we discovered a hidden door and decided to discover where it led."

"When we were finally able to get it open," Romilly said, picking up the story, "we found ourselves in a secret passage."

Kirill sent Romilly an unamused look. "Should we call it something so dramatic?"

"It's the most accurate term," Romilly insisted.

"And it led you here?" the king asked, cutting through the disagreement.

"Yes, but there's another branch to the corridor as well," Kirill said. "It ends in a small room with no other entrances. There's a desk and shelves. I think we may find the information we're looking for there."

"Show me." Lysander strode around the bed and followed Romilly and Kirill through this room's secret door without another word.

Sascha glanced around for a moment, taking in his surroundings now that he was reasonably certain he was awake. A bedchamber with his trunk in it and a secret passage connecting it to Jannik's bedchamber. Had this room been meant to be Sascha's? The thought made Sascha shudder. It also made him not want to be in the room alone.

He hesitated briefly—because it really wasn't his place—then gave in and dashed after the king, Romilly, and Kirill.

The secret passage, because, yes, the name fit even if it was overly dramatic, had smooth stone walls and a tiled floor, worn with age and use. How often did Jannik make this secret trip from his bedchamber to the one meant for Sascha? Did he always house his concubines there? He pushed the question aside—best not to think about it.

The others weren't far ahead, and Sascha crept quietly after them, not trying to sneak so much as to not get in the way. All right, he knew he would likely be sent back as soon as they noticed him, so it was best to go unnoticed.

The smooth tiles of the floor were slick and cool under his stocking feet. The cold radiated upward into his legs, then the rest of him, leaving him chilled and longing for shoes and cloak. Had someone carried him up to a bedchamber but left his clothing behind? He shouldn't have taken them off. What if he never got them back? He didn't often get such nice new things.

Was it the pretty new clothing, made only to enhance Sascha's attractiveness to Jannik, that drew the king's attention? Sascha was aware of his appearance, and since the king barely knew him, it was the only thing that might tempt him into making Sascha his concubine. Because it seemed King Lysander was contemplating such an arrangement. Sascha had spent quite a bit of time thinking it through, but he'd come to no conclusions before exhaustion had dragged him into sleep.

Well, except to acknowledge that the king generally got his way. Was it possible Sascha was about to trade one arrangement he hadn't chosen for another? The king had said they should both think about it, but had he meant it? Or was he just trying to appear reasonable? Sascha had given himself a headache trying to puzzle out the king's motives; continuing to do so would only result in frustration.

Romilly and Kirill led the king around a bend in the corridor, and Sascha quickened his steps to catch up with them before they were out of sight. The candles Kirill carried here were the only light now that Sascha had left the dim illumination of the bedchamber behind. He had no desire to find himself alone in the dark. Around the corner, they didn't even walk a moment before they arrived at an open door—a real door, not one disguised as part of the wall.

"How did you get in?" the king asked. "Was it open like this?"

"No, Your Majesty," Kirill said. "Romilly picked the lock."

"And I'm running out of usable hairpins. If I need to do any more of it, I'll have to see if Sascha has any to contribute," Romilly put in. Their tone was light, but the complaint seemed real. If so, Sascha did in fact have hairpins to give Romilly.

"I'll bear that in mind." The king moved into the room, and without his broad-shouldered form blocking the doorway, Sascha could finally see inside.

The room was tiny, just big enough for the shelves lining the stone walls floor to ceiling, most full, and a desk and chair in the center. None of it was ornate or grand. The only thing with even a hint of the luxuriousness Jannik seemed to favor was the rug spread on the floor beneath the desk. Its plush, vibrantly patterned surface covered a floor made of the same tile as the passageway. Kirill began working his way around the room, lighting more candles with magic.

"It's a good bet we've found what we're looking for," King Lysander said as he surveyed the room.

"Most likely, Your Majesty." Romilly continued, uncertainty in their voice, "But why he would keep so much? Wouldn't it be safer to destroy it?"

"He might have been too arrogant," Kirill pointed out. "He might have assumed no one would find his secret room and everything would be safe."

"Or he might have decided keeping information implicating other members of the conspiracy was worth the risk," King Lysander mused.

Sascha hovered in the doorway behind Romilly, peeking around them at the two men inside listening avidly. Romilly had to know he was there, but they said nothing.

"You're thinking blackmail, Your Majesty? Or control?" Kirill asked.

"Perhaps, or a safeguard." The king surveyed the small

room. "Or, as you said, arrogance. We can ask him about it, though I doubt he'll answer."

"I'm not certain it matters why, Your Majesty," Romilly said. "If there's information about the plot here, we have it now and can use it."

"True." King Lysander frowned. The expression should've made his face less attractive, but, somehow, it didn't, and the fact Sascha was even noticing it disturbed him. "I want to know what's here, and we need to decode those letters we found in the study. It's strange he would keep them there when he had a more secure location."

"Perhaps the letters don't pertain to this matter at all," Kirill suggested.

"Or perhaps they're decoys," was Romilly's contribution. "Or he just received them."

The king's frown deepened. "Do your best to decode them, and we'll match them up to what we find here. If everything is in code, I'm afraid you'll have quite a bit of work ahead of you."

Sascha couldn't see Romilly's face, but he imagined it didn't change despite the size of the task in front of them. All Romilly said was "Yes, Your Majesty."

"We need to know what their next step is, and we need to know who is involved." The king almost looked pained for a second. "There isn't room for all of us in here so I'll go back to the contracts we found and gather a list of names to investigate. How far did you get, Romilly?"

"My notes are on the table in the study, Your Majesty. I can fetch them for you, or I can work on them once I finish here."

"No, you have enough to do here. It infuriates me that Jannik and the families of his concubines entered into such restrictive and outdated contracts. And the ages of some of his concubines! Barely more than children." The king shook his head. "For people ready to discard tradition and risk all our safety to reveal who we are to the world, they're also quite willing to invoke the most old-fashioned, hidebound customs we discarded years ago. How do they reconcile it?"

"Because it isn't about tradition or lack thereof." Sascha's eyes went wide as the king, Kirill, and Romilly turned to face him. Romilly had a rueful look on their face, and dismay flooded Sascha. He hadn't intended to speak.

The king fixed him with a sharp stare. "In a moment, we'll discuss what you're doing here. For now, explain what you meant."

Sascha firmed his spine, even as his cheeks heated and his heart began to race. "Yes, Your Majesty. I only meant it sounds as if they aren't concerned with tradition, or not entirely. They're thinking about power."

"How do you mean?" the king asked, the question almost snapped out.

"Well," Sascha said slowly, considering his words carefully. He had no knowledge of this conspiracy or its members—and hoped his speaking didn't make the king think he did. The thought was just there and it had slipped out, but now he had to articulate whatever instinctive impulses had brought him to the conclusion he'd made, even as his thoughts began to scatter. "Well. If they want to reveal the existence and reality of dragons to the world, they believe those with the dragon Talent are more powerful, perhaps more worthy."

Sascha hesitated, but no one spoke, so he made himself continue. "My parents... They value my older brothers who have the dragon Talent more. Timur and Grigoriy have the responsibility and the honor in the family. They are my parents' heirs. My oldest brother already has a son with the Talent as well. My sisters and I didn't inherit the Talent, and our only value to our parents is to be traded away for wealth and connections. With belief in that...hierarchy, perhaps someone wouldn't care about making things better for someone like me, as long as I'm useful." Sick to his stomach, he wanted to shrink back under the weight of their combined stares, but he refused to allow himself. "I could be wrong, of course. Your Majesty."

A moment passed in silence, then another. And Sascha fought the urge to slink away and hide. But then the king spoke. "What you say makes a lot of sense. It doesn't, however, do anything to take suspicion off of your parents."

"I know, Your Majesty."

The king nodded, his expression thoughtful. "Thank you for giving us something to think on."

The feeling of being a puppet with its strings cut swept through Sascha again when the king focused elsewhere. He sagged just a bit and let out a long breath, trying to inconspicuous about both actions. And even so, he only allowed himself an instant before he straightened and waited patiently once more.

"We need more help, Your Majesty," Kirill ventured to say.

"How long do you think searching this room will take you?" the king asked.

"It isn't so much the search as the time it will take to read and organize and decode—especially if the majority of the papers are in code," Romilly said. "I believe another set of eyes would be helpful."

The king sighed. "Who do you have in mind?"

Romilly and Kirill glanced at each other, seemingly conferring silently about the decision. Finally, Kirill said, "We could bring Galina here. She knows the situation and will be able to help."

King Lysander studied Kirill and Romilly for a moment. "All right. I'll send for her."

"Thank you, Your Majesty," Kirill and Romilly said.

"Get to work in here. I'll return to the study. Send for me if you come across anything."

"Yes, Your Majesty," they replied, once more in unison.

The king made his way out of the little room, pausing only to take up a branch of candles, and Romilly was forced to vacate their spot in front of Sascha to allow the king through the door. Sascha wanted to cringe again now he was in the king's sight, but he refused. He would not cower, especially in front of a man whose concubine he might be, even if he was the king.

King Lysander stopped in front of him and watched him for a moment, gaze searching. "Come along, Sascha. They need to work."

"Perhaps I could help? If they need it?" Sascha couldn't imagine what prompted him to offer. Oh, he would be happy to help, and he was certainly still curious to know the details of what Jannik had been up to, but he didn't expect King Lysander to agree. "I'd be happy to do anything I could, Your Majesty."

"I don't believe you're a part of this plot, Sascha, but neither can I let you learn more about it with your family under suspicion and your own innocence not entirely proven."

Sascha jolted and his stomach dropped. He fumbled for a defense. "I'm a loyal Ivrian. I had nothing to do with this. I didn't even know it was happening."

"I can't allow you access to this information if I don't know you're trustworthy. You might choose to share it, with your family or someone else. You might even inadvertently disclose it."

"But you have no intention of allowing me to go free, Your Majesty," Sascha said, suddenly bold, and horrified at himself, but if the king suspected him of treason, maybe it didn't matter. "You're going to keep me, as a prisoner maybe. Or as your concubine. Either way, you're keeping me here or with you or somewhere you choose. How would I pass along information to my family or anyone else?"

Sascha was shaking, his face hot, by the time he finished speaking. Being bold was one thing—bold might be admired or at least indulged—but what amounted to blatant insolence to the monarch? He could be in quite a lot of trouble.

King Lysander stared at him, his expression unfathomable, for long moments. Sascha looked down at his feet, studying his stockings, wishing for shoes, as he tried to keep himself from being ill all over himself or the king.

Finally, the king spoke. "Come with me."

"Your Majesty," Romilly said as the king took Sascha's arm in a firm grip.

"Do your work, Romilly." King Lysander didn't look back as he began walking, towing Sascha with him. Sascha glanced over his shoulder, his gaze landing on Romilly's worried face. He shook his head, trying to keep them from doing anything else. Sascha had spoken; whatever happened next was his own fault, his own responsibility. Romilly shouldn't get in trouble because Sascha had lost his head.

The king marched Sascha through the secret passage and back out into the bedchamber Sascha had woken in. But he didn't stop there—the king continued out into the corridor. The hold he had on Sascha's arm remained firm but not painful. He kept Sascha moving at his side but didn't drag him off his feet. The king was treating him with some courtesy. Would he do so if he was about to have Sascha punished for speaking out of turn?

The king guided him through corridors and down stairs and through more corridors to what looked to be a study. A very messy one with papers and books strewn about on all the flat surfaces. He wondered for a moment why Jannik would keep his private study in such a state, then realized the search of Jannik's papers and records had caused the disarray.

"Sit there." The king nudged him toward a chair, and Sascha hastened to obey his command. Once he was seated, he tried not to shrink back as the king loomed over him.

King Lysander frowned down at him, time stretching out around them as Sascha scrambled to anticipate what he would do, thoughts racing. Finally, the king spoke. "I'm going to excuse your outburst because you've had a trying day. Don't test me because I won't excuse another. Do you understand me?"

Wide-eyed, Sascha rushed to reply. "Yes, Your Majesty. Yes."

"Good. Stay where you are."

He nodded quickly. "Yes, Your Majesty."

When King Lysander turned away, Sascha let out a long, slow breath. The king could easily have punished him for the outburst—his parents would've done so if Sascha had dared to speak to them in such a way. Which he wouldn't have, so why had he dared to now? King Lysander seemed to want him as a concubine and that fate might be the safest for Sascha at this point, but the king could change his mind at any time if Sascha wasn't more cautious with his words.

CHAPTER 6

Lysander strode to the door and sent one of the soldiers stationed outside hurrying off to find Alan. While he waited for him, Lysander went to the desk. He glanced out of the corner of his eye at Sascha once he was seated. Sascha sat exactly where Lysander had left him, gaze trained down at his lap. Lysander stared at the top of his head, at the tumble of red waves cascading from it, as he couldn't see Sascha's face. Had he cowed Sascha completely? He didn't want to break him, certainly not after what sounded like the beginning of Jannik's efforts to do just that, but neither could he allow Sascha to defy him.

He shouldn't even care. What did it matter if he'd intimidated Sascha too much, if he'd scared him? Sascha was wrapped up in a plot against Ivria—might even be a part of it— so why should Ivria's king be disturbed to upset him? Maybe if Sascha was upset they'd get something out of him, some indication of his involvement, some information about what his family was doing.

Only Lysander couldn't quite make himself believe those

rationalizations. Alan might be right about him losing his head over Sascha.

"Your Majesty."

Sascha jumped slightly in his chair, sending his dark red hair swaying, at Alan's voice from the doorway, but he didn't look up. Lysander wanted to sigh, but instead, he stood and went to Alan. Leaving the door open and Sascha in full view, Lysander left the study and walked a few feet into the corridor with Alan. When he spoke, it was quietly, to keep his voice from carrying to the soldiers near the door and Sascha inside the study.

"I need you to send someone for Lady Galina. Kirill and Romilly found something big when they were searching Jannik's bedchamber, and they're going to need help."

Alan's eyebrows went up. "Of course, Your Majesty."

They could trust Alan's soldiers, but they'd be of little help to Romilly and Kirill in combing through the contents of the hidden room. His trust in Romilly and Kirill—and Galina—was the only thing keeping him from struggling through every encoded document himself.

"I'll send someone for her immediately, Your Majesty." Alan glanced into the study. He hesitated for a moment. "May I ask why Sascha is here?"

Lysander stifled another sigh and succinctly explained what had happened. Once he finished, he glared at Alan. "I know what you're going to say to me from the expression on your face."

"Do you?" Alan answered in as low a voice as Lysander had been using. This discussion was getting far more personal than he preferred in the open, but going into the study wasn't an option with Sascha there.

"You're going to say I was lenient with Sascha because of my fascination with him."

"I'll admit to thinking it was a factor, but I also don't think your reaction was necessarily wrong. Sascha was thrown into a bewildering situation, when he came here." Alan shook his head. "It seems he had no way to anticipate what Jannik was like, let alone the rest of this. I don't believe it's bad for you to have shown him some compassion, but I don't know that you need or want my approval."

"Perhaps not, but it's good know my judgment wasn't as clouded as I feared it might be."

Surprise flooded Alan's face. "Were you so worried about having your head turned by a pretty face?"

Lysander raised an eyebrow. "You accused me of just that earlier."

"I'm skeptical of the wisdom of taking him as a concubine before we confirm his loyalties, but I never doubted you would act sensibly and make the proper decisions." Alan glanced at Sascha again. "Neither of us believes he's part of this. True, he might be an exceptional actor who is fooling everyone, but, more likely, we're right. In which case, he really was trying to help and he became overwhelmed and upset. You were sympathetic to that. If it turns out we're wrong, I know you won't allow yourself to be distracted."

Lysander shouldn't need Alan's reassurance, but for some reason tonight, having someone else—someone he trusted—validate his judgment made him feel more confident in it. Which frustrated him. He hadn't felt the need for such a thing since the early days of his reign, and he'd hated how uncertain he'd felt then. He hated it more now.

"Thank you, Alan."

"You're welcome, Lysander." Alan nodded, and his manner became formal once more. "I'll send someone for Lady Galina immediately. Is there anyone in particular you'd like me to send?"

Lysander shook his head. "Whoever you think best."

Galina's lack of a dragon Talent meant she couldn't fly herself here. Traveling overland would take far too long, so someone would have to fly her back.

Lysander returned to the study when he and Alan parted ways. Sascha remained where he'd left him in what seemed to be the same position. Lysander thought he saw Sascha twitch when he walked back into the room, but he couldn't be certain. Should he say something to Sascha? Something to alleviate his fear?

Not yet.

Back at the desk, he pulled the stack of contracts and Romilly's notes in front of him and set to work. As the night wore on, he studied the contracts, making lists of names and dates, amounts of money changing hands, and any odd terms. They'd check into every one of these families. By the time he'd reached the end of the stack, he was thoroughly disturbed and never wanted to read another. He was also convinced of how odd Sascha's position as Jannik's concubine was, not because there was anything wrong with Sascha but because he was far older than Jannik's norm despite Sascha just being of age.

What would've caused Jannik to deviate from his pattern and tastes? Lysander's instincts told him the change had something to do with the conspiracy.

He moved on to reviewing Jannik's daughter's betrothal contract. Another old fashioned document—the terms did more to protect her future husband and his family and keep Jannik in a good financial position than to safeguard his daughter's wellbeing or happiness. Her soon-to-be husband and his family went on the list with a little star to mark them as especially suspicious. Whether or not the family proved to be traitors, Triana would have to be questioned. The dilemma was whether to retrieve her now and risk the entire operation being discovered sooner than they wanted, or to wait and risk her running if she was involved.

Lysander sat back in his chair and rubbed his eyes. He glanced over and found Sascha had finally moved. Not out of the chair, though. Sascha had curled up, his head at an awkward angle on the arm of the chair, and somehow fallen asleep. Lysander's neck ached just watching him. He couldn't leave Sascha that way.

How many times was he going to carry Sascha around while he was sleeping? As often as he had to. Lysander shook his head to rid himself of the thought and bent, sliding his arms carefully beneath Sascha. He lifted him slowly, then glanced down once he straightened. Sascha slept on. He was either a heavy sleeper or utterly exhausted. Lysander bet on the latter, if only because he'd also bet Sascha would be too anxious to sleep otherwise.

While Sascha would be more comfortable in a bed, he hadn't yet ordered another chamber prepared for him, and he wasn't going to leave Sascha in a bedchamber with access to the secret room. Instead, he carried Sascha to the couch against the wall and lowered him gently onto it. When he straightened up again, he surveyed his efforts. The couch didn't look particularly cozy, but Sascha would be better off than scrunched up in the chair. Lysander froze when Sascha moved, but he only curled up tighter and subsided into stillness again. He hesitated briefly, then went to the door. Outside, two soldiers snapped to attention as soon as he opened the door.

"Yes, Your Majesty?"

"Have someone fetch a blanket, please." He went back into the study after making his request, but it didn't take them long to fulfill it. There was a light tap on the door a few moments later, and one of the soldiers entered with the blanket. Lysander dismissed them with his thanks before he returned to Sascha's side. He laid the blanket over Sascha and then smoothed the hair out of his face with a light touch. He couldn't convince himself what he did was similar to covering his sleeping children against the cold, though he did try telling himself he was only being considerate—none of it had any impact. He was in trouble.

Lysander strode across the room and poked at the fire, coaxing it higher to warm the room...and realized he was doing it because Sascha looked cold. He shook his head and paced to the desk, then back. Was he really in trouble? If Sascha had no part in the plot against Ivria—aside from being treated as a commodity changing hands—there was nothing to stop Lysander from taking him as a concubine for as long as he desired. Assuming Sascha himself agreed. Lysander might have the right to keep Sascha in such a role, but he preferred his bedmates willing.

And if Sascha was a part of the conspiracy...Lysander wouldn't let his attraction stop him from doing what had to be done. Alan was right. He wasn't going to let a pretty face cloud his judgment when it counted. But he hoped he wouldn't have to. Not only because he wanted Sascha, but because he hated to think his instincts and Alan's were so off. Sascha couldn't have fooled them both, couldn't be so skilled at deception.

Lysander stared across the room at Sascha, sleeping deeply, utterly exhausted. He wanted him to be genuine.

He sat at the desk, but before he could return to his work, another knock sounded on the door. He glanced reflexively at Sascha, but he slept on. "Enter," Lysander called softly.

The door opened, and Kirill walked in. He bowed and frowned almost immediately when he straightened, confusion clouding his eyes as his gaze landed on Sascha. Lysander wondered if he would dare to ask anything.

"Romilly had wondered where you were taking their kinsman, Your Majesty. I'll, ah, let them know," Kirill said carefully.

Romilly would have been worried. They wouldn't have anticipated Lysander's leniency toward Sascha. "Tell Romilly their cousin is fine. After you report what you've found."

"We're not finished yet, Your Majesty. There is quite a bit to go through, and everything we've found so far is in code."

"I've sent for Galina."

"Thank you, Your Majesty. She will be a great help, I'm sure." Kirill seemed to settle himself more comfortably, though he was standing.

"In the meantime, what can you tell me?" He gestured for Kirill to sit in the chair in front of the desk, which he did before he began his report.

"As I said, everything is in code. Some of it seems to be in a personal code of Jannik's, or perhaps one we simply haven't seen other members of the conspiracy using so far. Romilly and I will study it, but we may need someone more skilled in these matters if we can't make sense of it." Kirill paused, and Lysander nodded. "For the moment, Romilly has been focusing on documents in the code we've seen before while I search."

"Has Romilly found anything of interest?"

Kirill nodded. "I have more names. Romilly also found some correspondence that implicates Sascha's parents."

Lysander couldn't say he hadn't expected it.

"However, what Romilly read indicates Sascha himself was kept entirely unaware. As we suspected, Sascha's parents were using their son to bargain for more wealth and connection, but the position they were looking for was within and among the plotters."

Everything inside Lysander lifted and spun. He had a chance to get what he wanted, if Sascha was agreeable—and Lysander tried not to think about how quickly Sascha had become what he wanted. But Sascha was beautiful and Lysander even liked his courage, so there was no reason he shouldn't want to take Sascha to bed. There was nothing more to it. There couldn't be anything more to it.

He considered briefly how this liaison might be perceived when the treasonous conspiracy was revealed and people found out the King's Concubine was the son of conspirators. But he dismissed his concerns just as quickly. He wasn't going to punish people who weren't to blame—not with anyone who shared familial or clan bonds with a conspirator and who proved not to be involved themselves. Lysander would handle the perceptions of others as they came.

"Suspicions or no, it's good to have the confirmation," he said finally, knowing he'd kept Kirill waiting while he thought.

"It will be a blow to Sascha. Romilly, as well."

"They'll handle it. I think Sascha is halfway to believing it already, maybe even more than that." Now, he glanced across the room at Sascha, who continued to sleep undisturbed by their low-voiced conversation.

"Yes, Your Majesty, I'm sure they will." Kirill turned to look at Sascha briefly as well. "Romilly will likely be reassured if they know Sascha will be safe and cared for."

Lysander raised an eyebrow. Kirill's statement was as close as he would get to asking what had happened and why Sascha was sleeping in the study while Lysander worked, and he was certainly asking on Romilly's behalf. "Sascha is an adult. I'm sure he can see to his own safety and care."

"He is, but he's also in a bad situation, one that leaves him without power of his own. And family is important."

Lysander inclined his head, agreeing. Family was important, and he shouldn't forget it. Sascha would be grateful for Romilly's concern. "As you say. Tell me what else you've found so far."

"Yes, Your Majesty."

Lysander leaned back in his chair and listened to Kirill's

recitation attentively, tapping his fingers against the arm of the chair as he let the information settle into his mind. He wrote nothing down—Kirill and Romilly would be making note of any pertinent information, names, dates they would need. When Kirill finished, Lysander was quiet for a moment more, turning everything over again.

"All right. We need to strategize," Lysander said finally. "Continue working until Galina arrives, then let her take over and come down here. I'll have Alan come in as well. We'll put together everything we have and decide on a next step."

"Yes, Your Majesty."

After Kirill left, Lysander remained as he was, lounging back in the chair, not going back to the papers on the desk. He suddenly found it difficult to keep his eyes open, and no wonder —a glance out the window showed him dawn just lighting the horizon. True daylight was still a ways off yet, but he'd been awake for a full day, and not a leisurely one.

He wanted a bed and to sleep for even an hour. And was more tempted than he should have been to take Sascha and go find one because sleeping with Sascha pressed against him also seemed like an excellent idea.

Instead, he settled himself more comfortably against the chair's cushions. Another throne-like chair, similar to the one in the dining room, which said something about Jannik and his mindset, but Lysander wouldn't examine that now. For the moment, he closed his eyes. He'd let himself have a brief nap. And he'd make certain to tell Alan, Kirill, and Romilly to get some rest after. It was his last thought before sleep took him.

~

SASCHA BLINKED his way to wakefulness slowly. He shifted,

rubbing at his eyes. And teetered precariously. Flailing, he just managed to save himself from tumbling off the couch.

He pressed a hand to his chest over his pounding heart, very much awake now. The last thing he remembered was trying to make himself less noticeable by staying still and quiet in his chair. He must have fallen asleep, and someone had moved him. Again.

Surveying his surroundings, he found himself still in the study. And....and the king appeared to be asleep in the chair behind the desk. Sascha pushed himself up to a sitting position, the blanket tangling around his legs. He had a blanket now too. Interesting. Who had moved him and gotten him a blanket? Who had cared enough to see to his comfort?

His gaze strayed to King Lysander behind the desk. Could he have...?

The king was the only one here, had been the only one in the room last Sascha remembered. Logically, the king was most likely to have moved him and covered him. But would he have? Was the king concerned enough about him to do so? If so, it was...stunning.

Sascha sat, still tangled up in the blanket, and studied the king—Lysander—while a warm wave of something sweet moved through him, leaving him feeling safe, as if he was something important. It was likely all in his head. He was assigning far too much significance to a simple action. But what the king had done, especially after his compassion earlier, felt significant.

He frowned, hesitating, then gathered up the blanket and swung his legs off the couch. His stocking feet met the chill of the floor, reminding him he still had no shoes. He'd have to find them soon. He stood and made his way across the room. A glimpse of the sky through the window had him changing direction. He stopped at the window and stared outside. The horizon was pink with the dawn. The whole day and night gone. So little time. He felt as if he'd been here for weeks.

And he still had no idea what would happen to him.

Shaking his head, he turned and continued on his original path. He hesitated again when he reached the desk but firmed his resolve and moved forward. With light, quick movements, he tucked the blanket around the king where he slept in the chair. Once he had, he stepped back immediately, but he hadn't even made it a step when a voice froze him in place.

"What are you doing?" The king's voice was sleep-roughened, but his tone didn't seem harsh.

"I'm sorry. I didn't mean to wake you," Sascha said, the words tumbling out in a fast whisper as his heart began to pound.

"I didn't intend to sleep long." King Lysander answered in something close to a whisper as well, and suddenly, the conversation began to feel intimate.

"You should sleep a little longer. It's barely dawn, and I'm sure you have a long day ahead of you." He was being bold again, perhaps too bold, but at least this time he wasn't being insolent with it. Something inside him wanted to care for the king. Obviously, King Lysander had no one looking out for him here—the soldiers would protect him from danger, but there were other important ways of watching out for someone. Did he have anyone to do so when he was at home? "Sleep. I'll go sit on the couch while you do. I promise I won't move from there. Or I could go out in the corridor where the soldiers could watch me?"

The king shook his head. "You don't have to. Your concubinage contract is on top of that pile. Romilly said you wanted to see it. Sit and read it if you like."

"Thank you, Your Majesty. I would like to." Even though he

dreaded what it would say, given the suspicions against his parents. "But you should still sleep."

Something softer came into the king's eyes. Amusement and...affection? No, it couldn't be. "I'll sleep a little while longer."

Sascha smiled. "Good."

He began to move away again, but this time, the king reached out and caught Sascha's hand in his. Sascha shivered at the intensity of the king's gaze. King Lysander watched him steadily as he slowly raised Sascha's hand to his lips. Sascha's breath caught when the king's lips brushed over his knuckles, then stopped entirely when he flipped his hand over and pressed his lips to the center of his palm. A tingling warmth raced through him from that spot. It was like nothing Sascha had ever experienced, and when Lysander released his hold, Sascha felt as if he were floating, disconnected from the floor beneath his feet. Then the king smiled, just slightly, but a real smile, and it did odd and unfamiliar things to Sascha's insides.

"Read your contract, Sascha. We'll talk after I wake up."

"Yes, Your Majesty," Sascha whispered. This time, when he moved away, Lysander let him. He took the contract from the desk and went back across the room, feeling as if he was being watched the whole way, but when he turned and sat on the couch, the king's eyes were closed.

Sascha had no idea what was happening between him and the king, but it confused him. The king was considering keeping him as a concubine, so he'd assumed King Lysander desired him. But Sascha's own reactions were foreign to him. He'd never felt in such a way, never had anything like a physical reaction to another person. Hadn't been sure he was capable of it. Why now? And why the king?

But...perhaps he shouldn't worry over it. If the king did want him, having such a reaction to him was good. Helpful. So long as he didn't go and fall in love, everything would be fine. And what chances were there of him falling in love with the king?

Nerves somewhat calmer, he turned to the contract in his hands. Would he be able to understand it? Mother and Father hadn't thought it necessary for him to read it, had implied heavily he wouldn't be able to comprehend it. He could only try. The contract, though its language was formal and stilted, was easy enough, if a bit slow, to read. However, it wasn't easy for him to believe. He'd have to ask whether such harsh terms— with regard to him at least—were standard in this type of arrangement, but something told him they weren't. He wasn't surprised Jannik would want them—a few moments in the man's company had given him that information—but he was surprised his parents had agreed to them.

Or maybe he wasn't, if he believed they were involved in a treasonous plot with Jannik and who knew how many others. Sascha didn't want to, but what was the alternative? That they saw him as a disposable commodity? Perhaps they did either way; they certainly didn't view him and his sisters in the same way as they did his brothers. Sascha had accepted long ago the role he and his sisters were given in the family, but he hadn't seen quite how ruthless his parents would be or how little choice and respect he would have.

He sat back, letting the papers fall into his lap for a moment, and sighed. No matter the reason his parents had for signing such a contract on his behalf, they'd shown far more concern for themselves than for him. And he wouldn't go back to them and let them do it again. He was of age; he'd find his own way somehow. Unless the king kept him as a concubine. The king had at least asked Sascha his thoughts. King Lysander seemed to respect him, and he'd been kind. Sascha gazed across the room at the sleeping king and was struck by the trust it took for the king to sleep with Sascha in the room. Perhaps staying with him for a while wouldn't be bad.

With that thought, he picked up the papers in his lap and began reading the contract one more time.

Some time later, a quiet noise from across the room broke his concentration. He looked up. King Lysander was awake and watching him. Thoughts skipped through his head too quickly for him to grasp as he sat still under the force of that intense mahogany gaze. What came out of his mouth was, "My parents are part of this plot, aren't they?"

The king didn't even twitch in surprise. "Yes, they are. Romilly found proof while you were sleeping. I'm sorry."

Sascha nodded. He wouldn't say it was all right, when it wasn't. "Thank you. And me? Do you still believe I'm involved as well?"

"No, I don't."

Relief moved through Sascha in a wave. He stiffened his spine to keep from sagging in his seat. He'd have a more emotional reaction to the revelations about his family at some point, perhaps soon, but his relief that he wouldn't be wrongfully accused or punished for their crimes was immediate and strong.

King Lysander looked on, quiet and patient, waiting.

"Thank you, Your Majesty," Sascha finally said.

Before the king could say anything else, a knock sounded on the study door. King Lysander still watched Sascha, but he called out, "Enter."

The commander opened the door and stepped inside. He bowed, but Sascha didn't think he was imagining the faint surprise in his eyes as he surveyed the scene in the study—Sascha on the couch with papers spread over his lap, the king behind the desk with the blanket still half over him.

"Your Majesty," the commander said. "Lady Galina has

arrived. I showed her upstairs. I believe Romilly and Kirill are on their way down, or will be shortly. Kirill said you wanted to meet with us."

"I do. It's time to decide our next steps. I need everything we've found so far." The king's gaze strayed back to Sascha, who remained on the couch. But something had changed from earlier when King Lysander had told him to sit in the chair and not move. He didn't feel he had to stay seated, still and small, anymore. The king wasn't going to do something to him if he moved.

"Yes, Your Majesty," the commander replied.

The king was still watching Sascha. If they were going to talk, he couldn't be here. He'd offered to help, and the offer hadn't been received well, but even if it had, Sascha wouldn't have expected to be part of this meeting. Steeling himself, he gathered up the contract and stood, drawing the commander's attention as well.

"I can go, Your Majesty, so I don't intrude on your meeting. Perhaps I could clean up and change?"

King Lysander watched him for another moment, assessing. "I think that would be a good idea."

The king glanced at the commander, who understood what the king wanted without a word exchanged. "His trunk was moved to another bedchamber. I could show him up?" At the king's nod, the commander turned to Sascha. "If you'll come with me?"

Hiding his relief that his suggestion had been right, Sascha nodded in the elegant, almost regal, way he'd been taught. One of those things he'd been taught were important in the life he'd been chosen for. He'd need them if he became King's Concubine. Sascha walked closer to the desk and bowed to the king, taking more care to make the movements fluid and graceful. "Thank you, Your Majesty."

"Go. After I finish here, we'll have something to eat."

He concealed his surprise at the king's words. "Yes, Your Majesty."

Sascha followed the commander from the room. Once they were out in the hallway, the commander only said, "This way," before he began walking. Sascha hurried after him but was reminded of his lack of shoes immediately by the shock of cold stone floors through his thin, delicate stockings—likely ruined now. Sascha, who had a fondness for pretty, delicate, lacy things, had been thrilled with the new clothing. His parents had thought the money worth spending so as to send him off looking a particular way—not that they hadn't outfitted their children appropriately all along. But new clothes, so many at a time and of such quality, were an unknown luxury. Ruining them made him sad and sorry.

The loss of a pair of stockings shouldn't disappoint him so, but all he had were the clothes he wore and the possessions in his trunk.

The commander led him back out to the entrance hall and up the stairs, then along a corridor. Sascha kept up, despite placing his feet carefully to avoid slipping on the stone. The bedchamber the commander led him into was slightly smaller than the other. The furniture was delicate, the colors pale. Sascha studied it from the doorway.

"We believe this was Jannik's daughter's bedchamber. It's clean and aired, which is more than can be said for the guest chambers," the commander said. "There's a bathing room, and your trunk is there."

Sascha followed his gestures to take in the door across the room and his trunk at the foot of the bed. He wasn't sure how he felt about using Triana's bedchamber, but he supposed it was a moot point. She had left, and if her attitude was anything to go by, she never intended to return. There was no reason for him to feel odd about using her room for the—hopefully short —time he would be residing at the castle.

"Thank you, Commander," Sascha said to the stony-faced man. The commander was being respectful, certainly, but Sascha could determine nothing of this thoughts from his face or bronze eyes. Perhaps he had no opinion about Sascha's presence, but Sascha couldn't quite believe that, not about the commander of the King's Guard in regard to something potentially affecting the king's safety. His inability to even hazard a guess frustrated and worried him.

The king would make his decision about Sascha's fate, and Sascha couldn't make him choose one thing over another. But he could show himself to best advantage—his looks, yes, but also his personality and the grace and manner that had been trained into him as well. Perhaps even his intelligence. Romilly had always told him he was, and maybe they were right. Maybe the king would value intelligence. Only time would tell.

Once the commander had left him alone, Sascha went to his trunk and flipped open the lid. He wasn't surprised to see the jumble of his belongings, but dejection filled him nonetheless. Then anger popped up out of nowhere, directed at the nameless soldier who had so carelessly pawed through his things, burning through him like fire. Sascha clenched his fists, wanting to hit something, but just as quickly, a wave of weariness swept through him, drowning the anger. He sank down on the bed. The soldiers were doing their jobs, even though Sascha hated the idea of what little privacy he had being breached, of someone's hands all over his possessions, of everything being in such disarray.

But there was nothing to be done about the cause of the mess. He could only clean it up. With a sigh, he pushed himself to his feet and went to investigate the bathing room. He'd start himself a bath and then begin putting his trunk to rights.

CHAPTER 7

"What have you found so far?" Lysander asked as he settled himself more comfortably in the chair behind the desk. The blanket was back on the couch; Alan had said nothing about the way he'd found Lysander and Sascha when he'd returned, likely only because Kirill and Romilly were already present. It would've provoked less attention to have been found kissing Sascha or having him on the desk—but waking from a nap while Sascha sat on the couch for all the world as if he were watching over Lysander was another thing.

Lysander had more important matters to deal with now. Alan could keep his thoughts to himself for a while—forever would be fine. "Have you gotten Galina settled?"

"Yes, Your Majesty. She's upstairs continuing where we left off," Kirill said. "It's going to take all three of us some time to go through everything in that room."

"I have my people searching for other concealed rooms or passages," Alan remarked from where he leaned against a cabinet. "If there's one, there might be more."

Lysander was so tired of being here already; the thought of additional time at Grau was almost too much. But he tried not to show his impatience. "True. We need a plan of action. The longer we stay here, the more likely it is someone finds out and the conspirators go to ground."

"They may do that anyway, Your Majesty. Jannik will no longer be here. Someone will try to contact him," Romilly said, fatigue obvious in their blue eyes. "His son will return at some point too. And there's a castle full of servants we have to worry about."

"We aren't going to be able to leave the castle unattended," Lysander said. "We can't let the staff go abruptly, both for their well-being and for our ability to keep this quiet."

"And keep the castle under your control," Alan added.

"Yes. I can't stay here indefinitely." Though he'd have to return at some point to check on matters with Jannik's holdings, even after he installed someone he trusted here to make sense of the more mundane aspects of them. "I'll appoint someone to stay. I don't want to leave any of you here."

Or at all. Romilly and Kirill had other places he needed them to be, and he needed Alan with him.

"Do you have an estimate of how long it could take you and Galina to search through everything upstairs? If no other hidden rooms are found, of course." Lysander drummed his fingers on the arm of his chair. "Or would it be easier to pack everything up now and bring it back with us for you to finish?"

"We'd bring it back with us anyway, wouldn't we?" Romilly asked with a glance at Kirill. "I wouldn't think we'd want to leave such things here, even with someone to watch over the castle, Your Majesty. Evidence shouldn't be left behind."

"In which case, it might be just as easy to pack it all up and bring it with us now as opposed to staying," Kirill suggested.

"We could do so, leave the search of the castle under the supervision of whomever you choose, Your Majesty, and return home to continue sorting through the evidence of Jannik's crimes," Alan added.

"It seems the consensus is to leave quickly," Lysander said dryly. The three people facing him looked back with bland expressions on their faces. "Fine. We'll plan to return home as soon as possible. I do want to talk to Hannes and perhaps Jannik again before we go now that we know more. I also would like to know where Jannik's son is. I'm worried most about him. If he comes home and finds his father gone and gets away before we can apprehend him... It will be everywhere that we have Jannik. And the rest of the conspirators will go to ground."

"And we aren't ready to snap them all up yet," Alan mused. "If we were, I'd say to go after them and get it over now."

"Going after them all at once would mitigate the risk of losing them, but we don't know who they all are yet," Kirill pointed out. "With everything upstairs, we'll get a lot of names, and we'll have to figure out who was part of this and how. But I don't know if we'll have all the names once we've gone through everything."

"We have to piece together as much as we can," Lysander said. "I want us to know all the major players in this and as many of the minor ones as possible before we move."

"How likely is that? It means keeping knowledge of Jannik's arrest and the seizure of his holdings from getting out," Kirill said.

"That's the question, isn't it?" And Lysander wasn't sure of the answer. "We can't dawdle, but we can't move too quickly either."

"We're walking a fine line, Your Majesty," Alan said.

"Start by finding Jannik's son," Lysander said firmly. "I want him located and quietly taken into custody. Let's find out if he's involved."

"And the daughter?" Alan asked.

"With his views and what we've seen, do any of us believe she's part of this?" Romilly asked.

"No, but we need to know, and we will need to talk to her." Lysander drummed his fingers on the desk again. "Finding her and watching her are all we can do for now if we don't want to give anything away. Get someone close if we can. We'll bring her in immediately if we see an indication she's involved. If not, we wait and watch."

"You don't think we need what she might be able to tell us now?" Alan asked. "I think we need all the information we can get."

"I do too, but I'm trying to balance our need for information with the necessity of not revealing our plans." Lysander shrugged. "We're walking a fine line, as you said, and I'm not certain yet how to manage it, but this seems like the right course for now."

Alan contemplated him for a moment, then nodded. "Yes, Your Majesty. If we have the right person watching her, we might be able to get some information on the husband and his family. If Jannik married her off to someone else in on the plot, it could be useful."

Lysander had thought of that, especially with what Jannik and Sascha's parents had done to Sascha. "Talk to Felix. He can give you information about the family to help you."

"Has Prince Felix been told? Should he be?" Alan asked with a raised brow.

Lysander sighed. "He hasn't, but he should be. I've been reluctant to involve too many people, but we need Felix if we're going to manage this properly. Unless you know of a reason he isn't trustworthy?"

"Not at all," Alan said quickly, and Romilly and Kirill voiced their agreement more convincingly. Lysander didn't have time to determine Alan's reservations.

"All right. I'll inform him when we get back." He made the decision with more confidence than he had in other recent decisions. Not because he believed Felix wasn't to be trusted—far from it. But a treasonous plot had caught him entirely unaware and he was second-guessing every move. Lysander hadn't had so little confidence in his judgment since he first became king. He couldn't afford such uncertainty.

"So, we'll try to keep knowledge of Jannik's arrest from getting out until we gather enough information to have a good sense of the scope of the conspiracy. We need to apprehend everyone as near to simultaneously as possible—unless we get a hint of the information getting out. Then we'll move early and deal with the consequences later." Perhaps they shouldn't have even come here yet, but he'd thought it a necessary risk. They needed more information, and Jannik seemed the most likely source of it. "Comments? Feel free to tell me if I've overlooked something important."

Kirill, Romilly, and Alan all assured him they couldn't think of anything, and he ended the meeting. He'd wanted more details of what Kirill and Romilly had found, but at this point, it seemed easier to let them continue unless they found something urgent. Especially since the job of packing up Jannik's papers was a large one. They dispersed with the agreement to meet for a meal shortly. Only Romilly remained.

"Yes, Romilly?"

"I thought I'd go up and get Sascha, if he'll be eating with us, Your Majesty?"

Did it seem as if Romilly was fishing for information? If they wanted to act as a protective family member for Sascha, they'd have to be more direct. Lysander knew they were well capable of it, even with their smooth court manners.

"Yes, he's welcome to join us, and I told him so. If he's changed his mind, he doesn't have to come down. You can ask if you like," he said with studied nonchalance.

Romilly watched him for a moment, then nodded. "I will. Thank you, Your Majesty."

Lysander watched as they left, knowing Romilly would likely say something to him again, perhaps after speaking with Sascha. And he would allow it, to a point. He understood and respected the need to protect family. Sascha's parents hadn't seen fit to do so, but Romilly was taking up for him. Lysander would see what happened—what Romilly did, what Sascha said when Lysander spoke to him about his future. About his future with Lysander.

Odd how much he liked the idea of a future with Sascha in it. He didn't know Sascha. But he wanted to. He was intrigued by the man, and Sascha's grace and compassion, his strength and bravery, only deepened Lysander's fascination. And, yes, he wanted Sascha in his bed, soon and often.

Perhaps it wasn't so odd, then. But Lysander didn't often have time or judge it wise to indulge his attractions—a king had to be careful. Did he trust Sascha? No...but they would see. If trust grew between them, if they enjoyed each other, he could see the potential for the arrangement to last. If not, well, he'd treat Sascha far better than his parents or Jannik had.

Sascha didn't allow himself the long, relaxing bath he would have liked, despite the warm water fragrant with the soothing scent of his own bath oil. The bathing room was decorated in the same style as the bedchamber, with a certain amount of luxury in the large tub and the crystal sconces set with long tapers. Under other circumstances, lingering in such surroundings would be pleasant. But he wasn't certain when the king would call for him...and even more importantly, the bedchamber and bathing room doors had no locks.

He hadn't noticed if the other bedchamber—the one that would've been his—had a lock on its door. Of course, the presence of a lock wouldn't have mattered with that secret passage opening into the room. In any case, he didn't feel comfortable lazing about in the bath when anyone could come in. There were too many people wandering the halls, or patrolling them, that he didn't want potentially walking in on him naked.

He could've used a nice long soak too.

Sascha hauled himself out of the deep tub and dried himself with a towel he'd found in the cupboard beside it. Then he slipped into the dressing gown he'd pulled from his trunk. The wool was warm and soft against his skin in the slight chill of the room, and more welcome as he walked out into the even chillier bedchamber. He needed to put on clothes, but he couldn't wear just anything with the king here.

Sighing, he surveyed the bedchamber...where he'd unpacked and laid out everything that had been in the trunk while the tub filled, hoping to save it from ruin, organize it, and somehow make it all fit back in the trunk again. The task was monumental. Fatigue and worry and the press of emotion probably made it seem so when it shouldn't. That logical thought did not help.

Even though the trunk had been packed meticulously for the journey here with every article inside fitting like a piece of a puzzle, he didn't know if he could manage the same again, especially without the help of his sister and a maid. But he'd have to try.

After he found something to wear.

Actually, first he needed slippers. The floor was far too cold.

Which reminded him a pair of his shoes was somewhere in this castle and he'd need to retrieve them before he left.

Slippers were surprisingly easy to find, and he slid his cold feet into them with some relief. Underclothes were as well, as he'd left them in a pile on the bed with his night clothes. He donned them quickly but still enjoyed the feel of silk on his skin, then wrapped himself in the gown again. Dressed enough to not feel cold or too vulnerable, he set about organizing the chaos of his belongings so he could find proper attire. Whatever proper attire was in this situation.

A knock came on the door before he was near finished and made him nearly jump out of his skin. He pressed a hand to his chest and took a breath, hoping to slow his racing heart, and asked, "Who's there?"

"It's Romilly," came the reply from the corridor.

As he called for Romilly to enter, Sascha sagged a bit in relief. Romilly was one of the few people here Sascha actually wanted to see. Sascha frowned—one of the few? Shouldn't Romilly be the only person he wanted to see? Why did Sascha keep thinking of the king?

"Are you all right?" Romilly asked.

Sascha blinked himself out of his musing and forced the frown from his face. "Yes, of course."

"I doubt there's any 'of course' about it with everything you've fallen into." Romilly stepped into the room and shut the door behind them. "I..."

Romilly surveyed the bedchamber, their eyes widening. "What's all this?"

Sascha looked around himself. If anything, the mess appeared worse. Rather like the trunk had exploded, sending clothing and assorted items everywhere. "Oh, well. My trunk was a mess after someone searched it. I've been trying to put everything to rights, but I've made it worse."

Romilly's expression turned to one of dismay. "I'm sorry, Sascha."

"It's not your fault." He glanced around again. "I'll get it all back in again, hopefully without doing too much damage."

"I'll help you."

He smiled at them. "Thank you, but I'm sure you have more important things to worry about than my wardrobe."

"Your wardrobe would make a pleasant distraction." Romilly rubbed at their eyes, and Sascha looked more closely at his cousin. He frowned. There were purplish smudges beneath Romilly's eyes, and their usually impeccable posture was absent. "Are you all right? You look exhausted."

"I am tired. Kirill and I didn't sleep last night—we haven't had much sleep for a while." Romilly sighed. "It's all right."

"No, it isn't." Guilt filled Sascha—he'd slept, a little at least. "Why don't you nap? I'll clear the bed for you."

For Romilly, he would dump everything on the floor and worry about it later.

They smiled, but there was weariness in the expression. "Thank you, but I can't yet. I only came to fetch you so we could eat with the king. After, I'll check in with Galina, and then maybe I can rest."

"You need sleep, Romilly. You won't help the king or anyone if you collapse in the middle of your work," he said sternly, perfectly comfortable scolding Romilly, despite his cousin's more elevated station. He'd even consider saying something to the king, for Romilly.

"I promise I'll sleep after." They smiled again, still tired but fond, then pushed at the locks of hair that had escaped from the band holding it back in a tail and made a face.

Sascha studied them for a moment, assessing. He'd seen

Romilly's face pull into the same lines many times before, when they were beginning to feel wrong in their own skin. "Well, sit and let me do something about your hair at least. Maybe it will make you feel better."

"You don't have to."

"I want to." Sascha gestured at the vanity stool, waiting expectantly until Romilly sat. Once they had, Sascha grabbed up his hairbrush and a couple of ribbons and went to stand behind them. He loosened the hair tie and pulled it free, letting Romilly's red hair fall over their shoulders, then he began to gently brush the knots out.

He worked in silence, the tug of the brush meditative for him, hopefully soothing for Romilly as well. After a few moments, Romilly said, "The king told you about your parents."

Sascha froze for just an instant, the brush hovering as he lifted it from Romilly's hair. But he'd known Romilly would say something—he wasn't truly surprised they did now. He set the brush down carefully and picked up one of the blue ribbons. He held it up in question to Romilly and got a nod in return. "He did. I read the contract they signed as well."

"How are you doing?"

He focused on braiding, methodically weaving hair and ribbons together, letting the action ground him. Romilly stayed quiet, letting him work their red locks into an intricate braid and giving him time to gather his thoughts. Sascha chewed on his lip, an unattractive habit his mother had broken him of long ago. It had apparently returned with the tense situation. "I... I'm not certain. I feel betrayed, but it's all just a step removed somehow. I think I'm going to feel a lot about it later—I might even completely fall apart—but not now."

"Understandable." Romilly reached back and took his wrist, giving it a comforting squeeze. "I'm here."

A rush of gratitude filled Sascha. What would he have done

if Romilly hadn't been here? Sascha could stand on his own two feet quite well, or he thought he could, but his time here had been so far outside his experience. He swallowed and spoke past the lump in his throat. "I know. Thank you."

"Of course."

"How are you? You aren't close to my parents, but they're family, if distant. And something like this in the family…" He couldn't say the word treason.

Romilly sighed. "I'm not sure either. The very fact that such a plot exists is almost unthinkable. That our own family is a part of it is…too much. But I can't deny it, so we'll have to learn to accept it and what comes next."

Sascha shuddered. "I'm not ready to think about what comes next. I know I should, but I can't yet."

"It's all right. I don't want to think about it either."

They fell into silence then, and Sascha focused on Romilly's hair, keeping the braid neat and pretty, and tying it off with another ribbon. He scrutinized it for a moment, making sure his work was up to being seen by the king, then nodded. "All done."

Romilly twisted a bit to see what they could of Sascha's work and smiled. "Thank you. It's lovely."

Sascha smiled too. Romilly had relaxed a little when they'd seen their hair, and he was happy to have helped. "You're welcome. I just need to dress quickly. I haven't held us up, have I?"

He hadn't thought about keeping the king waiting, and he should've. If he stayed with the king, he'd have to remember, have to be far more careful.

"No, not at all." Romilly smiled as they turned on the stool. "They didn't expect us back immediately. We had a little time."

Romilly wouldn't lie, even to make him feel better, especially with the king waiting. Nevertheless, he needed to dress quickly. He turned to the bed and the clothing covering it. "I'll still hurry. Do you need to go down?"

"I can wait for you, unless you'd prefer I didn't."

"Of course you can stay," he said absently as he considered his options. What was the proper attire for breakfast with the king in the castle of a traitor when one's parents were also traitors and one was potentially about to become concubine to the king? He hadn't learned the rules for such a situation. "I don't know what to wear," he finally admitted with a helpless laugh. "It's silly, but...the king is waiting."

"You've met him already, and this isn't a court presentation —that, we'd have to spend much more time planning for—but I can understand why you're thinking about it so much." Romilly came up beside him and surveyed the piles on the bed. "The king wants you to be his concubine?"

Butterflies exploded in Sascha's stomach, making him slightly ill. "He mentioned it, but before he had the proof about my parents. So, I don't know."

"He isn't going to hold the actions of your parents against you." Romilly began gathering clothing from the bed. "Do you want to stay with him?"

Sascha plucked at his dressing gown. "I..."

"You can tell me to stop asking." Romilly handed him a shirt and gave him a penetrating stare. "I won't be offended."

"I know, but I don't mind that you're asking. I'm just not sure what to say. If he wants me for his concubine, I don't see how there's another option."

"Put these on." Romilly passed him a pair of pants. "There are other options. The king wouldn't force you, no matter what he could do by rights. He wouldn't want you unwilling. And though you couldn't go back to your parents, mine would take you in. I'll be leaving Ivria again on the king's business, but we can ask if you could come. Maybe go to university there? If you want."

Sascha's head began spinning with only the couple of options Romilly presented. And...university? Him? He was decorative, not studious. To settle himself, he began dressing.

After a moment, Romilly turned with a jacket in their hands. They studied Sascha, now wearing the slim plum pants and white shirt, and nodded in approval. Holding out the jacket, Romilly said, "Or you can stay with the king. I believe he'll ask you to, and I believe he'll treat you well for as long as you're with him."

Sascha took the jacket, a pretty silvery gray with white lace at the cuffs, and ran a hand over the soft material. "I might want to stay with him."

"There's nothing wrong with wanting to." Romilly leaned against the bed. "Are you ready for what it means?"

"To live with the king? Be so close to him and among the highest of Ivria's nobility?" Nervousness pulled an awkward laugh from him. "Probably not. I was prepared to be someone's concubine or husband, but no one expected me to move in such circles."

Romilly huffed. "I don't know why. You're beautiful and clever and everything someone like the king would want."

"Oh. I..." He closed his mouth when he realized he had no words.

They waved a hand. "Sorry. Obviously I've never been in the position you would be with the king, but I've moved in those circles. I'll help as much as I can."

"I'll gladly take your advice, if I stay. Thank you."

Romilly hesitated. "Um. What about sleeping with him?"

"Well, it's expected."

They rolled their eyes. "I'm aware. And I assume part of

preparing you to come here was explaining the mechanics of it all."

"You assume correctly." Sascha was frankly surprised his cheeks weren't burning. They had been while everything Jannik might have wanted from him had been explained.

Romilly floundered a little but continued on. "How do you feel about the idea? You and I... We've always been similar in that we don't see people and feel attracted that way."

Sascha had known they had that in common for a while now, as Romilly had been the only person he felt comfortable speaking to about it, especially after his sisters began mooning over people—though they weren't allowed any freedom to act on those feelings—and he hadn't. "I've never just seen someone and wanted to kiss them or go to bed with them. It's always seemed odd anyone would."

Romilly laughed. "Agreed."

"But I'm...intrigued by the king. He was kind to me when he didn't have to be. He showed compassion when he could've punished. He didn't assume I was involved in the schemes of Jannik and my parents when he would've been justified to. I feel something." Sascha only wished he knew what the something was—and that it didn't make him so nervous. "I want to be around him more. And I don't think I'd mind going to bed with him."

His stomach swooped as he said it, but the feeling wasn't all anxiety—he recognized a little anticipation as well. Which was something else to think about. It was all perplexing and new and he didn't think he was explaining it well to Romilly when he didn't understand it himself.

Romilly studied him for a moment longer, then nodded as if everything had been decided. And maybe it had. "All right. If you change your mind, please tell me. I'll help."

"I know you will." He stepped forward and gave Romilly a

quick hug. "For now, help me find a pair of shoes, will you? I left a pair in the parlor, but I don't have time to search for them now."

Romilly laughed and went to do as he asked while Sascha tugged on the long jacket. "I'm sure the king will buy you a trunkful of shoes if you stay with him, but never fear, we'll find the missing pair anyway."

"You didn't tell me I'd be getting new shoes," Sascha said, putting on a mischievous grin. "I wouldn't have hesitated at all."

Romilly only rolled their eyes.

CHAPTER 8

Lysander watched as his breakfast companions began scattering after the meal, though he was supposed to be reviewing the missive he'd just received from Wyndward. Kirill and Galina—a tall, golden-haired woman with a sharp gaze and a quick mind, not to mention a formidable Talent—were deep in discussion as they made their way toward the door. Alan was already out in the corridor talking with one of his people. But Lysander would've been lying if he denied his attention was mostly on Sascha.

Sascha and Romilly were whispering to each other, their heads bent close, shining red hair gleaming in the light. Romilly had returned with Sascha for the meal with their hair twisted into a complicated braided arrangement. Sascha's hair remained loose, but he'd changed into fresh clothing that looked quite well on him, highlighting his slender frame and long legs. Just one reason Lysander was having a difficult time keeping his eyes off of him.

Sascha nodded to something Romilly said, and, after darting a quick glance at Lysander, bowed and slipped from the room behind Kirill and Galina. Lysander raised a brow as Romilly turned to him. "Where is Sascha going?"

He'd told them all they could leave, but he hadn't expected Sascha to go off somewhere alone.

"A pair of his shoes were left behind in the parlor where he spent most of yesterday. He's gone to fetch them. He didn't want to trouble anyone," Romilly replied.

Lysander's fault probably. "He shouldn't hesitate to ask if he can't find them. We can make sure he retrieves them before we leave."

"Thank you, Your Majesty. I'll tell him." Romilly hesitated. "Your Majesty, I spoke with Sascha about his future. Obviously, he can't go home now. I offered to take him with me when I leave Ivria if he wants to go—with your permission and if you choose to cancel the contract, of course."

He stared at Romilly for a few moments. He wanted to be annoyed at Romilly's presumption, but he couldn't, not with the strength of the familial bond between them and Sascha. "I don't want to release Sascha from the contract." He held up a hand to forestall Romilly's protest. "I will if he wants me to, and I will consider allowing him to leave with you if he wants to. But I would prefer to keep him with me."

Romilly nodded slowly. "The terms of the contract..."

"Are far too harsh toward Sascha. A new contract will be presented to Sascha for his approval." He wouldn't force Romilly or Sascha to trust his word. Sascha's own parents had betrayed him—why should he trust a stranger, even if the stranger was his king?

"Thank you, Your Majesty."

"I'm going to talk with him this morning. I want us to leave soon, and I want Sascha's answer by the time we do."

Romilly nodded slowly again. "It's a big decision for him to make."

"I know."

"If he agrees, will you release him later if you don't suit?" Romilly asked.

"I don't want an unwilling concubine, Romilly. I'm not Jannik. If Sascha and I find we don't suit after a period of time, I'll see him happily settled elsewhere. Perhaps even send him to you." Lysander studied them. "Have I sufficiently reassured you?"

"Yes, Your Majesty. Thank you," Romilly said. Though the tone of their voice seemed to say 'for now' more than anything else. Romilly's loyalty was something Lysander had never questioned and never would, but he couldn't help wondering how far it went when up against their loyalty to family. Lysander didn't intend to give himself a reason to find out.

"Good. I'm sure Kirill and Galina could use your help?"

Romilly hesitated again. "I'll just find Sascha first."

"No, I'll find him. You get back to work—the sooner we finish up here, the better."

If Romilly was still reluctant, they didn't show it when faced with Lysander's unwavering stare. They nodded, then bowed and left the room.

Once he was alone, Lysander glanced down at the report in his hand. Then he folded it back up and stood. He had something more pressing to do—or at least something he had to do before he could concentrate on what he should be doing.

Out in the corridor, he waved Alan off when the man looked about to follow Lysander. He would catch up to Alan after; he didn't need his cousin with him for this. Alan's soldiers were still a presence in all the corridors, searching the castle, now looking for any secret passages and rooms in addition to papers and hidden wealth. Lysander acknowledged them as he walked but didn't ask about their progress. He would hear about it later. For now, he found his way back to the little parlor where he'd found Sascha asleep on the couch yesterday—was it only yesterday? That day felt like a month.

Sascha was still there, eliminating a need for Lysander to track him down. He was straightening from a crouch when Lysander walked into the room, and he whirled in a graceful spin, rich red hair lifting gently from his shoulders, to face Lysander.

His blue eyes were wide and surprised. "Oh! Your Majesty. I just came to get my shoes."

A pair of gray low-heeled shoes dangled from the fingers of one of his hands. He lifted it slightly then let his hand fall back to his side almost immediately, as if he regretted the gesture. Lysander found the slight awkwardness endearing, which was disturbing. Would this odd fascination ease when he finally took Sascha to bed? Would it clear Sascha from his thoughts entirely? He hoped not entirely—he doubted he'd be ready to be done with Sascha so soon.

The slight awkwardness detracted not at all from Sascha's loveliness. Sascha's current clothing flattered him as much as his previous had, obviously carefully chosen for the purpose. But Sascha wore the clothes well, and after a little rest, his beauty was even more apparent. He would be a jewel on anyone's arm, including the king's. As exquisite as Sascha looked now, Lysander dreamed of stripping him of the clothing and seeing him bare, creamy skin glowing in candlelight, dark red hair spread around him. He forced the images from his mind.

"Romilly told me. I wanted to talk to you," Lysander said, keeping his gaze intent on Sascha, examining him, his demeanor. Though it was easy to get lost in Sascha's beauty, Lysander wanted to be certain he was steady enough to make the decision Lysander was about to put to him.

"Yes, Your Majesty?"

"We'll be leaving soon, and the question of your future is one we have to settle before we go. I would like to keep your contract in place, amended, of course, to give you the protections you should have, and ask you to be my concubine. Is that something you would like?"

Sascha contemplated his question in silence; Lysander liked that he didn't jump to an answer—of any kind—too quickly. "Yes, Your Majesty, I would."

Triumph coursed through Lysander, but he forced himself not to swoop Sascha up and carry him off to start fulfilling his fantasies. He wouldn't, not now, not yet. He did prowl closer as Sascha watched him, eyes still wide. Lysander only stopped when he was so close Sascha had to tilt his head up to meet Lysander's eyes. Lysander liked that he did—he didn't want someone who wouldn't look into his eyes, not as a lover, not in his bed.

He wanted to just take, but he wouldn't. "May I kiss you?"

Sascha blinked his large eyes, his lips parting again in surprise. But his voice was sure was he spoke. "Yes."

Lysander couldn't help his smile—satisfied, anticipating—as he bent closer to Sascha. He slid one hand around the back of Sascha's neck, the other around his trim waist, and bent his head to touch his lips to Sascha's. The contact was like lightning arcing through him. Sascha made a little noise in his throat and brought a hand up to Lysander's chest, but he didn't push Lysander away. He just pressed his palm there, perhaps anchoring himself, perhaps keeping a little distance. Or perhaps some other reason entirely.

Lysander didn't intend to do more than kiss Sascha now, but he couldn't go another moment without a taste. And though it would just be a taste, it didn't have to be quick. He savored, his lips moving gently and carefully over Sascha's for long moments. Then, slowly, reluctantly, Lysander lifted his lips from Sascha's and straightened, though he kept his light hold on him. Sascha's eyes were wide and dazed, his lips reddened and kiss swollen, his cheeks delicately flushed. He looked delectable. But Lysander was quite aware this had likely been the first time he'd been kissed, and he refused to do anything to overwhelm Sascha. Until he knew what Sascha was comfortable with, what he wanted, Lysander wouldn't rush.

"All right?" he asked, gently massaging the back of Sascha's neck.

Sascha watched him for a couple of breaths, the look in his eyes unfathomable, and then his lips curved in a little smile, sweet with just a bit of mischief to it. "Yes, very much all right."

Lysander chuckled. "I'd very much like to kiss you again if you're amenable to the idea, but unfortunately I have to return to the study."

"Of course, Your Majesty. What you're doing is more important."

He had a feeling Sascha could become quite important to him if he let him. But he dismissed the idea. Just because he found Sascha beautiful and intriguing didn't mean anything more would come of it.

"Thank you for understanding."

"Perhaps I could return to the bedchamber I was given, Your Majesty?"

He saw no guile in Sascha's eyes. "If you'd be most comfortable there."

"Yes, please."

"I'll walk you up."

"Oh, you don't have to, Your Majesty. I know you're busy."

"Not at all. I'll walk you." He could've ordered a soldier to do so, but he wanted to see Sascha safely to the bedchamber himself. Partly to make certain Sascha didn't wander where he shouldn't, though he saw no indication Sascha would after the incident in the secret passage. He presented a demure image, but there were flashes of stubbornness and boldness that made Lysander both curious and cautious. A vulnerability that made Lysander protective. He wanted to talk with Sascha—soon and at length, potentially while sipping wine in bed with Sascha clad only in sapphires—to learn all there was to know about him. Now was not the time though. And though Sascha likely wasn't part of this plot they were trying to counter, Lysander had learned long ago that someone in his position needed to be careful letting people close too quickly.

"Are we speaking to Jannik?" Alan asked as they strode down the stairs into the castle cellars.

"No. He isn't going to give us anything," Lysander replied with a shake of his head. "Not yet. He still thinks he's untouchable."

The man's arrogance was galling, and Lysander was going to be pleased to see him brought down from it.

"Hannes, then. You think he's going to talk? He's remained stubbornly loyal to his master and tight-lipped this whole time." Alan wasn't wrong—Hannes was either extremely loyal or a believer in the cause, or both. From what little experience Lysander had of the man, Hannes seemed to be well-suited to a place with Jannik.

Lysander nodded to the guard at the bottom of the stairs but didn't pause. "I'm done asking politely."

"We were asking politely before?" Surprise threaded through Alan's voice.

Lysander didn't bother answering.

They were keeping Hannes on the west side of the cellars, separated by the entire floor and its maze of storerooms from

Jannik. With the soldiers down here—some guarding the prisoners and others searching—Hannes would find escape difficult, but if he managed to, the distance made him unlikely to reach Jannik without being caught. And made it impossible for the two men to communicate.

"What's the plan for not asking politely?" Alan asked in a low voice as they turned the corner closest to Hannes's makeshift cell.

Lysander nodded to the woman waiting for them there.

Galina stood calmly a few feet from the guard, her hands folded at her waist, her face serene. For all the world as if she were in an elegant parlor.

"Ah," Alan replied.

"Your Majesty." Galina dipped into a curtsy as he approached.

"Thank you for coming down. Are you ready?"

"Yes, Your Majesty." Her ice blue gaze was steady.

"Let's go, then." Lysander gestured for the guard to unlock the door. They'd found a few of these small rooms—bare and windowless with locks already on the doors—down here. They were probably storerooms, unused now but once holding items valuable to the household. Or, at least, Lysander hoped.

Inside, Hannes stood waiting for them in the center of the room. He appeared somewhat the worse for wear, but his demeanor had not softened.

"We have more questions for you," Alan began.

"I don't have any answers for you," Hannes snarled back. Unsurprising.

Lysander nodded at Galina. At his side, she said nothing but moved one hand in a short, graceful gesture.

Hannes flew backward into the stone wall with a pained grunt.

Galina's hand kept moving, just slightly, fingers dancing through the air.

And roots burst forth from...somewhere...to bind Hannes thoroughly in place against the wall, suspended a foot in the air.

She could do much more—and Lysander might ask her to if it proved necessary—but they would start here, as they'd discussed briefly earlier. He hoped a little fear and intimidation might loosen Hannes's tongue.

"As I was saying," Alan said after a moment of silence broken only by Hannes's panicked gasps and struggles, "we have some questions for you."

THE THREE OF them trooped back up from the cellars a while later, leaving Hannes locked in again, unharmed but far less confident. Lysander was grimly pleased at the change in the arrogant man's attitude. He had allowed Alan to do the questioning, while Galina had kept Hannes trussed up and hovered several inches above the floor. Sometimes moving him about the room when he wouldn't speak. They'd gotten more from him this time. Not everything...but Lysander believed most of it. He couldn't imagine Jannik would trust too much to Hannes— he may have relied on his henchman, but Jannik wasn't the type to make a partner of him.

Lysander led Galina and Alan to the study. None of them spoke until the door was shut behind them. And even then, Lysander took a moment to study Galina in better light, but she appeared as unruffled as she had before she began using her magic. She was powerful and knew her limits, so he hadn't expected her to be physically affected, but he would be remiss if he didn't check. And doing what she had done could certainly affect someone mentally, even though she'd only scared and threatened with her magic, not physically harmed. But her calm did not appear to have been shaken either.

"Do you think he told us everything?" Alan asked. "And if what he told us is the truth."

Lysander glanced at Galina, then spoke. "He was too scared to make up so much information in the moment. Unless he rehearsed stories for such an eventuality..."

"He might have, but he doesn't seem the type," Alan mused.

"We'll give the information all due consideration." Lysander rounded the desk and sat, gesturing for the other two to take seats opposite. "We'll verify everything we can—the names, the meetings. His impressions are another story, but...we'll see what makes sense with Jannik's papers."

"I'll continue decoding," Galina said from the straight-backed chair she gracefully perched on. "How long will you stay, Your Majesty? If you'll permit me to say, your continued absence could be suspicious."

Lysander waved a hand, dismissing any insult. The truth was, he couldn't stay much longer. Not only would his absence be remarked upon soon, but he had a duty he could not put aside even for this. "I'm going back in the morning. But we need to make arrangements here."

"The search hasn't been completed." Alan frowned. "And that was before Hannes told us where more papers might be. Are we going to pack everything up and take it with us tomorrow?"

"I'm not sure we could have it all ready in time," Galina said. "And if there's more we haven't found yet, we'd be leaving it."

"We'll bring anything that we can reasonably load up by morning." Lysander leaned back in his chair and studied Galina. "Galina, I'd like you to stay and continue working through

Jannik's papers. No one can know we have Jannik, and when his son returns, we need him apprehended as well. Alan will leave soldiers with you to protect the castle while you work. I trust you can make everything appear normal here. You're in charge."

If anything, Galina sat even straighter. "Of course, Your Majesty."

"Good."

Once Galina had left, Alan turned to Lysander. "I'll begin making arrangements for our departure and choosing people to stay. Shall I make arrangements for Sascha as well? Will he be staying here for the time being, or are you sending him elsewhere?"

"Sascha is coming with me."

"You'll have to permit me this time, but I think that's a mistake," Alan said after a moment.

"I know you don't entirely trust him—"

"I don't trust him," Alan interrupted. "I don't trust anyone who might be a danger to your safety. Furthermore, in your position, you shouldn't trust him. We don't believe he's part of this plot, fine. He may not be, but he may put you at risk in other ways."

Lysander kept his voice even. "I'm quite aware of my position and all that goes with it. I don't have to know everything about Sascha to take him as a concubine."

"You're trusting too easily."

"I'm really not. At some point, we'll have a discussion about how you trust no one at all, but this isn't the time."

Alan frowned at his flippancy. "You need to be serious. Besides, even if you care nothing for your own safety, how are you going to explain Sascha? What if someone realizes he's supposed to be here? It could jeopardize our ability to end this threat."

That was a valid concern. But Lysander couldn't bring

himself to leave Sascha here, a place that had been so upsetting to him, to exile or imprison him for an indeterminate amount of time because of something out of his control. Perhaps those feelings made Lysander weak—Alan would say he was being influenced by a pretty face—but he couldn't do it all the same. "We'll come up with a plan to explain his presence and who he is."

"If you say so."

"I do." Lysander hardened his tone and gave Alan a sharp look.

"Yes, Your Majesty."

CHAPTER 9

Sascha was shocked when he thought about how short a time he'd actually been at Grau—it felt like months. And though he was still uncertain about the future, he couldn't wait to be anywhere else. He'd dressed warmly and secured his hair in a tight braid in deference to their method of travel, and now he stood in the castle entry, once again swathed in his cloak, gloves clutched in one hand, waiting.

Romilly was beside him, and Sascha was grateful for their presence, though Sascha's cousin probably had other things they could be doing—supervising the last of the packing of whatever they'd found, perhaps. Sascha hadn't asked about what they were doing since he'd been marched out of that secret room, but he assumed staying with him was not the best use of Romilly's time. Romilly had gently dismissed his suggestion that he would be fine on his own, though, so they were both here, waiting for the king to be ready to leave. Keeping out of the way of the soldiers preparing for their departure.

Sascha watched the flurry of activity swirling through the hall, but it did little to distract him from his thoughts. From worries of what might wait for him at Wyndward Castle. He'd never been there. Romilly's parents had wanted him to accompany them a couple of years ago, as they had the rank and connections to bring him to the king's court, but his parents had refused. Sascha had been bitterly disappointed—and somewhat confused, since the invitation had seemed like an opportunity his parents wouldn't want to pass up—because he'd been alive with curiosity to see the place, to see something beyond his clan's lands and the small corner of them his family occupied. His clan was respected and noble, but he came from a branch of it that was neither titled nor particularly wealthy—he wouldn't have been asked to the king's court any other way.

Was his parents' refusal then because they were already involved in treason and planned to put Sascha to use? He couldn't help but wonder, and he should probably mention it to...someone. Romilly, in case they didn't remember the incident. There was no reason they should—Romilly had been disappointed on Sascha's behalf, but the decision certainly hadn't affected them the way it had Sascha.

A part of him was still curious to see Wyndward, to experience the Ivrian king's court...but another part of him was nervous to do so. He'd been taught courtly manners, but he'd never expected to use them at the royal court, not after his parents' refusal, and certainly never in such a position. King's Concubine was a rank and position at court that would put him under the eyes of everyone, yet set above them. For an outsider who had never been anywhere or done anything and was well aware of that disadvantage, the thought was enough to make anxiety surge through him in a sickening wave.

And that was before he added in what he would be to the king. King Lysander had not kissed him again nor pressed him for anything else after their interlude in the parlor. And Sascha...was fine with the lack of attention. A revised version of the concubinage contract had been delivered to him the night before, and he'd stayed awake quite late studying it. Sascha had found it far more generous to, and protective of, him than the original had been, which stoked his anger at his parents even as it calmed some of his fears. He was still turning over what his role—especially the part of it involving the king's bed—would be, trying to get his thoughts and emotions in order over it. It wasn't that he hadn't considered the more physical aspects of being someone's concubine, just the opposite, but it had been somewhat academic. Abstract. He'd been taught what to expect in a man's bed, but he'd never felt the giddy attractions his siblings had, never had the temptation to defy the rules and put what he'd been taught into practice. Nerves and something like dread had filled him when he found he'd be handed over to someone he'd never met, but he'd hoped he would suddenly feel those sparks for Jannik.

All he'd felt for Jannik was revulsion.

Sascha wasn't revolted by the king, far from it. The kiss had been...more than pleasant. Sascha had been left a bit dazed and warm with a swoop in his stomach he'd never felt before. He wanted to feel it again. He wanted the king to kiss him again. He was curious about what it would be like when he went to bed with him. Which worried him a little. Or perhaps what worried him was how captivated he was with King Lysander. He'd never felt anything like that either.

His curiosity about the man was growing by the moment, but he was a concubine, not a husband, not a consort. He didn't have any claim on the king or his feelings, on permanence. Sascha couldn't allow himself to begin down a road that included emotion or the possibility of it. Despite the odd sense of connection he was developing for the man. Something was developing between them, or maybe just in Sascha. He had no way of knowing what the king felt—no experience in these matters—but he could remind himself not to care too much about someone who would never be his.

But if nothing else, the king had been...careful of him. He'd seemed concerned with not overwhelming or frightening Sascha, not doing anything he didn't want. After his short experience with Jannik, Sascha appreciated someone showing him that respect. All he could do was hope it would continue, as the king could do whatever he pleased.

"Are you all right?"

Sascha jumped when Romilly spoke quietly beside him. "Fine. Just thinking."

Too deeply, apparently, if he'd lost all sense of his surroundings.

"Serious thoughts. Anything I can help with?" Romilly offered in the same quiet voice, trying not to be overheard.

"Not really. My mind is running away with me. Getting me all tangled up." He stifled a sigh and spoke even more quietly. "I'm ready to leave."

The statement felt like an admission of weakness—and he'd been far too weak for far too long—but Romilly would never hold it against him.

"Soon, very soon. And I don't blame you—I want to leave as well, and I didn't have half as much happen to me here as you did."

"Not all that much happened."

Romilly nudged Sascha until he looked at them and found them frowning. "It seems like a fair amount to me. Between the way Jannik treated you and the shock of soldiers bursting in and the revelation of what your parents are doing and the worry over what would happen to you—"

"Yes, all right, I suppose it was a lot." Sascha spoke quickly; though he hated to be rude to Romilly, he also didn't much like hearing the list.

"It won't all disappear when we go, but at least we won't be here."

Sascha nodded.

Romilly opened their mouth to speak again, then closed it as their attention was drawn to something over Sascha's shoulder. "Here we are."

Sascha turned to see the king striding into the entrance hall with the commander and Kirill at his heels. One of the soldiers met them halfway across the room and bowed, then began to update them on the progress of the preparations, or so it sounded to Sascha. He didn't try to listen closely—all he cared about was that they were leaving.

"His Majesty had a revised contract brought to me last night," Sascha murmured to Romilly.

They turned to regard him with a raised brow.

"What? I read through it, and it's much better for me than the other one."

"I would've read through it with you if you wanted. You could have come for me."

"I know you would've, but I didn't want to bother you."

Romilly appeared almost hurt. "It wouldn't have been a bother."

"You had things to do, and I hope one of them was sleeping." Sascha fixed them with a stern look. "It didn't matter if I stayed awake late, but you needed the rest. I won't have anything to do except sit while we travel today—it will be far more tiring for you."

Sascha knew well the expression that came over Romilly's face—some mix of knowing they were wrong but wanting to be stubborn about it, but Romilly was an adult now, and they only sighed. "I can look at it later if you want another opinion. We'll have to stop before we reach Wyndward, probably for the night unless they've determined it's safer to press on after some rest."

He absorbed that information, which no one had bothered to tell him before. "I'd like that. Thank you."

A flash of uncertainty crossed Romilly's—still rather tired—face. "I don't mean to force myself where I'm not wanted. You're fully capable of reading a contract that affects your own life, and I don't want to imply you aren't. I just...worry."

Sascha smiled and reached out to grasp Romilly's hand. "I know you do. And I don't think you believe I'm not capable of it." Though Sascha was well-aware of his own shortcomings in education and experience with things like the document in his pocket. "I would welcome your thoughts if you have time to give them."

"I'll always make time for you, cousin."

"Everything all right?"

Both Sascha and Romilly whirled to face the origin of the new voice. Kirill stood near them, but he took a half step back at their movement.

"The resemblance between you really is uncanny sometimes," Kirill muttered. Romilly appeared to be about to say something to that startling statement, but Kirill spoke before they could. "I came to tell you we're almost ready to go, but I can leave you to your conversation. It looked serious."

"No, it's fine," Romilly said. "You don't have to. It's almost time, then?"

"Yes. The king is just speaking with Galina. Last minute instructions, I assume." Kirill nodded back toward the king, who was in the same spot but now speaking with Lady Galina. Sascha had only seen her at a couple of meals since she'd arrived at the castle, but he was impressed by her unflappable demeanor and elegance. She was wearing a divided skirt and heeled boots today, her gold hair twisted back in a thick braided knot at the back of her head, but she could have been in court dress with the way she carried herself.

Most of the soldiers had gone outside while Sascha was absorbed in his whispered conversation with Romilly, and the commander was on his way out, as well. Perhaps the soldiers still inside were the ones staying.

King Lysander finished his conversation and strode toward the door. Galina followed, and Kirill and Romilly fell in beside her. Sascha was quick to move, staying on their heels. They wouldn't leave him behind, of course, but he couldn't keep himself from feeling nervous about potentially being over-looked in the confusion of leave-taking. Only, when he stepped out into the weak morning sunshine, he saw there was no confusion. Many of the soldiers had already transformed into dragons, and others were helping them secure the baggage they needed to carry.

Even more than the lack of chaos, what struck Sascha and nearly made him miss a step was the sheer number of dragons present. He'd seen people using their Talents to transform into dragons, obviously, and often. But there were *so many* out on the cobblestones in front of the castle. It was beautiful.

King Lysander took his leave of Galina and strode out to where the commander stood among the soldiers.

"Well, I guess it's time to go," Romilly remarked, to no one in particular.

"Yes," Kirill said far more seriously. He turned to Galina and wished her farewell before he stepped away as well.

"Take care of yourself," Romilly told Galina. "I know you'll keep the king informed, but send word if you need anything. Kirill and I will be in Ivria for a while longer, and I'll make sure to let you know before we leave."

"Thank you, Romilly." They clasped hands for a moment. "You take care too."

Sascha didn't want to think about Romilly leaving at some unspecified time not too far in the future, and he didn't care for the thread that ran through both Romilly's and Galina's voices when they told each other to take care—because it sounded more like an instruction to be careful. But he reached for a smile when Galina looked at him. Sascha bowed slightly, the correct amount for someone of Galina's rank. "It was lovely to meet you, despite the circumstances."

Galina's smile was a wry twist of lips. "I'm sure we'll meet again, hopefully under better ones."

Sascha's eyes flew wide when she bobbed a short curtsy. "What—"

She shook her head. "You're King's Concubine. You need to get used to the status that comes with it. And you need to take care of yourself too."

His head spun. "Oh, yes. I will. Thank you."

"Good."

"Sascha?" Romilly called.

"Yes, coming." He nodded to Galina, then hurried to where Romilly stood, not wanting to keep everyone waiting, but no one seemed impatient.

"We're just about ready," Romilly told him. "You're all right riding with me?"

Sascha caught a glimpse of something cross the king's face where he stood a few feet away, but it was gone before he could identify it. "Yes, of course."

The soldiers had moved aside once they were transformed to give the king, the commander, Romilly, and Kirill space. But Sascha noted as they walked into the cleared area that the soldiers hadn't just moved aside, they'd formed a ring around where the king and the others would use their Talents, keeping them protected. Sascha just stayed out of the way. There didn't seem to be a protocol about who used their Talent first, or not one he could discern. Romilly quickly closed their eyes and called up their Talent. Immediately, they were surrounded by silvery light, a cloud of which swirled and grew and sparkled as Romilly's body changed from person to dragon. It faded as quickly as it had appeared, leaving Romilly standing there as a dragon.

Sascha had long since gotten over any jealousy or disappointment he'd had at not inheriting the dragon Talent himself, but every time he saw Romilly's scales, he couldn't help thinking his likely would've been a similar color to the rich blue that perfectly matched Romilly's eyes, and he felt just a bit of longing for what he'd never have. Romilly stretched their long, sinuous body for a moment before nodding, and one of the soldiers who remained human-shaped strode over to help them into the harness used when a carrying a passenger for any length of time.

Kirill had pulled on his Talent while Sascha was watching Romilly, and he now stood stretching his long neck and wings nearby. Shimmering light faded from around the commander to reveal a muscular bronze dragon—he wasted no time stretching or working kinks out of this shape, but, instead, turned to look down at the king. King Lysander stood surrounded by dragons but was the only one traveling today who hadn't transformed yet. Well, who could. Sascha seemed to be the only person without the dragon Talent in the group.

"Sir?" The soldier who had been helping Romilly appeared at his elbow. "Honorable Romilly is ready for you."

"Thank you."

Romilly was lying down to make it easier for Sascha, but he still had a climb ahead of him to get himself settled. It wasn't anything he hadn't done before with Romilly, but they'd been younger and unobserved then. Sascha hadn't had to be graceful as he scrambled into place. He bit back a sigh and steeled himself to do his best.

"Allow me to help you." It was the king's voice this time.

Sascha whirled to find him on his other side, holding out a hand.

Sascha couldn't very well refuse, even if he didn't want to be seen as needing the help. He put his hand in the king's. His fingers were warm around Sascha's, kindling an odd heat inside him. "Thank you, Your Majesty."

The king led him to Romilly and helped him climb carefully up, his hands steady and strong, then waited beside Romilly as Sascha settled himself in the harness. He didn't seem to notice Sascha was trembling. "You know how to secure everything?"

"Yes, Your Majesty." Sascha turned to the straps, making sure everything was fastened and fit snugly but comfortably around him, and then arranged his cloak with more care than necessary. He could still feel the king's gaze burning into him.

King Lysander nodded and strode away, back to the center of the group, the most protected place among them. "Are we ready, Commander?"

At the commander's affirmative, the king finally used his Talent. The transformation was the quickest Sascha had ever seen—the king's Talent was formidable. And so was the king's dragon. His scales were a rich, deep red, and they gleamed even in the poor light of the cloudy morning. The king didn't stretch or shake either, but he did draw himself up to his full height and pause there for a long moment, as if letting everyone see him, see their king. He was majestic.

Sascha realized he was clenching his hand, the one the king had taken, the one that seemed to tingle with echoes of his hold. But that was ridiculous, and he was being silly. He quickly drew on his gloves and pulled up his hood against the morning chill.

And not a moment too soon. There must have been some signal Sascha didn't see or didn't recognize, but some of the soldiers leaped into the air. Sascha looked up to watch as they gained altitude and began to circle the castle, scales bright against the clouds.

"Our turn is coming," Romilly said. "Ready?"

Sascha took hold of the straps in front of him. He hadn't been flying in so long, he wasn't sure whether he was excited or nervous. "Yes."

A moment later, Romilly was spreading powerful wings and taking to the air. Sascha couldn't hold in a gasp, but it was lost in the rush of wind and beating wings as not only Romilly, but the king, the commander, and Kirill took flight. In those first few minutes in the air, Sascha forgot about every single one of his worries and fears. Romilly darted upward through the chill morning air, and Sascha grinned madly. Flying was exhilarating; he'd loved it from the first time Romilly had flown him in lazy circles over the forest, silly that he'd almost forgotten.

Soon, the rest of the soldiers were in flight, and they arranged themselves in a formation everyone seemed to know, keeping the king, Romilly, and Kirill surrounded on all sides by soldiers. Protected from potential attack. Certainly the king always had guards, but with the plot they'd uncovered... Did they expect an attack? Sascha's hands tightened convulsively on the leather, his grin falling away. He hadn't thought about the possibility, not really. He'd been so wrapped up in the revelations about his parents and the existence of such a plot in the first place. Sascha hadn't considered real, physical danger to the king.

Suddenly, he was far less thrilled by the joy of flight and far more wary of what dangers might be ahead of them.

As purple twilight fell, they landed in a large clearing. Alan had sent a couple of his people ahead to scout and secure the area. Lysander couldn't imagine anyone could be waiting for them there, but he didn't object. They began using their Talents to let go of their dragons as soon as they landed, those not carrying packs efficiently helping those who did remove them. As the soldiers went about setting up camp, Lysander found his attention drawn to Sascha. He was already climbing down, and Lysander was almost annoyed he hadn't been able to help him. Almost as irritated as he'd been not to be able to have Sascha ride with him.

He could have, he supposed. He was the king, and no one would have gainsaid him. No one would've argued, even if they would have whispered about it later. Just because it wasn't done, didn't mean he couldn't have carried Sascha. But it wasn't done—a king did not allow such a thing, not in public. Perhaps exceptions could be made for a consort. But for a concubine? A new one? No, and flouting tradition would only bring more attention to Sascha. There would be plenty of attention soon enough, and it would be best if they had a story to explain his presence and identity before the talk began.

Knowing that didn't soothe Lysander's possessive thoughts. Dragons may have faded into legends in the world outside Ivria, legends that were more fantastical than anything else, but there was some grain of truth in the stories of dragons hoarding that existed in the wider world. Lysander wanted to grab Sascha and carry him away far from others, wanted nothing more than to drape Sascha in jewels and keep him in his bed forever.

But he was more than his urges and instincts, his lusts and desires. He was king and had responsibilities and duties. He was a man who wouldn't frighten or push Sascha.

Lysander took a breath and forced himself to look away from Sascha and search out Alan in the bustle of soldiers making camp. Alan found him first.

"I know you want to be back at Wyndward," Alan said when

he reached Lysander's side, "and I do too, frankly—I don't like being so exposed out here—but it's not worth the risk of flying so far on a moonless night."

Lysander nodded. "I know. I don't like being in the open with everything we took from Jannik, but no one knows we're stopping here."

"And we weren't followed."

They would be fine for one night, despite Lysander's impatience to be home. "We'll leave at dawn. We should be home by midday."

Alan nodded. "They're getting the fires going and a couple of tents put up. Everyone will be ready for sleep after a meal. I already have the watches set."

Lysander would've expected no less.

"Sascha can sleep in the tent with Kirill and Romilly. I'll share with you when I'm not taking my watch," Alan said with no particular emphasis, but Lysander fixed him with a stare. "Your Majesty, don't make me worry about him killing you in your sleep and taking off into the woods with none of us aware."

He barked out a laugh. "If he wanted me dead, he could've murdered me any number of times in the last few days, and he'll have more opportunities once he's living in my apartments and spending time in my bed."

"At least then it's unlikely he'd escape easily," Alan said with a frown.

"I'd still be dead in this scenario of yours, so thank you for that." Lysander shook his head. "You can't believe he wants to kill me."

"My job is to assume everyone wants to kill you and make sure it doesn't happen."

"Or just make sure my murderer is caught before he escapes." This time, Lysander rolled his eyes. "Fine, I won't share a tent with him tonight to ease your mind. I'm too tired to make it worthwhile anyway. Go check on whatever you need to check on and stop bothering me."

It was Alan's turn to roll his eyes. "Yes, Your Majesty."

In other parts of the world, spring was already beginning, but here in Ivria's north, winter stubbornly clung on. The already chilly temperature dropped as night fell, and they gathered around the warmth of the fires to eat their evening meal. They'd brought food with them that had been prepared back in the kitchen of Grau; it was simple traveler's food, but it was filling and it had seen them through the midday and evening meals today. Lysander assumed there was something left to break their fast with in the morning. By lunch, they'd be at Wyndward.

The soldiers not on watch clustered around their own fires to eat, and Lysander could hear some of the usual joking and stories common to these situations. Lysander shared a fire with Alan, Kirill, Romilly, and Sascha. None of them were particularly talkative after the long day, fatigue or preoccupation weighing on them. Lysander and Alan exchanged a few words here and there, and, every so often, Romilly and Sascha whispered to each other where they huddled together on the other side of the fire. Sascha's white cloak was dusty, and the food was probably not what he was used to, but he hadn't complained and had a perfectly pleasant, if weary, expression on his face.

Even rumpled and tired from travel, he was beautiful. The firelight played over his pale skin and made dark pools of his blue eyes, while it teased out sparks in his rich red hair. He smiled at something Romilly said and then turned, and his eyes met Lysander's across the fire. They widened, and Lysander couldn't be certain in the firelight, but he thought Sascha might be blushing. Their gazes held as a few moments slowly spun by, tension tightening between them. Lysander began to wonder if easing Alan's mind was really so important. It didn't seem more important than a night with Sascha.

Sascha jumped slightly and jerked away to face Romilly, who must have said something to him. With the connexion broken, Lysander stifled a sigh and looked away from the captivating man to survey the rest of the camp. Nothing appeared out of place; certainly nothing existed that was intriguing enough to distract him from Sascha. Just Alan's soldiers settling in for the night.

"I'm going to check on everyone once more. Make sure the first watch is doing as they should," Alan said, breaking into Lysander's thoughts. "I'm taking a later watch, so I'll be in to sleep shortly."

Alan didn't have to take a watch, but he always did when he was out of the castle with his soldiers. He'd been the right choice as a commander—and for all Alan often said Lysander was raised to be king and Alan to ensure his safety, he wouldn't be in such a position if he hadn't been best suited to it.

Lysander began to tell Alan to find somewhere else to sleep, but stopped himself. "I can't imagine your people are doing anything but what they're supposed to."

"Best to make sure. I won't be long."

He waved a hand at his cousin negligently, letting him know to take his time. Alan would understand the gesture. As Alan strode away to speak to whoever he needed to, Lysander turned his attention back across the fire, where Sascha was sneaking glances at him from under his lashes. Shyness? Nerves? Attraction? Lysander couldn't be sure, and—putting aside Alan's suspicions and worries entirely—a tent in the middle of a camp filled with soldiers wasn't the place to find out what those little looks meant.

Lysander pushed himself to his feet and waved a hand

when the others around the fire began to move. "Don't get up. We're hardly standing on protocol in the middle of the woods. I'm going to my tent. I'll see you all in the morning."

As they said their good nights to him, he rounded the fire and stopped near Sascha. Sascha turned and tilted his face up to Lysander. Confusion swirled in Sascha's eyes, but nothing of it showed on his face. Lysander held out a hand, and Sascha slowly put his into it. He was expecting the spark of heat and awareness when their skin touched, though he doubted he would ever get used to the strength of it. With a smile, he lifted Sascha's hand to his lips and brushed a kiss over his knuckles. "Sleep well, Sascha."

"Thank you, Your Majesty," Sascha whispered.

Lysander released his hand with another smile and went to his tent. He couldn't imagine he would sleep well tonight.

CHAPTER 10

And he was right. Dawn came far too quickly, after far too little sleep. At least he was thinking about Sascha. It made for a pleasant change from being kept awake worrying about treason. He was alone in the tent, so he allowed himself a quiet groan before he pulled himself together. The camp was bustling when he emerged, with soldiers doing the last of the packing and preparations to depart.

Kirill and Romilly were sitting with Sascha between them, eating breakfast and talking over Sascha's head. Mostly, it seemed, because Sascha was sleepy and hunched over a steaming cup. Not a morning person, then, or at least not someone who enjoyed rising with the sun. Somehow, it was adorable.

Alan came to his side and handed him food to break his fast, then surveyed the campsite. "We'll be ready to leave shortly."

"Good. The sooner the better." Behind him, someone had already begun to break down the tent they'd slept in. Lysander knew better than to try to do so himself among this group—it was another of those things the king wasn't supposed to do. "I want to get back."

"Impatient to get Sascha into your bed?"

He was, but that hadn't been what prompted his statement and he didn't care for Alan saying it. "No. And watch your tongue. He's to be treated with respect."

"I was teasing."

"He's been through enough—he doesn't need to deal with teasing." Lysander put a hand up to forestall Alan's words. "I know he didn't hear it, but others could. And then other people will decide it's all right. The court will be watching. Let's not give them license to be horrible to him."

Alan nodded. "You're right, of course."

Lysander stared at him for another moment, making sure Alan understood his seriousness, then turned back toward the activity in the camp. It seemed to be winding down. Lysander began to eat, not wanting to hold up the departure himself. They couldn't leave without him, but he didn't want to be delayed a single moment.

Sascha glanced over his shoulder at Lysander as he, Romilly, and Kirill began to move off toward where the soldiers were preparing to transform. Yes, he wanted Sascha in his bed—and would have him there tonight if he had his way—but his concern at the moment was how long he'd been gone from Wyndward. He trusted Thalia and Felix to see to matters, but this trip had shown him just how many people were potentially involved in the plot against Ivria. Lysander couldn't help worrying about what could happen in his absence.

Sascha's first look at Wyndward Castle came from the air. He'd been tired and grumpy and doing all he could to hide it when they'd flown away from the campsite at dawn—Sascha was not someone who greeted early mornings cheerfully and even less so after a night sleeping on the ground. He'd never camped before, and he didn't want to again. The chilly air woke him quickly enough during the flight, and he was more alert when they stopped for a break midmorning. Kirill had told him they should arrive around noon, and Sascha had spent the second part of the morning's journey studying the countryside that passed below him. He only realized the castle in the distance was Wyndward when the dragons banked in that direction.

Even with clouds obscuring the sun, Wyndward was beautiful. It perched on a rocky slope above the town of the same name that now sprawled over the eastern shore of the vast lake below. Wyndward sat at the heart of Ivria, central to all the clans and farthest from the world beyond the mountains that protected the kingdom. When their ancestors had come here, they'd been looking for sanctuary, a safe place to live away from those who sought to kill or control those with the dragon Talent. Dragons were once plentiful, but their numbers dwindled as the dragon hunts swept across the world. And so the dragons and their allies fled and found an uninhabited land sheltered by impassible mountains. Impassible, except by wing.

Over the generations since then, they had spread throughout Ivria and built a kingdom. From his history reading, Sascha knew it hadn't been easy for people from all over the world with different languages and customs to come together, but they'd had the common goal of survival, of finding a home free from the dangers that had plagued them. And they'd done it.

Now some people were trying to undo it.

The unpleasant thought came unbidden, marring his first sight of Wyndward and its towers reaching toward the sky. And he had too little time to smooth over the bitterness and try to appreciate the majestic view before they were descending toward one of those towers. Most of their traveling party—all of the soldiers and their commander, along with Kirill—veered off to land elsewhere. Only Romilly followed the king to the wide, flat top of the tallest tower. Romilly landed lightly on the stone, not far from the large red dragon. Sascha immediately began to extricate himself from the straps so he could climb down and allow Romilly to change back. Romilly lowered themself to the floor so Sascha could slide down, which he scrambled to do. Sascha sucked in a breath as strong hands closed around his waist and guided him down. He teetered a bit when his feet hit the ground, more from the shock of the touch than the stiffness in his legs. His back came into contact with the king's broad chest for just an instant, the heat searing into him even through the layers of cloak and clothing.

Sascha froze there. He wanted to believe the shock of it was just the contrast to the chill that had seeped into him on the flight, but he knew that wasn't true. Knew the reaction was purely to the proximity of the king's body, so much broader and taller than his own. What would it be like to be held, enveloped, covered by that body, by this man? Sascha trembled, a combination of fear and desire. Perhaps fear of the desire. He'd never known what it could be like.

Romilly was suddenly standing in front of him as a person instead of a dragon, and Sascha blinked wide eyes, the sight of his cousin jerking him from his thoughts. Sascha straightened slightly but didn't pull away from the king. King Lysander squeezed his waist lightly, briefly, then let go and stepped to Sascha's side. Sascha took a long breath and turned to face him.

"Welcome to Wyndward, Sascha." The king offered his arm.

Guards opened the doors for them, and Sascha walked inside on the king's arm with Romilly following behind them. The king led them down a flight of winding stone stairs and through another door, also guarded. "These are my private apartments. My children and I are the only residents. And now you, of course."

Surprise flashed through him. Sascha hadn't expected to be housed in the king's own apartments. He surreptitiously took in his surroundings as they walked. Gently glowing orbs in silver sconces were attached to the stone walls, the magically charged globes illuminating the hallway with a soft light. Finely woven tapestries hung between them—Sascha wished he could stop and study the exquisite work, see what scenes they depicted, but he'd have time if he was really going to live here. What an odd thought—this would be...home? Could it feel that way? Should he even let it? How long could he possibly keep the attention of the King of Ivria?

Those questions distracted him long enough for the king to usher him and Romilly through a door into what proved to be a sitting room. It was a comfortable room—cozy, even, which Sascha wouldn't have expected in a royal residence—with chairs that seemed perfect to curl up in upholstered in soft fabrics. The windows looked out over the town and the lake, curtains drawn back to frame the view.

"I'm sure you'd like to settle into your chamber, but we'll have to give them a little while to bring your things up," the king said as he lit the fire with a flick of his fingers and a tossed ball of flame. "In the meantime, I'll send for lunch."

"Thank you, Your Majesty," Sascha replied as the king reached for his cloak. Sascha allowed him to help him out of the garment, sadly somewhat the worse for travel. White had been impractical, but his mother had insisted and Sascha had adored it once it was in his hands. He hoped it could be cleaned.

"Romilly, are your parents in town?"

"My father is, Your Majesty. Do you have need of him?" Romilly replied.

"Yes. We need to create something of a fiction about why

Sascha is here, should it be needed, and I want him involved, if you don't think he would object." The king turned to Sascha. "You're supposed to be with Jannik, and we don't know who knew that—your parents at the very least, but possibly others. Perhaps I should've left you with Galina or sent you somewhere else until we sort this mess out." The king made a dismissive gesture. "We need an explanation for your presence ready."

"My father will be pleased to help and honored to have your trust in such a matter," Romilly responded smoothly. "He'll be happy to find Sascha well."

The king nodded. "Good. Ask him to come for dinner this evening. I'm going to have Felix join us as well. We'll make plans."

After lunch, the king showed Sascha to the bedchamber that would be his and excused himself to visit his children and speak with his sister, who had been in charge in his absence. The door closed behind him, leaving Sascha and Romilly in the center of another comfortable room. Much larger and grander than Sascha's bedchamber in his parents' home, it had every-thing Sascha could imagine needing, including its own well-appointed bathing room—and a lock on the door. He went over and fiddled with the key. The king might have one as well, but the gesture of a door Sascha could lock between him and the world was appreciated.

"Should we look for entrances to secret passages?" Sascha joked wearily, suddenly more than a little overwhelmed.

"I think you're safe from that here." Romilly came forward and pulled him into a hug. "We'll make sure you're safe here entirely, or I'll take you with me no matter what anyone says."

Sascha laughed weakly and rested his head on their shoul-der. They stood that way for a while, taking comfort. "Thank you," Sascha finally said.

"Of course, dearest." Romilly stepped back but kept hold of

Sascha's shoulders, examining him with a keen eye. "I have to see Father—I'd send a message, but I think this demands going in person."

He nodded. "It'll be good to see him."

Romilly smiled. "He'll be glad to see you too."

"Who's Felix?" Sascha asked, the question popping out without much thought. His mind was skipping all over. "Sorry. The king said he was inviting him as well?"

"Oh, yes." Romilly shook their head as if to clear it. "Prince Felix is the king's cousin, his uncle's child. He was the ward of the old king after his parents died and grew up here. He and I were at school together, and we've stayed close. Felix knows everyone and everything, it seems. He's a good friend to have."

Sascha hoped Felix would be his friend, then.

"Will you be all right for a while? I need to see Father and get cleaned up and changed before dinner."

"Of course." Sascha didn't need Romilly to think he couldn't survive on his own for an afternoon. He was stronger than that. "I need to get cleaned up myself."

Romilly studied him closely for another moment. "Do that and get some rest. Settle in. You can call for a maid if you want some help unpacking or getting your clothes presentable after so long in a trunk."

"I'll be fine. Go on." Sascha shooed them toward the door. "I'll see you later."

Romilly probably only left because the king had given them a task, but they slipped out the door at last. Final reminders that he could call a maid to get his clothes in order or send for Romilly—they had rooms in the castle—if Sascha needed, following them out the door. Sascha closed it and leaned back for a moment, just a moment, to catch his breath.

He would need more than a moment, but he didn't think he had the time.

Oh, literally, certainly. There was time before dinner. He would unpack and soak in a bath, maybe even nap. He had time to see what state his wardrobe was in and decide what was appropriate to wear for dinner with Romilly, his clan head, the king, and the king's cousin in the king's private rooms. Sascha would have time to wonder and worry about what would happen after dinner when he was alone with the king.

But Sascha would have no time at all to reckon with the complete change in his life before he was meant to sit down to dinner with that small group of people. And there was no use grumbling about it.

He pushed himself away from the door and went to his trunk.

LYSANDER WAS SITTING at the desk in his study, reviewing papers his sister had left for him and studiously not thinking about what Sascha might be doing in the bedchamber down the hall —his visit with his children had been a much better distraction than these documents—when the knock came at the door. He expected Felix, but Alan stepped into the room at his call. Alan bowed briefly.

"Everything all right?" Lysander asked.

"That was going to be my question."

"Oh?" Though Lysander could guess why.

"I could've come with you when we landed." Alan had made variations on the statement already—before they left camp and when they stopped for a rest. Lysander wasn't certain what he expected Sascha to do. Wait until they were in his apartments at Wyndward and murder him? With guards and people all around?

Lysander sat back. "You were needed elsewhere. Everything is fine here. What do you have to report?"

Alan frowned slightly, but he didn't argue. "My people brought the papers we retrieved from Jannik up as you asked."

"Good." It wasn't a long-term solution, but everything was safer up here secured away from potentially prying eyes. Before Lysander could say anything else, another knock came.

This time, it was Felix who glided into the room at Lysander's call. Lysander thought Alan frowned briefly again, but he might just be perpetually frowning these days. Felix bowed and glanced between Lysander and Alan. "I'm sorry if I'm interrupting. I was told you wanted to see me, Your Majesty."

"I do." He faced Alan again. "I must speak with Prince Felix. Is there anything else you need to tell me?"

"No, Your Majesty."

"I'm sure you gave your people some time to themselves. You should take some yourself." Lysander could predict how Alan would react to that suggestion.

"He's going to go right back to work," Felix mused once the door was firmly shut behind Alan.

Lysander laughed a little. Felix knew that much about Alan as well—the two men were both Lysander's cousins, though not related to each other, with Felix the son of his father's brother and Alan the son of his mother's. The two men had never been close, mostly because of some attitude of Alan's toward the younger man. Felix probably knew what it signified; information was his trade, as it were, though few saw past the striking face to the mind beneath. "Yes, he is."

Felix took the chair Lysander gestured to without a word. He was unfailingly proper in front of others, but he allowed those mannerisms to drop when it was just them. Lysander was king, but Felix was royalty too—before the children were born he was second in line for the throne—and family. "How was your trip? Are you finally going to tell me what took you away for so long?"

"I should be glad you don't know yet with your propensity for hearing everything."

"You kept this frustratingly quiet," Felix said flippantly, then became sober abruptly. "But it isn't a joking matter, is it?"

"No, and I'm going to tell you all of it, but first, is there anything I need to know since the last report?" As far as everyone else was concerned, Lysander left his younger sister in charge whenever he had to be away for any prolonged period of time, and Thalia was, but not alone. Felix shared the responsibility with her, though he preferred not to have that fact well known. It suited his purposes to be seen as nothing more than the charming, social prince, and since it had suited Lysander's purposes as well these last several years, he was inclined to let the situation stand. Thalia was less inclined, but only because, as she didn't live here year round, she sometimes had to be called back to Wyndward to take up those duties, while Felix made the castle his permanent home.

Felix gave a short shake of his head and brushed at the lock of dark hair that fell into his eye with the movement. "It's been quiet. There aren't many people back in town yet. Which you took into account when you planned the timing of this little trip."

"I did." Lysander took a moment to gather his thoughts. "All right. I have a lot to tell you."

He started at the beginning, with the plot itself. With a nebulous group of Ivrians deciding it was time for the world to know dragons were real and then to rule that world, which would have to involve an overthrow of Ivria's ruler. Because

Lysander would never support such a thing. The secrecy kept them safe, and their Talent didn't mean they deserved to rule over all.

By the time Lysander got through a description of his trip and an explanation of who Sascha was, Felix was wide-eyed and slack-jawed. Lysander had never seen him so utterly surprised—even when Felix had been a child, the several-years-older Lysander could never shock him—and amusement bubbled inside him despite the seriousness of the situation.

"Well." Felix fell silent after that one word.

"Yes," Lysander said. "You can see why I need your help."

"And you have it, of course. You would have had it sooner if you'd told me before now." Felix didn't ask why Lysander hadn't, but the question was implied. As was the one about whether Lysander trusted him, though he had to know Lysander did.

"I should've."

Felix nodded his acceptance of that statement and let the matter go. "Does anyone else know, other than those you told me about?"

"The conspirators?"

"I didn't mean them, but all right. Tell me what you need of me."

There was no one who had more information about the lives and relationships of the leading families of Ivria than Felix, and his knowledge likely went further than that. People told him things or spoke freely around him or tried to impress him, and Felix had a memory nothing escaped and a frighteningly quick mind when it came to making connections. For now, Lysander needed that.

Felix nodded. "Of course. I'll take a look at all the names and see what I know or can find out. I assume you want my help with Sascha too? You're going to need a good story in reserve at the very least, and he'll need some help navigating Wyndward."

"I'd appreciate it more than I can say."

Felix raised a brow, but only said, "I'll do what I can to smooth the way."

CHAPTER 11

Sascha examined his reflection in the mirror in his bedchamber, looking for any flaw, anything inappropriate to the occasion. What even was the occasion? A small dinner with family in the king's private apartment? A strategy meeting?

He hadn't been educated about these situations.

But he'd done the best he could. Clothing was armor as much as it was expression of self. His options were limited—and he'd had to call for a maid after all when he'd seen how hopelessly creased everything was; she'd worked magic in fixing it. Perhaps literally, who knew? But he'd decided on a vivid blue velvet jacket that buttoned high at the neck over a lace-trimmed white shirt and slim pants in a blue so dark it was nearly black. He owned no jewelry except for an intricately worked pair of silver hoops that he'd threaded into his ears, wincing a little as he hadn't worn them in so long. He'd brushed his hair out until it gleamed and then left it to fall loose. Objectively, he looked good.

He was pale as death.

Sascha shook the comparison away and pinched his cheeks, a bit harder than necessary, to restore some color to them.

His heart kicked up at the soft knock at his door, but Romilly's voice announcing themself through the wood soothed it once more. Sascha let them in, and they studied each other for a moment. Romilly was wearing a pale gray silk jacket over a darker gray shirt and a long skirt slit up the middle to reveal pants much like the ones Sascha wore. Pearls gleamed at their ears. They looked wonderful, rested and more settled.

"You looked wonderful," Romilly said.

"I was thinking the same about you."

Romilly waved that away, though they did murmur their thanks. "That doesn't matter so much. I know you're worried about making the right impression."

"Is it obvious?"

"I know you." Romilly took Sascha's hand and squeezed encouragingly. "Try to calm down. The king wants you here. He chose *you*. You belong at Wyndward, as much as anyone does. You are not inferior to anyone. Everything else can be figured out, including what to do if you decide *you* don't want to be here. Remember that."

Sascha nodded. "I will."

Romilly studied him for another moment. "All right. Let's go."

Sascha took a deep breath and followed Romilly from the room. They walked together through the king's apartments, Romilly murmuring information about the rooms they passed and what was where. Sascha wanted to ask how Romilly knew so much, considering these were the family's private apartments, but it didn't seem the right time. They took a short flight of stairs briskly and came out on the floor below where they walked almost immediately into a small dining room.

For a moment, Sascha thought the room was empty—no one sat at the table, which was already laid for dinner with five place settings. But movement by the window caught Sascha's attention. Romilly's father turned from the view of the lake to face them. A smile spread across his broad face, though concern shadowed his eyes. Nevertheless, the smile remained as he came forward, hands out for Sascha's. "Sascha."

He was a duke and the head of Sascha's clan—there was a formal way Sascha should've greeted him. But Florestan was also Romilly's father and had become Sascha's uncle despite their more tenuous blood connection. Sascha and Romilly had become inseparable as children even though Sascha was younger, and from then, Uncle Florestan had taken an interest.

"Uncle." Sascha smiled and put his hands in Florestan's, letting him squeeze them as he looked over Sascha, the way he had so many times before, to assure himself Sascha was well. "It's so good to see you."

"And you. Are you all right? Romilly told me what happened." He frowned, a flash of anger joining the worry in his eyes. "I wish I'd known your parents were considering a contract with Jannik."

Sascha shook his head, jumping quickly to reassure him. "You couldn't have done anything. They were set on it."

He wasn't certain how much his uncle knew, and he wouldn't be the person who revealed a treasonous plot. He wouldn't betray the trust in him.

If anything, Florestan's face darkened further. Sascha would've been nervous if he didn't know his uncle well enough to be sure the emotion wasn't directed at him. "Yes, Romilly told me that, too, and why. Don't imagine I wouldn't have forbidden it—I'm the head of this clan, and that means something."

"Yes, sir."

"Stop that." Florestan seemed to make an effort to smile. "Tell me truly. You're all right now? And you want to be here?"

"Yes, to both questions."

Florestan nodded briskly, accepting Sascha had told him the truth. "Then I'll do everything I can to help."

"Thank you, Uncle."

"Good, we're all here." King Lysander's voice came from behind Sascha, and he turned immediately to bow along with Romilly and Florestan. But he caught a look at the king as he did—he wore dark green velvet, the fabric well tailored to his broad shoulders and muscular thighs. Intricate embroidery in gold thread meandered over the front of the jacket, somehow highlighting the firm breadth of his chest to Sascha's eyes, making it something mesmerizing, when he'd usually be more interested in the work on the clothing. "We have much to discuss."

"Don't forget dinner. You can't expect anyone to put forth inspired ideas on an empty stomach." The crisp voice drew Sascha's attention to the person who'd followed the king through the door.

The man was undeniably beautiful, if in a remote way. He was slender, not as tall as the king but not short either, with artfully tousled dark hair that swept over his forehead and waved around his pale face, just brushing his collar. A slight smile curved his finely wrought lips, showing that his statement wasn't meant to be disparaging—which Lysander hadn't seemed to take it as anyway. The rich plum of his jacket heightened his coloring, and the cut was both fashionable and flattering. He wore several delicate rings on elegant fingers, though none of them appeared to be a wedding band; his only other jewelry was a large amethyst pinned at his throat to secure his high collar. His gray eyes were sharp and studying Sascha just as closely as his were this man. Who had to be Prince Felix.

Sascha's assumption was proven correct when the king next spoke. "I could hardly forget that, Felix," he said with a chuckle. "Let me introduce you to Sascha."

The king presented Sascha to Felix, not as formally as if they were at a court function but not in a casual way either. Felix responded quite correctly, and Sascha could not fathom what the intimidatingly elegant man thought of him. Then there were greetings between Florestan and Felix—polite but not unfriendly—and between Romilly and Felix—much warmer. And they sorted themselves out at the table. Servants poured wine and set the first course in front of them, then melted back to stand at the sides of the room.

Conversation remained innocuous, likely due to the presence of the servants, during the meal. There would be no talk of treasonous plots or Sascha's situation in front of others, even those trusted to serve the royal family in their private rooms. Sascha was torn—he wanted to know what the others were thinking and what they wanted done, considering it concerned him, but he was eating a delicious meal in a lovely room and the light conversation flowing around him gave him time to calm.

Sooner than he could've imagined, dessert was placed in front of them—an apple cake full of fruit and nuts and redolent with spices—and the servants slipped from the room. They continued to eat and drink wine for a few moments before the king said, "Your Grace, Romilly told you why I asked you to join us?"

"Yes, Your Majesty, they did. I must say I'm shocked to hear of this plot against Ivria." Florestan leaned forward slightly in his seat. "You can be assured of my discretion in the matter and will have whatever help I can provide."

The king nodded. If King Lysander hadn't believed those things, Florestan wouldn't have been told, Sascha was certain. "I may call on you more, but for tonight, our concern is Sascha."

"I will, of course, claim him as a member of my family." Florestan flashed a fond look in Sascha's direction. "He's been a brother to Romilly since they were children. Will that be enough?"

"It's best not to say too much," Felix remarked. "There will be curiosity about Sascha and no little amount of jealousy. Claim him as part of your clan and family but keep things simple."

"And if someone knows he was contracted to be with Jannik?" Florestan asked.

"It's unlikely Jannik told anyone. He wasn't the type," King Lysander said as he sipped his wine.

"If he did say something," Felix said with a glance at the king, "we'll let it be known that the king saw him and wanted him for his own concubine. No one will say anything directly, but a few whispers in the right ears will have people convinced."

"Even if that isn't my normal behavior..."

Felix flicked another pointed glance at the king. "Even if."

"If someone involved in the plot knows, they may try to confirm the story with Jannik," Romilly said.

"Galina will intercept messages for us," the king said. "We'll make sure she's informed of the story."

Sascha felt like there were far too many uncertainties in this plan, but perhaps he was wrong. He wasn't experienced in...well, anything, but certainly nothing that would help him form any useful ideas in this situation. He was more relieved than he could express not to be with Jannik, happier than he could say not to be at Grau. Staying there, even with Galina in residence and Jannik nowhere near him, would've been unpleasant. He would've if he had to; he would've gone somewhere else to wait until his presence wouldn't put the king's plans at risk. But, as Romilly had reminded him, the king wanted him here. And Sascha wanted to be here too. As it was, he would trust their planning and do all he could to avoid detection.

Their little party broke up after some more discussion. They walked upstairs to the main doors of the apartment together, idly chatting as if dinner had been nothing more than a social occasion. Sascha did his best to keep up with the pretense. When they stopped just inside the closed doors to say their good nights, both Romilly and Florestan pulled Sascha into embraces. Florestan promised Sascha would see him soon; Romilly told Sascha they would come by tomorrow—but even with that promise, they seemed reluctant to leave Sascha. Florestan had to gently steer them out.

Once they'd left, Felix came to Sascha with a slender hand outstretched. "It was lovely to meet you, Sascha. I'll back in the morning to see you."

Felix's fingers were cool wrapped around his, his grip firm but not too tight. Sascha had absolutely no idea how to respond to Felix's statement—it wasn't an invitation or a question, but...

"We have a lot to do to get you settled in," Felix continued. "Best get a start on it quickly."

A broad, warm hand came to rest on Sascha's lower back. It pressed soothingly when Sascha startled. "Don't overwhelm him, Felix," Lysander said from where he now stood at Sascha's side. "He's had a trying time, and he's only just arrived."

"Don't treat him like a child," Felix shot back. "Yes, he's had a difficult few days, but unfortunately, he won't be able to hide away in these rooms. News of his arrival and that you've taken a concubine is already filtering through the castle. Better to begin now than to be caught unprepared."

Sascha was also right there, and he wanted to snap that at them, to tell them not to talk about him as if he wasn't.

But speaking so sharply to royalty seemed like a poor idea.

He couldn't imagine how they might react if he did, but...it could be bad.

Felix watched him shrewdly. Sascha had the sinking feeling the man had seen everything that had just run through his head. He steeled himself for how Felix would respond to those unspoken thoughts, but Felix only said, "I'll see you tomorrow morning, Sascha."

"Yes, Your Highness. Good night," Sascha replied in the only way he could.

Felix nodded and said his farewells to Lysander before slipping out the door and leaving Sascha alone with the king. And as worried as Sascha had been about everything else tonight... Well, it all disappeared in the face of another worry.

The king's hand moved over Sascha's back in long strokes that somehow both soothed and created new tension in Sascha. "Come have a drink," the king said.

"Oh. All right." Sascha let himself be ushered along the hallway and into the king's private sitting room.

"Sit, please." The king gestured at a couch in front of the fireplace where a cheerful fire dispelled the chill of the evening. As Sascha seated himself on one end of the couch, taking care to do so gracefully, King Lysander went to a sideboard. "You could have refused Felix, you know. You don't have to do everything he wants because he insists."

Though Sascha hadn't known how to respond to Felix informing him of their morning plans, he thought the king's characterization of what happened was a little uncharitable. "It's fine. He knows far more than I do about life here at Wyndward. I'm grateful for the guidance, especially in light of the... larger situation."

The king joined him on the couch and handed him a glass of deep red wine. "You can always ask me if you need to know anything about the court."

"Thank you, Your Majesty." Sascha sipped the wine, finding it rich and flavorful, then set the goblet down while he gathered his thoughts. "But you have so much you must put your attention to. I wouldn't want to take you away from more important matters, especially when Prince Felix has graciously offered to help me."

The king watched him levelly for a moment. "He's knowledgable about navigating life here, and it wouldn't be a bad thing for you to appear as if you have Felix's approval and support. He's popular among the court."

Sascha tried not to let the king's words about appearing to have Felix's support upset him. Of course Felix wasn't his friend —why would he want to be?—but he was willing to help.

The king reached out and gently swept a lock of Sascha's hair behind his ear before cupping his cheek. Sascha's lips parted on a soft exhale. "You should call me by my name when we're like this," the king—Lysander—said.

"If you want me to, Lysander," Sascha said softly.

Lysander smiled, a pleased and somehow sensual curve of lips. "I do."

He leaned forward, slowly enough that Sascha could've refused the kiss. But, well, it was why he was here, wasn't it? And he'd liked Lysander's kiss before. Sascha thought he'd like it again. Lysander's lips slid over Sascha's, a whisper of a kiss at first that deepened quickly into something consuming. Their first kiss had been revelatory to Sascha, but it had been nothing compared to this. This...this was...

His thoughts scattered as Lysander explored his mouth with lips and tongue. Lysander's large hands curved around his waist, gentle but sure, the heat of them burning through the layers of Sascha's clothing. Sascha realized he was gripping Lysander's jacket, but he couldn't force himself to untangle his fingers from the fine fabric and release what felt like his only anchor in the dizzying whirlwind of Lysander's kiss.

And then...the kiss was over. Sascha blinked his eyes open, trying to steady his spinning mind. Lysander's hands were still at his waist, the hold they had on him more steadying than anything else. Sascha dragged in a ragged breath and made his fingers release Lysander's jacket, though he left his hands where they were, flattening them on the firm expanse of Lysander's chest. He focused on that point of contact, on his pale, slender fingers against the dark green velvet. When Lysander said nothing, Sascha looked up into his eyes and found him gazing at Sascha, waiting patiently.

Sascha wished he knew what Lysander was waiting for. What he wanted from Sascha. An academic knowledge of what happened between men in bed was far from actual experience, something Sascha felt keenly now as he never had before. He wasn't embarrassed by his lack of experience or that Lysander knew of it—though he wasn't going to be quick to tell him he had never wanted to be with anyone before—but experience might have helped him divine what to do when Lysander looked at him that way.

Or he could ask.

"Lysander?" It came out quieter than Sascha would've liked. Calling the king by name would take getting used to. Also, the decision to ask what Lysander wanted didn't make doing so easier. "I don't know what you want me to do."

Lysander took a hand from Sascha's waist, and he immediately felt the loss of the contact, the warmth. But Lysander only lifted it to Sascha's cheek again. Sascha leaned into his palm, just a little, but forced himself not to let his eyes fall closed, to curl into the warmth of that touch. He needed to know what Lysander expected from him.

"What do you want to do, Sascha?"

Sascha blinked and stared, too startled for a moment to worry about how his reaction would look. But Lysander only smiled anyway and stroked his hand through Sascha's hair. Warmth slid through Sascha again.

"I don't want you to do anything you don't want."

"But…" His mother would surely have lectured him about the frown marring his brow if she'd seen it. Then again, Mother was a traitor to Ivria, so Sascha didn't feel much like listening to her lectures, even the ones he imagined. "But I'm here to please you."

It was what he'd been taught, what he'd been told for years. His duty as concubine or husband was to please and to be pleasant and graceful and decorative the rest of the time.

"I'll get no pleasure if you're doing something that doesn't please you too." Lysander continued to comb fingers through Sascha's hair, gentle and soothing but also…arousing. Sascha wanted to arch like a cat under the petting. "We're going to talk to each other, and you're going to tell me truthfully what you want or don't, what you like or don't. And if you don't, we won't do it. All right?"

Sascha nodded slowly, the words turning themselves over in his mind, erasing old assumptions, creating new patterns. He had no power in this situation, no power except what Lysander gave him in the contract they'd signed, and Sascha had known it, had come into this knowing where he stood and understanding the risk he took. Lysander's words threw that into disarray. If Sascha could trust them. He supposed he'd find out.

"Good. Do you want to come to bed with me tonight, Sascha, or shall we sit here together for a while longer before you go to your own?"

The question, the offer, seemed utterly sincere. If Sascha wanted, Lysander would sit here with him and sip wine, before sending him off to bed, perhaps with a kiss. Though Lysander seemed to want him, he would wait.

Sascha didn't want to wait.

He looked into Lysander's eyes. "I don't want to go to my bed alone."

Something hot flashed in Lysander's eyes. But he moved slowly as he leaned forward and kissed Sascha, long and deep. "Come to bed, then."

CHAPTER 12

Lysander took his hand as they walked to a door on the other side of the room. Sascha tried to fall back, to let Lysander go first, but Lysander kept him at his side, not allowing him to let the king enter the room first. In fact, Lysander opened the door and ushered Sascha through ahead of him. Sascha was too aware of Lysander following just behind him, of the heat of his body at Sascha's back, of the quick click of the door closing, to get more than impressions of the bedchamber. Soft light, a fire in the hearth, thick curtains drawn against the dark of the night. The large tester bed, hangings neatly tied with tasseled cords, blankets turned down.

It was probably the largest bed Sascha had ever seen, but Lysander was a tall man.

Sascha drew in a sharp breath when Lysander's hands came to rest on his shoulders. The large hands squeezed gently, comforting, grounding. Lysander's presence at his back somehow the same.

"All right?" Lysander asked quietly.

"Yes." Then again, in a stronger voice, "Yes."

"Nothing you don't want." Lysander massaged Sascha's shoulders.

"I know." And he was beginning to believe it. "But I do want."

He did. And not just in some vague wondering way of what it would be like, not with just anyone. He wanted Lysander. He wanted to be in Lysander's bed. Sascha would worry about what that could mean later.

"I do want," he repeated.

Lysander squeezed his shoulders again, then slowly ran his hands up and down Sascha's arms. Sascha's breath came faster at the steady drag of hands over clothes. "What do you want?" Lysander whispered in his ear.

Sascha blinked. He was glad Lysander was kissing his ear—he shivered delightfully as lips moved over his earlobe—and not looking at him because he was sure a stunned look had come over his face at the question. How was he supposed to answer?

Then Lysander began nibbling and kissing his neck, and Sascha's head dropped back as he moaned. "More of that, please."

Lysander's low chuckle had heat curling through Sascha's belly before he could wonder if he shouldn't have said it. Lysander returned to kissing along the side of Sascha's neck. His head rested against Lysander's firm chest, and his hands came up to clutch at Lysander's arms as they circled him. Lysander whispered words against his skin that Sascha couldn't quite understand as his body seemed to come alive. It was barely anything, what Lysander was doing, wasn't it? How would he survive more?

Lysander turned him carefully and bent his head to kiss him, pulling Sascha flush against his body. He explored Sascha's mouth—more than that, he devoured Sascha as if he was the most delectable sweet, and Sascha could do nothing but hold on through it and try to get closer. Going up on his toes and wrapping his arms around Lysander, sliding a hand into the hair at the back of his head, the strands surprising soft as they twined around Sascha's fingers. The kiss was consuming and overwhelming and it drove everything out of Sascha's head except want.

Sascha made a small noise of protest when Lysander's lips left his, but Lysander only chuckled low again and dragged his lips along Sascha's jaw, nibbling at his ear, kissing his neck again. He nuzzled in where Sascha's pulse jumped in his throat, the area just covered by the collar of his jacket.

"You look lovely in them, but you're wearing too many clothes," Lysander murmured in his ear, and Sascha gasped quietly. Lysander ran his hands up Sascha's back and then down to clasp his waist. "May I?"

Sascha's fuzzy mind took a moment to understand what Lysander was asking. Then he shivered. His voice was rough when he answered, "Yes."

Lysander looked into his eyes for a moment, then reached for the fastenings of Sascha's jacket. He moved slowly, dexterous fingers finding each one as he moved down the front of the jacket until the velvet finally parted and he slid it from Sascha's shoulders, letting it fall down his arms and to the floor. Sascha barely spared it a thought as Lysander turned to his shirt, slipping it just as deliberately from Sascha's body. Lysander stopped for a moment and just looked at Sascha, his gaze surely taking in every detail. Sascha stood and let him—he wanted to say something, but just the heat in Lysander's eyes had his thoughts going even more hazy.

Lysander put his hands on Sascha's waist, watching him for

a moment longer as Sascha's breath came more quickly. Then Lysander moved his hands, smoothing them over Sascha's stomach and up his chest, brushing his thumbs over Sascha's nipples. Sascha gasped at the bolt of sensation, his eyes widening then falling closed as Lysander continued his exploration. Up to Sascha's shoulders, pausing to knead them briefly, then sweeping his hands over his upper back. Dancing his fingers down the knobs of Sascha's spine. Palming the curves of his backside through the pants Sascha still wore. He gasped again.

The sound of Lysander's chuckle was utterly wicked. "I think it's time we got rid of these, don't you?"

Sascha didn't know if he actually wanted an answer, but Sascha gave him one anyway. "Yes."

Lysander's smile flashed, but he wasted no time in doing just as he said. Sascha helped by stepping out of his shoes and then pants. A bolt of anxiety shot through him as he stand before Lysander—before the King of Ivria—in nothing but silvery gray silk underthings, but Lysander's gaze burned as he swept it over Sascha's body, searing into him, tangible as a touch, leaving no room for anything but desire. Then Lysander's hands were on him again, running over skin and silk, and pulling Sascha against him and into another deep kiss.

He felt as if he might be swept away. Everything in his body was alight, blazing with want. The almost overwhelming reactions to...well, not a simple kiss. This was not a simple kiss. It couldn't be. It was more like being devoured, and he loved it. But it was also nearly too much all at once.

And still, disappointment flooded him when it ended. When Lysander pulled away, Sascha felt a brief moment of shock, of panic, wondering what he'd done wrong. What he could do to make it right, to fix it.

But Lysander didn't look upset, at least not until he saw Sascha's face. "Are you all right? We can stop." His voice was soothing, reassuring, but still rough with passion.

"No! I don't want to stop," Sascha said, making an effort to calm his voice after his first frantic exclamation. It came out a whisper when he spoke again. "I don't want to stop. But I don't want to disappoint you."

And this would, wouldn't it? What king wanted a concubine so unsure of himself and his abilities? A thought came unbidden that his parents would be disappointed, but Sascha crushed it. He refused to care what they would think.

"I won't be disappointed."

"You can't know—" Sascha cut his own interruption off even before Lysander began shaking his head.

"I do know." Lysander slid his hands up to cup Sascha's cheeks, then back into his hair. "I'm here with you and I want to kiss you." He did so, a soft brush of lips over his own. "Touch you." More soft kisses, this time along his jaw. "Be inside you." It was a whisper directly into Sascha's ear. A shiver ran through his whole body. From the words, the kisses Lysander trailed down his neck, both? Sascha's head was getting fuzzy again, and he almost couldn't care about his earlier worries anymore.

"Is that something you want?" Another rough whisper in Sascha's ear.

"Yes." It was little more than a breath of sound, but Lysander heard.

He brought his lips to Sascha's again, a firm kiss, before he stepped back. Sascha swayed briefly, caught off balance by the suddenness of the action. But Lysander was only stripping out of his own clothing, much more quickly and efficiently than he'd done with Sascha's. Sascha watched as more and more of his powerful body was revealed. The strong arms, the dusting of dark hair across a muscular chest, the—

Sascha was caught up in those arms and deposited on the bed, abruptly but carefully.

"Now," Lysander said, as he crawled over Sascha and began sliding the gray silk off his hips, "let's see if I can distract you sufficiently so you forget what you're worrying about."

Everything became sensations from there as Lysander bent himself to his task. The smooth, cool bedclothes beneath him. The heat of Lysander's body above him. Lysander doing just as he said he would, touching and kissing him everywhere, driving every worry from Sascha's head as he found new spots that made him gasp and shiver. His thoughts were slow, like pouring honey, until they almost stopped entirely, subsumed into waves of pleasure. Was this what it would feel like to be drunk?

Sascha's skin chilled briefly as Lysander moved away, but he was back before Sascha could form a question. Lysander's lips covered his again in a deep, claiming kiss. Those kisses... Sascha loved them, had no defense to them. He needed to guard himself, guard his heart, but his body was apparently quite happy to belong to Lysander. And thinking about it was far too difficult at the moment. He moaned as the kiss ended.

"I want to be inside you, Sascha," Lysander whispered roughly in his ear. "Do you want that?"

"Yes." There was no other answer. Lysander treated him with respect and would stop if he said so, Sascha had to believe that. But there was no other answer because Sascha ached. His whole body was on fire, lit from the inside and thrilling to each touch of Lysander's hands, lips. He couldn't stop now.

Lysander sat back and coated his fingers in oil, the bottle what he must have retrieved when he'd moved away earlier. Before Sascha could even get nervous, Lysander bent to kiss him again. Slippery fingers trailed over the skin of Sascha's abdomen, skimmed over the aching hardness of his cock, and down further, until a single finger slipped into him. Sascha gasped at the intrusion, at the oddness of the feeling, and then again at the jolt of pleasure when Lysander moved it over a particular spot. Sascha writhed as Lysander did more of the same, even as he added another finger.

Lysander's gaze burned into him, those dark eyes intense in their regard, as if to scrutinize Sascha's every reaction. Sascha didn't know what would please him, could see no guidance in the intensity of Lysander's face. Or perhaps he couldn't quite grasp it. Thoughts skittered away, driven out by the overwhelming sensations, by his response to them. Lysander above him, his fingers—three now, he thought—twisting inside him.

Lysander rubbed the calloused pad of his thumb across Sascha's nipple, just as his fingers brushed that spot inside him again. Sascha cried out and arched, his fingers tangling in the sheets beneath him, an anchor to keep him from flying right off the bed.

But no. Lysander was above him, leaning closer. He wouldn't let Sascha levitate away. Lysander kissed and nipped at Sascha's neck and even more heat rolled through him. What was it about that spot and how had Lysander known? Sascha let out a long, low moan.

"Beautiful," Lysander breathed against his skin. A shiver raced through Sascha at the sensation. At the word itself.

Lysander pulled his fingers out, and Sascha whined involuntarily at the sudden emptiness. Lysander soothed him even as he moved. Then the blunt head of his cock was at Sascha's entrance, slowly pressing inward. Lysander ran gentle hands over him. "Shh. Just relax and let me in."

Sascha could do nothing else as he was stretched and filled in a way that was beyond anything he'd imagined. Well, he could've told Lysander to stop, but he didn't want to. Lysander pushed inside him slowly, gently, and Sascha wasn't sure how much time had passed before Lysander stopped, before he was fully inside and they were connected. The feeling of it was... good, odd but good. And intimate. He'd known it would be, had to be, but the reality of it was different from anything he'd contemplated. Sascha was somehow glad it was Lysander.

"All right?" Lysander's words seem to vibrate through Sascha, they were so close now.

"Yes," he breathed.

"Good. Let go of the sheets and hold on to me." And Lysander began to move.

Sascha did as Lysander bid, grasping Lysander's arms tightly and wrapping his legs around his hips, as everything inside Sascha lit up with pleasure. His head pressed back into the pillow, and Lysander dragged his teeth over Sascha's throat. He couldn't have even described the noise he made, but Lysander chuckled, that dark, smooth chuckle again. "I love the sounds you make."

Sascha might have blushed, but he was certain his skin was already flushed, and he couldn't be embarrassed for anything that brought Lysander pleasure. It was what he was supposed to do. He was so very lucky Lysander seemed as attentive to Sascha's own.

Extremely attentive. And it was all extremely good. Each thrust ratcheted his pleasure higher and higher. Wound him tighter and tighter. Until it all just broke, a wave crashing as his release found him, sweeping him away.

"So beautiful." Sascha didn't think he'd imagined Lysander's whisper, and he tightened his arms and legs around Lysander as he kept moving, chasing his own pleasure, his own release and held him as he cried out with it.

Lysander lowered himself fully onto Sascha, resting there for a few moments. Sascha loved the weight of him, as he floated in a haze of lingering pleasure, would have kept him there forever. But too soon, Lysander nuzzled Sascha's temple briefly, then pulled himself away and left the bed. Sascha lay there, not sure his legs would hold him if Lysander meant for him to leave now. After a short while, Lysander returned and cleaned Sascha up with a cloth, then climbed back into bed beside him.

"Should I—"

Lysander pulled him close again. "It's been a long day. Let's sleep."

Sascha hadn't expected Lysander to want him to sleep in his bed. He'd assumed he would return to his own bedchamber after. Did this mean Lysander would want to have him again tonight? Or—

"You're thinking too hard." Lysander pulled the bedclothes up over them and pressed a kiss to Sascha's shoulder. "Just sleep."

~

SOMETHING PULLED SASCHA TO WAKEFULNESS—A gentle hand smoothing the hair from his forehead, lips placing a soft kiss there. "Lysander?" he asked in a whisper even as he opened his eyes.

Lysander stood over him at the side of the bed. He was already dressed and seemed to be smiling fondly down at him. "It's still early, but I have to go to a meeting, and I didn't want you to wake alone."

"Oh, I can..." Sascha moved, just awake enough to know he should slide from the bed and go back to his own bedchamber. After finding his clothes. He was still naked, the soft sheets against his bare skin an unusual but not unpleasant sensation.

Lysander stilled him with a hand to his shoulder. "No, stay. Sleep some more. There's a dressing gown in the bathing room for you when you want to get up. When I come back, we can have breakfast in the sitting room."

"Oh," Sascha said again, quite intelligently. "That would be lovely."

Lysander smiled—fond again, Sascha thought with some amount of wonder, unless he was dreaming—and brushed a kiss over Sascha's cheek this time. "Sleep. I'll be back soon."

Sascha closed his eyes again, but, though he drifted, sleep didn't return. There was too much in his head and all of it spinning around, one thing tumbling over the next to fight for his attention. All of it pushing at him more and more until he finally huffed out a breath and opened his eyes again. Folding his arms over his chest under the blankets, he stared up at the canopy, tracing its complex botanical design with his eyes as he breathed slowly. By the time everything settled enough for him to focus, he was irrevocably awake. He grumbled at that—a glance at the sky through the window showed him dawn wasn't long past, and as lovely as the day looked, he would have preferred to sleep.

Sighing, he sat up and let the blankets pool in his lap. He glanced around the room, which he hadn't had the opportunity —or desire—to study last night. His impression that it was dominated by the large bed was born out, but there were also two cozy chairs near the fireplace and thick rugs in rich jewel tones laid over the stone floor. It was a room designed for comfort, as a sanctuary. And wouldn't a king need one? Or perhaps Sascha was being fanciful. Either way, he liked the room, was comfortable in it himself, which was good, since it seemed he'd be spending a fair amount of time here.

He swung his legs over the side of the bed and stood, then realized once more he was naked. His clothes were nowhere to the seen—had Lysander picked them up or had a servant been in the room while they slept?—and the promised dressing gown was all the way in the bathing room. Sascha briefly considered wrapping himself in a blanket, but he was alone with the door closed. He didn't need to cover up. He couldn't stop himself from walking quickly anyway, but he would blame it on the chill in the air.

The bedchamber was chilly compared to the warmth of the cozy bed and soft blankets. It was almost enough for him to want to dive back under the covers, but he wouldn't sleep and staring and thinking would do him no good. Perhaps if he had a book, he'd be more inclined...but he didn't and he should be up and presentable when Lysander returned. And a glance in the mirror in the bathing room showed him his hair was an utter mess, so it might take a bit to make himself presentable. He considered going back to his own bedchamber and bathing room, but Lysander said he'd come back here and the loan of the dressing gown—because the one draped over a chair was not Sascha's own—seemed to imply Lysander assumed Sascha would stay.

Giving up on thinking it through, Sascha used Lysander's bathing room to clean up and then wrapped himself in the soft wool gown. Which was undoubtedly Lysander's and far too large on Sascha. But the thought that the king had left his own dressing gown for him was somehow warming in itself, so he knotted the belt tightly and turned back the cuffs. Then he set to untangling his hair.

When he emerged from the bathing room, he felt far more himself. The bedchamber was still empty. Sascha hesitated briefly, then opened the door to the sitting room. This room was empty too, except for the two spaniels lounging on the hearth. They lifted their glossy heads when Sascha walked into the room and watched him.

"Oh, hello there." Sascha hadn't known Lysander had dogs, but they didn't seem hostile. He dropped into a crouch and held out a hand to them. The two dogs stood and walked to him, nosing at his hand and then pushing into it, looking for attention. He laughed and sank down to sit on the rug and give them all they wanted. Perhaps the faint scent of Lysander that clung to the dressing gown—something Sascha found quite pleasant—made them more inclined to him, or perhaps they were just this friendly. Either way, Sascha was happy to have found them.

He wasn't sure how much time he spent on the floor with them, stroking their silky coats and rubbing their bellies and murmuring compliments to them and laughing at how excited they were. It lightened everything inside him, alleviated his worries, brought him such pure joy—he wished he had treats for them, to thank them for this time.

When the door opened, the dogs went still, turning their attention to whoever was coming in, but they didn't leave Sascha's side. As Lysander stepped inside, their tails began to wag, but they still didn't leave Sascha to go to their master. Sascha smiled up at Lysander from his spot on the floor with the dogs. He knew his happiness was shining out of the smile, and perhaps it was a little too much, a little too unguarded for Wyndward, but after last night, he didn't think it was too unguarded for Lysander. And, of course, as soon as he thought of last night, his cheeks heated.

Lysander had frozen in the doorway, but then his lips curved in a smile too. "I see you met Kore and Rion." He closed the door beside him and continued into the room. "And I see I've been replaced in their affections."

A denial was on the tip of Sascha's tongue, but then he saw the twinkle in Lysander's eyes. Lysander crouched beside Sascha to rub the dogs' heads, which meant he was very close to Sascha when he looked at him again. Sascha wouldn't have to move far to put his lips to Lysander's, if he were brave enough to do so. He wanted to, but he wasn't yet sure what would be welcome, so he waited, barely breathing, as warmth shivered through him at the intensity of Lysander's gaze.

Lysander closed the distance between them for a brief kiss. As he slowly pulled back, Sascha smiled at him again, unaccountably shy—ridiculous after last night. Lysander held his eyes, his gaze no less intense, and the moment stretched between them, tense with the same energy that had been in the air last night. Sascha held his breath, wondering if Lysander would kiss him again or take him back to bed, and finding he would be happy with either.

Then one of the dogs pushed between them, and they both began to laugh. Lysander playfully scolded the dog, petting him all the while. Lysander's manner toward the dogs thoroughly charmed Sascha. "I should've asked how you felt about dogs," Lysander said. "I'm glad to see you like them."

"I do, very much. Meeting them was a pleasant surprise this morning."

"Good—" Before Lysander could say anything else, a quiet knock came at the door. "That will be breakfast."

Lysander extricated himself from the dog and stood, then reached a hand down to Sascha. Sascha put his hand in Lysander's and allowed him to help him to his feet. Once he was standing, the dogs took up positions at his feet, as if to guard him from whatever dangers lurked outside the door. Lysander chuckled softly as he pulled Sascha closer to his side and called out for the person to enter.

A maid curtsied as she carried in the breakfast tray and set out plates of food and a silver pot on the small round table near the window. Once she'd arranged food, plates, and cups to her satisfaction, she asked if they needed anything further and receiving a negative answer and Lysander's thanks, curtsied again and left.

"Let's have something to eat before I'm pulled away."

Lysander ushered Sascha to the table and pulled out one of the four chairs for him. Sascha seated himself with a murmur of thanks and waited for Lysander to sit opposite him before he reached for the food. He made up a plate for Lysander first, filling it with the cheese, fruit, and cakes from the platter and handing it across the table to him before serving himself a portion of everything.

"You don't have to serve me," Lysander said after a moment, just as Sascha was reaching for the pot to pour them each a cup of whatever it contained—some sort of tisane from the scent.

"Oh." Sascha froze. He'd been instructed that whomever he contracted with might like or want such a thing, and Sascha hadn't minded the thought too much, since he'd been used to doing the same for his younger sisters. Though it felt very different doing this for Lysander. Intimate again. "I don't mind, but I don't have to if you don't want me to."

"I don't mind either," Lysander said, reaching across the table to take Sascha's hand, "but I want you to know that you don't have to. If I needed someone to serve my breakfast, I could've asked the maid to. I don't want you to feel obligated to do such things for me."

"All right. I don't." Sascha took Lysander's cup and filled it with the steaming liquid, allowing some mischief into his smile as he handed it to Lysander. He liked the fond amusement that came over Lysander's face, liked the honest laugh even more.

Breakfast was far more relaxed and comfortable than Sascha could've dreamed. Certainly, their conversation and even the silences between them were easier than he had imagined when he thought about what life would be like with the king—with Lysander. He hadn't even imagined quiet, private breakfasts together. Hadn't known he or Lysander would want them. But Sascha, at least, found he would be happy starting the day like this—across a sunny little table from Lysander with the dogs at their feet—every day.

A rap came at the sitting room door just as they finished eating. Sascha had poured them each another cup of the warming herbal tisane and settled back in his chair to sip from his cup, marveling at Lysander's attention. Lysander stifled a sigh at the interruption—was he enjoying this time together as much as Sascha was?—and called out, "Enter."

CHAPTER 13

Felix opened the door and glided inside, elegant again this morning in clothing that was less formal than what he'd worn the night before but no less beautiful. Sascha tried not to let his envy show; he supposed he'd end up coveting a lot of pretty clothes in his time at Wyndward, but it wouldn't do to show those feelings.

"Good morning." It was clear he and Lysander were on more informal terms when others weren't present. Sascha was briefly surprised to realize he didn't count as an outsider.

"Good morning, Felix," Lysander said.

"I've come for Sascha. Am I too early?" Felix flicked his gaze over Sascha in a quick glance that probably took in every detail of his appearance.

"That would be up to Sascha." Lysander turned a warm smile him. "I have meetings for the next several hours, so I'll have to leave you now anyway. But you can linger here and tell Felix to come back later."

Sascha couldn't imagine doing so. "No, that's not necessary." He turned to Felix. "But if you wouldn't mind waiting while I dress, Your Highness?"

"Of course, and do call me Felix."

Lysander studied the two of them for a moment, then stood and bent to kiss Sascha softly. Sascha's cheeks heated with a blush, which only seemed to delight Lysander. "I'll see you later."

He moved away from the table, but even when he called them, the dogs stayed right where they were, looking as if they had no intention of moving from their comfortable sprawl beneath the table. Lysander shook his head but only bid Sascha and Felix farewell and left them alone.

"I'll just go dress." Sascha stood, and the dogs did as well, eager to follow him wherever he planned to go.

A slight smile crossed Felix's face when Sascha froze. "Lysander won't mind if they come with us, if you don't."

"Of course not, if it isn't a problem." Truthfully, Sascha hadn't realized they were going anywhere. "I'll only be a few moments."

"No need to rush. I'll come with you."

Sascha could see no way to politely refuse. And though he was puzzled as to why Felix would want to accompany him when he could wait comfortably here, he had no real problem with the company.

They wound their way briskly through the halls, the dogs trotting happily at their heels. Their speed was Sascha's fault— he'd forgotten he was barefoot, and the stones of the corridor floor were far colder on his feet than the soft rugs of the sitting room and bedchamber. Inside Sascha's bedchamber, which he hadn't used since he dressed for dinner the night before and which showed it, he went directly to the wardrobe. "Is there a particular way I should dress? I don't know what you have planned for us."

"I'll show you around some of the castle and perhaps introduce you to some people. We can go into town too, perhaps lunch there, go to a couple of the shops."

Sascha supposed those things were sensibly part of settling in. After a moment's thought, he pulled clothing from the wardrobe and excused himself to his bathing room. When he emerged again, neatly dressed with his hair properly brushed and pulled back into a tail, Felix was searching through his clothing.

"What are you doing?" Sascha wasn't even sure what to say.

Felix's head popped up. He didn't appear guilty for snooping through Sascha's things. "Just seeing the extent of your wardrobe. Is this everything?"

"The maid took a few things to be cleaned yesterday, but this is most of it." He spared one more thought for his poor white cloak.

The corners of Felix's lips turned down just slightly for the briefest second. "What you have is quite nice, but it won't be enough to see you through life at Wyndward. We'll definitely stop at a few shops today, and I'll make an appointment for the woman who makes most of my clothes to come up to the castle and measure you for a few more things."

Sascha was shaking his head before he even realized it. "I can't afford any of that."

It was an understatement—he'd literally been sent off without a coin in his pocket. He doubted Felix knew that; Lysander probably suspected.

Felix shook his head right back. "Lysander will pay for it."

Despite joking with Romilly about the king giving him a wardrobe of shoes, Sascha wasn't sure how he felt about the idea of his clothing being provided by the king.

"Come on," Felix said before Sascha could answer, or he might have just seen the answer in Sascha's face. "Do you have a coat?"

He did, and he gathered it up before he followed Felix out, the dogs still happily with them. Felix guided him out the main door of the king's apartments, the first time Sascha had been out into Wyndward Castle.

"I'll show you around some now, but I think we'll go to town first," Felix said as they walked. "Then we can continue here this afternoon. Lysander and the children—and you now—have private rooms in the top of this tower. I have rooms in the top of the second and Princess Thalia has the other. You haven't met Lysander's sister yet, have you?"

"Not yet." Nor Lysander's children. Would Lysander introduce his children to his concubine?

"I'll introduce you later," Felix said briskly. He pointed out library and various receiving rooms and dining room as they continued through the castle. There were other people in the corridors looking at them—at him—with curiosity, so Sascha did his best to inspect his surroundings without gawking. The stone of the floors was laid in intricate patterns, and the walls were covered in art in the form of tapestries and paintings, all beautiful and fine. He'd never been anywhere so grand.

Felix ushered him out the main doors and into a large, flat courtyard, paved in cobblestones, from which led a road down the hill to the town on the shore of the lake. Sascha took in the view as they stopped for a moment to fasten coats and draw on gloves. Felix's were black leather with intricate cut-outs on the wrists; they were lovely, much nicer than Sacha's plain ones.

"I should've asked—do you mind walking? It's not far, but we could get horses or fly," Felix said, as he brushed at hair that had been blown into his eyes by the breeze.

"I don't mind walking."

The dogs were excited to be outside, but they contented themselves with frolicking around Sascha's and Felix's feet as they started down the road, two royal guards following behind them, far enough to give them their privacy but close enough for protection. Sascha assumed such precautions were necessary for a prince out of the castle. He supposed Felix was used to it, though it felt odd to Sascha.

"It's beautiful here." Sascha took a deep breath of the crisp air. It was chilly, and nothing had begun to bloom yet, but the sky was a brilliant blue and so were the waters of the lake. There were birds singing and dragons in the sky and playful dogs at his feet and…well, not a friend at his side but someone friendly whom he hoped could become a friend, and all of it make Sascha feel lighter.

"Yes, it is. A lovely place to live and to grow up." Felix's gaze went a bit hazy for a moment, perhaps remembering his childhood. Romilly had said Felix grew up here. "Lysander said you've never been to Wyndward before."

"No. My uncle—Romilly's father wanted to bring me, but my parents refused. I've never been anywhere except my parents' house and my uncle's."

"Well, you're here now, and I'm sure you'll get to see more of Ivria with Lysander."

Sascha was startled. "Do you think so?"

"I do." Felix put a hand on Sascha's arm as they reached the outskirts of the town. "This way."

The town was the largest Sascha had ever seen, housing, he was told by Felix, many who worked at the castle, shopkeepers and craftspeople, fishermen…so many people who made their livings because of Wyndward Castle's residents and those who visited or lived their lives in the vibrant town that had grown over the years in the shadow of the castle. The heads of the clans and the wealthiest nobles who spent time at court kept homes in town or just outside it, many on the banks of the lake. Felix pointed them out as they walked a loop of the town, the dogs now trotting calmly beside them.

Soon enough, Felix's route took them into a bustling town center. A market in a large square was crowded with people examining the wares at each of the stalls, but Felix passed it by in favor of the stores lining the street. "As I said, we'll make an appointment so you can have some more clothes made up, but for now, we can see if the shops have anything appropriate that will fit or that can be altered easily enough."

With that, Sascha was swept into the first of a series of shops, each time the guards waiting outside with the dogs. The shopkeepers obviously knew Felix and hurried to help them, showing Sascha pants and shirts, jackets and shoes, hats and gloves. It was an almost dizzying array of beautiful things, and he didn't need Felix to tell him—though he did—that Sascha had to think about what his appearance would say about him, about Lysander, to the court. Sascha thought carefully about his choices with that in mind and picked things he both liked, loved even, and that he believed would accomplish what he needed. Sascha expected Felix to make final decisions, but he never did, never pushed Sascha away from something he liked, only drew Sascha's attention to a few things he hadn't seen that Felix thought would flatter him.

Once Sascha had sorted through the options, had tried clothing on and had it pinned for alterations and was exhausted at the thought of more shopping, something he hadn't thought possible, Felix ushered him into one last shop. Sascha stopped abruptly just inside the door. Everywhere around him was silk and lace, but made into far more...intimate garments. Underthings, nightwear, stays, and stockings. And nothing plain or utilitarian in sight.

"When I was looking through your wardrobe, I happened to see you seemed to have a fondness for lace. I'm going to do my best not to imagine what Lysander thinks of it on you because he is my cousin, but I thought you might like to look around here, perhaps make some purchases." Felix's words were delicate, his voice quiet to avoid anyone overhearing, but he wasn't hesitant or judgmental of Sascha's preferences.

"Thank you," was all Sascha could think to say. He loved pretty things—clothes certainly, but he'd discovered a fondness for silk and lace undergarments too. A few fancier pieces had been made up with the new clothes he'd been given before he left to be with Jannik. His mother, who'd had charge of making the final decisions, had probably thought Jannik might like them—which nearly made Sascha shudder now—but Sascha hadn't considered how the garments might make anyone feel but himself. After last night and with his unexpected desire for Lysander, Sascha found himself wondering about Lysander's reaction, what he would like. It was a distinctly odd feeling.

He hadn't even been wearing anything as fancy as they made here last night. Would Lysander like him in lace? Did it matter since Sascha liked himself in lace? He ran a hand over a trim of deep purple. Sascha guessed he would find out.

AFTER A LUNCH with a handful of the clan heads, Lysander walked with his sister through the castle corridors. It was a monthly lunch, open to any of the clan heads who were at Wyndward or cared to make the journey to attend. The group most often used it to air grievances, both trivial and serious, but Lysander liked the opportunity to get a sense of changing conditions and dynamics and how what this group wanted to tell him matched with what he'd heard from other sources. His father had held such lunches, bringing him along once he reached an age when he could sit and listen and understand and then his sister as well when she did. Thalia usually accompanied Lysander now; she had been his heir until his children were born, was still his right hand, and would be his daughter's regent if anything happened to him. He hoped nothing ever would, but in his position—especially now—he had to plan.

The guard outside the anteroom of Lysander's office bowed and opened the door for them. The secretaries working inside did not bow—they knew by now he'd prefer they just continue on—and thankfully, no one appeared to be waiting to see him. "I have to speak with the princess," he said as they walked through the room. "Unless there's something urgent, leave us undisturbed."

"You just want to avoid any papers they want to stick in front of you for a while longer," Thalia said with a laugh after the office door closed behind them, leaving them alone.

"And you wouldn't?" Lysander asked as he rounded the desk. He did check to see if anything had been left for him, despite the teasing.

"Of course I would. I just spent too long standing in for you and thinking I might drown in paper under the stern eyes of your secretaries." Thalia lowered herself into one of the chairs near the large fireplace, the stone surrounding it carved in scenes from the founding of Ivria. She lounged there as she watched him.

"You know I'm grateful."

She waved a hand. "I do, and you know it's never something I would refuse. I'm glad you've finally told me what's going on though."

There was reproach in her stare that he knew he'd be seeing for a long time. And he deserved it. "I should've told you sooner."

"Yes, you should've." She sighed. "But enough of that. You've told me now, and we can deal with it and these people."

The tone of her voice reminded him of their father, unshakeable and implacable.

"You've told Felix as well?"

He joined her near the fireplace, taking the chair opposite. "Yes, when I returned, same as you."

"And I'm sure he feels much the same as I do."

Lysander was as well, though Felix wouldn't show it, unless he thought the display would be of advantage to him. Thalia laughed at whatever she saw on his face. "I'm sure he'll say something if he feels it necessary," she said. "At least you've provided us with an excuse for your absence. People were beginning to wonder, but coming home with a concubine makes everyone assume you went to get him and then hid your-selves away somewhere to get acquainted."

"I hadn't thought about it that way. I was more concerned about someone finding out where Sascha was meant to be than creating a reason for my time away."

"The distraction will help. You know how people here gossip—it might have nothing to do with treasonous activities, but they're all going to talk. This will divert the talk to some-thing that won't cause suspicion." She waved a hand again. "Yes, yes, I know you're worried about Sascha causing suspi-cion, but we'll have to hope the strategy you concocted last night will work."

"Would you have done something different?" Lysander asked mildly. Thalia was, more than anything, sensible. She probably wouldn't have brought Sascha here yet, or at all, if she were in Lysander's position.

"In regard to your Sascha? I don't know. I think the distrac-tion will be helpful, so maybe not. Just be careful how he inter-acts with people at court for a while. And who is allowed to get close to him."

"Hmm. Yes." Especially since he didn't know how Sascha would fare among the court. He'd done well in the small groups he'd been thrown into so far and his manners were quite pretty, but the court would be a whole different experience. Even without their extremely complicated situation, letting Sascha loose on his own was a poor idea.

"Where is he now?"

"With Felix," Lysander said. "He didn't give Sascha much of a choice. Something about a lot to do to get him ready to face the court."

Thalia nodded. "And of course you didn't ask what those things are. No, it's good that he's with Felix. Felix is probably the best person for him to be with." At Lysander's sour look, she laughed. "You know what I mean. Felix is an expert at navigating court politics and projecting exactly the image he wants and nothing else. If Sascha can learn that, he'll be well on his way."

"I think that's a skill Felix has been developing his whole life."

"Hopefully, your Sascha is smart enough to pick up what he needs."

Lysander bristled. "Sascha is plenty clever."

Thalia smiled, fond and amused. "You hardly know him and you're jumping to his defense. You are smitten, brother, aren't you?"

He had to fight to keep his mouth from dropping open. "Smitten?"

"Yes, smitten. Personally, I can't wait to meet the man who has you so infatuated you scooped him up and brought him back with you, ready, I'm sure to drape him in jewels and treat him like the most precious one of all."

Lysander glared at her, which only made her more delighted.

She rose from her seat and smoothed her hair and skirt. "I'll go and leave you to your paperwork, so you can get back to

Sascha more quickly." She frowned. "Where are the dogs? Still with the children?"

The dogs usually followed him to his office each day. When he was away from Wyndward, they stayed with the children. "I've been abandoned for Sascha."

Thalia looked startled for a moment, then let out peal of laughter. "Oh, I really can't wait to meet him now."

She kissed him on the cheek before heading for the door, a spring in her step.

"So glad I could amuse you."

His words only made her flash him a grin before she slipped out of the door. He only sighed and shook his head. Lysander had missed her, and he was happy to have her and Felix with him in dealing with this plot, and yes, to have their support and approval of his decision about Sascha too. Even if she did tease.

MOST OF SASCHA'S PURCHASES—THOUGH he had a difficult time thinking of them as his own, since he wasn't paying for them— would be delivered to the castle, but he carried a few small parcels as he and Felix walked back after lunch at an eating house overlooking the lake. The food, fish caught just that morning in that lake, had been excellent, and Felix delightful company, but they hadn't managed to eat uninterrupted. A few people had stopped by their little table to speak to Felix, perhaps to try to bring themselves to the prince's attention and favor, perhaps to satisfy their curiosity about Felix's companion.

Felix handled them all quite gracefully, giving them very little information but making it seem as if they had received all the latest news. What Sascha found most interesting, and what he pondered on the stroll back to the castle, was how different

Felix was with them. His manner had changed completely, or so it seemed to Sascha, though perhaps it was more subtle. Somehow, the clever, quick man Sascha had been getting to know was hidden in the blink of an eye. Sascha had seen it all morning, but the change was most stark among these visitors, who, from their appearance and words, had to be nobility who frequented the castle. Felix only let people see what he wanted them to see, and Sascha felt he'd been allowed to observe something of the real man, without the disguises and pretenses.

That Felix would be careful about what to share of himself with those who came to his cousin's court didn't surprise Sascha. What did surprise him was that Sascha had been let in. He assumed it was a matter of necessity, but he hoped to be worthy of the trust and to become friends with Felix in truth. Sascha liked him, which was far more important than any strategic considerations.

"Thank you," Sascha said as they approached the castle. He continued when Felix gave him an inquiring glance. "For today. For taking the time to help me."

His words seemed an inadequate expression of his gratitude and sounded awkward and juvenile to his own ears. Heat rose in his cheeks, and he could only hope the blush wasn't so noticeable with the color the brisk wind had likely already brought to his skin.

"You're welcome," Felix said, nothing but sincerity in his tone. "The shopping was my pleasure, and the rest... Well, I'm good at it. Lysander has been alone for a long time, and now he's brought you here. And I like the way he looks at you. I would've helped just because of that, but I rather like you too."

Sascha wasn't certain what the rest of Felix's help would entail—though Sascha had learned something just from watching him today. As for the remainder of what Felix said, Sascha wasn't sure how to respond. He'd known Felix was helping him for Lysander's sake—perhaps even for the sake of Ivria. He hadn't expected Felix to care to anything for Sascha himself. "I... Thank you."

Felix flashed him a smile. "Now, let's go back to the king's apartments. We'll call for some hot chocolate and cake and talk about what you should expect tonight."

"T-tonight?" Sascha stuttered, his mind flying back to last night and his time in Lysander's bed.

"Yes. Lysander will have to eat in the castle dining room tonight, given his absence, and, also given his absence, all of the nobility currently in the area will likely dine there as well, hoping to put themselves in his path. And to see you, with word already getting out."

"Oh." That made far more sense than Felix wanting to talk about...

Felix shot a quick sideways glance at him. "I can't imagine Lysander will leave you behind, so we should discuss what you should expect and do."

"Oh," Sascha repeated, then shook himself mentally. "Yes, of course."

The castle courtyard and hallways were more crowded now, and Sascha and Felix garnered more attention as they strolled through them. Perhaps because of the dogs. They'd stopped gamboling around without a word from Sascha or Felix and were now walking sedately at their sides. But they were the king's dogs with someone other than the king and obviously alert to threats, and Sascha wasn't surprised by the looks they received. No one said anything, though they greeted Felix with bows and pleasantries and barely veiled curiosity. Felix met them all with polite nods and walked on. He kept their pace steady—not overly quick, but not so slow as to invite someone to try to engage them in conversation—and kept an impassive, serene expression on his face. Sascha tried to emulate him.

They were nearly back to Lysander's apartments—as best Sascha could tell—and the corridor was empty, except for guards, when a feminine voice called Felix's name. This time, Felix stopped and turned with a slight smile on his face, so Sascha did as well, curious about who would cause that reaction. A woman was not far down the hallway, the skirts of her green silk gown swishing around her legs as she took long strides toward them. She had rich tawny gold skin and dark hair pinned up in thick coiled braids, and emeralds at her ears and throat. She had abundant curves flattered by an exquisite gown and strong features that would likely make people call her striking rather than traditionally beautiful...and that marked her as Lysander's sister.

Her eyes were nearly the same mahogany as Lysander's too, and they studied Sascha closely as she came near. He bowed, perfectly correctly, and took that moment to gather himself. Sascha wanted very much to make a good impression on her. It was certainly childish to want everyone to like him, but he did want Lysander's sister to like him, or at least not actively dislike him. Notwithstanding any status it might hold, he was Lysander's concubine, not his spouse, so maybe he was silly as well as childish. And yet.

Felix greeted her with more genuine warmth in his voice than he'd used with anyone else they'd encountered today. "Thalia, I don't believe you've met Sascha."

"I haven't," she responded. Her expression was pleasant, but her gaze was still assessing.

Felix made the introductions smoothly, the etiquette of them somewhere between casual and formal. Princess Thalia had names and titles Felix didn't include, but he didn't leave out the most important of them either.

"An honor to meet you, Your Highness," Sascha said when Felix finished.

She glanced down at the dogs sitting obediently at Sascha's feet, and her lips quirked into a small smile. "And you, Honorable Sascha."

The addition of the title still startled him. His family was not so highly placed for him to bear any noble title, unlike Romilly who'd had one from birth. The change would take some getting used to. He only hoped his reaction hadn't shown.

"My brother told me the dogs had deserted him for you." Her smile grew. "They are excellent judges of character."

"So she says," Felix remarked lightly.

"I can't help it if you choose not to take heed of their opinions," she replied to him just as lightly. Sascha was mystified by the whole exchange but couldn't ask. She turned back to Sascha. "It really was lovely to meet you, and I do want to get to know you better. Lysander is frustratingly close-mouthed. We'll find time soon."

Thalia swept away again a moment later, leaving Sascha somewhat stunned in her wake. Felix appeared to understand. "Thalia is something of a force of nature."

"All three of you are," Sascha blurted out without thinking. Heat burned in his cheeks immediately, but Felix only laughed.

"I suppose we are." Felix linked his arm through Sascha's and began walking again. "I think you'll manage just fine, though."

When they arrived at the entrance to Lysander's apartments a few moments later, Romilly was there, speaking with one of the guards. Romilly turned at a gesture from the guard and smiled when they saw Sascha and Felix, though their gaze searched Sascha. Sascha smiled back, trying to tell them he was all right without words. Romilly would ask once they were alone, Sascha was sure, but this might reassure them enough for now.

"Good afternoon, Romilly," Felix said. "How are you today?"

"Well, thank you." They glanced at Sascha again. "I came to see how you're settling in, dearest."

"Thank you, Romilly." Sascha smiled, once again trying to reassure his cousin, since he couldn't speak too candidly in front of the guards. They might well be trustworthy, but they didn't need to know anything personal about him. "I'm beginning to. Felix was kind enough to spend the morning with me."

"I decided to take up all of Sascha's time today, I'm afraid," Felix added. "We were about to call for cake. Why don't you join us?"

"Yes, please do." Sascha smiled again, brighter this time, hoping to convey how much he wanted Romilly to accept the invitation.

"I'd love to," Romilly said, needing little encouragement.

A guard opened the door for the three of them, and they walked through together, Romilly asking an innocuous question about their morning. By unspoken agreement, they chatted only about the shops until they were in a small parlor and Felix asked a maid to bring their cake. Once the door was closed behind her and they were alone, they let the conversation drop.

"I should've let you request our snack—I apologize," Felix said. Sascha blinked in surprise, but he continued before Sascha could speak. "Now, we have planning to do for later."

CHAPTER 14

Cautious optimism began to rise in Lysander about halfway through the long dinner that night. Sascha had obviously dressed with care for his first appearance before Lysander's court—though he seemed to always dress with care. He'd arranged his hair in a complicated braid that left the unreal loveliness of his face on full display. He wore blue again, but a paler shade that perfectly matched the small aquamarines set in the braided silver circle of the brooch fastened at his throat. Lysander thought he recognized the jewelry as Felix's, a gift from Lysander's parents that Felix hadn't worn in years as far as Lysander knew. Since Sascha wore the same earrings as he had the night before, Lysander could surmise he had little jewelry and Felix was trying to see him properly attired and adorned as concubine to the king. Lysander hadn't thought about Sascha's wardrobe, but he should have. He'd have to speak to Felix about it. Sascha likely wouldn't tell him he needed anything, but he couldn't have him at a disadvantage.

Even without the more ostentatious jewels and fashions many of the nobility were wearing, Sascha stood out, almost unbelievably beautiful. Lysander had to force himself to look at anything else, to think about anything else. And he had to, with the importance of tonight.

The assembled nobility had watched Sascha walk in on Lysander's arm with undisguised interest and avid curiosity. Sascha held up well under it, moving gracefully through the room, his expression calm and pleasant though color flushed his cheeks. Lysander had to quite deliberately not think about that either, or he would remember the delightful blushes that had stolen over Sascha's face the night before. And thinking about the night before would absolutely be a distraction he could not afford.

Sascha's presence meant a reshuffling of the seating at the royal table. Thalia kept her customary seat at Lysander's right, but Sascha now sat at his left with Felix moved one seat over to Sascha's other side, something Felix seemed to have no problem with. If Sascha knew his position as Lysander's concubine had changed the arrangement of the high table, he gave no indication. Felix and Thalia didn't always eat dinner here—neither did Lysander—but both were present tonight. Lysander hadn't asked but was grateful for support.

Felix, especially, seemed to put Sascha at ease, making quiet comments to him throughout the meal and receiving small smiles or equally hushed replies. Lysander took far too long to recognize the little niggle of jealousy within himself, and then spent far longer squashing it. Such a feeling was absurd. Felix wasn't interested in Sascha that way, and the appearance of an easy friendship between them would help both allay suspicions and increase acceptance of Sascha. As did Florestan's casual claiming of Sascha as a member of his clan and family. No one asked their specific relationship, and he didn't offer the information. The strong resemblance between Sascha and Romilly didn't hurt

By the time—the interminable—dinner was over, Lysander felt almost hopeful that Sascha's position as his concubine might go without undue scrutiny. He still had to search out traitors within his own country, but perhaps Sascha's presence wouldn't bring more danger down on them.

He and Sascha parted ways with Felix and Thalia after the meal ended and left the hall, Lysander in no mood to socialize further. For all the nobility's curiosity, none of them would expect him to linger, not with a new concubine. Back in Lysander's apartments, Sascha seemed to hesitate for an instant but continued to walk beside Lysander, on his arm, as Lysander led them into his sitting room.

"Would you like a drink?" Lysander asked.

Sascha clasped his hands together in front of him when Lysander stepped away and answered quietly, "All right."

Lysander studied him closely. "Is it? Are you? I apologize for leaving you on your own your first day here. I wouldn't have if there was any other option."

Had there been? He should've made certain Sascha was well.

"No, of course not! You have no need to apologize," Sascha rushed to say, dismay flitting across his features. "You're the king; you have important work. And I was fine—Felix and Romilly were kind enough to spend much of the day with me."

There was that odd and unusual pang of jealousy again. Lysander smothered it ruthlessly as he poured them each a glass of wine. He returned to Sascha and handed him a goblet. He asked gently, "Then what's wrong?"

Sascha paled, alabaster skin going stark white. "Nothing, Your—Lysander."

Alarmed at the reaction, Lysander slowly reached out and brushed his fingers lightly over Sascha's cheek. "It doesn't seem like nothing."

"It…" Sascha bit his lip just for a second before smoothing out his expression. "Nothing is wrong. I'm just not certain what to do. What you want me to do."

"Right now?" At Sascha's nod, Lysander continued, "I want you to relax, sit with me, and tell me about your day."

Sascha's brow furrowed slightly. "You want to hear about my day?"

"If you'd like to tell me."

"I'm sure it wasn't as interesting as your day. Nothing important happened."

He had to stop Sascha from thinking such things immediately or this would never work, not the way Lysander wanted it to. He drew Sascha down to sit beside him on the couch. "My day was long and tense. I'm hoping yours was more enjoyable and that you'll be willing to tell me about it, since I couldn't spend it with you."

"Oh." Sascha watch him for a moment, whatever was going on in his mind hidden behind those big blue eyes. Then he glanced at the bedchamber door. "You don't want us to…"

"Not yet. I'd like sit here with you and talk and share some wine. We can go to bed later, if you'd like to join me. Or you can go back to your own bedchamber to sleep if you would prefer."

Sascha considered him for another moment, then nodded. "I'd like to join you, later, after."

Lysander smiled as Sascha sipped his wine. "Then tell me how your day was. Did Felix overwhelm you completely?"

"Not at all! He was very kind." Sascha needed little more prompting tell Lysander of his day, though he watched him carefully from under his lashes as he spoke, as if making certain he wasn't boring him. He wasn't. Lysander enjoyed listening to him, hearing his first impressions of Wyndward castle and town. There was a sparkle in Sascha's blue eyes that Lysander found he adored. Lysander couldn't help his smile as Sascha talked.

Sascha abruptly stopped after describing how he met Thalia and bit his lip. "But I've been going on for far too long. You didn't want to hear all of that."

"I did. I enjoyed hearing every bit of it." He reached out and gently brushed a lock of red hair that had come free of his braid behind Sascha's ear.

"Oh," Sascha said, his voice slightly breathy.

"I'll always want to hear about your day," Lysander told him, surprising himself almost as much as Sascha with that truth. Before either of them could say anything else, Lysander closed the distance between them and kissed Sascha. The little sound Sascha made had Lysander deepening the kiss—wanting more of those noises, of the sweet taste of him—and dragging him into his lap. Sascha gasped but didn't pull away. Instead, he wrapped his arms around Lysander's shoulders to get closer as Lysander kissed him and ran his hands along his back and hips over the cloth of his jacket.

Soon, it wasn't enough. Lysander stood with Sascha in his arms. Sascha's eyes, which had gone half lidded, popped wide and he clutched arms and legs around Lysander. "I'm not going to drop you," he whispered.

Sascha relaxed just a little, though he didn't loosen the grip of his limbs on Lysander. He buried his face in Lysander's neck, pressing his lips against his skin, and Lysander stopped worrying that Sascha thought he would drop him. In the bedchamber, Lysander reluctantly set Sascha on his feet, loath to give up the feel of his long limbs and slender body pressed to Lysander's but also craving the feel of skin. He raised his hands to Sascha's jacket and stopped.

"May I?"

Sascha watched him from under his lashes, provocative whether deliberately so or not, and nodded. "Yes."

Lysander made short work of Sascha's clothing, not damaging anything, but not taking particular care either. He'd been thinking about Sascha's smooth pale skin and long legs all day. Forcing himself to banish the memory as he worked, as he spoke with people. Had he ever been so obsessed with someone? He pushed the question aside. Sascha was standing in front of him now, and he could indulge himself, indulge them both.

He stopped only when Sascha stood before him in his underthings—mostly of blue lace, held up on slender hips with a ribbon tied in the front. Sascha had worn something frivolous and beautiful and tantalizing last night as well, prompting Lysander to wonder if he wore such things habitually and to hope he did. Lysander reached out and traced the edge of the lace against Sascha's hip. Sascha shivered.

"Do you wear things like this because you like them or because you hope I will?"

Sascha contemplated him for a long moment, eyes unfathomable. Finally, he said, "Both."

"Good." Lysander pulled him into his arms and into another devouring kiss.

THE NEXT SEVERAL days passed in much the same way for Sascha. He spent every night in Lysander's bed. His own—quite comfortable—bed was only used when he sometimes stretched out on it to read. He often woke to Lysander rising in the morning but he always urged Sascha to sleep longer. Lysander would then return later to share breakfast with him. Romilly and Felix continued showing him around the castle and the town that bore its name, each taking time from their own obligations to help Sascha. He was grateful to them for it—and happy to spend time with Romilly before they left Ivria again—but he also felt like a burden.

They didn't make him feel that way, of course—no word or action of theirs gave him any indication that they resented the obligation—but Sascha couldn't help it. And he knew he had to rely on them for now. He hadn't been raised for life at Wyndward as King's Concubine, but he might have figured how to play that role more easily were it not for the specter of treasonous plots and the potential for discovery hanging over his head. Every time he was out, he felt eyes on him, and he couldn't help wondering if today was the day someone would realize he wasn't where he was supposed to be.

Though, even when he was alone in the king's apartments, he could stop himself from feeling as if he were somewhere he wasn't allowed to be. He was only truly at ease in his own bedchamber and, to some extent, in Lysander's sitting room and bedchamber. The feeling made him want to scurry through the halls so he wouldn't be caught.

It was ridiculous. And even if Sascha couldn't quite make the feeling go away, he refused to allow anyone to see it. He kept his steps measured, his breathing slow, and told himself it would all get better as he became more comfortable with his new surroundings. Well, perhaps not his fear of discovery and endangering Lysander or Ivria. The rest, though, he could work on, beginning slowly by going to Lysander's small private library and choosing a book. The walls of the large room were lined floor to ceiling with shelves, and cozy chairs were scattered around the edges of the room. He found a book and chose one of those chairs and defiantly read.

Thalia did, in fact, invite him to lunch. Sascha hadn't doubted she would, exactly, but he hadn't thought she would rush to either. Felix joined them in her private dining room. Sascha got the impression he hadn't been meant to be there.

"No one is serving. I wanted to get to know you a bit on our own," Thalia said as they sat down at a table laden with covered dishes. "Some people didn't seem to understand that."

Felix shrugged off the pointed look she sent his way. "I'm certain it was perfectly clear."

"Sascha doesn't need to be protected from me," she said.

"Of course he doesn't." Felix glanced at him. "But he doesn't quite know what to say to us now, so let's stop worrying him, hmm?"

"I apologize, Sascha." Thalia reached across the table and squeezed his hand with every evidence of contrition. Her be-ringed fingers were warm. "Let's eat lunch and talk. I want to hear all about you."

Over the course of their lunch, Thalia set to actually learning everything about Sascha. She wasn't interrogating him, but she was cheerfully relentless about her task. Felix broke in to joke or tease or deflect a bit, which Sascha realized quickly might have been why he'd insisted on joining them. Sascha was safe with Thalia; Felix didn't need to be here...but he wanted to help. Perhaps they might be moving toward a real friendship, not only the one they'd given the appearance of from the start.

And by the time the three of them got to the sweet at the end of the meal, Thalia had left off her questioning and was relaxed and smiling as they talked. So maybe Sascha had gained some measure of approval from her too. His hopes in that regard were solidified some when they ate their midday meal together again one day the next week.

Sascha wished he didn't feel the need to garner her approval, but, though his situation was far less dire than it had been at Grau, nothing seemed certain. He felt as if he hadn't had his feet on firm footing since he'd been sent away from home, and he hated it. He had to get his balance, and it was heartening for Felix and Thalia to include him, to be friendly and welcoming. He was Lysander's concubine and there was a treasonous plot to be uncovered, but Felix and Thalia didn't have to act like his friend in private.

He was so grateful they did.

Thalia sipped her wine and then sighed.

Felix raised a brow. "What's that about?"

"I have to meet with the steward."

Sascha frowned, not having any idea why Thalia appeared so frustrated, but Felix's lips twitched.

"Oh, don't you laugh." Thalia tossed her napkin at Felix, who did then laugh.

"I'm sorry, I'm sorry." He tried unsuccessfully to stifle laughter, as Thalia looked even more disgruntled. "We're confusing Sascha."

Sascha glanced between them and said with a self-deprecating smile, "Just a little." Then he added hastily, "It's all right, of course! You shouldn't worry about..."

Felix shook his head as Sascha trailed off, unable to finish his statement in any way that made sense. Why would they be concerned that he didn't know what they were talking about? Thalia waved a hand and smiled at him. "It's nothing. The steward is good at his work, but just...tedious. My mother handled all things relating to the castle when my father was king, and the steward either got used to that or is old-fashioned or something. When Lysander became king, Mother decided to retire away from Windward."

"The steward feels that the king is above such petty concerns as the running of the castle," Felix added with a roll of his eyes. "And since Lysander has no consort, the steward brings his concerns to Thalia."

Sascha frowned. "But... You're not even here all the time. What does he do when you're away?"

"He sends me a lot of letters." Thalia sighed. "He could easily go to Lysander or Felix, even—"

Horror flooded Felix's face. "You think I want to deal with him?"

"No, and I don't think he would go to you. He thinks he should be working for the lady of the castle"—the derision for that idea practically dripped from her words—"and I'm the closest there is. Maybe that will change if Lysander ever marries, though I do wonder what the steward's reaction would be if Lysander didn't marry a woman."

She seemed to find some amusement in the thought, but Sascha felt...odd at the mention of Lysander marrying, and the unsettled feeling followed him out of Thalia's cozy apartments and through the rest of the day.

LYSANDER STOOD at his office window and stared down into the castle courtyard. Sascha had just walked across it, Romilly at his side, the dogs frolicking at their feet, a guard following discreetly behind as they strolled through the gates. Nothing appeared wrong in Sascha's manner from this distance, but Lysander still frowned. Sascha had been...off...somehow when he'd seen him a few moments ago. Lysander couldn't quite put a name to it, but Sascha hadn't seemed his usual self. Not knowing why—and not knowing what to do about it—troubled Lysander.

A light tap sounded on the closed door. At Lysander's call to enter, one of his secretaries stepped inside and informed him that Thalia was here.

"Let her in, please."

A moment later, Thalia swept into the room, and the secretary closed the door behind her. She opened her mouth to speak but stopped, her brow furrowing. "What's wrong? What's happened?"

"Nothing." He stopped. "Nothing new. I've gotten a report from Galina."

She continued frowning as he returned to his desk to retrieve the report to show it to her. "Was the report particularly bad? Or is your frown just because this is happening at all?"

Lysander handed her the papers on which he'd translated Galina's original coded missive as she sank into a chair in front of the desk. He forcibly wrenched his mind from Sascha and back to the matter at hand—the serious matter at hand. "Isn't that reason enough to frown?"

Thalia hummed her agreement as she read. The report was succinct, imparting the results of the ongoing search of Jannick's castle and property. Jannick seemed to keep every scrap of paper that passed through his hands. Lysander couldn't guess his motivation for the habit, but he assumed Jannick kept some documents as leverage against any who might cross him or betray their plot. Of course, much of what they found had nothing to do with treason—though some of it hinted at other not entirely lawful activities Lysander would have to deal with—but everything had to be reviewed.

"If they keep finding places he's hidden documents, this will go on forever," Thalia said once she finished reading. She looked up at him with a frown on her own face. "What about the son?"

He flopped into his chair. "Traveling around Ivria, seemingly without a care in the world. Innocently visiting various families. Various families whose names are in his father's files.

We keep hearing about where he's been and who with just after he's left."

"Hmmm."

"Exactly," Lysander responded, correctly interpreting his sister's tone and facial expression. "We need to get ahead of him, but so far, he's been tight-lipped about his plans. On the bright side, he doesn't seem to know about his father yet."

"Small favors there." She drummed the fingers of one hand against the carved wood of the chair arm. "The daughter?"

"Triana is in Viera, married to the oldest son of the family, Arlo."

Thalia frowned. "Wait. Isn't he the one Father banished from court?"

"Yes." Years ago. Felix would remember when, but Lysander didn't plan to ask him, since part of the reason Arlo had been banished was his treatment of Felix. The rest was his deplorable behavior with a couple of young ladies and maids. Father wouldn't stand for it and wouldn't hear Arlo's protests either.

"Poor girl. Unless he's changed in the intervening years, but I doubt it."

"You'd be right." Lysander had heard that much from Felix, who'd gotten the knowledge through the vast network of gossip and information that flowed to him from seemingly everywhere. "She hasn't left their family home since she arrived, and we haven't been able to get anyone in to talk to her."

"If they traveled or came to Wyndward, it would be so much easier."

"I'm not inviting that piece of excrement back here. Personally, I wish Father had heaped more punishment on him."

"Me too." Thalia sighed. "You're having her watched?"

"As closely as we can."

Thalia was silent for a moment, then she said slowly, "Is

there a way for us to get word to her, or get her out of the house?"

"Get her out to talk to her? Or were you thinking of something more permanent?" Lysander knew the man was horrible, but was he a danger to his new wife?

She sighed. "I don't like the idea of anyone married to someone like that, but I haven't heard anything that makes me think he would physically harm her."

"We're trying to get a message to her without arousing suspicion. It would be easier if she left their property." And now he worried about why she might not. He'd assumed it was because her new husband and his traitorous family wanted to keep a close eye on her to reassure themselves of her loyalty, but now...

"Does she have any friends who could extend an invitation for a visit?"

"That we could subtly nudge into doing so?" He shrugged. "I have no idea. Maybe Felix would know."

Thalia's expression settled into one of thought. "She was only here briefly to be presented. I vaguely remember her, but I don't recall if she spent time with anyone in particular."

"And it seems her father kept her home otherwise." Always knowing he would arrange a marriage for her to his own advantage.

"Poor girl," Thalia repeated, then paused. "I mean, I assume so. We're assuming she isn't as bad as her father and in on the plot."

Lysander shook his head. "His papers say otherwise. And Sascha met her briefly. She was kind to him, warned him and seemed relieved to be getting out of her father's house. She's being used as much as he was."

"Then I'll say again: poor girl. At least Sascha is away from all of it. And we'll keep him well away from it, right?"

"Of course."

As much as he tried to concentrate after Thalia left, Lysander couldn't keep his mind from veering back to Sascha and how unlike himself he'd seemed earlier. But Thalia's words about Jannik's daughter did make him wonder if perhaps everything wasn't just catching up with Sascha. In a short amount of time, he'd been sent away from home to a terrible man, found out his parents were part of a plot against the Crown, and then been swept up to Wyndward. To be Lysander's concubine. In the middle of a precarious and unstable situation. Had Sascha ever come to terms with what his parents had done—were doing? Or was he too busy surviving at the castle, trying to keep secrets he shouldn't have to keep?

Alan would ask why Lysander was worrying about Sascha's state of mind at all. Except to determine whether the change in Sascha's demeanor meant he was plotting against Lysander, which would be Alan's first thought. Suspicion was Alan's natural state.

But Lysander didn't believe that. He couldn't delude himself into thinking he knew everything about Sascha yet, but he was getting to know him more each day. And he knew there wasn't a deceitful bone in Sascha's body, but it was plausible that his parents' betrayal and all the sudden changes were catching up with him. Lysander kicked himself for not thinking of it sooner. He needed pay more attention.

Alan would also wonder why he would do that, but if Lysander had just wanted someone to warm his bed, he wouldn't have named a concubine. Now he had Sascha, who was beautiful, but also kind and sweet and Lysander liked being around him. So he had to pay attention and make certain Sascha was all right.

Lysander found Sascha in the library in the royal apartments. Its collection was not as extensive as the castle's main library, but it had enough for Lysander's needs most days, both for entertainment and information. The library was also a warm, cozy room, one he enjoyed stretching out in with a book when he had the time or reading to the children with them curled up beside him. It was also the only place in his apartments that was spacious enough for him to transform into his dragon in, as long as he was careful not to extend his wings. During the long winters, the children thought it a fun game to climb all over his dragon, and he liked when they flopped down against him after and fell asleep. It reminded him of when they were babies sleeping on his chest, the small, precious, warm weight of them.

Sascha didn't look as relaxed as the comfort of the room warranted. He sat in a chair Lysander knew from experience was inviting enough to sleep in, but his posture was still straight as he focused on the book in his hands. Lysander frowned. He'd known Sascha used this library, though he'd never seen him in it. Sascha seemed to enjoy reading, and Lysander was perfectly happy for him to fill his time that way if he chose. He had just assumed Sascha would be more relaxed doing something he enjoyed.

Lysander took a step into the room, and Sascha looked up, something like alarm flashing in eyes for an instant. Why would he be alarmed? Lysander consciously made the frown drop from his face, smoothing his expression into something pleasant. "There you are."

Sascha rose gracefully, his book held to his chest. "I'm sorry."

"For what?"

The barest hint of anxiety ghosted over Sascha's fine features. "You were looking for me."

"You had no way of knowing that, and you were hardly difficult to find. So you have nothing to be sorry for." He continued into the room, walking up to Sascha and brushing his lips over Sascha's in a light kiss. When he straightened, a small smile was playing around the edges of Sascha's lips and his eyes were just fluttering open. The worry wasn't as prominent, but Lysander still wanted it banished entirely. He hated seeing it. "What are you reading?"

Lysander had meant to soothe Sascha with the question, but it was immediately obvious he'd missed the mark. Something complicated and indecipherable passed through Sascha's brilliant blue eyes, twining with the dregs of worry there, but nothing disturbed the serene set of his features. Which was even more disturbing. He didn't want masks from Sascha, not when they were together. But he knew better than to think he could order that from him. He could certainly order Sascha to tell him what he was reading instead of pleasantly asking, for whatever that was worth. Was it something Sascha didn't think he should be reading? Lysander couldn't imagine a book on these shelves he would care if Sascha read.

Finally, though it couldn't have been more than a breath later, Sascha turned the book to show him. "Just some history."

It was a history of the founding and early years of Ivria. A long, comprehensive telling, though far less dry than many such histories were. Now Lysander was even more puzzled and didn't care for the feeling. "Do you enjoy history?" he asked carefully. "I always liked studying it when I was younger. Learning all our ancestors did to keep us safe. It felt like a tale. Of course, it was far more complicated than that, but I didn't learn those bits until later."

Sascha smiled, but it faded quickly and Lysander could almost see the calculation, the indecision. The tension in his frame as he decided what to say next. Then, "I learned the sweeping tale parts of it when I was little too. My parents didn't think it was worth continuing my lessons along with my older brothers' after a point—I didn't need more for what they had planned for me. My grandfather made sure I could at least read as much as I wanted before he passed. He didn't think any education was wasted."

"I agree with your grandfather." Lysander ached for Sascha. There were schools all over Ivria, and children were required to be educated to a certain point, with plenty of opportunities to continue on or apprentice in a trade, but none of that stopped a parent from controlling the course of a child's education if the schooling was being done at home, something many of the more highly placed, wealthy families—or those who aspired to their behavior—opted for.

Sascha smiled again, a bit brighter, though not the dazzling one Lysander loved. "I still like to read. History, but other things too."

"I hope you know you can read anything you like from this library—and Wyndward's castle library, too, though you'll have to contend with the librarian there." As he'd hoped, that got a chuckle out of Sascha. He was calming down. "Make yourself at home here."

"Thank you, Lysander."

"Of course." He hesitated a moment. "Would you want to learn more formally?"

They could figure something out. Tutors?

But Sascha was shaking his head. "No, but thank you. I'm not like Romilly. I'm not meant for that. I doubt I'm smart enough for it."

"I don't think you give yourself enough credit," he said sincerely.

A faint blush tinged Sascha's cheeks, and Lysander could actually see him trying to decide if he could contradict Lysander's words. On the one hand, Lysander wanted Sascha to know that he didn't have to defer to him entirely when they were alone; on the other, he liked that Sascha wouldn't continue saying such self-deprecating things if it meant contradicting the king.

He changed the subject before Sascha could potentially get over those inhibitions. "I was looking for you to ask you to have dinner with me."

A slight frown wrinkled Sascha's forehead. Lysander shouldn't find it so adorable. "Dinner? Is there something special happening tonight that I wasn't aware of? Have I forgotten something?"

"Yes, dinner. But, no, you haven't forgotten anything. Just us tonight." He took Sascha's hand and raised it to his lips. "I'd like you all to myself."

He so often had to eat in front of the court or with various councillors or ministers or nobles. Sascha was with him, looking lovely and being charming, but it wasn't the same as having time alone with him. And perhaps it would help Sascha as well. Perhaps some time away from the eye of Wyndward's court would be good for him.

A smile bloomed over Sascha's face again. "You would?"

"Very much." He rested his hands on Sascha's arms, moving them slowly from shoulder to wrist, sliding the silk of his shirt beneath his hands.

Sascha's lips parted on an indrawn breath, and Lysander suddenly wanted to skip dinner entirely, or at least for the moment, and carry Sascha off to bed. Dinner could wait, surely? They could eat later, in bed even.

But, no, he planned on dinner, to spend time in Sascha's company without dozens of others looking on. He kissed Sascha, meaning for it to be brief but sinking into the sweetness of him for just a little longer, before straightening and offering his arm. "Shall we?"

CHAPTER 15

Sascha made his way through the castle, quite deliberately keeping his pace to a stroll. Rion paced beside him, probably hoping that Sascha was going to take him outside and let him run. The poor dog was going to be disappointed. Sascha glanced down at him—perhaps they could go out to the garden later. Nothing was in bloom yet, so it was almost always empty, or it had been the times Sascha had visited. Sascha wouldn't mind having the garden to himself.

For now, he kept walking, dog beside him, guard a few paces behind. The more public areas of the castle were not empty this afternoon. People greeted him, and Sascha responded politely, graciously, but not too effusively, and he didn't stop to talk to anyone. He didn't know these people. Felix had told him to decide who he would be, who others would see. After some thought, Sascha had found the idea not too far off what he already did. It was just a matter of choosing what face to show. Sascha had decided keeping a serene countenance and looking nothing less than exquisite every time he was seen, while still being kind and gracious, would be best. Holding on to an outward calm would be difficult enough at times. He wasn't going to try a more elaborate ruse, especially not with the potential for dire consequences.

As he took the stairs to Felix's rooms, Sascha's mind drifted to last night. It wasn't such an odd turn for his thoughts to take —they were often not far from Lysander, whether he worried about reflecting well on the king and not revealing the plot against him or daydreamed about the man. He found himself dropping some of his masks around Lysander. Sascha wanted to know him, wanted him to know Sascha, as frightening as that was. He was far too fond of Lysander already; if he married and set Sascha aside, it would hurt and he didn't think there was anything he could do about that. He hated the thought, but he hated the thought of pulling away from Lysander even more.

Sascha hadn't expected Lysander to invite him to a private dinner in such a sweet, personal way, as if it was special. Though really, it was just like Lysander; he was obviously and understandably busy, but he was thoughtful when he was with Sascha. Still, something had felt different last night. They ate breakfast alone together every morning, shared plenty of meals with others present as well, but last night... Had Lysander been more attentive? More curious about Sascha? More likely to casually touch? He was probably just imagining it.

The guard outside Felix's door let him in without announcing his presence or checking with anyone inside. Sascha hesitated for a breath before walking through the door, the dog at his heels. The door closed behind him, leaving him alone in the small entry. Felix was expecting him, but shouldn't someone have made him aware of Sascha's presence? He stood just inside the door and glanced around. No one was around. Sascha shifted from foot to foot. When he realized he'd curled his fingers into his sleeves, he forced himself to relax his hands. Rion whined quietly and leaned against his legs. Sascha stroked his silky head.

He was being ridiculous.

"Felix?" he called. "Are you here?"

Faint noises, movement overhead, then Felix appeared on the stairs to Sascha's left. "Sascha? Come upstairs."

Sascha relaxed and followed Felix, the dog trotting after. Though Sascha did raise a mental eyebrow at Felix's appearance. The man was barefoot, wearing a loosely belted dressing gown over his pants. At the top of the curving stairs, Felix led him across the hall into a large bedchamber that was luxurious in its sheer warmth and comfort. Felix gave Rion a pat and sent him off to curl up in front of the fire, before asking Sascha to come with him. A large cat sleeping on a chair didn't stir at their passage. They moved into a dressing room almost as large as the bedchamber.

"I'm sorry. I was held up at a lunch earlier, and now I'm running late, which I hate," Felix grumbled. Well, that explained his uncharacteristic appearance. "Do you mind if I finish dressing?"

"Of course not." Sascha was rather touched that Felix didn't mind Sascha seeing him without his usual armor of perfect, fashionable clothing.

"Thank you. I meant to be dressed before you arrived, but Lord Otto can go on." He scowled again as he shed his dressing gown—a soft gray velvet Sascha coveted immediately—and tossed it over a chair, baring a flash of pale chest flattened by short stays of silvery silk before he pulled a light green shirt over his head.

"It isn't a problem." Though he wasn't quite sure what to do with himself. The temptation to look through Felix's extensive wardrobe was strong, but he couldn't bring himself to do such a thing without invitation, no matter what Felix had done to his more meager one when they had first met. He finally leaned against a low dresser as the only chair in the room was occupied with the clothing Felix was changing into.

"If Otto hadn't also spilled wine on the jacket I was wearing, this wouldn't be a problem." Felix sighed. "While you're over there, the black bag is for you. Some more jewelry for you to borrow."

"You didn't have to do that." But he was picking up the velvet bag anyway. He itched to see what was in it.

Felix chuckled at his actions. "I know I don't. You're striking enough that you stand out in a room even without the jewels most cover themselves in, but you should have a few more things to choose from."

Sascha looked up sharply at Felix, but the man wasn't looking at him, too busy fastening a pair of short leather boots in a rich deep green. It was true—he hadn't realized just how much adornment many of the people here felt appropriate. Sascha thought some of them crossed a line into something gaudy, but he did sometimes wish he had more of his own.

"Lysander should've taken care of it." Felix shook his head in what felt like reproof, though he was still bent over his boots.

"Lysander is busy. He's the king and there's a treasonous plot. I'm sure it just slipped his mind. It's not a problem."

"You don't think anything is a problem. You can be too kind sometimes." Felix glanced up with a reassuring smile and a warmth in his eyes that took the sting out of his words. "I'm sure you're right about Lysander. Nevertheless, he has plenty of jewelry he's inherited stashed away that he could make available to you."

"That's likely set aside for his future consort." Sascha turned back to the dresser and fixed his attention down at it surface, beginning to empty the little bag. He didn't want Felix to see if anything of his conflicted feelings showed. He had said the word, but it ached, even though it shouldn't. He examined a pair of earrings set with deep purple amethysts, willing himself to not think about anything except how beautiful they were.

"Lysander isn't likely to marry any time soon."

Felix's words—and their tone, though Sascha couldn't quite parse it—had him raising his head...and meeting Felix's eyes in the mirror he'd forgotten was above the dresser. So much for hiding anything from Felix. Was that even possible? Felix always seemed to know everything.

As his cousin, he would probably know more about Lysander's plans when it came to marriage than Sascha did. But Sascha didn't want to talk about that subject now, not under Felix's perceptive gaze.

Sascha turned back to the jewelry and sorted through earrings, brooches, and a set of hair clips. All of it of excellent quality and finer and more valuable than anything he had ever worn in his life. "This is all beautiful. But...too much for me."

Felix stepped to his side on silent feet. "It's really not. You're King's Concubine." He held one of the clips—gold set with light blue stones—up to Sascha's hair and nodded. "This will all suit you far better than it does me. They're pieces I inherited but never wore. All lovely and appropriate for wear at Wyndward, nothing out of fashion, just not really to my taste."

He'd noticed that Felix wore comparatively few jewels when set against others at Wyndward, and those he did wear seemed quite carefully chosen, as was all his clothing. But Sascha stuck on another part of what Felix had said. "If they're family pieces, I wouldn't want to..."

Felix was shaking his head. "Take them. They don't have strong sentimental value to me and someone should use them." He plucked the other clip from Sascha's hand and moved behind him to fuss with Sascha's braid. "When my parents died, Lysander's parents—my uncle and aunt—took me in while my mother's parents took guardianship of my older brother. They needed an heir for the title and clan leadership, so he gave up his position in the succession to be raised for that position. They spilt our parents' property between us, including the jewels. These are some of what came to me, but I don't remember my parents wearing any of it. Except these clips. I remember my mother wearing them."

Felix stepped back to survey his work, then found a hand mirror in a drawer and gave it to Sascha. He angled it so he could see the back of his head. The clips were nestled in the complicated braid he'd woven his hair into this morning. He stared at them for a moment.

"Thank you for trusting me." With the jewelry, and the story, though he didn't say that.

Felix nodded. "Now, we have to go before I make us later than we should be."

Sascha didn't think Felix could be considered late to anything, but he acquiesced. He put the jewelry back into the bag and slipped it into his inner coat pocket while Felix finished dressing and donned his own coat.

"Are you certain I should be going to this?" Wyndward apparently had something like a festival to mark the beginning of spring—though this high in the mountains, early spring was a fickle thing. It had been flurrying yesterday when Sascha went for a walk with Romilly and was chilly today. Sascha's concern was less the weather and more the appropriateness of his attendance both as Lysander's concubine and as someone whose presence could conceivably give away their knowledge of the plot against Lysander.

"It can't be helped," Felix said. "With your position, people will expect you to be there. Your absence from too many events would be more suspicious. We'll have to hope our story holds."

Felix must have seen something of Sascha's feelings on his face because he continued, "Yes, I hate that plan too, but it's what we have. Come on. I think you'll enjoy this if you can stop worrying."

Sascha doubted he could, and he was certain Felix knew it, but he went without further comment.

Outside, the sharp breeze tugged at Sascha's coat and hair, trying to pull it from its braid. He could only hope it wasn't turning his nose as red as his hair. Eyes were on him and Felix as they strolled through the festival, located in a field outside town. Stalls sold various foods and wares, and Felix led him through all of them, making certain to share a few words with each vendor. Their gazes were bright and curious when they glanced at Sascha, but held no malice. Felix told him in an undertone that when Lysander and Thalia came down, they would do rounds of the merchants as well. Lysander's father had always done so, and this generation continued his tradition of meeting and talking to all the people they could. Another reason Lysander, and his father before him, was a popular and well-loved king.

Except by the people plotting against him, but Sascha pushed the thought away before it could darken his expression.

After a while, they made their way to a platform near an open area where performances were taking place. Chairs had been lined up under an awning that snapped in the wind for Lysander, Thalia, Felix, and him. Sascha wondered briefly as he followed Felix onto the platform if he would ever get used to having a seat among royalty. The spectators gave a cheer upon seeing them, and Felix smiled at them before taking his chair. Sascha sat beside him, happy to—theoretically, at least—no longer be the focus of people's attention.

He absolutely wasn't invisible, of course. Eyes would still find him, but sitting elegantly and putting a pleasant, attentive look on his face was something he could do with no thought by now. And if he felt the weight of stares, he tried to banish the idea that they were conspirators realizing who he was. The performances helped. Musicians, dancers, acrobats, and jugglers entertained the crowd. Warriors fought with swords and other weapons to display their skills, and a sorcerer performed illusions that had the audience gasping.

Sascha just managed to hold in his own gasps but couldn't repress a delighted smile. He didn't think the expression would be held against him. The smaller fairs and festivals he'd attended didn't compare to this one, and Felix had been right about him enjoying himself. If he could've banished the oppressive feeling of being watched, he would've enjoyed it all more, but nevertheless, it was a wonderful experience.

When Lysander and Thalia arrived as afternoon was moving toward evening, the crowd gave an even louder cheer. And another and some whistles when Lysander raised Sascha's hand to his lips, then kept it in his as they sat to watch the remainder of the performances. The whistles—bawdy, though seemingly good-natured—brought heat to Sascha's cheeks, which he hoped was indistinguishable from the color the chill of the breeze had likely whipped into them. He didn't want people seeing him blush and remarking on it; Lysander reacted with equanimity, only smiling slightly and directing his attention to the dancers. He didn't let go of Sascha's hand.

If Sascha wasn't already blushing, Lysander's continued hold on his hand might have made him, not out of embarrassment though. The contact, the very fact that Lysander wanted to hold his hand—and did so casually—in front of all these people, warmed Sascha through. It might mean nothing to Lysander. Sascha shouldn't assume it was important, but he couldn't stop it feeling important to him.

Caring for Lysander—Sascha could not use stronger words than that, even in his own head—was a bad idea. He and

Romilly had talked about that back at the beginning of this. Sascha hadn't thought it would be a problem.

He'd been wrong. So very wrong.

And he knew it, as he sat gracefully at Lysander's side smiling and exchanging a few words about the performances with the rest of the royal party, trying to ignore the curious stares from the crowd and the uneasy prickling sensation that perhaps someone less benign was watching.

As he strolled back to the castle with Sascha's hand in the crook of his arm, Lysander deemed the day a success. The people of Wyndward had enjoyed welcoming spring today— were continuing to enjoy it, performances giving way to dancing even as snow swirled in the evening air. Thalia and Felix had stayed. This year, with fears of plots and treason, Thalia and Felix would likely only dance once—under the careful eyes of their guards—and then sit to watch.

Being seen and seeing people, meeting them, talking with them—especially those from the town and surrounding countryside that their family wouldn't interact with on a daily basis —had always been why they attended. This year, Lysander believed it vital to do so. They'd heard no rumblings of wider discontent, but then, he hadn't realized there was a plot at all before it was brought to him. He wanted to be among his people, with the hope they wouldn't turn on him. How sad it was that he even had to consider that a serious possibility. His family had always taken pride in serving Ivria and its people, in protecting them and governing fairly.

Sascha shivered at his side, breaking Lysander from his dark thoughts. Lysander turned to look at him. Snowflakes had caught in Sascha's red hair, making his intricate braid look even more fanciful.

"Cold?" he asked quietly.

Sascha glanced up at him with a smile. "A bit."

More than a bit, Lysander guessed. The temperature had dropped as the sun set. Back at the festival, people were keeping warm at the bonfires or with dancing, and there was a heat spell on the platform where he and Sascha had been sitting. The change, now that they were on the road back to the castle with only the guards around them, was noticeable.

Lysander unwound his arm from Sascha's and put it around his shoulders, drawing him close against his side. Sascha made a soft, startled sound, then almost immediately leaned into Lysander, snuggling in closer to his warmth. Lysander chose to believe Sascha just wanted to be close—he'd caught the flush on Sascha's cheeks when he'd kissed his hand earlier—and the warmth was secondary. Having Sascha pressed against him was giving him ideas about what they could do when they got home and were finally alone. He squeezed Sascha's shoulders just a little more, and Sascha glanced up at him again. His cheeks were flushed again, more so than they'd been a moment ago. Lysander began to walk faster, startling a laugh out of Sascha. But his long legs let him keep up and kept him pressed to Lysander's side.

Inside the castle, Lysander didn't let go of Sascha. He slid his hand down Sascha's back and settled it at his waist as they walked through the corridors, not slackening their pace.

Sascha slanted a look in Lysander's direction, a smile curving one side of his full lips, but he only said, "It's quiet here tonight."

"Everyone is at the festival or home. There's no dinner or entertainments here. The staff are all given time to go enjoy themselves throughout the day." Lysander relished the quiet—

the ubiquitous guards keeping the castle safe, but few other people around to make demands on his time. "I should've asked if you wanted to stay at the festival instead of coming back with me."

"No, I wanted to come back with you. Do you always leave early?"

"Yes, let people enjoy themselves without worrying about their king's attention. My father always did the same." Before he became king, Lysander had stayed longer, joining in the dancing with his sister and Felix.

Sascha nodded.

"Did you enjoy yourself?"

"Oh, yes," Sascha replied brightly. "It was wonderful."

"I'm glad." He moved his fingers in teasing patterns along Sascha's side, satisfaction flooding him at Sascha's shiver. "Still cold?"

Sascha's smile turned just a bit wicked and sent a bolt of heat straight through Lysander. "I'm getting warmer."

"I wouldn't want you to be cold. I'll just have to see if I can warm you up," he whispered roughly.

Sascha's eyes were wide and dark. "Yes, please."

Those two words almost ripped a groan from him. He wanted to snatch Sascha up and run the rest of the way. But that action would alarm their guards and embarrass Sascha. He had to content himself with striding through the castle at a brisk pace, Sascha at his side.

They entered the royal apartments alone, leaving the guards at the doors. The children and their nursemaid were in the nursery, but the children were asleep—Lysander had gone to see them before he'd left for the festival—but otherwise, they were alone and hopefully would remain undisturbed. He drew Sascha close for a kiss, keeping it gentle, soft, though he wanted to devour.

"We can have something to eat brought up, but I think we should warm you up first."

"You've made a good start." Sascha tilted his face up in an invitation to kiss him again.

Lysander took the invitation but kept the kiss brief. "I should finish, then."

He drew Sascha through his sitting room and bedchamber into the large bathing room attached to it. Sascha had an inquiring expression on his face, but Lysander let him wait for his answers as he went to the tub that was easily large enough for two, though Lysander had never tested that, and set it filling with hot water.

"I didn't think you meant to run me a bath."

Lysander flashed a grin at Sascha as he moved around the bathing room, pulling out towels and bath oil and soap. "I'm not running you a bath."

Sascha's adorable frown appeared. "You're not?"

"No." He returned to Sascha for another kiss, this one a little longer, a little firmer. "I'm running us a bath."

"Oh."

Surprise gave way to intrigue on Sascha's face, and Lysander had to kiss him again. Sascha made a little humming noise and curved his body to Lysander's, circling his arms around his neck. Lysander held onto him, anchoring him close. He indulged them both with long, luscious kisses as the bath filled and the air of the bathing room became steamy and fragrant. Finally, Lysander pulled himself away. Sascha's lips were swollen and red, his eyes slightly glazed. The desire to kiss him again was overwhelming, but Lysander forced himself to step away. "Let's get you into the bath."

Sascha's lips parted on a long breath, then he nodded slowly. Lysander went to the tub to turn off the water before it overflowed, and when he turned back, Sascha had shed his coat and was winding his hair up on top of his head. Lysander stopped to watch him, enjoying the elegant arch of his back and the graceful movements. He wanted to see more.

Stepping up behind Sascha, he rested his hands on Sascha's hips and bent to kiss his newly bared neck. A shiver went through Sascha, so Lysander did it again. "Lysander," Sascha whispered.

"I'll help you undress." Lysander gently brushed Sascha's hands aside and carefully undressed him himself. Unfastening each piece of clothing and pulling it aside, laying kisses on bared skin. The curve of a shoulder, the pale expanse of chest, the jut of a hipbone when he dropped to his knees to pull off Sascha's pants and shoes. Sascha stared down at him, lips parted, aroused and shocked. Lysander stared back up at him, debating a moment, then stood and helped Sascha into the large tub.

Sascha sank into the hot water up to his neck and stayed there as Lysander undressed. He moved more quickly in removing his own clothes than he had Sascha's, tossing each garment aside with far less care than he had shown Sascha's, but Sascha watched his movements the whole time. Watched him as he approached the tub. Lysander loved Sascha's reactions, loved seeing what he felt play out across his expressive face. He urged Sascha forward and slipped into the tub behind him. Though he hadn't been as cold as Sascha had been, the hot water was perfect, loosening the tightness in his muscles, but it was Sascha's skin, silky and slick against his as Sascha leaned back against his chest, that was truly glorious. He pressed a kiss to Sascha's temple and then rested his cheek against Sascha's hair.

Sascha made a little humming noise and relaxed into Lysander even more. "Warmer now?" Lysander asked quietly.

Sascha chuckled. "Much. Thank you. This is perfect."

As much as Lysander wanted to continue what they'd started before they'd gotten in the tub, he had to admit that this was more than good all on its own. Being with Sascha always steadied him, for some reason, always lessened the tension of his day, of worrying about plots and treason. He let out a sigh himself and closed his eyes.

Lysander didn't know how long he drifted there, letting the hot water and Sascha's presence soothe him, when Sascha started trailing his fingertips along the arm Lysander had wrapped around him. That light touch was like lightning, a whisper of a caress that lit up every part of him and sent desire rushing through him again. He wanted to grab Sascha into a bruising kiss, but instead he reached for the soap. He wet and soaped a cloth and then ran it slowly and gently over Sascha's skin.

Sascha tilted his head to look at Lysander. "I can do that myself."

"I know you can, but I want to. It gives me pleasure," Lysander replied to what had sounded like a half-hearted protest. He continued washing Sascha, his movements as much caresses as anything else.

"Oh. Well, if it gives you pleasure, then by all means," Sascha said, a bit breathlessly. "I would never deny you something that brings you pleasure."

Lysander chuckled low. "You are so good to me."

Sascha laughed, still breathless under Lysander's ministrations. "If I were truly good to you, I would wash you too."

"I wouldn't object," Lysander said, loving that Sascha had made the suggestion. He didn't have the confidence yet to be too bold, or perhaps he wasn't yet certain it would be welcome —a notion Lysander would have to persuade him out of because boldness from Sascha was absolutely welcome and encouraged.

"Well." Sascha sat up and managed to turn to face Lysander without sloshing too much water on the floor. He was flushed and beautiful, his blue eyes large and brilliant, upswept hair leaving his face unframed and striking. He took the cloth from Lysander and added more soap, then with a glance from beneath his lashes at Lysander, he began smoothing it over Lysander's shoulders and chest. Sascha concentrated on his task, and his focus charmed Lysander even as his light caresses with cloth and hand maddened him. After a while, he couldn't take it anymore.

"Sascha," he said, his voice rougher than he'd expected. Sascha had barely looked up when Lysander reached out and pulled him into a deep kiss.

Sascha let out a noise of surprise immediately muffled in the kiss and wrapped his arms around Lysander's neck as he settled into Lysander's lap, straddling him. The bite of Sascha's short nails into Lysander's shoulders only made him more eager, kissing Sascha harder, holding him tighter. Finally, he slid a hand down between them and took both of their hard cocks in his grip. Sascha moaned against his lips as Lysander stroked them together, but he didn't pull away from the kiss. He just clutched Lysander tighter and closer. Only when he found his release did he break the kiss to cry out Lysander's name.

"Beautiful," Lysander whispered as Sascha slumped against him. His own release near, he kept stroking, Sascha shuddering against him, and grunted as his pleasure peaked. He relaxed into the side of the tub, Sascha a boneless weight on his chest, and turned his face into Sascha's hair, more content than he'd been in a long time.

CHAPTER 16

A few days after the festival, Sascha walked into town alone to have lunch with his uncle. Alone but for two guards and a dog trotting happily at his side. He wasn't entirely certain where the other was, but he assumed with Lysander or the children. He hadn't met Lysander's daughter and son yet. He heard them sometimes, faint childish voices or giggles, but he never encountered them, and he didn't go looking. Sascha wanted to meet them—was ridiculously curious about the young princess and prince because they were Lysander's—but he couldn't just introduce himself. It wouldn't be right. No matter how hurt he was that Lysander didn't want them to know each other. Sascha tried to stamp out those feelings. He was only Lysander's concubine; he had no right to know his children. He forced himself to push the hurt aside again.

At midday, the streets were bustling, and many of the people were fascinated with the King's Concubine. With his distinctive hair and the royal guards ensuring Sascha had plenty of space to walk along the winding streets, he was easily identifiable. Sascha wished he didn't stick out so much—he hated the attention, the possibility that someone involved in the plot would recognize him. But it couldn't be avoided. Perhaps one day, people would be used to seeing him and wouldn't stop to watch.

Perhaps one day soon, Lysander would catch all the conspirators and Sascha wouldn't have anything to fear from them.

His uncle's Wyndward home was separated from the narrow street by a stone wall with an ornate iron gate. The gate was opened immediately for Sascha, and he walked to the house through what would be a lovely little garden when it was in bloom. This early in spring, the trees were just starting to bud. The front door of the house was opened just as quickly and Sascha stepped inside. The maid, a pleasant girl he'd met on his last visit, took his coat and showed him through to a bright room at the back of the house. His uncle seemed to enjoy eating here, whether because the small room was more appropriate for meals with few guests or because it had a beautiful view out over the lake.

Florestan was already there. He stood when Sascha entered the room, his guard shadows taking up positions outside the door, which the maid closed as she left. "Sascha, my boy."

"Uncle. Have I kept you waiting?"

"Of course not. Come in, sit. Have some wine." Florestan was already pouring two goblets. "Lunch will be brought in shortly. It's just us today—Romilly has work."

Sascha sat in the indicated chair and thanked him for the wine. "They are working very hard to try to determine the extent of this conspiracy. They can't tell me much, but I hope they're making progress."

"Does the king not tell you?"

"Not really." Was that bad? He'd assumed this whole subject was being kept as quiet as possible, and who was he to push? But should Lysander tell him more? "I don't like to ask. I'm sure he'll tell me what I need to know."

Florestan was frowning slightly, but he nodded. "I'm sure you're right. Romilly obviously can't tell me much either. Though I do ask. Repeatedly."

Sascha laughed, as he was supposed to in the face of that comment, and the conversation moved on. They exchanged pleasantries until the maid returned with the food, a hearty fish stew that felt perfect for the brisk day.

"How did you enjoy the festival? I was only able to speak to you for a moment there." Florestan waved off Sascha's apology. "Completely understandable. No need to worry."

"Thank you, but I am sorry that we couldn't speak for longer. There were so many people coming to talk to the king or the prince or princess. I didn't expect it, and I would've liked to spend more time with you." He was still a little bemused by the entire day. "I did enjoy myself. It was just odd being in front of so many people."

"I'm sure it was." Florestan sighed. "I wish your parents would've let us bring you here when we asked. You could've explored the festival without the weight of such attention or obligations."

"I wish that too, Uncle, but please don't feel bad. My parents are..." Sascha wasn't certain how to finish that sentence, exactly what to say about them. They didn't deserve his loyalty or deference, but what could he say?

"Yes, they are," Florestan grumbled. "But you're free of them, and I'll make sure you're taken care of. How are you getting on with His Majesty? Romilly still talks about taking you with him when he leaves if you want to go, and your aunt and I would be happy to have you with us."

"Oh, I..." Sascha didn't know what to say in the face of such kindness. "Thank you, Uncle, but I'm happy with king for now. We're getting on quite well."

"But you'll tell me if something changes." Florestan leveled a stern look at him.

"I will. I promise." They were his family and he would need to rely on them when this was over until he figured out what came next.

"Good. I only want you to be happy. If you're happy with the king, then I'm happy for it."

"I am."

And he was. It was odd to think about with...everything else, but despite the worry and the fear and the uncertainty that nagged at him, he was happy where he was, with Lysander. He liked being around him, and he thought Lysander liked being near him in turn, perhaps took some comfort in Sascha's presence. More and more, they drifted toward each other. Sascha was glad to have his own bedchamber, but the idea of a private space was becoming more important than the reality of using it. He most often spent time in Lysander's sitting room, always slept in Lysander's bed. They took more quiet meals together, and Sascha often sat and read while Lysander went through papers or correspondence, just being in the same room together.

Sascha hadn't expected that when he came here, hadn't expected to be so comfortable in Lysander's presence, to want to spend so much time with him. He turned it over in his mind as he lay one morning, not quite ready to leave the cozy bed he had to remind himself often was Lysander's, not theirs. Sometimes it felt like theirs. Sometimes these rooms felt like home. Lysander had invited Sascha into his private rooms and seemed to enjoy finding him in them, even if all he was doing was reading in a chair by the fire. In turn, Sascha now felt comfortable here, even when he was alone. He hadn't felt so comfortable in many places in his whole life. It was extremely odd.

He sighed and forced himself out of bed. Perhaps if he got up he could stop his mind from spinning and worrying over the situation when he should just be glad it was working out for the moment. The cool air of the bedchamber hit his bare skin, and he hurried into his dressing gown before going into the bathing room to clean his teeth and wash up. Back in the bedchamber after, he dressed in a soft pair of pants and a shirt that had appeared in his wardrobe recently. He was almost certain the garments had not been among the many things Felix insisted he needed, but Sascha liked the soft, warm fabric and the shade of blue, so he wasn't going to argue with their inclusion. The clothes were obviously meant for lounging or sleeping, but their cut, the way they clung to his body, made it just as obvious they were meant to be seen.

Lysander liked him in them—and would likely appreciate them this morning when he returned for breakfast—though Sascha hadn't yet managed to wear them to sleep. Lysander also liked nothing between their skin in bed.

Sascha donned the dressing gown again. He'd find his book and pass the time until Lysander came back with it, perhaps ask a maid to bring him up a tisane. The first thing he heard as he opened the bedchamber door was the sound of delighted dogs. He was wondering if Lysander had returned early when he heard the giggling. Door all the way open, he stopped and stared at the two children playing with the dogs on the sitting room floor.

They were unmistakably Lysander's children. Even if it wasn't wildly unlikely for two other children to find their way into the royal apartments and Lysander's private sitting room, they looked just like him. The same tawny gold skin, the same thick dark hair. And when they realized they weren't alone and turned to face him, Sascha saw they had Lysander's eyes as well. They'd stopped laughing and were watching him curiously, even more so after one of the dogs trotted over to Sascha looking for attention. Sascha reached down and stroked his ears, but kept his focus on the children.

They stood and watched him for a while too. Princess Xanthe was six, her younger brother four, but at the moment, their self-possession made them appear older. What was Sascha supposed to do in this situation? Bow? Introduce himself? Ask why they were here? Hide?

Cassian made the decision for him when he asked, "Who are you?"

Sascha let go of the door and bowed, smiling warmly. "I'm Sascha, Your Highnesses. I'm...a friend of your father's."

If that wasn't the most ridiculous thing to say, he didn't know what was. But he wasn't going to tell them he was their father's concubine. Would they know what it meant? Did they know Sascha existed? He doubted it, and he was not going to explain any of it to them.

"You were in his bedroom," Xanthe said.

"Yes, I was." He was not going to explain that either. He could only hope they wouldn't ask.

The other dog abandoned the children, who were now ignoring her, and came to Sascha in search of her share of the attention he was giving Rion. Sascha crouched to pet them both, leaving the children to make their decision about what to do next. The dogs were certainly happy, and Sascha laughed a bit at their joy, though he kept the children in the corner of his eye. For a little while, they just watched him with the dogs. Finally, they turned to each other and something silent seemed to pass between them. Cassian nodded.

"Will you tell us a story?" Xanthe asked.

Sascha was so utterly flummoxed he nearly fell over. "Oh, um."

The two little faces were so hopeful, and so like Lysander, that Sascha couldn't refuse them.

"Do you have a book you'd like me to read to you?"

The children glanced at each other again.

"Our books are in the nursery," Cassian said.

"Do you want to go get one?" Sascha asked.

They shook their heads.

Sascha eyed them shrewdly. "Because you left without permission?"

This time they nodded.

"Won't your nursemaid worry?" He assumed a nursemaid minded them. They were still so young.

Xanthe spoke, "She'll know we won't have left the apartments."

Sascha should send them back immediately, should walk them back to make sure they went straight to the nursery. Their nursemaid wouldn't be happy they'd left—did they make a habit of escapes? Would she know where to look for them?

And, really, if Lysander had wanted him to spend time with his children, to know them at all, he would've introduced Sascha to them already. The hurt that he didn't and hadn't was fresh again, especially when faced with the sweet children in front of him.

He should take them back this instant.

Instead, he walked over, and to the delight of children and dogs, sat on the thick carpet in front of the couch. "A story, let me think."

Now the children seemed their ages. Giggling again, they scampered to him and sat at his sides. The dogs followed, likely not wanting to miss out on any belly rubs that might be offered. The children obliged eagerly in that regard while Sascha dredged a tale up out of the depths of his mind. Something he and his sisters had made up while they roamed the woods surrounding their house as children. He pushed aside the sadness and betrayal that crept in at the thought of his family and the bolt of worry for his sisters, powerless and young in their parents' house—he couldn't think of that right now—and began the story.

His youngest sister had loved stories of magic and danger and hunting for treasure, so they played that a lot. Probably why so much of the silliness was still in his memory, though he did have to embroider on it as he went. The children didn't seem to notice. In fact, they were hanging on his every word, eyes alight with their interest.

Until a sharp rap came on the door, which opened before Sascha could call out. The action left him stunned. No one did that, ever, not in Lysander's private sitting room. A stern-faced woman in a dark dress swept into the room. Her gaze swung immediately to the children. "There you are."

The nursemaid, then. Sascha still didn't care for her manner. "Excuse me." The words were out before Sascha consciously thought about saying them, and his tone was sharp and cold. His heart began to gallop and heat raced through him, as the nursemaid turned a disapproving—was that disdain in her eyes?—look on him. Sascha fought to hold on to the tone he'd taken, difficult as it was with his heart pounding and his awareness of his disheveled appearance. "You can't just come in here."

She drew herself up. "I am nursemaid to the prince and princess."

"And these are the king's private rooms. You cannot enter without an invitation."

The woman sniffed. She definitely looked disdainful now. "The king is not here, but my charges are."

"Actually, the king is behind you." Lysander's voice floated into the room from the hallway, and he didn't sound happy. Sascha's stomach swooped sickeningly.

"Your Majesty." She stepped aside and into a curtsy so quickly the movement was almost a hop. "I apologize. I wasn't aware you were there."

"It sounds as if you owe Honorable Sascha an apology as well. For coming in uninvited?"

"Your Majesty, the children snuck out of the nursery. I was searching for them."

"And Sascha is quite correct about my private chambers." Lysander was frowning, but not at Sascha, not yet at least. He turned to Sascha and the children who were still on the floor curled up with the dogs. "Did you sneak out of the nursery?"

"Yes, Father," Xanthe said, her tone contrite.

Cassian jumped in then and barely took a breath as he said, "But we wouldn't have left the apartments. And we found the dogs here and then Sascha found us and he's telling us a story. It's a good story too. Can he please finish?"

Sascha blinked at the rush of words. Lysander slid his gaze to Sascha. He tried to read it, to see what Lysander was thinking and if he was upset, but his expression gave nothing away. Finally, Lysander said, "You'll have to ask Sascha if he'll finish the story."

Both children turned to him, pulling his focus from Lysander. "Will you, Sascha, please?"

He had to clear his throat to be able to speak. "Oh, well, yes, of course."

"Your Majesty," the nursemaid interjected, "I really do think I should take the children back to the nursery."

"Oh?" Lysander turned his frown on her again. "Why is that?"

She seemed to be searching for a reason that wasn't that she didn't think the princess and prince should be spending time with a concubine. "They haven't had their breakfast yet."

"We haven't either. They can eat with us. Have their meals brought here. They'll be back before their morning lessons."

The nursemaid appeared as if she wanted to continue arguing but couldn't do so with the king. So she only dipped into a curtsy, then left the sitting room. Lysander closed the door behind her and turned to look down at them again. "We'll have a talk about leaving the nursery without saying anything to anyone later, hmm?"

"Yes, Father," Xanthe and Cassian said in unison.

"All right. Finish your story before breakfast arrives." A smile seemed to twitch at the corner of his lips when the children gave a little cheer. It turned into something warmer when his gaze shifted to Sascha, and Sascha's heart finally started to slow as he saw it, as he looked into Lysander's eyes.

"Sascha?" Xanthe asked quietly.

Sascha's attention snapped back to the children. He would have to finish calming himself down later. They needed their story. "Yes. Where was I?"

Lysander listened with half his attention as Sascha told a story that seemed to involve lots of searching through ancient ruins for treasure and running and magical artifacts and not a lot of actual story, though that didn't seem to bother the children. After trying to place it for some time, he realized Sascha must be spinning it as he went. He listened even more closely then.

The three of them made a charming picture curled together on the rug with the dogs sprawled over them. Lysander had been surprised to find them, but perhaps more surprised by how right they looked that way. How right Sascha looked with his children. He wasn't certain what to do with that thought. Lysander hadn't introduced the children to Sascha and hadn't planned to, or at least, hadn't thought about doing so. Not yet? Not ever? No, he would've had to at some point. The children were too big a portion of his lives, and they lived right here. Lysander should be more surprised that Sascha hadn't crossed paths with them sooner.

Sascha was good with them, seemed to enjoy them, and was quite patient with all of Cassian's questions. Lysander hadn't known if Sascha would even care to know Xanthe and Cassian. Sascha hadn't ever asked about them. But Sascha wouldn't if Lysander didn't say something first. Had Lysander ever spoken of them to Sascha? He sat back in his chair and tried to remember, as Sascha wound the story toward its dramatic conclusion. Lysander didn't think he had, but he talked about the children with very few people. Xanthe and Cassian would be in front of the court soon enough; he wanted them to have their childhoods separate from the intrigue and politicking and scrutiny.

But Sascha was not going to put the children through what they would receive at the hands of many who gathered close to power. Sascha was not going to put them in any kind of danger. So why hadn't he even asked if Sascha wanted to meet them? He didn't think it was inappropriate in regard to what Sascha was to him—unlike, it seemed, their nursemaid, which meant it was time for a change in the nursery. He would not have Xanthe and Cassian picking up that attitude.

Lysander hadn't brought Sascha to meet them because he thought they'd like Sascha and he didn't want them disappointed when Sascha left.

Only Sascha showed no signs of wanting to leave. Lysander supposed the real test would be if he asked to go with Romilly when they left Ivria, but if Sascha wanted to, Lysander believed he would've said something by now. If anything, he and Sascha seemed to be drawing closer. Lysander liked that they were. He liked that Sascha was here, a balm after a long, tense day.

He would disappointed if Sascha left.

He would just have to make certain Sascha didn't want to leave.

A knock signaled the arrival of breakfast and the end of that line of thinking for the moment. The maid didn't react to the cozy pile of children and dogs and Sascha when she brought the tray in, though Lysander assumed the tidbit of gossip would make the rounds in the kitchen and beyond soon enough. He cared only if it hurt the children or Sascha.

Cassian ran up to him after she left. "Father! Sascha tells good stories!"

Lysander scooped him up and into his lap. "Does he?"

"Yes!"

Sascha and Xanthe followed at a more sedate pace. Xanthe was holding his hand, and Sascha appeared vaguely bemused. But he smiled at Lysander's son. "I don't know about that."

"It was quite good, Sascha," Xanthe said as she hopped up into a chair and Lysander settled Cassian into one beside her.

"I'm happy you enjoyed it, but perhaps next time, I should just read you one of your books," Sascha said as he took his usual seat. Then he froze. "Oh, that is, if..."

Lysander reached out to take his hand. "If you want to read to them, I'm certain they would enjoy it."

Sascha turned a sweet smile on him, one that warmed Lysander down to his toes. "I would enjoy it too."

THE CHILDREN ADORED SASCHA. Lysander couldn't blame them— Sascha was easy to adore—but he was mildly shocked by how quickly it happened. Just as quickly, Sascha came to adore them. Lysander would've felt horrible if the children's feelings weren't returned. As it was, he had to put some rules into place to prevent Xanthe and Cassian from leaving the nursery at all hours of the day and night to look for Sascha without telling anyone. Thalia thought it was hilarious, but she also couldn't understand why he hadn't introduced Sascha to them before.

"Sascha is new and exciting. The novelty will wear off soon enough and they won't try to see him all the time," she'd said.

Lysander found it less amusing, not only because he didn't like the idea of the children wandering on their own, but also because he wanted time with Sascha himself too.

When he'd returned from his time away dealing with Jannik, Lysander had promised to take the children away for a few days as soon as he could. He hadn't managed it yet, but he'd finally given in and planned an overnight stay at an isolated house he owned a few hours flight from Wyndward. Before Xanthe and Cassian had been born, before his own father had died, Lysander had gone there alone whenever he could get away, enjoying the peace and quiet. It was a good place to take the children and let them run and play unbothered. He hated the idea of leaving Wyndward when they were still trying to gather information about the plot, but Lysander wasn't out gathering information himself. Felix was far better placed to hear anything at Wyndward itself, and Thalia was still there, able to handle everything else. There was no reason not to go.

The children asked him if Sascha was going with them. When he asked if they wanted Sascha with them, their answer was an enthusiastic yes.

Lysander hadn't planned to bring Sascha along, not back when he'd first returned home and made the promise to Xanthe and Cassian. He hadn't thought about Sascha at all then in relation to the trip. Recently, when he made firm plans about when to go, he'd felt bad about leaving Sascha behind. Lysander wanted Sascha with him, liked having the other man around all the time. He would miss Sascha, but he hadn't thought it right to bring him.

Now the children wanted him along too.

Sascha appeared more than pleased when Lysander asked if he wanted to join them. Surprised and pleased and happy. He smiled that bright, sweet smile, and Lysander had to kiss him.

When they left, it was with Alan and a squadron of hand-picked guards. Lysander once again flew without passengers. For safety reasons, he wasn't allowed to carry the children. They went to Alan, and Lysander personally checked the straps securing them and that they were dressed properly for the chill during the flight, though Sascha had also made sure they were bundled up well. He'd blushed when Lysander had caught him adjusting gloves and coats and stepped away immediately, likely thinking he'd overstepped. The new nursemaid—who had been assistant to the old head of the nursery but whose attitude was much better—had dressed the children and their care wasn't Sascha's responsibility or concern, but Lysander thought the action was sweet and so very Sascha.

One of the guards carried Sascha. Security reasons didn't prevent Lysander from flying Sascha himself, but the ridiculous protocols and traditions about it being below a monarch's dignity to carry passengers were strong and Lysander didn't want to draw more attention to himself or Sascha. He wanted to fly with Sascha though, wanted to have that experience. But he had to be sensible.

The day was crisp and clear, perfect for flying. They left Wyndward early in the morning and arrived at Eirini before lunch. The few bags they'd brought were carried in to be unpacked while Lysander and Sascha stayed outside to let the children stretch their legs after the flight. A few guards remained with them. The children were used to their presence and didn't notice that they were especially watchful as the children ran and Lysander and Sascha strolled after them.

They wandered behind the house where a small garden lay dormant and a stretch of grass led to some woods. Alan came out to report to Lysander about the security arrangements in the house, as Cassian tugged Sascha toward the trees, pointing at a bird on a bare branch and asking what it was. Xanthe skipped in circles and spun, dancing to music she hummed to herself. Lysander smiled fondly, watching his family while Alan talked to him. As if feeling his attention, Sascha looked over at him. Cassian still held his hand and was excitedly pointing out various things to him, but Sascha took a moment to smile at Lysander, a curve of lips that had a quality to it branding it as just for him.

Lysander was still watching Sascha, taking in the sun shining on his rich red hair, when the attack came and Sascha's smile was replaced by horror and fear.

CHAPTER 17

The dragons overhead appeared out of nowhere. One moment, a clear blue sky with hardly a cloud in sight. The next, several dragons circling above them, diving to attack. A strangled scream escaped Sascha's throat. The sound alerted Cassian that something was wrong, and the reminder of his presence did more to keep Sascha thinking than anything else. He grabbed the little boy and pushed him behind him, keeping a hand on him, keeping himself between Cassian and the attack.

Lysander and the commander had both used their Talents; in an instant, they were dragons, ready to defend against their attackers. The other guards were coming closer, some changing into dragons, others drawing weapons as they ran. Sascha's gaze darted around the scene, trying to figure out what to do—he couldn't stand here unarmed and frozen with Cassian behind him—and then he saw Xanthe. She was on her own, none of the guards close. Her head whipped back and forth, watching her father and the guards fight. Otherwise, she stood utterly still.

Her paralysis broke his own. He couldn't run to her, not and drag her brother into the open and he couldn't leave the little boy alone. "Xanthe!"

He worried about drawing attention to her, but there was so much noise, roars of dragons and yells in human voices and the clash of blades. Hopefully, they wouldn't hear. Hopefully, she would. He had to risk it. When she looked at him, he motioned frantically for her to come to him. Xanthe didn't hesitate, just turned and ran. She wasn't far and she was quick, but Sascha didn't breathe again until she was in his arms.

How had he come to care so quickly for these children?

She clung to him as he crouched on the ground just inside the tree line, Cassian behind him gripping his coat. Sascha felt the wet of her tears against his neck and murmured soothing nonsense to her as he looked over her shoulder at the fight, at Lysander. Seeing him all right—fighting off another dragon, but all right—made Sascha sag toward the ground a little more.

Speaking of...how had he come to care so much so quickly for Lysander?

He pushed thoughts and realizations aside. He and the children were not safe here. All of the guards were fighting, going to their king's aid. Did they not see Sascha and the children, or did they think fighting off the attack the best way to protect them? It hardly mattered when no one was coming to protect them. Sascha forced himself to breath slowly and think. He had to get the children—and himself—somewhere safe. The woods were at their backs, but he didn't know them. If these were the woods he'd grown up wandering, he would've known where to hide. He couldn't ask the children. They were too young and too scared.

They had to get to the house. And hope no one meaning them harm had made it inside. Even if somehow had, Sascha could barricade them inside a room until help arrived.

He hoped there wasn't anyone inside.

Sascha drew the children closer and whispered to them, "We have to go to the house and get inside. We're going to be very quick and very quiet. Can you do that with me?"

Both children watched him with wide, fearful eyes. Eyes that were also full of trust for him, which shook Sascha almost as much as the sudden attack. He waited until they nodded, then got to his feet and took the children by the hands, leading them deeper into the trees, hoping for a little more cover as they began to move.

Sascha's heartbeat was so loud he couldn't believe everyone didn't hear it. Every second felt like an hour, as they moved through the trees. The crackle of twigs and leaves underfoot had Sascha checking constantly if they'd been heard, but it was impossible to be completely silent with two small children. After a few moments, he scooped Cassian up and carried him. Xanthe stayed close beside him without having to be told.

He stopped when they got as close as they could to the house while staying under cover of the evergreens. When he looked at the distance they would have to cross—not so far, but a good distance when running from an attack with children—he almost wanted to stay right here, hunkered down among the trees, and hope no one found them. But he couldn't risk it. He crouched again and whispered to Xanthe, "Can you run as fast as you can to the house with me?"

She nodded silently.

"All right. As fast as you can straight to the door."

And as soon as he said to go, she did. Sascha ran beside her, still holding Cassian and glad he wasn't heavier or Sascha never would've been able to run with him. He heard a shout as they ran, something different from the sounds of the fight he'd been listening to as they crept through the woods. A shock of fear went through him that they might have been seen. All he could do was keep moving and urge Xanthe on faster.

She seized the door handle when they reached it, Sascha's hand gripping it a fraction of a second later, and they pulled the door open together and tumbled through it. He had a moment to be grateful that it hadn't been locked—something he hadn't thought of earlier and told himself not to dwell on now. He set Cassian down and latched the door himself.

"Let's find somewhere to hide until your father comes for us." He had to believe Lysander would be fine and would come.

Xanthe and Cassian each grabbed one of his hands and pulled him along the corridor. He was willing to let them lead, as they knew the house better than he did. They brought him to a small windowless store room filled with shelves of linens. When they stepped inside, a light globe flared to life, the magic triggered by their movements. Sascha was relieved they weren't left in darkness when he closed the door, but he rather wished there was something heavy to push in front of it.

Sascha sank to the floor and sat against the door, the children immediately coming to him and curling into him, one on either side. He untangled his arms from under them and wrapped them around the children. They were crying again, which was the only thing holding back Sascha's own tears.

"We're fine. We're going to be just fine." Sascha wasn't certain he should be making that promise, but if he knew Lysander at all, he would be fighting to get to his children. "Let it out, darlings. I'm here."

"Don't leave," Cassian whispered.

"I'm not going anywhere," he whispered back fiercely. "We're going to stay right here together." He held them and stroked their hair and murmured words he hoped were at least a little comforting. He'd soothed his sisters after nightmares and through childhood hurts and fears, but never anything like this.

Sascha didn't know how long they were there. It could've

been hours or minutes; it felt like days. The children stopped crying but made no attempt to move away from him, so Sascha just kept holding them and trying not to envision all the disasters that could be happening outside. It was difficult—every horrible outcome rushed to his mind, each worse that the last, all in vivid detail—but he made himself try. He had to stay calm, or appear calm, for Xanthe and Cassian.

Noise shattered the silence of the house. The children stiffened against him, and Sascha clutched them closer. But the sound resolved itself into calls of their names, the loudest voice Lysander's. Sascha let out a long, shuddering breath. The children realized it too and scrambled up. Sascha unfolded himself from the floor more slowly, legs stiff from being in one place for so long, but the children waited for him instead of rushing past to get to their father. Sascha opened the door himself, and they stepped through together.

Lysander wasn't immediately visible but a guard was, and he called out that they were here. Lysander appeared a moment later, eyes wild with worry. He was disheveled and dirty with some blood on his sleeve, but he strode toward them with no sign of injury. The children only left Sascha's side when Lysander dropped to his knees in front of them. He gathered them close, closing his eyes as he held them.

Sascha stood awkwardly. He considered stepping away, letting Lysander have this time with his children when he must have been frantic with worry. But Sascha was selfish—he couldn't bring himself to go when all he wanted was to be near Lysander, to prove to himself that Lysander was alive and safe.

Lysander opened his eyes and looked up at Sascha, his gaze searching. Sascha dredged up a small, wobbly smile for him, which Lysander returned. Then Lysander reached out a hand to him, and Sascha clasped it, just that contact helping him breathe easier. Lysander tugged gently and Sascha went to his knees on the carpet, leaning into Lysander's side as he held his children.

"Are you all right?" Lysander asked roughly after a while. "Are any of you hurt?"

"No. We aren't hurt," Sascha answered. "Are you?"

"I'm fine."

Sascha glanced down at the blood on his sleeve and back up at him with an inquiring expression. Lysander just shook his head, but Sascha wasn't certain if it was because he was truly fine or because he didn't want to upset the children. Sascha worried it was the latter. He straightened away from Lysander and knelt up. Slowly, carefully, gaze flicking to Lysander's face often, Sascha reached out to Lysander's arm and gently pulled his sleeve aside. It was made easier by the slash torn through the heavy fabric. Fear and worry made him glare at Lysander. When he realized what he was doing, he bent to his task again, moving carefully so as to avoid hurting Lysander or alerting the children to what he was doing.

He bared Lysander's forearm and found a long, shallow cut that was still sluggishly bleeding. His lips pulled down in a frown at the sight.

"Don't worry about it," Lysander whispered.

Sascha let out an exasperated huff and studied the cut. He quite deliberately did not think about how Lysander might have gotten it but did his best to assess how severe it was. His knowledge of injuries and healing was woefully lacking, but he thought he could handle this one. He laid his hand gently over the cut and closed his eyes. His healing Talent was barely a spark inside him—not worth training even if his parents hadn't had other plans for Sascha—but he'd spent the years since it manifested healing the scrapes and bruises and sniffles that he and his sisters had picked up, learning through instinct and doing and the couple of books in the house's small library. He couldn't do anything complicated or involved, but he could close a cut, even this one. He took deep breaths and pushed his magic to heal the injury. His stomach did a nauseating loop as the cut slowly healed, leaving only a thin, pink line as evidence it was ever there. Good.

Sascha sagged back to sit on the floor against Lysander's side, letting his his head fall onto Lysander's shoulder and closing his eyes.

LYSANDER WANTED the children and Sascha back behind Wyndward's walls immediately, but traveling now wouldn't be prudent. Or so Alan insisted. A few of their attackers had escaped and with the guards tired or injured from the fight, it was best to stay here and wait for reinforcements from Wyndward, additional guards to protect them on the flight home and a sorcerer who could hopefully detect whatever magic had been used to hide the attacking dragons until the very last second. Lysander had to agree that the course of action made sense, despite his every instinct screaming at him.

He spent some time with the children, getting them cleaned up, soothing their fears, listening to them talk about how Sascha had saved them and taken care of them. Hiding his own emotions from them. He'd been terrified for them and Sascha during the attack—he hadn't been near any of them, hadn't been able to get to them. He could only hope while he fought that the guards had. When he realized they hadn't... He didn't think he'd breathed properly until he saw all three of them safe.

After a while, they wound down and dropped into sleep, and Lysander left them napping with a maid in the room to watch over them. He couldn't bear to leave them alone, but he couldn't stay. Though he wanted to go directly to Sascha, he forced himself to check in with Alan and make plans. They might have to stay the night, depending on when the additional guards arrived. Spending the night had been the original plan, but Lysander wanted them home. He also didn't want to travel at night, so remaining here would be the prudent action, unless the guards broke all speed records to get here.

Finally free of Alan, Lysander made his way to his own bedchamber where he'd sent Sascha to bathe and rest. Sascha wasn't in the bedchamber, but the bathing room door was open, so Lysander went through and stopped. Sascha sat shivering in the bath, wet hair plastered to his head, arms wrapped around his bent knees. He looked up when Lysander stepped in, eyes wide and dark and lost.

"Sascha."

Picking up a couple of towels, he went to the tub and coaxed Sascha to stand and step out. He wrapped one around Sascha along with his arms, embracing him and drying him at the same time. For a while, as Lysander rubbed the soft cloth over his skin, Sascha just stood still and let him; then Sascha let out a shuddering breath and collapsed into Lysander's chest. Lysander held him there for a moment, murmuring to him that everything was all right. Once Sascha's hands came up to hold Lysander's hips, he kissed Sascha temple, then briskly rubbed his hair with another towel to get the worst of the wet out. Sascha probably wouldn't thank him for it when he had to untangle the long red locks, but Lysander wanted him warm.

Lysander dropped the towels to the floor and bundled Sascha into a dressing gown. Then he scooped him up in his arms and carried him out into the bedchamber. Only then did Sascha speak, and it was to protest. "Oh. No, you shouldn't. Your arm—"

"Hush. My arm is fine, thanks to you." And they would talk about that surprising ability of Sascha's later. He got Sascha into bed and under the blankets, then stripped off his own clothes and joined him. He'd been looking forward to a bath of his own, but Sascha was more important, and he didn't hate the idea of lying down anyway.

Sascha curled into his arms as soon as Lysander joined him under the blankets. He didn't cry, but he did tremble as he took long, quiet, shaking breaths. Lysander held him close with one arm and used the other hand to stroke his hair, his back, trying to soothe. He didn't say anything, wasn't sure what he could say that would help, but he could be there and offer comfort with his presence. And do whatever Sascha asked.

After a long while, Sascha whispered, "I'm sorry."

"For what?"

"I fell to pieces all over you."

"You also saved yourself and my children, and then kept all of you safe and calm through a terrifying experience." He kissed Sascha's forehead. "You're allowed to fall apart now."

"It's ridiculous to fall apart now though. It's over. We're safe. I should be able to hold myself together." Sascha's words had a bitter edge to them that told Lysander someone had lectured Sascha about something like this. Lysander had noticed Sascha's nerves—though Sascha hid them well—but he wondered how much difficulty they'd caused him and how much judgment his family had heaped on him for them.

Rage, white hot and intense, surprising him with its strength, flashed through Lysander at the thought. Sascha's parents had chosen to use him to better their own situation— and while it wasn't by any means uncommon for families to seek advantageous marriages or liaisons for their children, Sascha's parents had done so with no care for his well-being. They had chosen to commit treason and use Sascha as an unwitting pawn. It shouldn't surprise him that they would have little care for his well-being while he was still with them.

He forced the anger down. Expressing it wouldn't help and might very well upset Sascha further. "It isn't ridiculous. You were in danger and scared with two young children depending on you. That is enough to make anyone fall apart, but you are strong enough that you got through it and fell apart now when it's safe for you to react to how horrible it was."

Sascha lifted his head to stare at Lysander, his eyes bewildered. "I'm not strong."

"Yes, you are." He drew Sascha close for a soft kiss. "So very strong."

CHAPTER 18

They returned to the palace first thing the next day. Lysander had never been so grateful to be at Wyndward than he was that morning. The return trip was uneventful, whether because of the increased guard presence or because their attackers had left to regroup, but everyone had been on guard the entire flight. The children weren't quite their usual selves, but they did talk and giggle through breakfast and preparations to leave. They also quite obviously kept both Lysander and Sascha within sight, and often touching distance, at all times.

Sascha noticed too, or at least Lysander thought he did. He certainly made a special effort to stay close to the children. Lysander worried that there would be a problem when it came time to leave and the children would have to be separated from them for the flight back, but Sascha crouched between them and whispered to them, gesturing with his graceful hands toward the dragons already transformed and waiting for them. Whatever he said made Xanthe and Cassian nod and hug him, then hold his hands as he walked them to where Lysander waited for them beside Alan's dragon.

Lysander had secured them in place and then walked Sascha to the dragon he would fly back with, helped him up, and made certain he was secure as well. Sascha watched him the whole time, faintly bemused. Lysander only lifted his gloved hand to his lips for a kiss, then forced himself to walk away and transform into his own dragon. He wanted to carry Sascha and the children back himself, wanted to know they were all safe with him, but it wouldn't have been smart in the event of another attack. He'd been tense the whole journey, expecting one, but they'd reached home unbothered.

Thalia and Felix had come to meet their arrival, sharp gazes searching them for injury, though the message they'd sent had said there were none. As soon as they landed, Felix went to the children and helped them down. By the time Lysander had triggered his magic and changed back, Sascha had joined them and the children were holding his hands. Lysander walked over to them, Thalia meeting up with him on the way. She sent an inquiring look his way after glancing at Sascha and the children, but he shook his head slightly to delay her questions.

"I have to talk to Felix and Thalia," Lysander told Sascha and the children, hoping they wouldn't react poorly to his absence. Granted, he was more worried about the children, but Sascha had been too quiet and withdrawn that morning for Lysander's comfort.

"Why don't I take Xanthe and Cassian to the nursery then?" Sascha asked, infusing his voice with cheer as he looked down at the children.

"That would be wonderful," Lysander replied, hoping to forestall protests from Xanthe and Cassian. They were well-behaved and normally wouldn't argue in front of so many people, but it had not been a normal couple of days.

Sascha seemed to realize the same because he said, "Perhaps we can find the dogs first. I'm sure they missed you."

That got the children's attention. Xanthe looked up at Sascha. "They missed you and Father too."

Sascha smiled at her. "Well, the three of us can spend some time with them now, and your father will come as soon as he's finished with his important work, all right?"

The plan was deemed agreeable to all parties, and Sascha left with the children and their guards while Lysander led Thalia and Felix to his study. Once inside with the door closed, Lysander slumped into the chair behind his desk and let out a long breath, closing his eyes.

"Are you all right?" Thalia asked as she took one of chairs across from the desk, Felix sitting in the other.

He nodded. "I'm not injured." Though he thought about the minor wound Sascha had healed for him. "Sascha and the children are unhurt as well. But I am exhausted and worried." He opened his eyes in time to see them exchange a glance.

"Tell us what happened. Your message lacked detail," Thalia said sternly.

"I apologize. We were pressed for time." Lysander launched into the story, both what he'd experienced and what he learned later had happened to Sascha and the children. Thalia and Felix listened to the entire recitation without interrupting, though neither hid their reactions.

Thalia cursed long and low when he finished.

Felix slanted her a teasing look. "Not that I don't agree with all of that, but if your mother heard you..."

She whacked him lightly on the arm, shaking her head. The moment of levity helped, but they quickly returned to seriousness.

"I'm trying not to think about how lucky you were," Thalia said. "Especially the children."

"I'm going to have nightmares about it for the rest of my life. They weren't far away from us. I didn't think we needed guards a step away the whole time." Lysander shook his head. He was going to have to rethink security. "They went right to Sascha, though, and he got them into the house and hiding."

"They trust him," Felix said. "I could see it this morning. And he's good with them."

"He is," Lysander agreed. He couldn't quite identify the quality Felix's voice had taken on, though, and he was slightly suspicious of it, but Felix didn't seem inclined to say anything to elucidate what he was thinking and Lysander was too tired to worry about it.

"I'm glad of that," Thalia said. "I'm grateful he took care of them and relieved all of you are all right. I can't believe this happened."

"I want to know how it happened." Felix drummed his fingers on the arm of his chair. "How did they know where you were going?"

"Or that you were going," Thalia added. "There weren't many people who did."

"They have someone at Wyndward." Lysander had thought about it often since the attack. They had assumed the conspirators probably had people at court; this incident seemed to confirm it.

Felix nodded slowly. "Who knew your plans? Us. Some servants. The guards going with you."

"Alan trusts his people. He's been very careful," Lysander replied to Felix's musings.

"Everyone makes mistakes."

"You want to tell him that?" Thalia inquired of Felix.

Felix frowned. "If it becomes necessary. He needs to acknowledge the possibility that someone in the wider guard, if not in Lysander's personal guard, might be sympathetic to this plot. If he isn't looking into that, he's a fool."

"We can't discount someone at the house," Thalia suggested. "It's a small staff and they've been with you forever, but they were informed of your visit so they could make the house ready."

"It could also have been someone getting information out of the staff there or here by whatever means," Lysander added. "Paying them, getting them drunk, tricking them…"

"True," Thalia acknowledged. "Alan's investigating?"

"Hopefully without rousing suspicions."

"Hardly a pressing worry. Someone tried to kill you. I'd call that tipping their hand." Felix kept drumming his fingers as he thought. "They have to know this would make you suspicious and wary, even if you had no idea about the existence of this plot."

"Only if it didn't succeed," Thalia pointed out. "If it did, what Lysander thought hardly mattered."

"What a pleasant thought," Lysander murmured.

"Sorry."

"It does make me wonder what their objective was," Felix put in.

Thalia frowned. "I would think that's obvious."

Felix waved a hand. "Yes, they attacked Lysander. But were they trying to assassinate only him? Were they hoping to kill the children too? Or take them? What is their plan if Lysander were out of the way?"

Thalia sat back in her chair, a thoughtful look on her face, then stood and began pacing. After Lysander had controlled the jolt of sheer terror at the idea of his children being targeted, he spoke. "If what they want is to reveal our secrets and potentially go out into the world creating some sort of dragon empire, they would need me dead and someone more amenable on the throne."

"They might believe with Xanthe on the throne, they could maneuver a regent into place who would be swayed to their goals. Or is part of their conspiracy. That would be safer for them," Thalia said. "They'd have to get rid of me and Felix for that."

"Unless they thought one of us could be swayed." The look on Felix's face eloquently said what he thought of that idea.

"It would be safer for them to install their own regent. Or their own monarch." Lysander rubbed a hand over his face.

"The question becomes who," Felix mused. "Someone further down the line of succession? If they had someone in the family in their group, or just thought they could be used..."

Thalia stopped walking and blinked at him in surprise. "Are we suspecting family now?"

"I know neither of you are involved if that makes you feel better," Lysander told her.

She rolled her eyes. "Oh, so much better."

"I don't think any of us will be feeling much better until this is over," Felix said quietly. "Especially since you and I are in as much danger as Lysander and the children. After this attack, we have to assume they want us out of the way, if not Xanthe and Cassian."

Thalia took to pacing around the study again, letting out another litany of foul language as she did. Lysander and Felix waited patiently until she finished cursing. She was expressing Lysander's own thoughts anyway.

"Both of you need to be even more careful." Lysander rubbed a hand over his face again. He couldn't lose Thalia and Felix. "We don't know who informed them of my plans. We don't know who might be watching."

"We knew someone could be watching before," Thalia said as she reached the end of the room and turned for another circuit.

"We just didn't know they would go so far," Felix replied. "Oh, there was always a possibility, but I don't think any of us thought they were at this point yet."

"I'd hoped we would break this conspiracy before they got there." Lysander had certainly known assassination was a likely step, but he'd believed they had time. Who knew why. "Since we haven't, we all need to be wary. Alan will assign more guards. I beg you both to accept them for the time being and be cautious of where you go and with whom."

They both nodded, though Lysander doubted either was pleased. They were close to the throne and already had guards, but both were used to more freedom of movement.

"I think we both understand why it's necessary," Felix said, "so of course we will. Now, who has ideas about how we can find the traitors in our midst?"

"You want to ask again, don't you?" Sascha asked into the comfortable silence.

Romilly started laughing.

They were lying side by side on the bed in the bedchamber Sascha never used, staring up at the bed's canopy, like they had when they were younger and Sascha had visited Romilly. These days, they normally would've gone for a walk—Romilly helping Sascha explore Wyndward and its surroundings—but after last week's attack, Sascha didn't feel comfortable being so exposed. He knew quite well they hadn't been trying to hurt him, but he couldn't get out of his mind the attacking dragons cloaked by magic until they dropped out of the sky. Romilly hadn't argued the change.

They were worried too.

"You know me too well," Romilly said. "And since you know me, I'm going to ask. How are you doing? Are you all right?"

"I'm...getting there." There was no use in lying to Romilly. They knew Sascha too. "It was horrible."

"I can only imagine." Romilly's hand found Sascha's on the blanket between them and took it, giving it a comforting squeeze.

Knowledge of the attack had been allowed to get out, though Lysander was still holding his own awareness of the treasonous conspiracy back. And though there was no evidence proving they were related, it seemed implausible for it to be anything else. The attack had shocked the court, and those ripples of shock were moving out over Ivria as the news spread. Felix was watching for anyone whose reaction seemed wrong, hoping to catch the conspirators or their informants at Wynd-ward. Sascha wasn't certain he was supposed to know that, but he certainly wouldn't tell anyone.

Romilly and Florestan had come straight to the castle and Sascha as soon as they'd heard about the attack, needing to see for themselves that Sascha was uninjured. His parents might be horrible, but Romilly and Florestan cared about him. And amazingly Felix and Thalia too. They had both seemed to be as concerned for him as they were for Lysander and the children. Their concern was a balm to his fears and anxieties.

"Of all the things I worried about when I came here, I never imagined...something like that." Sascha wasn't even certain what to call it. He'd known about the plot, the conspiracy, but somehow, that had never translated itself into the potential for violence in his mind. Violence against people he...cared about deeply. Violence he might get caught up in himself.

"I know." Romilly squeezed his hand again. "We should've talked about it more. Though even I would've had a hard time conceiving of such a brazen attack."

Sascha deliberately took a long breath in and let it out slowly, then another, trying to keep himself calm. The silence stretched between them again for a while.

"I..." Romilly's voice was tentative. "I have to leave soon."

Sascha's heart kicked up again. "Is everything resolved? The king doesn't need you here anymore?"

He hadn't been told, but he wasn't told everything. As much as he felt involved, he had no part in this business. They didn't have to inform him of anything, and he refused to feel hurt when they didn't.

"No, it isn't," Romilly said, making Sascha's hopes plummet. "And he does need me and Kirill here. But he also needs us there."

"Oh." Sascha's heart sped up even more. Romilly was leaving, and Sascha would be...not alone, but without the person who perhaps knew him best.

"I tried to delay," Romilly said in a rush. "I thought perhaps Kirill could go on without me, but the king refused."

"You argued with Lysander?" Sascha shouldn't have been surprised but he was.

"I don't want to leave you, not when you're in the middle of all this." Romilly lifted their other hand and waved it, as if to encompass the attack and the entire mess of a situation.

"I'll be all right," Sascha said quietly, not even convincing himself but wanting Romilly to feel better.

Romilly slanted a look in his direction. "You will, but that doesn't mean you don't need me. And King Lysander does too. The circle of people he can trust in this is frustratingly small. But he refused, and I have to remind myself that he has those people. The princess and the commander. Felix and Galina. You."

"Me?" Shock zipped through Sascha. "I can't help him."

He wished he could, but he had neither the knowledge nor the skills to help Lysander unravel this plot.

"You can. Maybe not the way the others can, the way Galina is or the commander or Felix. But only because you aren't familiar with the players yet. You haven't spent much time at court or among the noble families of the other clans. Not because you aren't smart enough or capable." Romilly's voice was fierce.

"Um, then how..."

"You're there for him," Romilly said simply. "He trusts you to be there for him, and now for the princess and prince as well, I would think. To someone in the king's position, I have to believe that's everything."

Sascha shook his head, unable to find words. What they said couldn't be right. "Romilly."

"And even though I've just said that, and I obviously want the king to have what he needs, I'm going to ask one last time—do you want to come with me?"

"Romilly!" Sascha looked over at them sharply.

"I know, I know. You're happy here, and you care about him and the children, and I'm glad of that. I want you to be happy. But I'm also worried about your safety, so I have to ask." Romilly continued after only a breath's pause. "I don't expect you to come with me. I'd love it if you did—I'd love to have your company and I want you safe. But I think I know what your answer is going to be."

"I need to stay." No, that wasn't right, or at least that wasn't all. "I *want* to stay. I'm sorry."

Romilly looked at him. "Don't be sorry. Just promise to send for me if you need me, and know that you can always come, that I'll always want you with me."

Sascha nodded. "I will. I going to miss you."

He'd gotten used to seeing Romilly daily. He hated the idea of them being so far away.

"I'll miss you too. But I'll visit and we'll write. It won't be forever."

It wouldn't, but it would be another change, and an unpleasant one, just when Sascha was getting used to the drastic changes in his life up to now. "Of course."

CHAPTER 19

ook unopened in his hands, Sascha stared out of the
window at the lake and the town crowded along its
shore, the wide road leading up from it to Wyndward
castle. The lake was calm under a gray sky in which only a few
dragons flew. The morning seemed peaceful, though the town
probably bustled with people going about their morning business. He'd woken when Lysander had and grumbled enough
when he began to slide from the bed and Sascha's side that
Lysander had returned briefly to kiss his cheek and tell him to
go back to sleep, a thread of amusement running through his
voice.

But Sascha hadn't been able to sleep again. Lysander had
taken his warmth with him and the bed felt cold without him.
Colder than usual, but perhaps that was just Sascha. Romilly
had left yesterday, and Sascha couldn't help feeling somewhat
bereft. Once Lysander had gone, off to early meetings, Sascha
had risen, unable to lie in bed with his thoughts swirling
endlessly. He'd thought to read, wrapped in his dressing gown
and a blanket, until Lysander returned so they could breakfast

together, or sent word that he couldn't. Sascha hoped he could today.

A soft knock sounded on the door, and he called out for whoever it was to enter as he turned from the window. Few people would bother him. And when the door opened, he found it was his favorite of the few. The children's new nursemaid had knocked, but she remained in the corridor as the children came in.

"We weren't sure if you were awake, sir, but the children wanted to visit," she said. She was always very formal, but it seemed absurd to speak of visiting as if they lived far away.

"And I'm very happy for the visit." He smiled at the children, at her, then directed his attention to Xanthe and Cassian. "Would you like to stay for a little while?"

At their enthusiastic agreement, he turned back to the nursemaid. "You can leave us for now. Thank you."

As soon as the door closed behind her, the children rushed to him. He laughed and sank to the floor, his dressing gown pooling around him, to catch them. Xanthe reached him first, her longer legs carrying her there faster, but Cassian wasn't far behind, flinging himself into Sascha's arms right after his sister. Sascha cuddled them as they spoke excitedly about their morning so far, marveling at how they could have so much to say when they'd risen from their beds not long before.

And simply enjoying being here with them. He'd never expected to have this when he'd agreed to be Lysander's concubine. Never expected to love them so much, so quickly.

He had little experience with children and hadn't known if he would be any good with them, but Lysander's children didn't seem to care that he hadn't known what to do at first, that he'd been unsure. Now he just delighted in spending time with them and was honored that Lysander allowed him to.

"Have you eaten your breakfast?" he asked when they

trailed off. "Are you going to stay and eat with me and your father?"

They drew back a little, to stand in front of him as he knelt on the thick carpet. He marveled again at how Lysander was stamped all over their features. They had his eyes and his hair and a certain look of stubbornness. But, oh, they were the sweetest children too. The little girl standing in front of him would be queen one day, long in the future, but at this moment, in these private rooms, Xanthe was able to be simply herself—just as her father could—and even at such a young age, she knew what that meant.

Only, today, her little forehead was wrinkled in a frown.

Concern flooded Sascha. Was it something to do with the attack? He gently smoothed her dark hair back. "What's wrong, sweetheart?"

"I feel funny," she said.

His concern deepened. "Funny, how? Do you feel ill?"

He was already planning to call for a healer when Xanthe shook her head. "Not ill. Just funny."

Well, that wasn't helpful, though he wouldn't express his frustration to her. "Does something hurt?"

She shook her head again. "I'm all...itchy."

Sascha frowned. "Itchy?"

Xanthe nodded. "I feel..."

She gasped as her eyes widened. Sparkling light flared up to surround her, and only then did Sascha realize what was happening.

"Sascha?" Cassian's high voice was filled with fear and worry for his sister.

"It's all right, dearest. Come over by me now. Your sister will be just fine." He held out a hand to Cassian and smiled reassuringly when he took it, even as he hoped he hadn't lied to the boy. What did he know about what was happening to Xanthe?

Beyond the fact it was happening far earlier than such a thing normally did. Talents didn't usually manifest until the early teens, and she was only six. All he could do was wait and hope… and wish Lysander was here. But Sascha wasn't leaving the children for even the short time it would take to send for him.

When the light faded away, a tiny burgundy dragon stood where Xanthe had been. Cassian was staring at her with wide eyes and a mouth in the shape of an O. Xanthe's eyes were just as wide. Sascha had never seen a dragon look so startled before. And maybe just a little afraid.

"Look at you, sweetheart," he crooned, trying to soothe. "You are such a beautiful dragon, and so clever. No one expected you to come into your Talent for years."

She still quivered, and he did the only thing he could. He opened his arms and let her scamper into him. She practically climbed him, little claws catching in his dressing gown, and he winced for the velvet, though damage to the garment meant nothing when compared to Xanthe's well-being. She twined herself around him and he closed his arms around her, stroking a hand over her back to calm her.

Cassian's eyes were still wide as saucers. "Xanthe is a dragon."

"Yes, she is." Sascha smiled at him.

"Will I be a dragon?"

"Someday." Cassian had the dragon Talent. Those who did were born with scale-like markings on their backs as a sign. It was just a matter of when it became active.

Cassian sighed in a far too heavy way for a four-year-old, even when that child was a prince. "I want to be a dragon."

"You are. You will. It just might take a while longer for you to find your wings." Potentially ten years, but Sascha wasn't going to tell him that right now, when he wanted to do the same things his sister did. Instead, he beckoned and Cassian came to lean against his shoulder, to be close and included, while Sascha continued to cradle the shaking Xanthe and whisper reassurances to her.

Her trembling had finally slowed, though she continued to cling to him, when the door to the sitting room opened. When Sascha glanced up, Lysander was standing in the doorway, staring at them. An instant later, Lysander shut the door and came toward them, a look of shock and wonder spreading over his handsome features.

Sascha smiled somewhat tremulously at Lysander, then bent his head and whispered to Xanthe that her father was there, even as he kept his eyes on Lysander. He expected her to abandon him and run to Lysander, but she didn't move, continuing to hold tight. Trepidation washed through Sascha—this was a family moment, something to be shared between father and daughter, something monumental since she was so young —and Sascha wasn't...

Lysander dropped to his knees in front of Sascha. Instead of taking Xanthe from him, he reached out and gathered them both—and Cassian too—into his arms. All of Sascha's tension drained away. He wouldn't have blamed Lysander for nudging him out of such an important moment, but something like joy bubbled up inside him that Lysander hadn't, that he included Sascha, made him feel like he belonged there, like a part of the family. Maybe he read far too much into Lysander's action, but he couldn't care, not while held by Lysander with his sweet girl finally calming. Even as she curled into her father, her tail wrapped around Sascha's waist, anchoring her to him. Cassian still leaned into him, and Sascha freed an arm to wrap around him, bringing him close. The action united them, made Sascha feel even more strongly that they were a family.

It was a dangerous thought.

And a seductive one. Sascha wanted it, wanted this to be his family. He loved these children as if they were his own, something he hadn't imagined before coming here, and he... He loved Lysander too.

Dangerous, so dangerous. He couldn't love the king, or at least, he couldn't expect more than he had because he did. Sascha couldn't forget his position, his role.

"Xanthe." Lysander's quiet voice snapped Sascha out of thoughts that could easily have become panicked. "How wonderful. I'm so proud of you. So happy for you."

That Xanthe had come into her Talent so early was an indication of the strength of her magic, and the heir's early transformation would reflect well on her and the whole ruling family. But Lysander wasn't talking about that; he wasn't thinking of it now. He was only thinking of his daughter and the need to make her comfortable with all that had just happened. Lysander may have had children for the succession, but he adored them for themselves. How he felt about them shone through in his every word and gesture.

If Sascha didn't love him already, he might have fallen right then and there. He shook the thought off. Lysander glanced at him quizzically, but he smiled, reassuring. Lysander still appeared skeptical, so Sascha turned to Xanthe, hoping to deflect a little attention and concern from himself and put it back where it belonged. "All right, sweetheart?" he asked. He glanced at Lysander. "I think she scared herself. It happened rather suddenly."

What an inane statement to make. Of course Xanthe's transformation was sudden and unexpected—she wouldn't have been trying to transform at her age. But Lysander didn't chide him. He only smiled and turned back to his daughter.

"Did you startle yourself? I can see how, but having your Talent is good, and I'll teach you so you can control it and not startle yourself again. All right?"

"All right, Father." Her voice had more of a lisp than it usually did, but they all understood the quietly spoken words.

"Good girl." Lysander kissed the top of her head, just as he did when she was human-shaped, and she cuddled closer. "Why don't we go to the library and I'll change too? Would that make you feel better?"

Xanthe nodded. "Can Sascha and Cass come too?"

Before Sascha could get over his shock at being asked, Lysander answered her. "Of course. Shall we go?"

Xanthe nodded and immediately transferred her hold from Lysander to Sascha. He let out a soft, surprised noise as her little claws gently grabbed onto him again. He lifted a bemused gaze to Lysander, who laughed softly.

"You don't have to hang onto Sascha—he's coming with us."

Xanthe didn't let go, but she might have relaxed just slightly.

Sascha couldn't help his smile. "It's all right. I've got her."

Lysander looked as if he might argue, but he eventually nodded and stood. He held out a hand to Cassian. "Come on."

Cassian dashed from Sascha's side to his father's, allowing Sascha to hold Xanthe more securely and balance her as he carefully climbed to his feet. Lysander stayed close and put a hand to Sascha's elbow to steady him. That warm hand was care and comfort, and Sascha was a little afraid everything he felt was shining in his eyes. But if Lysander saw any of it, he didn't react. He only bent to kiss Sascha lightly and briefly. As he pulled away, Xanthe sighed in every appearance of contentment and snuggled in closer against Sascha.

They walked together out of the sitting room and along the corridor to the library, the only place in the royal apartments large enough for Lysander to transform. With the door closed behind them, they were alone in the large room. Plush rugs woven in intricate patterns covered the stone floor, and paintings and cases of books lined the walls. Cassian left his father's side to wait by Sascha as Lysander moved to the middle of the room. A glistening cloud of golden light wrapped around him. Sascha held his breath as he always did, not because he worried, but because he was still in awe of Lysander this way. Sascha had seen other people use their Talents to transform—it was impossible to live in Ivria and avoid it—but there was something about Lysander doing so.

The light shifted and grew around Lysander, grew with him, until it filled the center of the room. Then it faded away, leaving the deep red dragon visible.

Would the sight of Lysander's dragon ever not fill Sascha with awe? It swelled up within him, breaking over him like a wave. Before he could stare too long, Xanthe squirmed a little in his arms. He turned his attention to her.

She hesitated a moment. "Down, please," she lisped.

He smiled and let her down. Once she was on the floor, she scampered to Lysander who had settled in the middle of the room, curling up on the carpets. He gathered her in, his much larger claws gentle. She cuddled close to him for a few moments and finally seemed seemed to calm from her shock. Once she did, excitement began to take over. Sascha smiled as she began to practically vibrate with it and then hopped out of his hold to gambol around him.

Cassian squeezed Sascha's hand. Sascha looked down into his hopeful, inquiring face and nodded. He ran off to join his father and sister with a laugh. Lysander chuckled, deep and rumbly, and caught Cassian handily, pulling him in too.

Sascha melted a little watching Lysander with his children —this wasn't the first time he'd had the reaction, but it was something more today, sharing in this moment, in their joy and pride and love for each other, even only from the edges. The children darted around Lysander and climbed onto him, laughing and shrieking their delight as they played and he reached out to catch them then allowed them to slip away again. Sascha laughed too, hardly realizing he was doing it, until Lysander's mahogany gaze found him. It was filled with affection, and Sascha's smile gentled into something else, something just for Lysander. He had to see what Sascha was feeling, didn't he? There was no way Sascha was hiding it in this moment.

Lysander reached out a hand toward Sascha and said in his rumbling voice, "Come here."

Sascha went. Not because Lysander was king and Sascha had to obey him—he'd learned in personal matters that wasn't the case—but because he wanted to be a part of what was happening. Be a part of their family. Which meant he should've turned and run, but he wasn't strong enough to do so.

Lysander pulled him close as soon as he was within reach and nuzzled his much larger dragon's head against him. Sascha laughed again and stroked his hands over the silky scales at Lysander's cheeks and neck, awed that he was allowed to, that Lysander pushed further into his hands, encouraging him. He leaned closer and brushed his lips over the scales above Lysander's mouth. Then Cassian threw his arms around Sascha's leg and Xanthe came to dance at his side. And for the moment at least, Sascha was part of everything.

WHEN LYSANDER RETURNED to his bedchamber that night—after a strategy meeting gone long and looking in on his sleeping children—he found Sascha curled in a chair near the fireplace with a book. His rich red hair tumbled around his shoulders, and he wore the blue velvet dressing gown Lysander had gotten him because the color matched his eyes. All Lysander wanted to do was drape him in sapphires of the exact same shade. When this was over, he would do just that.

Sascha glanced up from his book and a smile lit his face in welcome. There was something in Sascha's eyes, some emotion Lysander thought he could identify but wasn't certain he should, though he craved it. But why shouldn't he? Why should he ignore the affection—the love—in Sascha's eyes? He'd brought Sascha here to be his concubine, and there was no reason Sascha couldn't stay here forever, no reason they couldn't love each other. No reason they...

"Is everything all right?" Sascha asked as he closed his book and set it aside, turning all his attention to Lysander. He always did that, always gave Lysander his full attention. Always gave the children his full attention too. Lysander could have loved him for that alone, even without so many other reasons. But the care he showed Lysander and his children—especially the children because they were Lysander's world and Sascha had no obligation to them. Lysander hadn't expected it or required it. Sascha honestly liked them, not because he hoped to win favor for the action.

Sascha had only ever been genuinely himself, and Lysander was grateful he'd found him, grateful he'd trusted his instincts.

"It's better now." He went to Sascha and bent to kiss his lips, which had parted softly in surprise.

When the kiss ended, Lysander didn't go far. Though bending over Sascha in his chair wasn't comfortable, he didn't want to move away from him.

Sascha blinked large eyes at him. He still appeared surprised, his large eyes wide. "Just because..."

"Because you're here. Because you love my children, and you—" He cut himself off, not wanting to push Sascha.

"I do love them, so much. And I..." Sascha bit his lip.

Lysander reached out and brushed a thumb over the abused lip, gently freeing it. "You don't have to say anything if you aren't ready. Neither of us has to say anything yet. We know anyway, don't we? I think I do."

Sascha nodded slowly, hesitantly. "And you...?"

"You don't know?" But would Sascha? Would he be able to trust it if he thought he did know Lysander's feelings? Lysander, though he tried to put them on more equal footing in many ways, was still the king, and Sascha was his concubine—and their acquaintance had begun while Sascha was being used by his parents. No, Sascha wouldn't.

"I..." Sascha swallowed. "I have a hard time believing. I'm sorry."

"Don't be sorry. Shall I tell you?" He would. He would say the words and hope Sascha believed him then, even if Sascha wasn't ready to give him the words in return. And he would battle the sense of vulnerability he had at the thought of saying those words to anyone outside his family, despite an almost bone-deep knowledge that Sascha would cherish them, wouldn't betray him. That Sascha could be—was already?—family.

Sascha regarded him for a long moment before straightening and lifting a hand to his cheek. Love lit Sascha's eyes and with it something else—wonder. "You don't have to, not yet. Not if you're not ready to say the words."

Lysander smiled, full of warmth and affection toward the man in his arms. "We'll both wait then, until we're ready. But we can just be here together and happy even without the words."

"Because we know anyway." Sascha smiled brilliantly and surged up to kiss Lysander fiercely.

Lysander let himself be drawn into the kiss, loving the uninhibited exuberance of it, loving that Sascha had initiated it. Or the way he had—it wasn't that Sascha never did, but he was quieter, waiting for Lysander most times, which made sense given Sascha's position, as much as Lysander tried not to hold strictly to it. Perhaps with some assurance of Lysander's feelings, Sascha had gained more confidence. It made Lysander want to give him more, everything, but something inside him balked. He wasn't quite ready to open himself up so much. But he could show Sascha.

He fell into the effervescent kiss, letting Sascha lead, letting the joy and desire fill him as well.

Sascha's graceful, elegant hands were soft and sure as they caressed Lysander's face and shoulders, as they curled around his neck and Sascha's lips moved over his, sure and sweet, lighting fires inside Lysander. He'd been innocent when Lysander had brought him here—well, inexperienced, untouched, but not ignorant—and though the reality of that had changed now, Sascha still had an innocent quality to him, to his sensuality, that was more seductive than anything else to Lysander. He craved Sascha in a way he never had anyone before, the feeling frightening but also thrilling.

Sascha pulled his lips from Lysander's and blinked up at him as he sucked in a breath. "Take me to bed."

Sascha never demanded. He hardly asked for anything, even when Lysander wished he would. So with the words barely out of his mouth, Lysander was pulling him up from the chair and swooping him into his arms. Sascha let out a gasp and wrapped himself around him with slim arms and legs, the strength in his limbs belying how slender they were. Everything about Sascha was contrasts. The softness, the delicateness, the elegance, the boldness, the uncertainty, the strength. All of it captivated Lysander.

He laid Sascha on the bed and crawled over him, then reached for the tie to his robe. His fingers collided with Sascha's at the knot in the sash. Sascha's heated gaze flew to Lysander's and whatever he saw there made him let go, leaving Lysander to unwrap him like the gift he was. When Sascha's hands had fallen to the pillow beside his head, Lysander went to work. The knot yielded to his fingers, and, with Sascha's smoldering eyes burning into him, almost a tangible sensation—that gaze and the knowledge of what he would find had the anticipation searing through him—he spread the sides of robe, exposing what lay underneath to his eyes. Never had he been more grateful for Sascha's penchant for silk and lace. The lace adorning Sascha's porcelain skin was the same rich blue as his eyes. Lysander had never known he'd love such frivolous, beautiful garments on someone so much, not until he'd seen Sascha in them. And something about how Sascha wore them, because he himself enjoyed them made it even better. Sascha hadn't done this for Lysander, but he was certainly pleased with Lysander's reaction.

"Sascha," he breathed and ran a hand down the center of Sascha's chest over smooth lace and silk.

Sascha arched into his touch with something like a purr. Lysander sat back and just took in the sight of Sascha spread before him, tumbled red hair, pale skin delicately flushed, rich sapphire blue lace wrapping his slender body.

"Lysander?"

He met Sascha's gaze and found the blue depths swirling with want. "You're beautiful."

A smile curved Sascha's lips. "Come here."

Lysander was chuckling as he lowered himself to Sascha but that ended as soon as their lips met. Heat flared inside Lysander and he groaned. Sascha reached up to curl his hands around Lysander's neck. The velvet of his robe cocooned them both as he held on, as if he wanted to make certain Lysander didn't separate from him—something Lysander had no intention of doing. He could happily keep kissing Sascha all night. He would, too, if Sascha wanted. Kissing Sascha was a joy and a pleasure all in itself. If they did nothing else tonight, after the excitement and stress of the day, after the profound unspoken revelations of tonight, he wouldn't be in the least disappointed. Losing himself in Sascha's arms, in his kisses, was all he wanted.

All he wanted. Now...forever. He only wanted to be kissing Sascha, only wanted to lose himself in Sascha's embrace and find peace and passion there.

Sascha seemed to agree, at least about tonight. He tightened his arms around Lysander, short neat nails digging in to Lysander's back just slightly. They kissed for a long time, deep and passionate and drugging.

Sascha wrapped a leg around Lysander's hip and pressed up into him, rubbing their hard lengths together. Lysander groaned and tore his lips from Sascha's, only to begin kissing and nibbling at his neck. Sascha's fingers threaded into Lysander's hair and tightened, holding him there.

"I'm not going anywhere," Lysander murmured into Sascha's skin, a smile curving his lips. When Sascha's grip tightened briefly, Lysander raised his head to look at him.

Sascha's eyes were wide and dark with passion, but there was something else there as well. He slid a hand around to Lysander's cheek, cupping it in his smooth palm, sweeping his thumb gently over his cheekbone. "Promise?" Sascha immediately bit his lip and shook his head.

But before he could speak again, Lysander swooped down and kissed him, brief and hard. "I promise."

Sascha shook his head. "I shouldn't ask and you shouldn't promise."

Lysander laid a finger gently over Sascha's lips and bit back a smile when he narrowed his eyes. "I promise," he repeated softly, sincerely. Maybe he shouldn't—maybe Sascha shouldn't have asked—but Lysander couldn't care. He had no intention of letting Sascha go.

Sascha's expression softened and he pressed a kiss to the fingertip resting over his lips, the action so sweet and so unexpected. When Lysander lifted his hand away, ready to kiss him again, Sascha said, "I promise too."

It had the solemnity of a vow, much more than anything they'd said earlier, and he was humbled by it. And honored to have Sascha at his side, at his back.

"Sascha."

Sascha pulled him down again. The kiss ignited as soon as their lips touched. Lysander groaned into it as Sascha clutched at him. He wanted to devour him, to possess him utterly, and Sascha, arching and writhing against him, seemed to be quite happy with the plan.

After a while, Sascha tore his lips from Lysander's and gasped. "I want you inside me, if..."

"Yes." Oh, yes.

Their hands tangled as they rid Lysander of his clothes and Sascha of just enough of his. Lysander liked the way the lace looked against his skin too much to let it all go. Sascha only smiled, affection and indulgence and no small amount of satisfaction in it, and while Lysander loved seeing it, he wanted more. To that end, he snatched up the oil from the bedside table and unstoppered it. He coated his fingers with the oil and proceeded to drive Sascha a little out of his mind, using all he'd learned of him in their time together.

"Lysander." Sascha tightened his grip on Lysander's arm. "Now. I'm ready. Now."

He chuckled low in his throat and considered continuing just what he was doing, but he was ready as well, ready to be connected to Sascha in that way. Only he wanted something else too.

He rolled them over, ignoring Sascha's furrowed brow and positioned Sascha over him. Sascha's kiss-swollen lips parted slightly in surprise and comprehension. He eagerly moved to take Lysander inside him. Lysander held his hips, both to steady him and to get his hands on him. The tight heat of Sascha surrounding his cock had his fingers tightening on Sascha's flesh.

Then Sascha began to move. And he was glorious. His red hair rippling with his movements, his pale skin flushed and glistening, the rich blue lace clinging to his torso. And the sounds he made—the breathy little gasps and whimpers Lysander loved.

One of Sascha's hands came down to cover Lysander's, and he twined their fingers together. With his other hand, Lysander explored the lace-covered skin as Sascha rode him. It didn't take long for Sascha find his peak, calling out Lysander's name as he did. Lysander wanted it to last longer, but they were both too far gone with desire and half spoken revelations. Sascha collapsed onto him, and Lysander drove up into him a few more times before pleasure exploded through him as well.

They lay together, Sascha draped over Lysander's chest, as their breathing slowed to normal again. He stroked a hand up and down Sascha's back, soothing for him and for Sascha. And for the sheer joy of touch, of being so close to the man he loved. He welcomed Sascha's weight on him, and was amused at how Sascha understood he was happy to be his pillow, happy to have Sascha sprawled over him, boneless and sated.

Sascha hummed, a noise of utter contentment. Lysander smiled just hearing it and kept stroking, moving his hand up into the tangled silk of Sascha's hair. If anything, Sascha sounded even more content now.

He stirred a bit at Lysander's satisfied chuckle, but he didn't move, much to Lysander's satisfaction. "What is it?" Sascha asked, his voice slightly slurred with sleepy pleasure.

Lysander didn't want it to disappear. "Nothing. You seem happy."

Sascha hummed again. "I am. Are you? You looked like you had a difficult day."

"I did, but you made it better."

"I'm glad." Sascha nuzzled into his chest. "Do you want to talk about it"

Did he? Sascha always asked and never pushed if Lysander refused. There were things he couldn't tell Sascha, but fewer now that he knew he could trust Sascha. And, yes, he did want to talk to Sascha. Sascha's calm, sincere way of listening was a comfort—Sascha wasn't his advisor, wasn't well-versed in all Lysander had to handle as king but none of that meant he couldn't be a help and support to him.

"It's what it always is. We're moving too slowly. We know some conspirators but not all of them. We don't know who they have here, but they must have someone."

Sascha stiffened in his arms.

Lysander cursed himself and held Sascha tighter. "I'm sorry. I shouldn't have mentioned it."

Sascha lifted his head and looked at him. "No, I asked."

He contemplated Sascha for a moment, but he seemed steady. "All right, if you're sure. We assumed they would try to get someone close even before the attack. It could be one or more conspirators spending a lot of time at court or they could have someone working here or any number of possibilities."

"How can we trust anyone then?" Fear filled his blue eyes.

Lysander lifted a hand to Sascha's cheek. "There are people we can trust. And we have guards to protect us."

"How do you know they're loyal?" Sascha asked somberly.

"I trust Alan with my life and I know he'd give his for me." Though he never wanted him to have to. "Alan knows his people and the oaths of my personal guard are enforced by magic. We're as safe as we can be."

The twist to Sascha's lips said he wasn't quite satisfied, but he didn't push. "All right. What else?"

"The longer this goes on, the more I worry they're spreading tales throughout Ivria, poisoning people against me and our traditions." He'd tasked Felix with listening for rumors and discovering if they were spreading discontent. "I need to make certain the country isn't turning from me. We need to end this."

Sascha's gaze was entirely understanding. "You must have made progress."

"We have. We are. But timing is delicate. I have people watching and listening, trying to determine the extent of it." He didn't want do more too soon and lose parts of the conspiracy, especially the leaders. But had he waited too long already? Waiting was a risk, too, especially with Jannik in custody. They'd heard no indication anyone had learned of his arrest yet, but how long would that last? If someone hadn't discovered it already, they would soon.

When he focused outward again, Sascha was watching him patiently. "I'm sorry."

Sascha smiled gently. "It's all right. You needed to think. Is there anything that can be done in the meantime? I mean, to encourage the people's support."

"There's one thing I can think of, but I hate to do it now. She's so young." Xanthe was the heir to the throne. She'd learn how much of her life Ivria would claim—he just didn't want her to yet.

Sascha nodded slowly, understanding washing over his face. "Ivria would be thrilled to hear Xanthe's come into her Talent. They'd celebrate for weeks."

"Probably."

"But you don't want to make it about them," Sascha added perceptively.

"I wanted to keep it inside the family for a little while longer." He sighed. "But we couldn't keep it a secret. Someone will see and talk. She doesn't have control yet. Even if she did, I wouldn't want to make her hide it."

"Of course you wouldn't." Sascha lifted a hand to his cheek and caressed it with his thumb.

"We're going to have to announce it and have a ceremony at court." He closed his eyes and let the slow movement of Sascha's fingers soothe him.

"You'll explain it to her, and she'll understand," Sascha said, tone comforting. "We'll get her through it."

He opened his eyes. "We?"

A flush spread across Sascha's cheeks. "Oh, well—"

"No, 'we' is good." With a smile, he drew Sascha to him for a gentle kiss.

CHAPTER 20

When Sascha had said they would help Xanthe through the experience—when he'd used the word we—he hadn't really thought about what he'd meant. Perhaps simply that he'd make certain she knew how much she was loved, how proud they were of her, that she was important to them just because she was herself. And since he loved her, he thought he could do that for her despite not being her parent. And maybe, after his conversation with Lysander during which they'd danced around confessing their feelings but might have said enough, Sascha wouldn't be overstepping if he did so.

What he didn't expect was to have any public role in the proceedings. Well, not a role, as such. He didn't have to do anything during the ceremony. But he would be there on the dais in front of everyone with Lysander and his family. He'd never dreamed it would be his place on such an important day, despite his position as King's Concubine. He still wasn't certain why he was being included—Lysander's unstated feelings notwithstanding, was it appropriate for Sascha to take such a place?

The councillor who came to him to discuss protocol for the event—a man old enough to be Sascha's grandfather with dark skin and kind eyes—didn't seem to think it odd, though. He was respectful, deferential even, as he told Sascha what would happen and what he would have to do. Stand in a particular place, for the most part. Wyndward's steward came with him and proved to be every bit as tedious as Thalia had said, fussy about the protocol and repeating the details multiple times.

Felix and Thalia were with him when he had to review designs for his clothing for the event. The royal seamstresses would be making new clothing for him, Lysander, and Xanthe, as well as Felix and Thalia, and the amount of work it would entail—especially after Sascha got a look at the designs—made his head spin. Felix and Thalia discussed the designs while the seamstress efficiently and quickly took his measurements and her assistant noted them down. As soon as they were finished, Sascha shrugged into his dressing gown. He'd worn some of his more plain underclothes, but the young assistant nevertheless looked scandalized and delighted at the lace trim. Sascha could only hope his undergarment preferences wouldn't be everywhere tomorrow.

"I like this one. Sascha, come look," Felix said, glancing up at him and beckoning him over.

Sascha went, stopping beside Felix where he sat next to Thalia on a couch. They were in the small sitting room attached to Sascha's bedchamber—he'd hardly set foot in the room, but it seemed an appropriate place for this endeavor, giving them space and privacy. Felix showed him the sketch, and Sascha took a moment to study it, resisting his first impulse to let Felix choose. Felix knew him and knew what was appropriate for this event and wouldn't steer him wrong, but Sascha needed to learn and to be confident.

After a few moments of scrutiny, Sascha decided he agreed with Felix. "I like it too. Where are the others?"

Thalia handed him the pages, and Sascha looked through them, considering each in turn with Thalia and Felix's patient attention and the furtive regard of the seamstresses. Thalia pointed out one she liked, and Sascha gave it a second look, but he thought it too much. Finally, he came back to the original design Felix had drawn his attention to.

"I think this one." He looked over at the seamstress. "But can it be done in blue instead of green?"

Felix craned his neck to study the drawing again. "Yes, in blue to match his eyes."

"Of course we can do that, Your Highness, sir. I have just the fabric," she said.

"Then this one in blue. As long as the color won't look out of place with what His Majesty and Their Highnesses will be wearing." Sascha had thought he would be fading into the background at this ceremony, but since he wasn't, he would do what he could to keep attention where it should be. Out of the corner of his eye, he saw Felix nod slightly, reinforcing that he was thinking of the right things. Appearances were important; they were armor in all the machinations that swirled through the nobility, the politics played by all the clan heads at the king's court. Sascha's proximity to the king made him someone of interest.

"Not at all, Honorable Sascha. I believe the blue will be perfect."

With the decisions made, the seamstresses gathered their tools and departed, telling Sascha they would notify him when he was needed for a fitting. Once they were gone, Sascha flopped into a chair.

"I still can't believe this is happening."

"I know." Felix gave him a sympathetic look. "But you'll be fine."

"You don't have to speak during the ceremony," Thalia pointed out. "Which I know you know. You just have to walk in at the appropriate time and sit in the place prepared for you, just as Felix and I will. You can do that."

Sascha let out a long breath. "Yes."

He'd been prepared all his life to be a concubine to as highly ranked a person as his parents could find to take him—and the joke was certainly on them that they'd try to use him as a pawn in their schemes and he'd ended up concubine to the king, from which they'd reap no benefits—so he'd learned to be elegant and graceful, to reflect well on that person either by carrying on an intelligent conversation or being lovely and silent. He almost resented it—maybe he did, some—but he was here with Lysander, who seemed, somehow, to love him for more than those things.

There was understanding in Felix's eyes, and he likely did understand as much as he could, from what Sascha had told him. "And you'll do it all just as you should," Felix added. "You'll be a credit to yourself and the king."

The reassurance lit a little glow inside Sascha, and he pushed himself up straighter in his chair. Yes, he would do this, and he would be a credit to Lysander. And more importantly, he would support Xanthe. She was the important part, not Sascha. As long as he did nothing that would reflect poorly on Lysander and he did well by her, Sascha would be content with his performance at this event.

"That's all I need."

"Personally, I'd want to stand out a bit myself if I were in your position," Thalia said with a grin.

"Sascha will stand out plenty," Felix said. "You know what

people would say if he gave any appearance of putting himself forward."

She nodded. "True."

Sascha had to walk a fine line, which he'd learned it very quickly with Felix's counsel. He had status as King's Concubine—Lysander's only concubine at that—but he wasn't the consort and he couldn't give the impression of putting himself in such a place. The plot against the king just added more complications.

Thalia left them a few moments later, on her way to a lunch engagement. Sascha turned to Felix. "I didn't upset her, did I? By not choosing what she liked?"

"No. She wasn't thinking about the choice from your perspective, your current position. Even if she had been, she wouldn't be upset that you had a different opinion."

Sascha let out a breath. "Good."

Felix reached out and patted his hand. "Don't worry."

"I have a lot to worry about." Though a difference of opinion about clothing was far down the list, which was headed by a treasonous plot against the man he loved. He couldn't help lightening a bit when he thought about Lysander, though, about loving him and being loved in return.

"Yet a smile keeps appearing."

Sascha looked at Felix sharply. "A smile?"

He chuckled. "The one that's been flitting around your face whenever your mind wanders."

"I didn't realize." He tried to be careful about how much of this emotions he gave away, but Felix had become someone he didn't need to hide from. "I'm in love with Lysander," Sascha blurted out before he could think about it. "And I think he loves me too."

"I can't say I'm surprised. It's easy to see you've grown close."

"Well…he didn't say it—I didn't either—but he said it without saying it, if that makes sense. We admitted it without the words."

A frown creased Felix's brow. "Why not just use the words, then? If it's what you both feel?"

Sascha searched for the words to explain. "It's…big, isn't it? For both of us, but perhaps especially for him. He's king. And a king who is threatened right now. As much as I would love to hear those words from him, I can wait. I can hold on to what he's given me."

"You don't feel as if you want more?" Felix took his hand. "I only ask because I want you to be happy. You shouldn't settle for less than that."

Emotion welled up Sascha. He and Felix had become friends, but he also never forgot that Felix was Lysander's cousin and his first loyalty would be to him. Felix's saying that… seemed to say Sascha was just as important. Sascha swallowed, briefly robbed of the ability to speak. "I am happy, with him. I know I have a place with him, a place in his heart even if he isn't ready to say it outright. With that understanding, I'm content here. And I'm content knowing he has the same understanding about me. I want to stay here at his side, to be a help and a comfort to him, for as long as he'll have me."

Certainly, a relationship such as theirs could be permanent… Sascha shied from the thought. He wouldn't hope for such an outcome. Sascha wouldn't think of forever.

Felix studied him for a long moment. "If you're happy, I'm happy for you. For both of you."

～

Lysander waited, trying valiantly not to give in to his impatience without much success. The ceremony was to begin shortly, and neither Sascha nor Xanthe was here. While he didn't have a problem keeping people waiting if it served a purpose, he didn't want to delay today. Everything had to go smoothly for Xanthe. This was her first official event with Lysander's court since her presentation as his heir after her birth, obviously not a day she remembered. He still had misgivings at pushing her in front of the court so young, despite the necessity of doing so, and making today as easy as possible for her was the only way he could think to assuage his own guilt.

And he wanted today to go well for Sascha, who would be making a more formal debut today as well. Though he'd been Lysander's official concubine for quite some time now, today's event was the first ceremonial one he would participate in at Lysander's side.

Before he could send someone off to look for them, Sascha and Xanthe entered the room, Xanthe's hand in Sascha's. Only her tight grip on Sascha's fingers betrayed her nerves. She appeared calm—for which he was proud of her—and far too grown up. Her dress was ankle-length and full skirted with the bell sleeves so fashionable at court, all in intricately worked sky blue and silver silk. Her slippers were silver as well, tied with ribbons around her ankles. Her hair had been braided back at the sides but left loose otherwise, and around her forehead was the diadem he'd picked for her, a delicate piece of silver set with pearls and aquamarines. Nothing about Xanthe's attire was inappropriate for a girl of her age, but seeing her in it made him feel the years slipping away too quickly.

"Are we late?" Sascha's voice, a little breathless, interrupted Lysander's thoughts before he could become too maudlin.

He tore his gaze away from Xanthe and turned it on Sascha, ready to say something about how they nearly were late—and found himself caught. Sascha wore new clothing as well, a formal set of court clothes in a vibrant sapphire blue that perfectly matched his eyes. The velvet jacket and slim pants were well tailored to highlight Sascha's slender build, the jacket's sleeves in the fashionable bell shape and revealing pale silvery gray shirt cuffs trimmed in lace. The traditional cape was draped around his shoulders and secured with a round silver brooch. His shoes were silver too, laced with ribbons of sapphire blue. Somehow, all of the formal garb managed to highlight Sascha's beauty, to make the gracefulness of his form and loveliness of his face the focal point, to enhance something Lysander had thought at its limit.

"Lysander?" Sascha's voice held a thread of uncertainty, which broke Lysander from the spell he'd fallen under.

His gaze snapped up to meet Sascha's. But perhaps how captivated he'd been was still in his eyes somewhere because Sascha's cheeks flushed fetchingly. If only he had time to act on the impulse that blush provoked.

"No, you aren't late," he said, finally answering Sascha's original question. "But you're cutting it fine."

"I'm sorry. It's my fault." Though his cheeks were still pink, Sascha appeared contrite. "We stopped to spend a little time with Cassian."

Of course Sascha would have thought to make sure the little boy didn't feel left out of a day that was about his sister, one that included Sascha but not him. Lysander had considered having Cassian with them, but he was so young, too young to be in front of the court unless absolutely necessary. But Sascha had wanted to make sure Cassian felt included. Lysander should've thought to do the same.

"Thank you for that."

A small, startled smile bloomed on Sascha's face.

So many words pushed into Lysander's head, so much he wanted suddenly to say... Lysander turned abruptly away from

Sascha and picked up the small box on the table. "I have something for you before we go in."

Sascha looked more than startled when Lysander turned back and held out the box to him. "For me?"

"Yes, for you. I thought you should have something to wear."

A little line furrowed Sascha's brow as he stared at the box. "I have clothes."

"Not clothes." He flipped open the lid on the box, revealing sapphire and diamond earrings on a bed of white velvet.

Sascha let out a little gasp. "Lysander."

"I'm happy they match your clothes, though. Will you wear them?"

Sascha lifted wide eyes to Lysander. "You want me to?"

"Very much."

"Then...yes, of course." Sascha reached hesitantly for the earrings, lifting first one then the other to his ears.

Lysander had only thought that Sascha needed jewelry to wear today. Their society and court did love their gems, and Sascha had, unsurprisingly, come to him with none. He hadn't gotten around to giving Sascha any before; he should have—Sascha was King's Concubine and should be attired as such. Felix had loaned him some things, likely including the brooch on his shoulder, so Sascha hadn't been completely without. Mostly Sascha was so much a gem himself that the lack of jewels almost wasn't noticeable, but he needed to show everyone Sascha's place at court today.

And he still had that desire to drape Sascha in sapphires.

Sascha slowly let his hands drop after he fastened the second earring, letting the dangling sapphires and diamonds sway. They flashed fire in the sunlight streaming through the windows, brilliant against the rich red of his hair. Yes, he wanted to see Sascha in more sapphires, only sapphires and the soft glow of candlelight. Sascha raised his gaze to Lysander's again, still a bit stunned and just a little questioning.

"Beautiful." Lysander lifted a hand to cup Sascha's cheek.

Sascha closed his eyes and leaned into Lysander's palm. "Oh, Lysander."

"You like them?"

"I love them. Thank you for letting me wear them."

"I'm giving them to you. They're yours."

Sascha's lips parted silently, then he whispered, "Lysander..."

"Oh, they're pretty!" Xanthe exclaimed from Sascha's side. Lysander was ashamed he'd almost forgotten she was standing there.

Sascha smiled down at her. "Yes, they are." Then he turned his smile on Lysander and it softened, turning into something else entirely, something just for him. "Thank you, Lysander."

"My pleasure." He took Sascha's hand, the one Xanthe hadn't reclaimed as soon as Sascha finished putting on the earrings, and lifted it to his lips. Sascha shivered when he flipped it over and pressed his lips to his palm. He wanted to kiss him properly, but they had no time. "And now we do have to go or we'll be late."

Sascha watched the entire ceremony from a delicate chair positioned a step down from the dais where Lysander, Xanthe, Felix, and Thalia sat. He concentrated on keeping a serene countenance. Concentrated on Lysander and Xanthe and ignored as best he could the crowd of nobles watching as Lysander ceremonially announced Xanthe's coming into her Talent. They would be far easier to ignore if they weren't nearly as interested in Sascha as in the announcement.

He'd expected it, especially with so many visitors to Wyndward who hadn't seen him before. He was new and unforeseen, and they didn't have his measure yet. Didn't know if they could use him to influence Lysander or displace him for someone of their own choosing. They didn't know how Lysander felt about him...but Sascha did, and the knowledge allowed him to sit gracefully under their scrutiny. He worried more about who in the crowd might be part of the conspiracy, and wished it wouldn't have looked odd for him to stay away from the event.

At least they seemed to be as attentive to the purpose of the ceremony, and genuinely proud—or at least satisfied—to find the heir to the throne had come into her Talent so young. A powerful heir was something that would please them, as Lysander had counted on. The assembled courtiers let out a cheer as the ceremony concluded, and Sascha added his own enthusiastic applause. Xanthe twitched just slightly at the explosion of sound in what had been an otherwise silent room, but Sascha doubted anyone who wasn't near to her would've noticed. Otherwise, she reacted exactly as she was supposed to, accepting the appreciation of her people. Pride swelled within Sascha.

Before the clapping died away, Lysander took her hand and began to descend from the dais. Sascha stood, ready to bow as they passed, but Lysander held out his arm to Sascha. He froze for just a second, then took the offered arm, hoping his brief, startled hesitation wasn't obvious. Lysander and Xanthe were meant to leave together, but Lysander obviously had a different plan.

Sascha walked carefully at his side through the long throne room and out of the towering double doors at the end, courtiers watching them all the way. His thoughts tumbled over themselves, spinning and tangling and never letting him get a purchase on any one that might answer the question of why

Lysander had deviated from the ceremony's planned conclusion. Lysander did not, however, seem to be deviating any further—he led Sascha and Xanthe across the wide corridor to another set of doors. At Lysander's nod, two guards pulled the doors open.

Sascha tried to step aside and disengage his arm from Lysander's, but Lysander glanced at him and shook his head with a smile. "Come with us."

He couldn't do anything but obey Lysander's gentle command. Sascha nodded just slightly and stepped out onto the balcony at the king's side.

The wide stone balcony overlooked the castle courtyard and the road winding down to the town on the shores of the lake. Today, the courtyard and road were filled with people, a crowd larger than any Sascha had ever seen before. His fingers tightened convulsively on Lysander's arm without his conscious control, but he forced them to relax—he didn't want Lysander worrying about him, or anyone noticing his momentary shock.

Anyone who couldn't fit in the throne room had gathered in the courtyard to see the princess, but he'd never expected the sheer number of people. He should have. Anyone in the castle, anyone living in the town, anyone within a reasonable traveling distance who could find lodgings or return home within the day had come to see their princess. Today's event was too important to miss. Everyone wanted to witness it.

And now Sascha stood in front of them at Lysander's side, the guards on the balcony and in the courtyard giving him only a little comfort. The people were here for Xanthe and Lysander, as those in the throne room had been, but they would notice Sascha. Notice and perhaps wonder. Perhaps recognize? He fell back on the only thing he knew to do, attempting to look the elegant and unobjectionable concubine. Let them talk about how pretty Lysander's concubine had been if they had to say anything at all. And let none of them realize he'd been meant to be somewhere else.

The crowd roared at the sight of them. Lysander guided them forward to the balustrade and Xanthe stepped up onto the footstool that had been positioned there for her, as she was too short to be visible over the balustrade. If anything, the crowd cheered louder. Lysander and Xanthe waved; Sascha smiled and stayed half a step back.

He watched them, Lysander especially once he was reassured Xanthe was handling the situation well. Sascha never forgot he was the lover of the king, never forgot the man he'd fallen in love with was the king, but today Sascha could think of nothing else. And he was afraid for himself and what his love for this man might bring him, and more for Lysander. Sascha could only hope today's spectacle would keep the people's favor with him, would do something to protect him—and Ivria as a whole—from those intent on hurting him.

After a few moments, Lysander bent to whisper in Xanthe's ear. She nodded solemnly. Lysander straightened and moved a fraction closer to Sascha. An instant later, Sascha understood why. A cloud of sparkling light surrounded Xanthe, obscuring her entirely for a moment and then fading away to reveal her dragon.

Pride welled up again in Sascha—for how brave she was being and for how hard she'd worked. She'd practiced to make calling up her Talent as smooth and controlled as she could, though she'd only just come into it, and so young too. But she'd had to demonstrate, to prove their claim, for those who came to witness.

The bright sun flashed off her scales and the crowd below roared even louder at the sight of their princess and heir as a dragon. As Lysander lifted her, making her more visible to the crowd, Sascha found himself hoping even harder this would serve its purpose, swaying public opinion and solidifying loyalty to the crown, and that the people here would carry the story of what they'd seen to the farthest corners of Ivria. He wanted to whisper the wish, to let the wind take it, but he didn't want Lysander to hear, so he kept it inside and hoped with everything he had.

Something wrapped around his wrist, and he jumped. But it was only Xanthe's tail. He couldn't stifle his laughter as she pulled him closer to her and Lysander even though he should have, even though he should've gently detached himself from her hold and moved away from her and Lysander. His place was not at their sides. Only, he couldn't quite make himself do so.

Warmth had begun to spread through him as soon as Xanthe tugged him closer and it rushed to fill him now as Lysander put a hand to his back. He glanced up and Lysander turned to him, flashing him a brief, devastating smile. The warmth changed to something entirely different, a dizzying heat that made him wish they were alone. Would that smile ever not have an effect on Sascha? He hoped not. He hoped a time never came when seeing that smile wouldn't make his knees weak and heat pool in his belly.

How long ago had it been when he'd never felt such a thing, never imagined he could? When he hadn't understood what this type of pull even was. Knowing Lysander had changed everything.

Lysander's gaze went slightly quizzical and just a bit concerned. "Are you all right?"

Sascha realized he'd been staring into Lysander's eyes for longer than he should have, considering where they were. Had he even blinked? He smiled softly, trying to reassure. "I'm fine. Don't worry."

Lysander didn't seem inclined to believe him, but he wasn't able to say anything more as calls and cries went up from the crowd. Sascha and Lysander turned to look and found dragons had taken to the sky. They swooped and looped and dove, soaring over the road, town, and lake. He didn't know who they were, but their joy was obvious. Did they live in the town? Or were they visitors, here to see the princess? Commoners or nobility? It didn't matter, not really. Their joy and pride were what mattered. Ivrians were always happy when someone came into their dragon Talent—and conversely some were disappointed at a child's lack of that Talent, but Sascha wouldn't think of such things today—and the feelings were magnified as it was their princess, their future queen.

Other dragons took to the sky as well. These Sascha recognized as members of the king's guard. They circled almost lazily, or so it appeared, but they were watchful and prepared to protect Lysander and Xanthe. Their presence was a comfort to Sascha after the attack and necessary because of it. Lysander had made a point of not being in such an exposed position since then, but today it couldn't be avoided, and the guard was prepared.

Lysander whispered to Xanthe and pointed to the dragons in the air. Sascha smiled as she bounced a little and clapped her hands in excitement. Lysander laughed and drew Sascha even closer, though Xanthe's hold, still firm on his wrist, kept him near. Then Lysander waved at the flying dragons and again at the crowd below and another cheer went up. Sascha clapped too—he didn't know what the etiquette was for him in this situation, but he had to show his appreciation as well.

CHAPTER 21

The celebration continued throughout the day and into the night. Lysander was informed of the revelry in the town and along the lakeshore, the music and dancing and bonfires. In his youth, before he had all the responsibilities he did now, he would've joined them, trying to remain anonymous—though believing he was a fiction. He couldn't do so now, despite the temptation of dancing around those bonfires with Sascha.

The celebrations in the castle were no less jovial—and as the night progressed, they would probably lose quite a bit of their decorum—but those parties in the town always seemed freer, or seemed to represent a sense of freedom, one he didn't have any longer. One he only had the illusion of before. He wouldn't complain, couldn't be so dismissive of the privilege of his position and the immense trust associated with it.

Even if dashing through the streets of the town with Sascha's hand in his did have a certain appeal.

He'd have to content himself with as many dances as he could claim with Sascha here after the feast. The long feast. The food was excellent, of course, the kitchen staff outdoing themselves to create a meal worthy of their princess, but many of the toasts to Xanthe and to Lysander himself offered up by the gathered nobility were long-winded and a bit too obsequious. Some were more sincere—or those delivering them just better at appearing so.

Lysander hated being so jaded. He knew well that there were plenty of people in the room loyal to him and to Ivria, but he also knew well there was a faction plotting against him and willing to embroil Ivria in conflict and war and risk their safety for the misguided aims of empire and domination. He scrutinized everyone, listened to every speech for hidden meaning and truthfulness. Lysander wasn't the only one doing so. Alan was watchful, Felix and Thalia as well. Those few who knew of the plot were taking this opportunity, with so many gathered who didn't often come to Wyndward, to study the assembly.

At his side, Sascha seemed watchful as well. Lysander wanted to tell him to relax, to enjoy himself, to leave the rest to him and the others, but Sascha wouldn't be able to. He cared too much and couldn't set aside worry. Both grateful for Sascha's devotion and hoping to soothe, Lysander reached to his left and took Sascha's hand, lifting it to his lips for a kiss. Sascha turned to him, lips parting in surprise and then curving in a sweet smile.

"What was that for?" Sascha asked, his voice just audible over the music and the hum of conversation in the room.

"Because I wanted to. I want to do this too." He gently drew Sascha forward, giving him plenty of opportunity to refuse, but Sascha allowed himself to be moved and was still smiling when Lysander lightly kissed his lips.

They tasted sweet, certainly from the honey in the cake Sascha was eating, but Lysander fancied the taste was just Sascha himself, naturally sweet in all ways. He wanted to linger, but he didn't want to share such a thing with all the eyes watching them, even though it wouldn't be unheard of—kings in generations past had done far more with their concubines in front of their courts, but such displays had fallen out of favor years ago and the idea of them had never appealed to Lysander in the slightest. Even if they had, he wouldn't have indulged in them with his daughter at his other side.

Sascha's cheeks were flushed a fetching shade of pink when Lysander drew back from him. His lashes lowered, veiling his large blue eyes for a moment, before they swept up again, and Sascha gave him a soft smile. His hand was still in Lysander's and he leaned forward, closing the small gap between them to brush a kiss over Lysander's cheek.

"What was that for?" he asked, echoing Sascha's question with as much flirtatiousness as he could.

Sascha's smile took on a hint of mischief. "Because I wanted to."

He chuckled appreciatively and squeezed Sascha's hand. He didn't let it go as they returned to their cake, and Sascha didn't try to take his hand back. After a few moments, he glanced past Lysander to where Xanthe sat. A smile of a different sort curved his lips, fond and almost paternal.

"She isn't going to make it much longer," he said to Lysander with a tilt of his head toward Xanthe.

Lysander turned to look and his own expression probably mirrored Sascha's. Xanthe slumped in the chair that was far too large for her, her spoon still in her hand, her eyelids drooping. She was so young—the long hours and expectations on her had been exhausting. He would've spared her if he could've, but as the one being honored, she had to be present for most of the day. And she had done everything expected of her without complaint.

Gently, trying not to startle her, he put a hand to her shoulder and whispered, "Time for bed, I think."

She blinked her eyes open and seemed to keep them that way through sheer force of will. "No, Father, I'm all right. I can stay."

"It's late, sweetheart, and you've done everything we asked perfectly. You don't have to stay any longer." He glanced behind him, searching for a servant to send for her nursemaid, but Sascha laid a hand on his arm.

"I'll take her," Sascha said when Lysander turned his attention to him.

"You don't have to do that."

"I don't mind."

Was Sascha hoping to escape the rest of the festivities himself? It was his first major court event as well. However gracefully he'd appeared to navigate it, it had likely been overwhelming for him as well. Lysander should let him go and indicate he didn't have to come back if he didn't want to, but Lysander selfishly wanted him here, wanted to dance with him.

"You'll come right back? The dancing will begin soon."

Sascha smiled as he stood. "I wouldn't miss it."

He rounded Lysander's chair and helped Xanthe down from hers. Lysander watched as they walked hand-in-hand from the dais. Others in the room noticed as well that the princess was leaving and who was accompanying her. Lysander glanced over his shoulder, this time to be certain that the guards weren't allowing Sascha and Xanthe to leave unescorted. He needn't have worried—two guards were already following. He returned his attention to Sascha and Xanthe making their way to the doors, Sascha appearing to politely deflect attempts to gain Xanthe's attention and time, or perhaps his own. They stopped as they reached the doors, and Sascha bent to Xanthe. Whatever he saw or she said caused him to lift the exhausted girl in his arms and carry her from the room.

Lysander stared at the empty doorway for some time after

they disappeared from sight, lost in thought. A servant came to refill his wine goblet and whisk Xanthe's abandoned plate away, pulling his attention back to the present where it needed to be. Alan strolled up to the table as the servant disappeared. He bowed to Lysander. When Alan straightened, Lysander waved him forward, gesturing toward Xanthe's place. "Come sit with me for a moment."

Another servant appeared, swiftly removing Xanthe's ornate chair and replacing it, then disappeared just as quickly. The switch was accomplished by the time Alan rounded the table. Lysander could've invited him to take Sascha's chair and the change wouldn't have been necessary but he wouldn't give away Sascha's seat when he would soon return. Besides, Felix's place was on the other side of Sascha's, and Lysander didn't want to risk conflict.

As Alan dropped down into the chair beside him, Lysander sipped his wine. "Anything?" he asked quietly.

Alan drank from his own goblet, giving the appearance their conversation wasn't of any particular import. "Nothing out of the ordinary. I've been watching, of course, and my guards are alert for any threats."

Lysander nodded.

"Felix will be listening too."

He nodded once more, his gaze straying to the man in the now circulating crowd of guests. Felix had stepped away from the table for a moment, but a group had gathered around him, making it difficult for him to return. As Felix laughed, Lysander mentally shook his head—if he didn't know better, he would've thought Felix nothing but a flirtatious, frivolous prince. But he did know better. Did Felix enjoy the flirtation as much as he appeared to or was all an act? Either way, the man chose to hide in plain sight by making himself appear utterly incapable of seriousness. Why had Felix made that choice, and why hadn't Lysander ever asked?

"He'll have a report for me tomorrow, I'm sure," Lysander said. And would certainly have gleaned a fair amount of information from those gathered tonight. Lysander could only hope some of it would pertain to their current problem.

He would've said something else about it, but the head of one of the southern clans approached the table. Lysander put his desire for a conversation with his cousin aside and gestured her forward. Thus began a steady stream of people, each staying a few moments, congratulating him on Xanthe's Talent —as if it were his accomplishment instead of luck and magic— perhaps flirting, perhaps mentioning sons or daughters of marriageable age. Some asked after Sascha, obviously hoping for information unknown to the assembly at large.

When a break came in the procession of people, Lysander made a point of turning to Alan and Thalia, a signal for them to be left alone for the moment.

Amusement danced in his sister's eyes above the rim of her goblet. She had her smile under control when she lowered it. "Well, that was to be expected."

"The parade of people wanting my attention? Of course it was. It happens every time."

"Yes, but she meant the interest in Sascha and your unmarried state." Alan stopped speaking as a servant refilled his goblet.

"Someone is always interested in my unmarried state. And many of the people here haven't seen Sascha before." He'd worried over it, whether anyone invited would know where Sascha was meant to be, whether letting Sascha be seen would give everything away. But he'd brought Sascha into Wyndward as his concubine and exposed him to the court already. The influx of people meant an increased risk, but keeping Sascha hidden would only raise suspicions and cause more talk. The King's Concubine would be expected to attend such an event.

Thalia fixed him with a keen gaze. "True. And none of them believed you were at all interested in taking a concubine prior to Sascha, so they're all hinting around the question, trying to determine if you would be interested in another or even in marrying, trying to see if one of their clan would be of interest to you."

"We should be alert to any overly curious inquiries about Sascha. If someone gets angry or jealous you've chosen him and don't intend to marry or contract another concubine, they might try to come at Sascha in some way, and we don't want anyone stumbling into other matters," Alan said in a low voice.

Lysander raised an eyebrow. "You think it might go so far?" He'd worried about putting Sascha in front of the assembled nobility, but not for that reason. "And why would they believe I wouldn't take another concubine? One might assume my willingness to contract one would mean I was more likely to take another."

"Well, they have eyes." Thalia's amusement became more pronounced even as she seemed to get more serious, the contrast startling. "You show no more interest now than you did before Sascha. If you were looking for someone else, they'd likely know, but they want to give you the opportunity to express an intent, especially those who haven't been here to see how you've been acting. So they mention their children or parade them in front of you in their finery"—she twirled a hand, as if to mimic the parading—"hoping you'll take an interest so they can reap the benefits of having a royal concubine in their clan."

"And if I was interested in another, I would be thinking of the implications of that." He already had, always had. Any liaison he made had some degree of risk, of one sort or the other, including the potential for politicking among the clans. Trying to gain favor or power or wealth through a connection with him. It was a factor in his decision to wait to wed and in his lack of desire to take an official concubine before. It had been a factor in how carefully he'd chosen the woman who'd carried his children. Now, well, any connection he made, anyone he let close would have to be even more carefully weighed to ascertain they weren't part of a plot against him.

Thalia nodded, understanding all Lysander hadn't said through the few words he had. She wasn't far from the throne herself, of course, and had been raised alongside Lysander and Felix, though he was slightly younger, with the knowledge that she would sit on the throne if something happened to Lysander. It gave her insight not many others had.

"They only have to pay attention to the way you look at Sascha and they'd know they have little chance anyway."

A flash of red caught Lysander's attention, and he turned to watch Sascha walking across the room toward him. Sascha's hair gleamed and the sapphires and diamonds in his earrings blazed in the light as he moved. "Hmm?"

Alan chuckled. "You're only proving her point."

Sascha noticed Lysander's regard and smiled, sweet and a little shy. Lysander loved that smile; it made him want to do wicked things to Sascha. "Proving your point how?" he asked Thalia absently.

"You haven't taken your eyes off him since he came back into the room, and the way you look at him..."

Now Lysander did tear his gaze from Sascha. "What?"

"Well, I can see you love him, but I know you well." Thalia said it quietly, matter of factly, with just a hint of gentleness.

"Excuse me?"

Her smile grew fond. "Did you think I wouldn't notice? Most people probably won't. I assume they believe the attraction will fade enough with time that you might be persuaded to wed one of their candidates or at least take a second concubine. But I can see it's more, and I'm glad for you. He's bringing you comfort and happiness in a time that isn't full of either, more so than usual. If I didn't like him already, I would just for that. Don't you agree, Alan?"

Alan was frowning, but Lysander was more concerned with Thalia's words at the moment. "Thalia—"

"Am I interrupting?" Sascha's voice drew their attention to the younger man as he stepped closer to the table. He bowed to Lysander, quite correctly and quite gracefully, and straightened with that sweet smile on his face.

"Of course not. Come sit with us." Lysander could continue his conversation with Thalia another time, when he had some idea what to say to her.

LYSANDER STRETCHED out a hand to Sascha as he rounded the table, and Sascha put his in it as soon as he was within reach, smiling at the sure clasp of his warm fingers. Lysander lifted his hand to his lips, brushing a kiss over his knuckles. The press of his lips made Sascha shiver, just a little, but Lysander knew—he always knew, and Sascha could see it in his eyes. Lysander kept hold of his hand as he lowered himself into his waiting chair and then used it to draw him forward.

Would Lysander kiss him again? Sascha craved his kiss, always. But he wasn't certain he wanted to share such things in front of everyone.

But Lysander only gently pulled him close until he could whisper into Sascha's ear. "I can't wait until we're alone. I'm going to strip you of everything you're wearing, except those earrings and whatever lacy surprise you have on under those clothes. Then I'm going take my time with you."

Heat flashed through Sascha at Lysander's words, a shiver running through him at the almost-touch of his lips to his ear. Sascha's lips parted, but the images, the anticipation, robbed him of words.

Lysander sat back but kept Sascha's hand in his, and eventually Sascha sank back into his chair as well, reaching for his goblet with his free hand, reaching for some sense of composure along with it. Some sense at all, as all thoughts seemed to have fled along with his wits. As Sascha scrambled for coherent thought, Lysander smiled, a wicked gleam in his eye. It broke Sascha from his stupor and he laughed. "You're horrible."

"No I'm not. And you love it," Lysander said, the gleam in his eye something intimate, just for Sascha.

Sascha shook his head, but meant exactly the opposite. He knew his smile was fond, and he hoped it didn't reveal more than he could afford in front of so many people. Keeping his emotions private from the court only seemed sensible.

But Lysander knew. He returned his smile and kissed his hand one more time, but he still didn't release it. Sascha was perfectly content that he didn't.

"Xanthe was all right?"

Sascha nodded. "Asleep before we made it to the nursery. Didn't even wake up when I laid her on her bed."

"She had a long day, full of excitement." Lysander squeezed his hand. "Thank you for taking her back."

"Of course." Sascha squeezed back. Before he got lost again in Lysander's pull, he leaned forward slightly to look past Lysander. "How has your evening been, Commander?"

"Uneventful." Alan gave him a gentle smile as he answered the question Sascha was really asking.

He smiled back, feeling just a bit guilty that he hadn't

expressed real interest in Alan's enjoyment of the festivities. "Have you found any time to enjoy yourself?" he asked quietly.

Something softened in Alan's eyes. "Not really why I'm here, but thank you for asking."

"You should be able to enjoy yourself at a party," Thalia put in. "It's why you supervise other guards."

"You know better. I can enjoy myself when I know you're all safe." Alan's tone was mildly scolding, sharper than most would take with the princess, and shock washed through Sascha. Thalia gave Alan a narrowed-eyed look, but said nothing either to scold him for his tone or to refute his statement.

"You should go enjoy yourself though," Alan continued. "It's about time for the dancing to begin. I'm sure you can find any number of people who want to dance with you, Thalia. Go dance with your concubine before someone wonders why you're just sitting here."

That last statement was directed at Lysander. Sascha stared at Alan as Lysander turned to him as well, probably leveling a look at him that Alan would understand but the majority of the room wouldn't.

"I'm watching. I have trusted people watching." Alan gestured at the space where the dancing would be once Lysander signaled for it to begin. "I don't think they'll do anything here in full view of the court with little chance of escape. That doesn't seem to be the way they're operating."

Lysander finally nodded sharply and turned back to Sascha. "Shall we?"

More time in front of the court with all their eyes on him. But their eyes would be on him even if he and Lysander didn't dance. They always watched him, always would if he stayed at Lysander's side, and he refused to be anywhere else. Lysander had chosen to bring him into the court's focus today even more than he had been and Sascha found he...didn't mind. Because he loved Lysander, and for good or ill, this was Lysander showing everyone Sascha was important.

He smiled. "Yes, let's."

They danced. And after a moment, Sascha didn't care one bit that everyone watched, that they were wondering about him and Lysander and how he could be manipulated or used. He couldn't quite forget about the threat to Lysander, but it faded slightly with the feel of Lysander's strong arms around him, the steady pressure of his hand guiding him through the steps. The warmth of the touch burned through layers of clothing as if nothing separated Lysander's broad palm from Sascha's skin.

Sascha hoped everyone attributed the flush of his cheeks to the exertions of the dance.

Lysander knew though—Sascha could see the knowledge in his eyes. The heat that followed in them lit fires in Sascha's body. He vividly remembered Lysander's promise of what would happen when they returned to his rooms. Lysander was thinking of it too, or planning what he would do with Sascha when they were alone, his gaze hot and intense on Sascha as they circled each other in the pattern of the dance.

Sascha felt almost...hunted. But in the best possible way, a way that left a delicious warmth flooding through him, that he never could have imagined only a few months ago. Lysander might have been the hunter in this scenario, but Sascha didn't mind being prey. He felt powerful with the certainty that Lysander wanted him and no one else, that Lysander felt for him as he felt for no one else. The exhilaration of it was almost as great as the desire, and they filled him, twining inside him, making him giddy, as Lysander pursued and guided him through the dance, as Sascha cast teasing glances at him from under his lashes while keeping just a little bit out of reach.

And Lysander... Lysander loved what he was doing; Sascha

could tell. Every move Sascha made, every flick of his eyelashes, Lysander noticed, and his attention only sharpened as a smile flirted with the corners of his mouth. And though this dance they were doing—both literal and otherwise—was exhilarating, when Lysander chuckled low in his throat as the steps brought Sascha close in to Lysander's body, Sascha very much wanted them to be alone somewhere.

Unfortunately, they were unable to be alone for some time as Lysander's obligation would keep them at the party. Then Sascha saw the gleam in Lysander's eyes. He narrowed his own in as much of a glare as he could give the king in full view of his court. Lysander only laughed, and the sound was so delighted Sascha had a difficult time holding on to his annoyance.

A lifetime seemed to pass before they were alone. Sascha preceded Lysander into the royal apartments, their guards left behind outside. He could feel Lysander's gaze on him, burning into him. They went directly to Lysander's bedchamber in unspoken agreement.

As soon as they were through the door, Lysander's hands clasped Sascha's shoulders. Sascha's breath caught in his throat at the press of those large hands. At the heat of Lysander's body along back. Lysander squeezed slightly, then ran his palms down Sascha's arms, trailing warmth in his wake. As Lysander's fingers tangled briefly with his own, Sascha let out a long shuddering breath.

Lysander's chuckle was soft, closer to a rumble of sensation than a sound but Sascha heard it, felt it. Lysander brushed Sascha's hair aside and pressed a soft kiss to his neck, just above his collar, just behind the glittering fall of jewels at his ear. Jewels Sascha still couldn't believe Lysander had given him. "Lysander," he whispered.

"Sascha." Lysander's hands were back on his shoulders, shockingly warm. His voice was a whisper too, one that spread heat through Sascha's body. Another brush of a kiss against his neck, and another as Lysander swept his hands down again, this time along Sascha's sides until they came to rest at his waist. Kisses turned to nibbles and, without thought, Sascha tilted his head to give Lysander better access. Another chuckle rumbled low in Lysander's throat and a nibble turned into a sharper nip. Sascha jumped slightly, and Lysander squeezed his waist.

"If you don't want your clothes ruined, you should take them off right now."

"What?" Sascha gasped, a laugh nearly breaking free, and twisted to look at Lysander. All thought of laughter died when he saw the burning desire in Lysander's eyes. If he didn't strip immediately, Lysander was going to rip these clothes right off him. And wasn't that a thrilling thought? He was tempted to not move, to let Lysander do as he would...but the clothes were new and beautiful. Ruining them would be an awful waste, even if the experience would surely be delightful. Stepping back from Lysander almost regretfully, he kicked off his shoes and unfastening his cape, brought his hands to the fastenings of his jacket and began undoing them as quickly as the sudden clumsiness of fingers allowed.

For an instant, he wasn't certain what to do with his clothing—it was the finest he'd ever worn and it seemed as wrong to drop it on the floor as to let Lysander ruin it. But looking at Lysander, at the smoldering heat in his eyes, he couldn't imagine why his mind was contemplating such ultimately unimportant things. Sascha tossed each article of clothing over the back of a nearby chair. When he was only left in the brief bit of silk and lace hanging low on his hips, he stopped and let his arms fall to his sides. Lysander always did like him in lace, and if he ripped this garment... Well, the destruction would be worth it.

Sascha watched Lysander through the curtain of hair that had fallen across his face while he'd undressed—something he should've tried to do seductively instead of frantically. He kicked himself, but Lysander didn't seem upset. Quite the opposite, in fact. Lysander still stared at him heatedly, still appeared as if he wanted to devour Sascha, as if he absolutely would. Sascha wanted him to. So he stopped, standing before Lysander in nothing but a bit of lace and a pair of sparkling earrings, and waited.

Lysander crossed the two steps to him in a heartbeat and jerked him into his arms. His large hands were everywhere, just rough enough to thrill Sascha with the urgency Lysander felt but still cherishing, always with that underlying care. The combination of urgent passion and aching tenderness was enough to melt Sascha. Lysander pulled Sascha against him and into a kiss. It was a little rough too, forceful, that feeling of being devoured Sascha had craved just moments ago. He went up on tiptoe to press himself closer, even as his knees went wobbly at the depth of the kiss. He clutched the velvet of Lysander's jacket to steady himself. Lysander hadn't undressed yet. Sascha wanted Lysander's skin against his, but the feel of the velvet against his bare skin, the thought of himself nearly naked while Lysander remained clothed, was somehow wicked and delicious. He shivered delightfully at the sensation.

Lysander tore his mouth from Sascha's and began laying a line of nipping little kisses along his jaw back to his ear. He nibbled and sucked at Sascha's earlobe, and Sascha gasped, clutching tighter to Lysander's jacket at the unexpected burst of pleasure. After a few moments, Lysander whispered in his ear, "Do you remember what I told you earlier? What I planned to do to you?"

Sascha had to think a moment longer than he should have to remember, the pleasure slowing his mind. But he did. *And then I'm going take my time with you.* The noise he made was somewhere between a gasp and a moan. Lysander's chuckle vibrated in his chest. Something shivered through Sascha in its wake—nerves, anticipation, all-consuming and almost over-whelming. Then Lysander kissed him, deep and thorough as his hands, so large and strong, wandered over Sascha again, explor-ing, grasping greedily at every part of Sascha he could reach. All the while, the kisses didn't stop. Drugging kisses that drove every remaining thought from Sascha's head. He tried to think, needed to do something other than cling to Lysander. He was past the point of believing it his duty to serve Lysander in bed, but he always wanted to give him pleasure. But under Lysander's determined onslaught, he could only hold on and feel.

Lysander swept Sascha up and carried him to the bed. Sascha's world tilted before he could even gasp at the sudden change, and he was deposited in the center of the plush cover-let. He'd barely registered the feel of the velvet beneath him, barely felt the world stop spinning, when Lysander was over him, lowering himself to Sascha's body, taking his lips in another intoxicating kiss.

Time lost all meaning then. Sascha drowned in sensation, swept under by the tide of it Lysander created with lips and teeth and hands. He could do nothing but let it happen, give himself over to Lysander's whims, knowing it would be both their pleasure. And if he had Sascha shaking and sobbing by the time he filled him, if he left him shattered by long awaited release, he also cleaned him up and tucked his limp body under the covers and into Lysander's arms, holding him close as sleep claimed him.

CHAPTER 22

Lysander woke slowly, reluctantly. He didn't want to get up, didn't want to leave his bed and Sacha, warm and boneless with sleep in his arms. But what he wanted didn't much matter. He had a meeting with Thalia, Felix, and Alan this morning, and his desire to remain wrapped around Sascha couldn't be allowed to distract him from the importance of the meeting, working to ensure the safety of Ivria and his own family. Sascha would probably take the necessity better than he was at the moment.

Giving in to the inevitability, he began to slowly extract himself from Sascha and the blankets twisted around them. Usually, no matter how careful he was, he couldn't leave the bed without Sascha noticing, even if all he did was stir and give a sleepy murmur of protest. Today was an exception; as Lysander pulled away, Sascha didn't move. Lysander stood and gazed down at him. Sascha sprawled among the velvet and fur of the bedclothes. His red hair fanned around his head on the pillow. His skin was sleep flushed, his lips still swollen from Lysander's kisses. His throat was pink in spots from the drag of Lysander's beard. There were probably other places just like it hidden by the blankets. He still wore the sapphire earrings; they were the only things he wore. Sascha looked utterly debauched and all Lysander wanted was to climb back into bed and see how much more he could muss him up.

Instead, he bent to brush a light kiss over Sascha's cheek and left to ready himself for the day.

A short while later, he strode into his private library to find Thalia, Felix, and Alan already there waiting for him. Felix was saying sharply, that tone a clear sign his large supply of patience had reached its end, "Just because I'm younger—"

"I never said being young and pretty made you incapable of—"

"You think I'm pretty?" Felix interrupted with an exaggerated sweet tone and an outrageous flutter of lashes.

From where she sat, Thalia saw Lysander first and gave a shrug and roll of her eyes in response to his inquiring look. Well, that was helpful. What had Alan said to irritate Felix so much? Did he even want to know? Lysander cleared his throat, drawing the attention of the two men before Alan could reply. They turned sharply at the sound, obviously startled. Felix's eyes flashed with the irritation Lysander had expected and a glimmer of hurt, which he hadn't, but as Lysander watched, the emotion drained away. Felix murmured a greeting, but gave no explanation, and Alan only bowed. Lysander was in no mood to deal with this.

"Sit, both of you."

As Lysander went to his desk and sat behind it, Felix followed and took the chair beside Thalia. Alan came closer but chose to stand instead of bringing over another chair. Lysander stifled a sigh. Why had he had to leave bed again? "You're really going to stand there the whole time? Get a chair."

Alan frowned but obeyed. As he did, Lysander surveyed

Thalia and Felix. "You both look revoltingly bright-eyed after such a late night."

Many at last night's revelry would've been shocked to see Felix in such a condition. They likely believed he would be in bed until noon, perhaps with a partner, and Felix likely wouldn't care they had such an image of him in their heads. Lysander glanced at Alan, who was seating himself in a chair he'd brought from the table and placed on Thalia's other side; perhaps Lysander wasn't entirely correct.

But carefree frivolity was the image Felix preferred to cultivate, for reasons entirely of his own. Felix was trusted family and deserved his privacy. Lysander didn't need to know his motivations, even if he was increasingly curious about them as time went on.

"You spent a lot of time mingling among the guests last night, Felix. Did you hear anything interesting?" Lysander asked.

The face that had captivated so much of Lysander's court last night was set in serious lines. "There was a lot of genuine and widespread happiness and excitement about Xanthe. Everywhere I turned people were expressing their pride in her and their optimism for the future of Ivria and the strength of its ruling family."

Lysander thought it had gone well—Xanthe had certainly done all he'd had to ask of her. At least it wasn't in vain. Hopefully, the attitude of the guests would filter out into Ivria and keep public sentiment on their side.

"Happy to hear it," Lysander said.

"That can't be all," Alan said. "I could've guessed people were happy just from walking through the party."

Before Lysander could turn more than a mild look of surprise at Alan for his rudeness, Felix had raised a graceful brow. "There's plenty more, most of it the usual rounds of power maneuvering and politicking. The leader of the northern clan was extremely impressed both by Xanthe's Talent and Sascha's beauty, and she plans to send us a case of the latest vintage of their ice wine. She also mentioned her grandchildren who are around Xanthe's age and should visit Wyndward. She's hoping for either a future match or an influential friendship. Bruccio, the old bastard, is somewhat reassured by today. After decades of kings, he was unsure about the idea of a queen. He also is scheming to get his grandchildren close.

"That's all normal and expected and there's more of it. I'll spare you for now. The few we know are involved didn't do anything obvious, but Triana's father by marriage attended and spent a fair amount of time huddling with each of those few at various times. Which I think is telling. I was interested in Malo and Floi. I would've expected far more power brokering from them, especially at yesterday's festivities. Mostly, they were quiet, watchful, and that isn't like them." Felix frowned and focused somewhere over Lysander's shoulder as he thought. "I don't think their names have come up in anything we've found yet, but my instincts say something is off there. Whether it's this plot, I can't yet say."

Lysander shook his head when Alan opened his mouth, forestalling whatever comment he was about to make. Alan seemed to be in an oddly antagonistic mood toward Felix today, and Lysander had no patience for it. Besides, Felix's instincts were generally solid when it came to the mood of the court and when something was brewing. Felix still couldn't understand how he'd missed the existence of a plot on the scale of the one they were trying to uncover. Lysander would have loved to blame him for the lapse, but he'd seen no sign of the plot either, no sign of any serious discontent that would lead to it, and neither had anyone else.

"I trust your instincts," Lysander assured him. "I'll have

Galina look for anything in Jannik's papers. Keep an eye on them until they leave."

Alan nodded in response to the inquiring look Lysander sent him. "Yes, Your Majesty."

He turned back to Felix. "Did you hear anything else of interest?"

"A lot of the conversation and speculation yesterday centered around you and Sascha," Felix said.

"Unsurprising," Alan remarked. "They swarmed you any time he wasn't at your side."

Felix glanced at Alan from the corner of his eye. "It isn't surprising. They'd seen no prior indication you were considering taking a concubine, and now that you have, they wonder if they might tempt you with another in the form of their own child. They also wonder if your acquisition of a concubine might speak to a loneliness that could lead you to marry, and they hope again to put their own children in your path if that might be a possibility."

"Acquisition?" Thalia repeated, wrinkling her noise.

Felix shrugged. "You know it's how many of them think of it, though I agree it's a distasteful attitude."

Lysander was more irked that Felix's observations echoed Thalia and Alan's. "If that's all they were thinking about, I'm not overly worried."

"There was something else," Felix replied. "A lot of interest in Sascha himself. Most of the guests had never seen him before, some hadn't even heard about his existence, and you showed your regard for him quite clearly. Some will think about his importance to you in a strategic way—considering whether and how they could use him. But others... Others were more curious than anything else. Sascha has gotten a fair amount of attention since you brought him here, but nothing like this. People are wondering about him—who he is, where he comes from, what influence he has over you, especially as your relationship seems close. I wonder if our story about him will hold up to more intense scrutiny if people start asking questions. If they haven't already."

Lysander was so struck by Felix's casual remark about his feelings for Sascha and how apparent they were to everyone, he almost missed the rest of what Felix said. "What are they saying?"

Felix didn't flinch at his sharp tone. "Nothing yet, but as I said, they're curious. There were the usual comments about his appearance and his manner and how you behaved toward each other, but also a lot of questions about where he comes from and how he came to be here. I heard the vague information you put about circulating—Florestan confirming it as well—but for some of these people, it won't be enough. Certainly people were curious before, but for most, there wasn't as much urgency." Felix paused, seeming to gather his thoughts. "Anyone would wonder about him, but the people who might care the most didn't see him enough or see you together looking the way you did yesterday. It allowed them to let the questions go in favor of higher priorities because it seemed that Sascha was just a concubine and perhaps not very important."

"And how did we look yesterday?"

He watched Lysander levelly, calmly. "Devoted. You looked devoted to each other."

Lysander didn't doubt Felix's observations or his conclusions, but he wanted to. He didn't want to believe he'd been so obvious and overlooked something that could jeopardize everything. Thalia shifted in her seat, and Lysander turned his attention to her with an inquiring glance.

"Maybe it won't be as bad as that," Thalia said, though she didn't sound convinced herself. "Sascha's uncle will continue to back up what we've already divulged about Sascha."

"But will that be enough?" At the time he'd brought Sascha here, he'd considered the problem but thought they'd be all right. It hadn't appeared as if too many people had known about Jannik's deal with Sascha's parents, so his solution—the vague story he'd put out with the help of Sascha's uncle—had seemed sufficient. Especially as he hadn't assumed Sascha would be quite as visible as he was now or that his own feelings would be what they were now. "I should've taken into account how strong curiosity surrounding any relationship of mine would be. All it would take is one person connected with this mess asking a question of someone who knows Sascha is supposed to be with Jannik, and they'll know something happened."

Lysander cursed viciously, kicking himself for how he'd handled the situation back to the start. The safer option would have been to hide Sascha away somewhere until Lysander had exposed the entire plot, then he could've brought Sascha here as his concubine. He wouldn't have had to fabricate a story for who Sascha was and where he'd come from, which he hadn't put enough effort into. And still, his mind violently rejected the idea of not bringing Sascha with him, especially knowing now how he'd come to feel for him.

"There's no use beating yourself up over it. What's done is done," Thalia said firmly. "How do we proceed from here?"

Lysander took a breath. His sister was right. Regrets and doubts about his past actions would get him nowhere and would only hurt him if he let himself wallow in them. Or let them show. He'd felt enough doubt—in his actions, in his perceptions, in himself—since finding out about this plot to last a lifetime, certainly enough to cause problems if anyone managed to take advantage of it. But he couldn't doubt or second guess anymore; he had no time for it.

"You're right," he said with finality to his tone. "We need to move forward from here under the assumption that they're going to find out we know something, if they haven't already. We need to move faster before we lose them all."

"You want to arrest them now," Alan said slowly.

"Or as near to now as we can." Resolve filled him, pushing out the doubt and regret. Later he might wonder if he should've done this even sooner, if waiting at all had been a mistake, but it wouldn't help now. "If we move quickly, we can get everyone we know of. Then use them to get the rest."

"We could lose some anyway. They could disappear when they hear of what happened," Alan said, as close as he would come to criticism of Lysander.

"And we could lose them all if they realize we know and go to ground. I don't want them to menace me and put my family at risk for years to come as we begin all over again trying to find them."

Alan nodded, conceding his point.

"From here, we need a plan." Lysander sat back in his chair. "We'll need a report from Galina—I know she sent one recently, but we need everything she has compiled, every name."

"You want to go after everyone at once." Understanding was dawning in Alan's eyes, even if he still appeared somewhat troubled.

"It's the best way to minimize the chance of our targets escaping us. Do you have enough people we can trust with this?" He hated to ask such a thing, to doubt his own soldiers and elite guards—Alan's people—but he had to, and Alan would have to face the issue as well.

Alan nodded brusquely. "I still have a few I'm unsure of, but the rest are loyal, I'm certain of it."

Felix, who had been silent while he and Alan began to discuss strategy, spoke up. "Give me their names. I'll see what I can find out."

Lysander could almost see the thoughts flitting through Alan's head, the questions about how Felix could ascertain their loyalty if he himself couldn't; he would have to have a conversation with Alan about trusting Felix's abilities. But he didn't have the time now. He cut in before Alan could speak, "Good. Let us know what you find."

"Of course," Felix said with a graceful nod and no indication he'd noticed Alan's skepticism—though Lysander doubted that.

He turned back to Alan. "Get Galina here as soon as possible. Probably best if she gives this report in person."

Alan nodded. "We'll need all we can get, and everything she couldn't trust to a written report. I'll send for her as soon as we're done here."

"I think we're finished for now. Give those names to Felix, and send for Galina. Think about your people and who you want to trust with this. We'll reconvene once she's back to make plans."

"Yes, Your Majesty." Taking his words for the dismissal they were, Alan stood strode from the room, closing the door behind himself.

After Alan was gone, Felix's lips twitched minutely. "He doesn't understand why I'm here or why you trust me."

No, Alan didn't, but Lysander would have to deal with it later. "He doesn't have to. You know I trust you."

"Me too," Thalia said with a smile. "Alan is dependable but he always has been just a bit thick about some things."

Lysander didn't want to agree with that statement, said in good humor though it was, but he could disagree either. "Anything else we should discuss?"

Felix glanced at Thalia briefly, then asked, "May I ask you a question?"

Lysander felt some trepidation at the request; Felix would usually just ask. "All right."

"Why haven't you just married Sascha? Or announced a betrothal?" Felix continued when Lysander didn't immediately answer him. "I said before it's easy to see how you feel for him, or at least, we can see how deep it goes." He gestured between himself and Thalia with a graceful hand. "You waited to marry because you didn't want to tie yourself to just anyone when it might risk power struggles between the clans, but he's important to you. You could end all the speculation and the posturing and scheming to trap you into marriage for some family's gain. And you'd have Sascha."

Lysander made the conscious decision not to sharply end this discussion in a way that would hurt his cousin. "I already have Sascha."

"But is it the same?" Thalia asked. "We can see you love him. And we can see he loves you."

"And we can see how much of a help he is to you," Felix said, picking up where she left off. "There's no reason for you not to marry him. Some will certainly be upset you didn't choose someone from their own clan, but that would happen no matter who you marry."

"Who's to say I plan to marry at all?" He'd tried to put discussion of potential consorts off by having children. It hadn't worked. There were times he'd thought that perhaps it would be best if he never wed.

Thalia rolled her eyes. "I am, because I know you. Marriage is important to you. I've always known that if you fell in love with someone, you would keep them with you."

"Sascha isn't going anywhere," Lysander pointed out.

"Perhaps not," Thalia conceded. "But if you don't care whether it's as concubine or consort and you love him, then why not marry and end the machinations that will try to displace him and put someone else in your bed and on the throne next to you."

Lysander rubbed a hand over his face. He loved Thalia and Felix, but he'd had about enough today. "I think this discussion can end here."

"Of course," Thalia said immediately, but there was an unrepentant gleam in her eyes.

"Go. I'll let you both know when Galina is due to arrive. If you hear anything useful before then, let me know."

Once he was alone, he sat back in his chair and sighed. He should be thinking about what was to come later, the planning they needed to do to eliminate the threat to himself and Ivria. Instead, after Thalia and Felix's questions, he could only think about Sascha...and why he hadn't been considering marriage.

He loved Sascha—he could easily admit it to himself, even if he hadn't said the words aloud yet—and he was better with Sascha. Sascha supported him as no one ever had, made him happier than anyone ever had. Made his burdens lighter just by being there. He wanted Sascha with him always.

Had he just not gotten to the idea of marriage yet, with everything else he was dealing with? The urgency of the current situation certainly occupied every spare thought. And having Sascha as a concubine brought him close enough to the danger surrounding Lysander... But would the risk be worse if Sascha was his husband, his consort? Sascha had already been caught up in an attack against him. Protecting Sascha wasn't a reason not to marry him.

Was he looking for a reason not to marry Sascha? He hadn't wanted to rush to marry when he came to the throne, which was why he'd provided for the succession immediately, eliminating the biggest reason anyone would push him to wed. Though not the politicking. He'd let everyone think he was keeping himself free to marry as he needed to later, if he had to placate or reward one of the clans in particular. But he'd wanted to be able to choose whom he would wed based on his own feelings. Lysander hadn't confided that hope to anyone, though of course Thalia and Felix knew.

He wanted a spouse he could trust, not someone hoping to gain favor for themselves or their families, not someone pushed in front of him and simpering to get his attention. There had been too many of those. And he'd been too busy to look for someone who wasn't, if he could've found someone, if he could've convinced himself he wasn't shirking his duty in doing it. Easiest to put aside the idea entirely.

But now there was Sascha. Whom he hadn't sought, but who had appeared and burrowed into his heart, and there was nothing left for it. He couldn't imagine his life without Sascha by his side. Could he marry him?

Lysander realized suddenly the question he asked himself wasn't whether he wanted to marry Sascha but whether he could. He wanted to. And he was king; surely he could marry Sascha if he wanted—and if Sascha wanted, of course. If they were to wed, some people would be upset, but that would happen no matter who he married. He couldn't live entirely at the whims of the clan heads and courtiers, especially when it came to his own family.

The children loved Sascha already and he them. Lysander loved Sascha, and Sascha loved him. They could go on as they had been; once this plot was ended and its perpetrators brought to justice, their life together would be calmer, at least some- what. Sascha had status as his concubine, and whatever anyone thought, Lysander would only ever have him. Or, he could ask Sascha how he felt about marriage and perhaps they could build something else together, something that would make

Sascha his husband and consort and officially a second parent to his children. The more he considered it, the more he thought maybe they all needed that.

CHAPTER 23

Sascha woke alone in Lysander's large bed. Normally, he stirred when Lysander rose for the day, but today he seemed not to have. Understandable after yesterday, but he couldn't help but be disappointed to have missed him. Starting his day with even just a kiss and a few words from Lysander made the morning feel as if it would be a good one. Well, he would see Lysander soon enough, he was certain. Sascha rolled onto his back, lifting his arms and stretching his whole body. A few delicious aches made themselves known, and he smiled at the memory of what caused them.

With a sigh, he forced himself to get out of bed and ready himself for the day. He could have lazed about longer—with the ceremony over, there was far less to occupy his time—but he saw little reason to lay about in bed if Lysander wasn't with him. Someday, perhaps, they could spend the day in bed together. Or perhaps not—Lysander was king. Sighing again, because no one could see and fault him for it, he took himself off to the bathing room.

After dressing, he went out to the sitting room and called

for breakfast to be brought—with Lysander's busy morning, there was no sense waiting—and sat to write a letter to Romilly about yesterday's festivities. He wasn't yet particularly practiced at the code Romilly had taught him. Between the amount that had to be recounted and the slow speed at which he worked, he was still writing when the tray arrived and continued to do so as he ate.

Some time later, a knock sounded at the door. It opened at Sascha's call to reveal Felix, looking no worse the wear for last night's revelry. Sascha smiled in welcome and motioned his friend in. He was struck again, after yesterday and the preparations that had gone into it, after all the help and support Felix had given him, how grateful he was at the genuine friendship that had grown between them.

"Good morning, Sascha."

"Good morning. Come join me. I think there's some chocolate left." He gestured to the other chair at the table and reached for the little silver pot and a second cup. When he poured, the liquid was still hot.

"I don't have much time unfortunately." But Felix took the chair. "I wish I could sit here all day and gossip about yesterday over chocolate and pastry."

Sascha nudged the plate of apple nut twists toward Felix, even though he was disappointed."Have one anyway if you can take a moment."

"I have that much. Thank you for letting me steal your breakfast." He picked a pastry and began to delicately eat it, despite his haste.

"Is everything all right?" Sascha asked hesitantly. He didn't want to pry, since he knew Felix was to meet with Lysander, Thalia, and the commander this morning. And while Lysander seemed inclined to tell him more lately, he was well aware he wasn't to know everything.

Felix looked up at Sascha, his gray eyes serious. "Everything is moving quite quickly now, or is about to, anyway."

Alarm skittered through Sascha. "Did something happen last night? Did they try anything?"

Felix was shaking his head before Sascha had finished speaking. "No, no. Nothing like that. But…"

"But you can't tell me what you know," Sascha said without resentment.

"I don't know. Lysander didn't say. Of course, I didn't tell him I was going to stop in to see you before I meet with the commander." He shrugged helplessly. "But I gave Lysander some information that is going to accelerate the timeline. Ask him about it. I think he'll tell you."

"All right." He certainly wouldn't press Felix.

Felix took a last sip from his cup. "I'm sorry to rush out on you, but I have to go."

"Don't worry about it."

Felix rose gracefully but hesitated before leaving the table. "Will you do something for me?"

Sascha was baffled as to what Felix could need from him, but it didn't change his answer. "If I can."

"Carry this with you all the time." Felix held out a hand, in it a small dagger in a plain sheath.

Sascha drew back slightly, the reaction immediate and automatic. "What?"

"Lysander will tell you what's happening, but I've been thinking for a while that you need a way to defend yourself—you don't have magic to rely on. Maybe you have something else already, but if not…"

"No, I don't, but… I don't know how to fight with a dagger. I was never taught." Sascha hadn't been taught any weapons or any way to defend himself. He remembered watching his older brothers practice with swords and bows when he was a child, but he'd always been told it wasn't for him, and he'd accepted it well enough. Now, after the attack and with Felix holding a weapon out to him, it seeming like a glaring gap in his skills.

"You don't have to know anything fancy now. I can teach you later." Felix bit his lip, a rare expression of uncertainty from a man who always appeared so poised and confident. "You may not need it—you're surrounded by guards all the time—but I would feel better if you had something you could defend your-self with. Just in case, just until this is over."

The urgency in Felix's voice took root inside Sascha. Even after the attack, he hadn't really thought about danger to himself—to Lysander and the children, yes, but not to himself. Why would anyone want to hurt him?

He was Lysander's concubine. Was that enough of a reason?

"Do you know something?" Sascha asked as he slowly reached out a hand that trembled slightly to accept the knife.

"No, but I don't like thinking of my friend with no way to defend himself."

"All right." Sascha wasn't certain he was reassured, but Felix's concern touched him if nothing else. "I'll keep it with me."

"Thank you."

After Felix left, Sascha sat at the table for a long while staring blankly through the window, thinking about the odd conversation what it could mean. Sascha couldn't imagine he was in any physical danger on his own, not the way Lysander or even the children were in the face of the plot against Ivria. He shivered, the thought of Lysander and the children potentially being hurt enough to send cold fear coursing through him.

He stood abruptly, needing to see the children now, needing to see Lysander, too, but knowing it wasn't possible. He glanced down at the little knife on the table. Would he even be able to use it if he had to? He wouldn't have to. But he'd made a promise. Sascha slid the knife into a pocket and left the sitting room.

The children were happy to see him, something that never failed to warm his heart. That he had been accepted as family, that Lysander and his children felt in such a way about him, was a precious and unexpected gift. For as long as it lasted, he wouldn't take it for granted, and when or if it ended, he would cherish what he'd had. Sascha let got of everything else, playing games until they were ushered into lessons.

Leaving the nursery, he found himself somewhat adrift. He could go back to his letter; he should finish it and send it on its way. Who knew how long it would take to travel the distance to Romilly? And now he missed his cousin. Suddenly and quite a lot. Romilly had been a constant, a dear friend from the time of childhood, and Sascha couldn't have been more grateful to have them with him during this time of upset and upheaval. Sascha was trying not to feel bereft without them. He had Felix and Thalia, and his uncle. He wasn't completely alone, and this mood was ridiculous.

Sascha would go to the library and find himself something new to read. Then he would return and finish his letter, and after that, he would write a note to his uncle with an invitation to lunch tomorrow.

Decided, he slipped through the halls of the royal apartments on quiet feet until he reached the entrance to the private corridors. Lysander had shown them to him a while ago, remarking that they were a good way to quickly get to certain places in the castle without notice. Sascha found it ridiculous that there were secret passages here too, but he'd learned them, in case he wanted or needed to use them. There was one corridor ending in a hidden alcove across from the door to the castle library—he'd have tried to find something in Lysander's private library, but the door was still closed, something that only happened when Lysander was working there and didn't want to be disturbed, so the castle's library it would have to be.

The network of narrow corridors always seemed a bit eerie to him, deserted and silent, the smallest sounds echoing. It was worse today. The knife in his pocket felt heavier than it should, the silence oppressive, and Sascha began to think he'd made a mistake. Perhaps he should've used the public corridors and let a guard accompany him. But he'd come to the library this way before, and nothing had ever happened. Was today any different?

That prior trip had been before the attack.

He stopped abruptly. Felix hadn't told him what was happening today. He'd said he didn't think Sascha was in danger, hadn't he? But he'd also told Sascha Lysander would speak to him, and he'd given him a knife while extracting the promise he'd carry it all the time. That action put a different shade on everything.

Sascha stared down the corridor; the library was only a few turns away, but he hesitated. He stood for another moment, indecisive, then nodded. Yes, more sensible to wait or to go to the library with a guard. With that decided, he turned and retraced his steps. His feet moved him almost automatically— but quickly, quietly—as his mind again turned over worries and theories about what had prompted Felix's odd gift. He was so sunk into his own thoughts, he almost missed the voices.

But someone was talking, and Sascha stopped so abruptly he almost lost his balance. His heart began to race as he glanced up and down the corridor, frantically trying to find the speaker, suddenly infected with the desire not to be found here. Which was ridiculous—he was allowed to be here. But Felix's knife rested heavily in his pocket, his words heavier in Sascha's mind. He took a breath. There was no one there, but there were definitely voices, two of them, slightly muffled but not echoing as even low tones did in the corridor. So where were they coming from?

Sascha turned and found himself next to one of the doors leading out. He hadn't thought he'd be able to hear anything through the thickness of walls and doors—these corridors were meant to be secret, after all, and if footsteps or conversations from inside could be heard, it would defeat the purpose. He stepped closer, leaning in to put his ear to the door. The people were still talking; they didn't seem to have heard Sascha.

And they were obviously no threat to him. He would mention to Lysander that he'd been able to hear voices through the door in case it was a problem, but he should go now. Eavesdropping on someone's conversation wasn't right.

He began to step away when one of the voices got closer, and he heard his name. Sascha should probably still leave—just because someone was talking about him didn't mean he was entitled to hear it—but he moved closer to the door instead.

"—haven't found out anything about him. He's let nothing slip in public," said one person.

The first words the other person—a man? The voice sounded deeper, so perhaps—weren't decipherable, but then he said, "—matter. I know who he is, and I know he should be with Jannik."

"What? Lord Jannik?"

Ice flashed through Sascha, and his heart raced at the name.

"Yes, given to him as a concubine. And yet he's here, concubine to the king?"

Sascha leaned even closer, holding his breath and trying to keep his balance, not daring to touch the door in case it made a sound. He needed to know what these people knew. He needed to know who they were, but this exit had no way of observing the room on the other side of the door. Which seemed like an oversight in construction.

He only got a few words of the reply to the question—perhaps the speaker had moved farther away—but the inflection sounded as if it had been a question as well.

"I'm going to find out," said the deeper voice. "But Jannik wouldn't have let him go, not a pretty thing like him. So the king has to have gotten to Jannik."

"—much does he know?"

"I don't know. I've sent someone to scout out Grau. But we have to assume he knows something of our plot."

"How did he find out?" Did this speaker sound worried? The other seemed more angry, or at least that's what it sounded like through the roaring in Sascha's ears.

They knew where he'd come from. They knew, or surmised, Lysander was after them.

Sascha concentrated on calming himself, on listening. He didn't catch the answer to the question, whatever it was, but the tone of the next words was sharp. "—know yet. But our plans will have to change. For now, keep on as you were and tell me everything you learn immediately. Sascha has to have said something to someone. He's hardly bright enough not to."

He bristled at the insult to his intelligence.

"What will we do about him?" the person with the higher voice was asking when Sascha began to pay attention again. "Anything?"

"I've taken care of it. Lysander is obviously infatuated with the boy's looks. Why else would he have brought him here? If he's stupid enough to trust the boy, he's setting himself up to have his trust broken."

"How? Sascha isn't one of us, is he?"

"No, but the king can't be sure of that. And I've planted something in the boy's bedchamber that will convince

Lysander he's a traitor. That will get Sascha out of the way nicely." The deep voice had a satisfied quality to it that had a shiver racing through Sascha.

"Do we have to get him out of the way? If he's not a part of it and not bright enough to be of use to either side, can't we just—"

"No. He betrayed Jannik one way or another, and I want Lysander distracted and hurt as we put our plans in motion. Let him think Sascha was planted with him, to spy on him, perhaps to murder him. He won't see what's coming." There was a brief pause and Sascha strained to hear anything. "Get back to work."

Silence followed that last remark, even as Sascha remained frozen. The conversation seemed to be over—could he ease the door open and get a glimpse of the participants leaving? But what if they hadn't left? If one of them was still there and Sascha was caught... Well, he wasn't certain if it would be worse than what they already had planned for him, but he didn't want to find out.

Sascha raised a shaking hand to his mouth. Perhaps to keep in the sound that wanted to escape. They were going to implicate him in treason. They already had; it was only a matter of time before someone found whatever it was they'd concealed. Had a maid already found it?

He turned and ran back toward the royal apartments, his mind spinning all the way. If someone had already found whatever the item was, Sascha could be executed for treason. Lysander loved him—he wouldn't believe Sascha was betraying him, would he? Perhaps Sascha should forget whatever it was, pack a bag, and run. He could leave the country somehow, get to Romilly. Romilly would believe him. But no, he couldn't leave whatever it was for someone to find. He needed to get to it first. Then he could decide what to do.

Sascha sprinted along the passage, barely slowing to climb narrow, winding stairs, pelting around corners, stumbling more than once. What he would say if he met someone, he didn't know, and he didn't think about it—couldn't have come up with anything if he tried. At the entrance to the royal apartments, he forced himself to stop and try to slow his breathing. He couldn't quite manage it after more running than he'd done since childhood, on top of the fear coursing through him, so he just hoped no one saw him.

Luck was with him. Sascha dashed to his bedchamber without encountering anyone. After closing the door firmly, he put his back to it, leaning against the sturdy wood as he surveyed the room that was nominally his. He'd never slept here and hardly spent any time in this room. His clothing had even begun to migrate to Lysander's dressing room, filling up empty space there. When he'd arrived at Wyndward—bewildered and unsure of what was to become of him—the bedchamber had been a sanctuary, a haven of sorts. Now it felt odd to think of sleeping without Lysander beside him.

Sascha took a deep breath. He couldn't run and leave Lysander behind. He had to trust Lysander's feelings for him. If Lysander loved him, he wouldn't believe Sascha had betrayed him. Sascha would find whatever had been hidden here and go to Lysander.

Resolved, he pushed himself away from the door. It wasn't a large bedchamber, but there were plenty of places to conceal something small. And since he saw nothing immediately out of place, he assumed it had to be small and hidden somewhere not entirely obvious. It would help if he knew what he was looking for, but of course, he hadn't overhead that critical piece of information.

He went to the writing desk positioned under the window. It was as good a place as any to start. Perhaps a very good place if what they were hiding was a letter or some other written evidence. The top of the desk was neat and almost bare—he'd taken to using the little desk in the sitting room and most often didn't bring his things back here. He took up the first book in the short stack on the corner of the desk and flipped through it to see if anything had been slipped inside. Then he tossed it aside when he found nothing, not even wincing at his poor treatment of a book. He took up the next and did the same.

The few books contained nothing. Something could have been hidden in a binding, he supposed, but such an action would defeat the purpose of making sure the item was found. He moved on to the box containing writing supplies, rifling through it quickly, but all he found were the expected pens and half-full ink bottles. He checked underneath the box and under the candle holder. Nothing. Increasingly frantic, he pulled the drawer open so hard it came out of the desk and spilled its contents onto the floor.

With a wordless sound of frustration, he dropped to his knees. A jumble of paper and journals and sundry items that had somehow accumulated in the desk spread out before him. He clenched his shaking hands into fists and forced himself to take a steadying breath, to close his eyes and try to clear his wavering vision. Then he turned to the mess in front of him. His hands still shook as he began shuffling through handfuls of writing paper and focusing was difficult, but it couldn't be helped. He just needed to slow down and search methodically. He tossed the paper into the drawer and grabbed for more, panic rising within him despite his best efforts.

"Sascha! What are you doing?"

Sascha gasped and whipped around, losing his balance and falling to his backside as he did. Lysander stood in the doorway to his room, Felix just visible behind his shoulder. Sascha hadn't even heard the door open.

Lysander's shocked expression changed immediately to concern as he came toward Sascha. "Are you hurt? What's wrong?"

Sascha considered lying, and he was immediately ashamed of the impulse—hadn't he told himself he had to trust Lysander, that he could trust Lysander? "I…" He swallowed against his suddenly dry throat as Lysander knelt in front of him and took his hands. The care in the gesture did something inside Sascha, warmed him, steadied him. He dragged in a shuddering breath. "I overheard something."

The story spilled out of him. He focused on Lysander, though he was dimly aware of Felix closing the door and coming closer. When he finished, silence greeted him. As it stretched out, Sascha's breathing sped up, his heart racing. Then Lysander squeezed his hands gently.

"Just breathe, in and out, slowly. Good. You're all right."

Sascha nodded. He was all right. Lysander was holding his hands, looking at him with such concern in his eyes, believing him. "I am."

Lysander let go of one of his hands to smooth Sascha's hair back from his face—he probably looked a fright, but Lysander didn't seem to care. He drew Sascha gently into his arms and kissed him softly, carefully.

When Lysander sat back, Sascha was steadier. "I'm all right," he repeated.

"Good." Lysander glanced over his shoulder, and Sascha remembered Felix was there. "You were right."

Sascha frowned. Felix had been right about what?

Felix shrugged where he sat in the desk chair. "I didn't expect this to happen, though."

"At least we know about it." Lysander turned back to Sascha. "Do you remember where they were?"

"Oh. Yes." Sascha always kept track of where he was in the

secret passages. He worried about getting turned around and lost—even though he could just let himself out and find his way back through the castle, he couldn't stop himself. "That little sitting room, by the smaller dining room. The one you said no one ever uses."

His cheeks heated as he said it, and he truly hoped neither Lysander nor Felix noticed, though of course they would. He couldn't help the reaction—when Lysander had told him that, it had been part of a teasing seductive explanation of what Lysander could do to him in that particular room.

But Lysander didn't mention his blush. He only frowned. "Which would make it perfect for a secret meeting. They're probably long gone now, but I'll have Alan check and then set a watch on that room in case they use it habitually."

"Sascha, did they say what they hid in here? Have you found it yet?" Felix asked when Lysander seemed to drop into thought for a moment.

"They didn't say, and I haven't found anything. I'd just started with the desk..." His reasoning was probably wrong in some way—what did he know about anything like this situation?—but he explained anyway. "I assumed it would be something in a fairly obvious place but perhaps easy for me to overlook, assuming they believe I still use this room regularly. Because they wouldn't want me to discover it—they'd want a maid or perhaps Lysander to find it. If I did and destroyed it or brought it to Lysander, their scheme would be foiled. I suppose if they knew I'm hardly ever here, that might change where they'd hide something... I don't know. I started with the desk because I thought maybe a letter or something slipped in with the papers, though I suppose hiding it in the drawer would defeat the purpose. I have no idea what I'm doing."

And he was rambling on top of it.

"I think you have the right idea," Felix said with no indication he thought Sascha ridiculous. "Everything you said made sense to me. You don't use this room at all anymore?"

"Not really."

"You hardly need your own bedchamber, unless you want it," Lysander commented. "Perhaps we should turn this room into something else for you. A study of your own?"

Sascha frowned, trying to puzzle out why Lysander thought that necessary and how the conversation had gone in this direction but not quite able to manage it. "I hardly need one."

"You will," Felix said. Lysander shot a sharp glance at Felix who looked on with a bland expression. "But that's neither here nor there at the moment."

"All right," Sascha said slowly. He was so confused, and he couldn't figure out if it was because his thoughts were still skittering around chaotically or if the conversation was as strange as it seemed.

"So, they couldn't have known you're hardly here or whatever they left might have been more obvious," Felix said briskly, ignoring Sascha's puzzlement. "Something that would just beg a maid to pick it up."

"Which tells me the servants in this wing haven't been talking," Lysander remarked. "We have to find what they left. We'll lock this room and keep the maids out if we can't, but I want to know what it is."

Sascha did too. "I'll keep looking."

"I can help," Felix offered.

"I wish I could stay and do the same, but I need to tell Alan about this before meeting with the heads of the southern clans." Lysander sounded truly regretful.

"It's all right." Sascha realized he and Lysander were still on the floor, Lysander holding one of his hands and stroking Sascha's hair. It was a shockingly intimate position to be in with someone else present, even if that person was Felix, but Sascha couldn't care. "I don't know what's going on."

Did he sound as plaintive as he thought?

Lysander cupped Sascha's cheek. "I know. I'm sorry. I need to tell you what's happened and I will. Can I ask you to be patient for a little while longer?"

"Yes, Lysander, of course." What other answer could he give?

"Thank you." Lysander leaned close and kissed him softly. "I have to go."

Sascha nodded. Lysander stood and reached down to help Sascha to his feet as well. "You'll be all right?" Lysander waited for Sascha's assent. "Don't leave the apartments. Please?"

"I won't." Leaving was the furthest thing from his mind. Staying here felt safe.

"Thank you. I'll be back as soon as I can." After another careful kiss, Lysander strode from the room.

Once he was gone, Felix went to the door and locked it. "So no one walks in on us and wonders what we're doing."

Sascha nodded.

"Shall we start by finishing with the desk?"

"Probably best." Sascha eyed the mess he'd made with some measure of frustration and embarrassment. "I'm not very good at this."

"You're doing fine." Felix sank gracefully to the floor. "We'll find it, whatever it is."

Sascha nodded and sat as well. "Thank you for your help."

"No thanks necessary." Felix pulled Sascha into a surprising hug. He repeated, "We'll find it. Let's get to work."

They found nothing in the contents of the desk. Nothing in the wardrobe or the books he'd left on the bedside table. There was nothing on the floor or anywhere waiting to be swept up by a maid. Frustrated, Sascha surveyed the small room. The only place they hadn't checked was the bed. He walked over and pulled the coverlet back. Nothing lay on the pristine sheets, so Sascha grabbed for the pillows while Felix shook out the blankets. He searched each before tossing it aside.

And there, under the last pillow, was a folded up piece of paper. Sascha froze.

"Look."

CHAPTER 24

Felix dropped the blanket he held and came over to stand beside Sascha. "Well, that's a ridiculous place to hide something—I mean, if they want anyone to believe you'd hidden it," he continued when Sascha turned to stare at him. "King's Concubine hiding something he didn't want the king to find in his bed? Ridiculous. Do they think we're all stupid?"

Sascha gaped at him, but the disgust in Felix's voice soon had him giggling uncontrollably. "Sorry, sorry. I have no idea why I'm laughing."

"I do. It's all right," Felix said gently and pulled him into another hug, letting him rest against Felix's shoulder until he had himself under control again. "Shall we see what it is?"

"Yes," Sascha said emphatically. He wasn't going to be kept in the dark about this.

Sascha carefully unfolded the intricate folds of the paper, not wanting to tear it as his hands were still shaking slightly. Felix said nothing about his care or the tremor in his hands, just stood patiently at his side and let Sascha do it.

But when the paper was open in his hands, Sascha's heart sank. "It's in code."

"Of course it is." Felix's expression became disgruntled. "Why would they make it easy for us?"

"I suppose it makes sense. They exchange their letters in code, don't they?"

"Yes, but putting this in code doesn't seem well thought out. If Lysander didn't know how to break their code, this could be anything. You could explain it away as—oh, I don't know—that you and Romilly have written in code to each other since you were children as a game."

Sascha frowned. "Under my pillow?"

Felix threw his hands up. "You know what I mean. I suppose they might think Lysander would assume it's from a lover and repudiate you for it."

"They believe I'm incredibly stupid," Sascha muttered.

"But anyone who saw you and him yesterday would know it's delusional to think you have another lover," Felix continued, perhaps mostly to himself. "Besides, they said they wanted to implicate you in the plot."

Sascha began nodding but stopped abruptly. "Wait. What about yesterday?"

"The way Lysander looks at you, the way you look at him." Felix waved a hand to forestall more questions, and Sascha glared at him but bit them back in the face of more pressing matters. "They must assume Lysander has their code."

"They wouldn't keep using it then."

"Not if they're smart. But...how much do they think we know? We should take this to Lysander."

"Let's go."

Once they were out in the hallway, Sascha closed the door behind them and hesitated briefly, wondering if he should lock it. Then something else occurred to him. He reached out and pulled Felix close, linking their arms. "How did they get into the royal apartments?"

Felix's eyes widened slightly. "Let's go now."

Sascha nodded. He wanted to run, but there were always servants around who might see. He kicked himself for running earlier, though he didn't think anyone had seen him. They didn't need anyone speculating. Keeping his arm linked through Felix's, as if they were having a gossip as they walked, he kept to Felix's sedate pace.

"What is it?" Felix's voice was so low only Sascha would hear him, though the hallway appeared empty.

"I made myself obvious before. I'm so stupid. I wasn't thinking, running around like that."

Felix squeezed his arm. "You're not stupid, not at all. And if someone saw, there's nothing to be done now."

Sascha nodded, pulling himself together once more. He'd been falling apart this whole time, making Lysander and Felix reassure him when they had far more important things to do. Sascha was stronger than this, or he should be.

The door to Lysander's study was shut firmly. Any other time, Sascha would've left him undisturbed, as he had in the library earlier, but now he lifted a hand and knocked. Lysander's voice came from behind the door, calling for them to enter. Sascha opened the door and stepped inside, Felix at his heels.

Lysander was behind his desk, but he wasn't alone in the study. Alan was standing near the window, and a woman, dressed in a divided skirt and boots, her braided blonde hair windswept, sat in a chair in front of the desk. She turned as they walked into the room, and Sascha recognized her as Galina.

"Come in, and close the door behind you," Lysander said. "You found it?"

"Yes." Sascha walked to Lysander, rounding the desk to his side.

"It was in the bed of all places," Felix added as Sascha handed Lysander the note. "I don't know what they were thinking."

After Lysander took the note, Sascha began to move away, but Lysander took his hand, lacing their fingers together and keeping him at his side. Felix had a rather knowing expression on his face again that Sascha couldn't decipher but would ask him about the next time they were alone. Meanwhile, Lysander glanced at the paper and shook his head.

"It's in code." Lysander looked up. "Galina?"

She took the paper when he handed it across the desk to her. "If it's the same code, it won't take me long."

"Do we think the information there is real?" Alan asked.

"No, but I need to know what they want us to believe Sascha is involved in," Lysander replied. Sascha stayed quiet beside him. His position should have been awkward, but he only felt good standing there with Lysander's fingers wrapped around his.

"If they even believe you can break their code," Alan said.

"No code is unbreakable. And they must believe we can or an encoded message is too much of a risk."

"Felix said the same when we found it," Sascha ventured to say. "Too easy to explain away."

"Perhaps. Let's see what it says."

"Shall I work on it now, Your Majesty?" Galina asked.

"Yes."

Lysander tried to hold onto his patience as Galina set to work decoding the short note Sascha had found in his bed. They all waited, watching her work, though if she was aware of the weight of their scrutiny, she didn't show it. She just pored over the paper she'd smoothed out in front of her and scribbled in the notebook she pulled from her bag. Lysander was glad now that she'd arrived sooner than expected—their message had found her already on her way—since she was the most proficient of them with this code.

Sascha remained at his side. He'd made no move to let go of Lysander's hand or step away. Lysander wanted to pull Sascha into his lap, but he didn't know how Sascha would feel about such a display of affection in front of others. But Lysander wanted him close—always and particularly after today's revelations and Sascha's upset. Lysander felt sick when he remembered how he'd found Sascha, white-faced and wild eyed. Every instinct Lysander had was screaming at him to keep Sascha safe and protected, to wrap him up and hide him away from all who might wish him harm. Someone had been inside Sascha's bedchamber, inside the royal apartments. The thought of what else they could've done made his blood run cold.

He resisted the urge to pull Sascha closer and began to make plans to tighten security even further around Sascha and the children. If these people could get in to plant a note, they could do the same for another purpose, one far more sinister. He'd thought them safe here of all places, but he'd been wrong.

"Finished, Your Majesty." Galina straightened from where she'd been hunched over her work. "It's rather vague, if I'm translating properly, and I believe I am. It seems to be instructions to continue to watch the king and wait for contact to pass along the information."

"Makes sense," Alan said. "Keeping it vague, I mean. If it was too detailed, it could be verified."

"And they wouldn't want to give anything away," Felix said. He'd been leaning elegantly against the edge of a table, but his gaze was sharp. "The more detail they put in—even if they were making it up—the more chance of inadvertently letting something slip."

Lysander nodded. "True on both counts, and unhelpful for us."

"Unfortunately, yes." Galina tidied up her pen and ink and put the original note and her translation together neatly. "I don't suppose anyone recognizes the handwriting?"

"Are we lucky enough for that?" Lysander remarked as Alan came forward to look over Galina's shoulder—he was the only one in the room who hadn't yet seen the writing himself. Lysander couldn't tell who had written the short, slightly smudged missive just from looking at it, and, apparently, Alan couldn't either as he stepped back to his original place with a shake of his head.

"All right." Lysander glanced at the people standing in his office, some of the very few he trusted. "We have plans to make. This development doesn't change that fact. We already knew they had to have someone here."

After acknowledgments from Felix, Alan, and Galina, Lysander turned to Sascha. "Will you wait for me in the sitting room? Once I'm done here, I'll come to you and explain."

A slight frown creased Sascha's brow, but he nodded. "Of course."

Lysander didn't like the frown. He lifted Sascha's hand to his lips and pressed a kiss to his knuckles, then his palm. "Thank you. I'll be there as soon as I can."

Sascha's expression smoothed out and he squeezed Lysander's hand gently. "I'll wait for you."

He let go of Lysander's hand and walked toward the door, and Lysander tore his gaze from Sascha's slim figure with some difficultly—he loathed the very idea of letting him out of his sight—to turn his attention to Felix who had straightened up.

"It's crowded in here and you'll want to spread out. If you don't need me at the moment, I'll keep Sascha company, if he'd like? Then I'll be nearby when you do."

Sascha appeared bewildered but nodded. "I wouldn't mind the company at all."

With Lysander's agreement, Felix followed Sascha from the room.

Alan came forward and dropped into the other chair across from the desk as soon as the door closed. "Will we need Prince Felix for this?"

Galina turned an icy gaze on Alan but said nothing. Lysander spread a map out on his desk. "We very well might, as you should know. Now, let's turn to the matter at hand. We have plans to make."

Much later, Lysander let himself into the sitting room adjoining his bedchamber. Sascha and Felix were both there, sitting on one of the couches together, glasses of brandy in hand. Felix had been in and out of the study all afternoon as they planned, when Lysander had needed the type of information Felix seemed to have in abundance, but he always returned to the sitting room and Sascha. Lysander was grateful for that— it had relieved some of his worry to know Sascha wasn't alone. Alan had spoken with the guards, and they were doing all they could to make certain no one could gain entrance to the royal apartments who didn't belong there. The problem, of course, was that so many people did. While only he, Sascha, and the children and their nursemaid lived here, so many others were in and out.

He had to keep his family safe, but the only way to do so was to end this plot once and for all.

Sascha and Felix looked cozy in the warm glow of the fire. Two beautiful men, one bright as flame, one luminous as a moonlit night. It was no wonder they drew attention wherever they went. Long ago, there were a few who had thought Lysander should marry Felix, but unions of first cousins had fallen out of favor at least a century ago, and even if they hadn't, Lysander felt brotherly toward Felix, though he was aware of his beauty as much as of his shrewd mind.

Sascha saw Lysander first, and a smile bloomed on his face, though tension still tightened the skin around his eyes. Felix looked up an instant later, the tension less obvious in his face but still present.

"We're done for the day," Lysander told them.

"When will you move? Have you decided?" Felix asked, swiftly adding, "If you can tell us."

"Day after tomorrow. We need some time to get everyone into place as quietly as possible." It went without saying that Lysander wanted them to keep that information to themselves; he wouldn't insult their intelligence by telling them so.

Felix stood. "As much as I'd like to retire to my rooms with a dinner tray, I'll change and eat out, see what I can hear, especially about those you're watching who are still at Wyndward. Send for me if you need me."

Lysander nodded, and Sascha said, standing as well, "Be careful."

"I always am," Felix replied with a reassuring smile. He made his farewells to them both before slipping out of the room.

Which left Lysander alone with Sascha. For a moment, Sascha watched him from the other side of the room and finally asked, "Will you tell me? At least, as much as you can?"

He opened his arms, and Sascha walked into them, letting Lysander hold him and take comfort in knowing he was here and safe, giving comfort to Sascha who still seemed to be practically vibrating with worry. "Yes, I'll tell you."

Sascha tightened his hold on Lysander, in thanks or appreciation, and then stepped away, taking Lysander's hand. He led him to the couch where he'd been sitting with Felix, and they sat together, all without letting go. Lysander took in Sascha's face, his expression so concerned, his eyes clouded with worry, and he hated it, hated that he would add to it by telling Sascha more of what was happening. But he didn't want to keep anything from him, not more than he had to.

"All right." He began with his morning meeting, which felt more like a year ago, and explained everything that had happened. Sascha listened with rapt attention, his eyes going wider as Lysander spoke, his fingers tightening around Lysander's.

"It's my fault, then?" Sascha asked when he finished speaking.

Shock had Lysander freezing for an instant. "Of course not. Why would you think so?"

"Because if those people hadn't recognized me and if everyone wasn't so curious about me, you wouldn't have to rush. You wouldn't have to do this now—you could wait until you're ready." His words tumbled out faster and faster. "It's my fault."

"No, Sascha, no. It isn't your fault at all," Lysander said as he gathered Sascha close. "It's my fault."

Sascha pulled back sharply, his expression fierce, as if he was ready to defend Lysander against himself. "What? No, it isn't."

Lysander held back an affectionate laugh. "It is, darling. I brought you here and hoped no one would question who you are." He could've said many things about why he'd done it, but that didn't matter now. "Maybe they would've been fooled if I'd let you fade into the background, but I always want you at my side. People were curious because they could see it."

Sascha's forehead creased with a frown. "See what?"

He brushed Sascha's hair back. "How important you are to me. And because you're important to me, they're looking at you harder, speculating about you. The conspirators would've found out about you after yesterday soon enough, even if one of them hadn't realized immediately. But that isn't your fault. It's mine, for not thinking and not hiding my feelings for you,"

Sascha watched him with wide eyes. He said nothing.

"I didn't want to," Lysander finally continued. "I hadn't thought about it, but as much as I wasn't ready to shout from the rooftops, I also didn't want to hide you or your importance to me. I should've just gone up to the highest tower and shouted for all to hear."

Sascha let out a little laugh, though he seemed bemused at Lysander's words. "That would've been something to see."

"Would you like me to do it?"

Sascha's laugh burbled out again, brighter this time. "No, I don't. I don't need you to do that."

He grinned. "Maybe I need to."

Sascha shook his head, though he still smiled. "You don't."

"You're right. I only need you to know how I feel." He lifted a hand to cup Sascha's cheek and smiled gently when he leaned into it. "I need you to know that I want you with me always. That I love you."

Sascha's lips parted on a soft exhalation. "Oh. Lysander... I love you too."

His heart swelled hearing the words—he'd known, but hearing Sascha say the words was something else entirely. Something more. He drew Sascha close again and kissed him, carefully, reverently. Sascha melted into him, wrapped himself around him, and Lysander wanted nothing more than to carry him off to bed. No, there was one thing he suddenly wanted more.

When he ended the kiss, Sascha was smiling as he opened his eyes. Lysander loved that smile, loved those eyes.

"Marry me."

Sascha's eyes went wide. "What?"

Lysander couldn't hold in a low chuckle this time. "Marry me, Sascha."

"But..." He still appeared completely flummoxed, though fetchingly so, something Lysander probably wouldn't tell him.

"I want to marry you. I want you beside me, as my love and my consort, as a parent to my children. I want to sleep and wake with you for the rest of my life. Do you want those things too?"

"I... Yes, of course." Sascha laughed as Lysander yanked him close and stood, Sascha's toes not quite touching the ground. "But, wait! Are you certain? Really?"

"I am." He spun Sascha around just for the joy of hearing his laughter, then kissed his smiling lips. "Why wouldn't I be serious?"

Sascha was still smiling, his eyes still sparkling, but he shook his head. "Because I'm...no one special. No one who should be marrying a king."

"Sascha..." He let out a long breath. "You are everything. Absolutely everything to me."

Sascha's eyes lit with wonder, but he still shook his head, slowly, as if in disbelief. Lysander didn't want to see anything except happiness, so he caught Sascha's gaze and held it, letting him see how serious he was. "Absolutely everything."

Now there was joy and wonder drowning out the disbelief, the confusion that had so puzzled Lysander, but he only had an instant to take note of the change before Sascha surged forward and claimed his lips in a hard kiss.

CHAPTER 25

Sascha paced. The sitting room, normally so snug and cozy, felt confined and confining. He'd been out of the royal apartments only once since they'd discovered someone had tried to implicate him in the plot against Lysander. They'd eaten last night with the court in an effort to appear as if everything was normal. He hoped they'd managed it, because nothing was normal. Sascha had felt horribly exposed. Hunted. Only Lysander's steady presence at his side— and the weight of the ring on his finger, so new and so delightful—kept him somewhat calm. He'd wanted to study everyone in the room, trying to figure out who it was, but he kept his gaze steady, focusing on eating or on Lysander, on Thalia's conversation from Lysander's other side. Sascha would not risk ruining Lysander's plans.

Which was the other reason he paced. Lysander was here in the castle—when he'd left their bed before dawn, he'd promised to come to Sascha first if he had to leave to join any of the squadrons. Despite the assurance, Sascha hadn't been able to sleep after he'd let Lysander go. He worried his ring—intricately worked gold with a central sapphire flanked by diamonds that Lysander had placed on his finger yesterday to seal the betrothal they'd announce when this was all over and they were safe. He stopped and stared out of the window, barely seeing the landscape before him.

Let this all be over soon. He said it silently, then repeated it in a whisper, a wish given to the wind in a childish ritual.

Sascha knew little of Lysander's plans, only that Alan's handpicked people were riding and flying the length and breadth of Ivria, putting themselves into position for a well-timed strike against the conspirators. Would he be less worried if he knew more details? Probably not. He wouldn't stop worrying until it was all over. Until the plot was exposed and its masterminds apprehended. Then they would be safe.

And Sascha would be planning a wedding. His wedding to the king of Ivria. To Lysander.

He looked down at the betrothal ring. A smile curved his lips despite his fears. It hadn't been made for him but had come to Lysander from his grandfather. Sascha thought perhaps that history made it more special, and it fit his finger as if it had been crafted just for him. He'd worn the earrings Lysander had given him when they'd gone to dinner the night before as well, knowing how much Lysander liked to see them on him. He was wearing them again now, for no reason except the sense of comfort they gave him.

Sascha transferred his attention to the view outside the window again. He wouldn't have been able to tell something so important was happening from the tranquil, everyday scene below. It created such an odd dissonance in him. Outside their little bubble, the world continued apace as if everything was normal. But today wasn't normal.

And he was making himself crazy pacing around this room thinking about it.

He wouldn't be able to concentrate on much, and his

options were limited, as he'd been asked to stay in the apartments, but he could visit with the children. They would distract him, just by being themselves, and then perhaps later, Felix could visit. Even if Felix couldn't take his mind off his worries, they could worry together. Sascha dashed off a quick note asking if Felix was free to join him for lunch and left the sitting room. He asked one of the guards to send a messenger to Felix with it, then turned his steps toward the nursery.

He'd just gone around a corner—out of sight of the door guards but not yet in view of the guard stationed outside the nursery—when he was grabbed. He froze for an instant, then, as arms banded around him, he began to flail and drew in breath to scream. A hand clamped over his mouth, muffling the noise, and he was dragged backward and through a doorway he'd never seen before but dimly realized was the entrance to another secret passage. He kicked out and struggled, trying to grab onto anything to stop them taking him. Nothing he did made a difference and he couldn't get a hand down to his pocket for the knife Felix had given him. He wouldn't stop though; maybe if he maybe enough fuss, someone would hear.

"Shut him up," a voice whispered harshly. The person behind him, holding him, Sascha thought. "If he keeps on, we'll be caught."

"I wasn't expecting him to just walk up, was I?" Another whispering voice. "Here. Watch out."

Sascha was roughly turned and had a glimpse of a face that seemed familiar before the woman was blowing a powder into his face. He'd inhaled it before he even realized, and immediately dizziness swept through him. His movements became uncoordinated, his limbs heavy, until he couldn't get them to move at all. Darkness swam at the edges of his vision, and he fought to keep it at bay, to move, to scream, to do anything. But it was a losing battle. They were in the passage now, cut off from the corridor and the guards. Someone lifted him, not gently. There were more whispered words, but he couldn't make sense of them, everything garbled and echoing. They were moving swiftly through the dim light when blackness took him.

LYSANDER RETURNED to the royal apartments with the hope of sharing a quiet meal with Sascha before he had to go back to appearing to carry on as if nothing was wrong while also impatiently awaiting news of those he'd sent out. When he arrived, he found Felix in the sitting room but no Sascha. Felix lounged in his elegant, graceful way, though tension was evident in his frame. Was he here hoping to hear news?

"Sascha invited me to join him for lunch," Felix said, explaining his presence without being asked.

Lysander tamped down his disappointment. Sascha had every right to make his own lunch plans, especially when he didn't know Lysander's, and though Lysander could have sent Felix away, he wouldn't do that to Sascha. "Ah, of course. Where is Sascha?"

He wouldn't interrupt their lunch, but he wanted to see Sascha.

"I don't know." Felix's forehead furrowed as he frowned slightly. "He hasn't come in. I thought perhaps he was with you and lost track of time."

"I haven't seen him, and losing track of time isn't like him."

Felix's frown deepened. "No, it isn't."

"Go ask the guards if they've seen him while I look."

Felix nodded and hurried from the room. Lysander was already striding to the door leading to the adjoining bedchamber. The room was empty and exactly how they had left it that morning—surely Sascha would've heard them and come out if he'd been in this room anyway. Nevertheless, Lysander checked the dressing and bathing rooms as well. He returned to the sitting room and glanced around for any hint as to where Sascha had gone and what had delayed his return. He wouldn't have left the apartment. Perhaps he'd gone to see the children?

Felix was returning as Lysander headed for the door. He hopped aside neatly and followed Lysander. "They haven't seen him since he gave them a note for me a couple of hours ago. You and I are the only people to have come in."

He nodded but didn't stop moving. "I'm going to check the nursery."

"Oh, of course. He's probably with the children." A measure of relief came into Felix's voice.

Sascha spent a lot of time with the children—the nursery was a perfectly logical place for him to be, and perhaps the one place he might have lost track of time. But Lysander wouldn't be able to quell this worry until he saw Sascha.

But Sascha wasn't in the nursery, and the guard at the door hadn't seen him at all that morning. Lysander's worry deepened. Sascha could have left through the passages but Lysander trusted that he wouldn't. He knew how dangerous the situation could be. Sascha had to be somewhere in these rooms because Lysander didn't want to imagine the alternative. They'd just not found him yet—and Sascha somehow hadn't realized they were searching.

He turned a corner to find Felix crouching, one hand braced against a tapestry hanging on the wall, the other plucking at something at the join of wall and floor. Lysander hadn't even realized he wasn't still following. Whatever Felix had been pulling at came free, and he rose in a fluid movement. He looked up and his gaze, bleak and fearful, landed on Lysander.

He held up what he'd found. "Isn't this Sascha's?"

The glitter of sapphires and diamonds flashed on the earring dangling from Felix's fingers.

"Yes, it is," he said slowly and gently took the earring from Felix. "Where exactly did you find it?"

"Here." He bent again and pointed. "It was wedged in between those two stones. I don't know how it could have even happened."

Felix only appeared puzzled, but alarm raced through Lysander. "It's supposed to be sealed off."

"What is? Wait, do you mean—"

Lysander nodded and nudged him aside. The passage had been created as an escape route for the royal family when the castle was first built and the situation in the world far less stable. "I didn't like how close it was to the nursery when Xanthe was born. I had it sealed up." While he spoke, he pushed the tapestry out of his way—Felix caught and held it for him— and searched for the hidden latch. It took him a moment, as he hadn't used it for years, but he found it, and the section of wall swung silently inward. Lysander cursed viciously.

He only had to take a single step inside before he found a scrap of lace caught on a bracket on the wall. Sascha had a jacket trimmed in this lace. Lysander liked it on him. He plucked the lace from the bit of metal it had snagged on. The earring wedged beneath the door, the torn lace. Sascha hadn't known this passage existed.

"They've taken Sascha."

LYSANDER HAD WANTED to charge off down the passage immediately, but Felix held him back. And though Lysander had wanted to rage at him for it, he'd been right. Lysander couldn't run off after Sascha's abductors, as much as he wanted to. He'd called for his guards and sent them into the passage and the tunnel it led to. The passage wound its way through the castle, a narrow corridor punctuated at various points by twisting stairs that opened into a tunnel running underground to the edge of the lake. He'd ordered both entrances blocked and magic used to ensure they stayed that way, but obviously they had been reopened at some point. Perhaps Sascha wouldn't have been snatched from a place he should've been safe if Lysander had ordered the whole tunnel filled in. At the time, he hadn't wanted to draw attention to its existence, but someone had learned of it anyway.

He would find out who.

Lysander hoped the guards would reach Sascha before they left the tunnel, but he had to assume they wouldn't and plan from there. He paced his private study like a caged beast. He wanted out, wanted to go after Sascha. He just needed to know where to go and who to rip limb from limb for this.

Felix strode into the room. "It doesn't appear as if anything of Sascha's was disturbed in his bedchamber. Everything is as it was when he and I were searching the room."

Lysander leaned back against his desk. "So they didn't take anything to make it look as if he left on his own. Were they not able to? Was it an oversight?"

"Or are they done trying to cast blame on him?" Felix added.

Alan arrived before Lysander could even attempt to speculate. His gaze swept over Felix before coming to rest on Lysander. "What's happened?"

Lysander steeled himself to say it again. "Sascha had been abducted."

Shock washed over Alan's features for an instant before he banished it. "Tell me."

Lysander told him everything he knew, which was precious

little. When he finished, Alan cursed. "I should ask if you're certain he didn't leave on his own."

Lysander forced himself not to bristle at Alan's words.

"He wouldn't have left that earring behind," Felix said tartly. "Even if we ignore how much they mean to him, it would be utterly ridiculous to leave something so valuable when you'll need funds. Silly not to take anything with you either if you were going to run."

Alan was staring at Felix with some amount of shock and reproof.

"Quite," Lysander said. "And silly of them not to make it appear as if he'd done just that. What are they expecting me to do?"

Thinking about that felt wrong. Everything in him was focused on Sascha, on fear and worry and getting him back. But he had to consider the other as well, had to think of possibilities and implications and strategy. He was king and had to act like it, even though Sascha was the man he loved, even though all he wanted to do was tear the people who'd taken him apart and then set whatever remained on fire. If they harmed a hair on Sascha's head, he would.

"That probably depends on whether they think you found the note they planted," Alan replied. "Or if they assume you'll find it once Sascha is discovered missing."

"Either way, they have to know I'll search for him."

"I suppose it's a matter of why you're searching, then," Felix mused slowly. "To rescue a beloved concubine or retrieve a suspected traitor."

And Sascha's abductors had no idea he was actually Lysander's betrothed. Maybe it was better they didn't—would knowledge of their true relationship put Sascha in more danger?

"Either way, it wouldn't go well for them once I found

Sascha—I'd either punish the kidnappers of my beloved concubine or the conspirators found with the suspected traitor. It doesn't make sense, and it won't until we know who's taken him." Well, there was one way the plan made sense—if they were just going to kill Sascha to assure he was either never found or found dead with nothing to link his death to anyone. Lysander refused to entertain the possibility they wouldn't find Sascha alive. Why take him just to kill him? Still, the fear burrowed into him. "Let's focus on finding them. On getting him back."

Felix nodded resolutely, but Alan looked as if he might argue. A knock on the study door prevented him from speaking.

"Enter," Lysander called out.

The door opened to reveal one of the guards he'd sent after Sascha. The man bowed, but Lysander was focused only on what he held. It was a shoe—a whimsical thing embroidered in silvery gray and laced with ribbon...and he'd last seen it on Sascha's foot. The cold fear rose up to choke him, and he ruthlessly forced it down.

"What have you found, Guardsman?" His voice was steady; he ignored Felix's close attention.

"The Honorable Sascha and his abductors were already gone when we reached the end of the tunnel. We found this in the grass not far from the tunnel's exit." He handed the shoe to Lysander.

"Sascha's," he said in confirmation, wrapping his fingers around the delicate shoe. "Anything else?"

"We did a search of the area, and found a woman whom we believe saw them."

"What did she see? Where is she?" Alan snapped out before Lysander could.

The guard showed no reaction to Alan's tone. "She told us she saw two people walking along the shore where a third person waited. One of the pair was carrying a person with long red hair. They spoke for a few moments. Then the one waiting and one of the pair transformed into dragons. One of the dragons took Honorable Sascha, and they flew away—southeast, it appeared. The third person began walking back toward the castle. She described the three people as best she could. We brought her back with us. She's waiting to answer your questions."

"Good," Lysander said, eager to make any progress toward finding Sascha and bringing him home safe. "Thank you, Guardsman."

After the man had bowed and left, Lysander turned and forced himself to set Sascha's shoe on the desk—it felt like leaving a link to him behind, but he couldn't very well carry a shoe around the castle with him. He had the earring stowed safely in his pocket, though, and he'd return it to Sascha soon.

"Let me go talk to her," Alan said as soon as the door closed.

"You can come with me, but I'll to speak with her myself."

"Yes, Your Majesty." Alan might have decided not to argue, but he also wasn't in agreement with Lysander's decision. Lysander didn't much care—he wasn't going to intimidate this woman who was their only witness, their only link to who had taken Sascha. He needed to hear what she said himself, not filtered through even Alan's perspective.

"Let's go." Lysander began striding for the door when Felix fell into step beside him and took his arm. Lysander didn't stop —he didn't have the time—but he turned a look on Felix.

Felix barely reacted to it, stern though it was. "I'm coming with you, and I'm walking on your arm to try to make things look just a bit more normal. If you go striding around like a thundercloud, people are going to wonder what's going on, and I assume you don't want speculation at this point."

"That's something." Lysander glanced at Alan who was

following. "Do you think they know of our plans and are trying to distract us? Or was the timing a coincidence?"

"I hope it was a coincidence. Otherwise, everything is about to fall apart."

Lysander could only agree.

Though he felt like everything was falling apart already.

THE WOMAN STOOD and dropped into a curtsy as soon as Lysander walked through the door, Felix still on his arm. Whether it had made him look less like he was about to explode in fury during their walk through the castle, Lysander didn't know, but his cousin's—brother, really in all the important ways—hand on his arm was grounding. The woman looked to be in her early forties, dressed in a neat blue gown and shawl, perhaps a shopkeeper by her appearance.

"Your Majesty."

He gestured for her to return to her chair and took a seat across from her. "Mistress, my guards say you witnessed what happened down by the lake. I need you to tell me what you saw."

"Of course, Your Majesty. I was walking out to visit my mother to take her a few things," she began. The story that followed was the same as the guard had told them in the study.

"The people you saw—can you describe them for us?" he asked when she finished.

"I can try, Your Majesty. I stopped at the edge of the trees when I saw them, so I wasn't too close. It seemed so odd, with the one person being carried like that. And they weren't all together long. The one waiting at the edge of the lake was tall and broad shouldered with very short dark hair. Pale skin and very nice clothes—good materials and decoration. It seemed strange for someone dressed so nicely to just be standing around there like that. He transformed into a large amber drag-on." She continued when Lysander gave her an encouraging nod. "The other two, coming from the direction of the castle. One had a long blond braid and tanned skin and was wearing dark clothes. A jacket and a split skirt with boots. I'm a seam-stress, so I notice clothing."

"Of course." Lysander found a smile for her. "Please go on."

"Yes, Your Majesty. The woman changed into a pale blue dragon. Almost silvery in the light. The last—he was the one carrying the other person. He wasn't as tall as the other man, but not short either. A bit stocky. He had silver hair, very bright and thick, and collar-length, and I thought his clothing looked like the castle's livery. I could be wrong, but..."

"But you notice clothing." His smile was gentle, and she gave him one in return. "Did you see anything else?"

"Not really, Your Majesty. It happened quickly. But, the person he was carrying... I only got a glimpse of hair, and that red is very distinctive. The Honorable Sascha came into our shop a few times, and it seemed the same." She didn't ask, but her statements were questions in themselves.

"You see why it was so important for me to talk to you," he said, realizing it was worthless to deny it. "I ask that you not tell anyone what you saw, for safety's sake."

Her eyes were huge. "Of course, Your Majesty. I hope he's all right. He was very kind to us."

Once a guard had escorted her from the room, Lysander turned to Alan and Felix. "Thoughts?"

"I think she's lucky they didn't see her," Alan said. "I can't imagine she would've faired well caught witnessing the abduc-tion of the King's Concubine."

Lysander didn't think so either.

"The man with the silver hair—so bright and thick," Felix

broke in. "Am I the only one who thinks that sounds like the head steward?"

"No, you're not." Lysander had immediately thought so too.

"Did anyone else wonder why he would be so stupid as to do this in royal livery? His appearance would make him distinctive," Alan said.

Privately, Lysander thought the same. Perhaps he'd assumed they wouldn't be seen. They'd gone most of the way in the tunnel, and the exit wasn't out in the open. Or perhaps it was just arrogance. Whatever the reason, Lysander wasn't going to be ungrateful for his own good fortune. "Find him, and we can ask. After we ask where they've taken Sascha."

"Yes, Your Majesty." Alan stalked from the room immediately to carry out Lysander's orders.

"You're just going to ask politely?" Felix leaned back against a table.

"I'm going to ask politely to start. If he doesn't answer, we'll move on to less polite ways of asking."

Felix nodded and settled in, obviously unconcerned with— maybe even approving of— whatever violence might follow. Lysander wasn't going to chase him away. Though the difference in their ages was large enough he couldn't exactly say they'd grown up together, it was as near as anything. He trusted Felix implicitly, both to be a part of this and to handle whatever happened.

"What do you know about the steward?" Lysander asked. The man had been employed at the castle Lysander's entire life and given his current position during his father's reign. Lysander knew the man's work in keeping the castle running properly was impeccable; he'd never heard of any trouble from him, which meant nothing in this context, but he'd had few dealings with him himself.

"I try not to come in contact with him often. Thalia has to

deal with him, and she finds him extremely tedious." Felix shrugged elegantly at Lysander's look but continued without further prompting, telling him of the steward's peculiarities in work, and then saying, "Everyone knows the servants know everything—or they should be aware of it if they're going to survive for any length of time in a noble house. He always seems to be deliberately watchful. As if he wants to gather as many secrets, as much knowledge, as possible for his own purposes, and his purposes are to help himself. Or, I suppose, this plot he's a part of. I'm kicking myself for not paying more attention now, but his behavior seemed normal, if tedious."

"Not your fault." He hadn't seen any of this coming, and he'd blame himself for that for a very long time, but he didn't have time now for regret or recriminations, not with conspirators to round up and Sascha to find. "We go on from here."

Felix watched him, then nodded resolutely. "All right. What next?"

"Nothing until we talk to the steward." He contemplated their surroundings for a moment. "I think that conversation needs a different setting, though."

A sharp grin flashed across Felix's face. "Somewhere more appropriately intimidating?"

"Just what I was thinking." Whether it would intimidate a man who had worked in the castle on the periphery of the royal clan for decades remained to be seen.

Lysander offered his arm to Felix this time, and he took it was another anticipatory grin. They would get the information they needed one way or another—Felix was with him in that—and they would bring Sascha home. They swept from the room, leaving a message for Alan about where to find them, and went off to set the scene.

CHAPTER 26

When Alan and two of his guards brought the steward to Lysander, he was ensconced in a receiving room that had long been known as the small throne room. He'd briefly considered the echoing chamber that was the actual throne room but discarded it as ridiculous. This room, with its ornate throne and hangings, its historic art and heavy velvet curtains, was just enough. Lysander had changed his jacket into something slightly more formal—what he'd wear for an audience day instead of one working in his office—and put on a circlet. He sat on the throne with Felix standing to his left, somehow both elegant and imposing—he'd already been dressed as the adornment to the court he'd made himself into.

Lysander studied the steward as he was marched into the room. The man seemed uneasy but not overly so—a good actor? Perhaps he should've called for him in a way less likely to cause suspicion. He couldn't remember the last time he'd met with the man, but they could've had Thalia send for him... Set up a real ambush. Too late now.

The steward bowed low when he reached the proper

distance from the throne and did not look at Alan, hovering a few steps behind him, or the two guards near the door. He did flick a glance at Felix.

"Steward."

"Your Majesty, you had need of me?" he asked as he straightened.

"I have need of answers from you."

"Answers, Your Majesty?" The steward's voice was gently puzzled and politely deferential. Lysander couldn't imagine the man didn't know why he'd been brought here, but he wasn't surprised he'd chosen this tack. If you were committing treason, surely it would be the first thing you thought of when hauled before the king by royal guards?

"Yes, answers." He leaned forward slightly in his seat. "I would like to know where Honorable Sascha is."

"I apologize, Your Majesty, but I wouldn't know. Doesn't the King's Concubine spend much of his time in the royal apartments?" The steward's puzzled expression remained, but there was something else in his eyes.

"I know quite well where Sascha spends his time. I also know he was abducted from the royal apartments this morning. What you don't seem to know is that *you were seen*. You were seen carrying Sascha out of the castle and giving him to someone who flew him away. I could ask why you did it, but I have some idea already and reasons can wait. I need you to tell me where they took him. Now."

"Your Majesty, I don't know what you mean," the steward protested, his gaze now flicking to Felix and Alan.

"You do, and I'm going to give you one more chance to tell me what I need to know." Lysander kept his voice even but held up a hand when the steward opened his mouth. "One more chance for this to be easy. Then, well, you'll give me the information I seek, but this will go significantly worse for you." He glanced at Felix. "Perhaps we should've stayed downstairs. Do you think blood will stain these floors?"

Felix shrugged—elegant, unconcerned, playing his part beautifully, though Lysander hadn't explained exactly what he needed. Then again, he might not be acting. "A shame to make more work for the staff, but I'm certain they could remove any stains. There's probably some magic that would do it. I'd say we could ask the steward—he does seem to know so much about everything that goes on in the castle—but he has other matters to concern himself with at the moment."

The steward flinched slightly at Felix's smooth words and the implications of them.

"I suppose the state of the floor is the least of our concerns. Certainly the least of his," Lysander remarked and returned his attention to the steward. "I'm rapidly losing patience. I'm asking you one last time. Where is Sascha?"

"Your Majesty, I-I don't understand," he stuttered. But they were right about him; Lysander could see it, could see the knowledge in his eyes. Could see him searching for a way out.

"You do. Denying it will do you no good." Lysander gestured at Alan, who stepped up to the steward, grabbed him, and flung him to the floor.

The man went down with a startled cry and immediately began trying to scuttle away from Alan who loomed over him. If he thought to run, he wouldn't get far.

"You will tell His Majesty what he wants to know." Alan reached for the steward when he just shook his head.

It didn't take long after that. The steward finally cried out that they'd forced him to aid in the abduction.

Lysander could feel Felix's disbelief and disgust. "They did, did they? Then you should have no problem telling us all about 'them' and how they forced you to kidnap the royal concubine."

The man only stared up at him from the floor.

Felix made a little scoffing sound after a moment. "You should really have your lies planned in advance, or did you never think you could be caught? That was poor planning too."

The anger that flashed in the steward's eyes at Felix's comments was interesting.

"I was forced into this. I would never wish harm on the king or his concubine," the steward exclaimed indignantly. "You must believe me, Your Majesty."

"I don't have to do any such thing. I don't have to do anything at all. What I am going to do is have you hauled down to the dungeon where you will await sentencing for treason."

Alarm flooded the steward's face. It didn't look false—he truly hadn't believed he could be caught. Lysander gestured again, and the two guards came forward to haul him to his feet. He struggled as he was pulled up. "Wait, wait! They really did force me into it! I don't know who they were, but they said they were taking the royal concubine back to his parents. That's all I know, truly!"

"You weren't a part of their plot. They forced you to help them. But they also told you their plan." Lysander shook his head. "That doesn't sound very smart of them, whoever they are."

The man's eyes widened fractionally. "I overheard them talking—they didn't realize!"

"Take him. Try not be noticed. Knock him out if you have to," Lysander ordered, giving no indication he'd heard that last bit of invention or seen the steward's increased struggles. "I want this kept quiet."

"Yes, Your Majesty," the guards replied.

The two guards dragged the man out, and Alan closed the door firmly behind them before turning to face Lysander. "Do you believe they're taking him back to his parents?"

Lysander rubbed a hand over his face, resisting the urge to

slump in his seat. "I don't know. It's entirely possible he was lying—he was obviously lying about being forced into this."

"Yes, but he could also be telling the truth about their destination," Felix mused. "The man clearly has problems thinking quickly—utterly ridiculous that he didn't have plans for what to do and say if he was suspected—and he might not have been able to come up with anything else. All he could think to do was deny the accusations and try to save himself when he couldn't."

Alan frowned at him. "And when we go there? He'd be exposing his co-conspirators."

Felix lifted his hands and let them fall. "Maybe, or maybe they have some contingency plan in place. Or maybe he doesn't care if Sascha's parents are caught. I've never met Sascha's parents, so I couldn't hazard a guess as to what they would do in that situation. Maybe he's just assuming we won't believe him."

"Too many maybes, but it's all we have at the moment. We need to check. If he's there, we'll bring Sascha home. If he isn't..." Lysander let out a long breath. "Alan, I need you to remain here and coordinate the operation we already have in place. I'm not losing my chance because of this. Everything goes forward as planned."

"You're not thinking of going after Sascha yourself?" Alan barked. "You can't, and you certainly can't go alone."

"I don't plan to go alone. I'll take my guards and meet up with the group already in place there."

"Let them retrieve Sascha as well. We'll send a message with the new orders," Alan said.

"No," Lysander replied firmly, his tone allowing no disagreement. "I'm going. I'll take Galina. Her magic may come in handy."

"I'll go with you as well." Felix spoke quietly but in an unwavering tone.

Alan crossed his arms over his chest. "You aren't a fighter."

"No, but I can set things on fire just as well as you can." Felix's gaze was hard and fierce as he stared down at Alan. He flicked his fingers and formed a small flame that he let dance along his knuckles.

"Be that as it may, two members of the royal family flying into danger is even worse," Alan thundered.

"Felix can come." Lysander shook his head when Alan began to protest. "Thalia will stay here at Wyndward. She knows the details of today's plan and has my authority. Brief your people. We're leaving within the hour."

He was going to get Sascha back.

SASCHA WOKE SLOWLY. His head throbbed and his mouth was dry and really his whole body ached. A shiver wracked him and even that hurt. He was cold and...on the ground? Damp, chill stone pressed into his cheek. What had happened?

Then it all flooded back—the people grabbing him, drugging him. He almost cried out at the realization but swallowed it back. He forced himself to remain quiet, to remain still, then forced himself to loosen tense muscles to appear as if he hadn't woken up. Was someone here with him? He couldn't tell, couldn't hear anything over the frantic pounding of his own heart. Couldn't think over the pain in his head and his rising panic.

He could do something about the pain. Once his head stopped hurting, he could figure out what to do next. It took him a long time to focus, but he managed eventually and directed his meager healing talent to soothe his tender head. Finally, finally, the pain receded, and Sascha let the magic go. But with the easing of pain came another wave of fear. It coursed through him, cold and sickening. And he had to breathe past that too because he had to think, to plan, if he was going to...what? What could he possibly do?

No. Sascha would not panic, would not allow himself to fall apart.

What did he know? Very little. He could surmise that whoever had abducted him was connected to the plot against Lysander. Maybe one or both of the people he'd overheard talking about him. It seemed ludicrous that there could be another, completely unconnected plot against Lysander or him —loving the king of Ivria was complicated and potentially dangerous, but that would be beyond belief.

Slowly, carefully, he cracked his eyes open just a bit, just enough to see something of where he was. The room—he assumed, as it didn't feel like outdoors despite the chill—was dark, but not pitch black. Light filtered in from somewhere... Somewhere above? Weak sunlight? Not the same quality as flame or magically created light, anyway. There was no one in front of him, so he took the chance and opened his eyes wider. No one anywhere he could see, and when he closed his eyes again and held his breath, no one he could hear either. He was alone. He might be able to chance moving.

Sascha lay on his side, head on the ground, pebbles digging into his cheek, one arm twisted beneath him. Had they dumped him here and left him as he fell? Such an action shouldn't be surprising, as he'd been kidnapped. The reminder, the word itself, had panic rising again, but he ruthlessly forced it back. He couldn't allow it, not if he wanted to get through this, and he did. He would. He would do all he could to keep himself alive at the very least, escape if he could. Lysander would find him, would come for him—Sascha knew that with every breath in his body. He would do all he could to help himself in the meantime.

Whether he could actually rescue himself was doubtful, but he refused to do nothing.

Cautiously, taking pains to be as quiet as he could, he pushed himself up to sit. The arm that had been twisted under him flared into painful tingling, and he bit his lip hard to keep from making a sound. But it seemed no one had heard him move—or no one cared. If he was locked in, they might not care what he did in here. Rubbing at his arm, he studied his surroundings. As his eyes adjusted to the gloom, the rough stone walls of the little room came into focus. High above him was a small, grimy window, the source of the meager light. He didn't want to think about what night would be like.

So, he should find a way out of here before then.

Sascha hauled himself to his feet, bruises making themselves known as he moved. Another glance around gave him no additional information, but something nagged at him, a sense of...familiarity? Why would this place be familiar?

The door appeared sturdy despite the air of abandonment in this place, but he checked it all the same. Throwing himself against it seemed unlikely to cause anything but injury and potentially alerting his captors he was awake. So he moved on. He trailed his fingers over the walls and crouched to explore the floor, working his way around the room as methodically as he could. In the far corner, his searching fingers encountered something small. He stood and held it up to the light. A silver hair pin, tarnished almost black by time and exposure to the elements.

His hair pin.

He'd lost it years ago—had he been ten? eleven?—and between the loss and coming home with dirty clothes, he'd been punished severely. His sister Inna had been along on that adventure with one of their older brothers instigating it—Timur hadn't been punished, though. Childhood resentments were not worth dwelling on at the moment. The important part was what the hair pin told him. He'd lost it exploring an old, crumbling building on his family's property. His brother had said it was the original house on the land. Whether Timur's assertion was true, Sascha had no idea, but the building had been little more than a ruin with no roof and most of the walls collapsing or pulled down for building materials. The cellar rooms had been more intact, and they'd run through them, exploring and hiding from each other. Now he was being held prisoner in one. They'd brought him home.

No, not home, not anymore.

Faint voices had Sascha freezing in place. Had someone heard him? The voices weren't coming through the door, but from above. He looked up at the dirty window with its thick, bubbled glass; it seemed to be cracked in places, a chunk in the corner missing. The urge to cry out for help was strong, but he wasn't stupid—anyone out there was likely well aware he was down here. Still, he listened, hope burning inside him.

"—don't know why you brought him here." The voice belonged to Sascha's father, and his stomach plummeted, though he wasn't surprised. "What do you want us to do with him?"

"You think we would give him back to you after you let him slip out of Lord Jannik's grasp?" Sascha recognized the voice from the dim memories of his abduction, and he shivered. "You would only find a way to make something off of him again, even if he has been the king's whore all this time. Why would we reward you?"

"We have no idea how he got away from Lord Jannik and ended up with the king of all people." Sascha's mother this time. He shouldn't feel anything at his parents' actions anymore, but there was still a dull throb of pain at their words.

"We assumed he was as pleasing to his lordship as we thought he would be."

"You were furthering your own ends, and you don't get to do that now when his presence with the king might have put everything in jeopardy," his abductor snapped.

"He doesn't know anything. He didn't suspect anything when we sent him to Lord Jannik," Father protested. "Sascha is useless for anything except warming some man's bed."

Anger, bright and hot, burned the hurt away.

"What will you do with him, then?" Mother asked, sounding almost bored.

"We had reasons for taking him from the king when we did, but the rest isn't as settled. He'll have to die of course—we can't have him speaking about this—but whether we kill him now or let some higher placed men in our organization take their pleasure of him first is yet to be determined." A pause. "You did say that was all he was good for."

Sascha shuddered, fear and revulsion coursing through him at the coldly spoken words.

"But—"

Sascha's kidnapper interrupted his father. "What? Are you going to beg for his life?"

"We understand he has to die."

"Oh, were you hoping for some compensation? You had that when you sold him to Lord Jannik. Don't think you deserve more. You'll be lucky not to share his fate. Just hope no harm comes to our cause from this." There was a brief pause—to wait for some sort of reaction from his parents? "He stays down there for the time being. I'll be close by and Lev will return shortly. Your son should remain unconscious for a while longer. We would be displeased if you tried to remove him."

"Why would we? We're loyal to the cause." Father's words

were the last Sascha heard, as footsteps crunching over the forest floor carried them away.

When it was quiet again, Sascha slumped against the wall. He'd known his parents were part of it, known they'd sold him to Jannik for their own gain, but this... They didn't care if he died? He wanted to believe they were lying and would come for him as soon as they had an opportunity, but they wouldn't. Because he also knew his parents and how they sounded when they were absolutely serious. They didn't care about him.

Lysander was coming, though. Lysander loved him, was going to marry him. He and the children—and Felix and Romilly and Uncle Florestan and Thalia—were Sascha's family. His parents didn't matter. Sascha wouldn't let them.

For now, he had to stay alive. If he thought too hard about their plans for him, he'd end up curled up in a corner shaking. So he wouldn't. He had to figure out what to do. If he could escape, he could hide in the woods until rescue came. Sascha didn't delude himself into thinking he could make it far enough on foot to actually get to safety—especially since one of his shoes was missing and the other was hardly sturdy enough for rough terrain—but concealing himself he could potentially manage; he'd had hiding places in this forest from the time he was a child.

"All right," he whispered to himself and took a deep breath. Then he began to examine the room again. He found nothing else, but he did realize his abductors hadn't taken his knife from him. Had they searched him? Or had they thought him so useless they hadn't even bothered? Their oversight left him with a weapon.

The door must have been barred from the outside. There would be no picking a lock with the hair pin, not that he knew how. So he was left with the window. He stared up at it, assessing. If he could get up there and break it or push it open, he could fit through. It wasn't horribly high, but it was above his head and well out of reach. He chewed on his bottom lip as he examined the wall below the window. Rough stone blocks formed the surface. He might be able to climb up.

It was slow going. Years had passed since he'd last climbed trees, which had been the total of his climbing experience. The stone was damp and he kept slipping, adding bruises to his body and scrapes to his hands. Every time he got close, he wasn't able to get the window open while holding himself up with one hand. He ached and he was tired and he wanted Lysander. And he couldn't imagine how no one had heard him yet. But he wasn't going to give up.

He took a moment to catch his breath and use his Talent just a bit to ease the scrapes on his palms. Then he looked up at the window again and nearly shrieked when he saw a face there. He jumped backward, pressing a hand to his galloping heart as the figure in the window rubbed at the grime there with a handkerchief. As the glass became marginally cleaner, he frowned. It couldn't be...

"Sascha?" That was definitely his sister's voice

"Inna?" He stepped closer, peering up at her. "What are you doing here?"

"Me? I think that question is better asked of you." She spoke just loudly enough for him to hear through the broken bits of the window.

"I'll explain another time." He hoped he had the opportunity. "But you shouldn't be here. It isn't safe."

"It isn't safe for you either. They told us to stay in our bedchambers, but I wanted to know what was going on, and I heard them talking about you." Tears clogged her voice. "I needed to know if it was true."

Sascha didn't want to know what she'd heard. More, he didn't want her to have heard it.

"And I guess it is. We have to get you out of there."

"You have to get back inside before someone sees you. I don't want you to be hurt." Just the thought of the people who'd taken him finding her made his blood run cold. He couldn't believe they'd let her go back home safe after seeing him here.

"I don't want you to be hurt either," she said with the stubbornness she'd never grown out of. "Where's the door?"

He doubted she was strong enough to move whatever they'd barred the door with. And he didn't want her seen— every moment she was out there terrified him. "Can you get the window open? I can climb up."

"Will you be able to fit?" The frown was obvious in her voice, even through the murky glass. "Let me try."

Sascha couldn't see what she was doing, her body blocking the light. He almost told her to find a rock and break the rest of the glass, but he worried about the noise. It felt like hours as he waited, berating himself for putting her in danger, expecting someone to grab her and jerk her away at any moment, but likely only minutes had passed by the time the rickety window came loose in her hands and swung outward.

Inna stuck her head into the open space, and even in the shadows, he could see the flash of her grin—or maybe he just remembered that triumphant curve of lips. "Hurry."

She shouldn't have had to tell him. He jumped into motion, reminding himself to be careful as he climbed—so close to freedom, he couldn't fall. With the window open, he was able to grab for purchase outside as he continued to push up with his legs. Inna held the window open with one hand and gripped the back of his jacket with her other, pulling with all her strength. An indeterminate and exhausting time later, he was through and flopped over onto his back on the grass to catch his breath for a brief instant. Then he hauled himself up and caught Inna's hand, tugging her with him as he jogged deeper into the cover of the trees.

Once they were out of sight, he stopped and turned to her. She was a bit wild-eyed but otherwise calm, and he pulled her to him and into a tight hug. "Thank you."

"Of course. As if I would leave you there. But..." She pulled away enough to look into his eyes. "Mother and Father said you were going to be killed, and they didn't seem to care. How could they... I don't understand."

"I'm not sure I understand either, even though I know why." And he still wouldn't let himself feel anything or he would fall apart and he couldn't because he wasn't out of danger. "I promise I'll explain everything, but not now, not when they could discover I'm gone and come looking. Can you get back into your bedchamber without anyone seeing you?"

"Yes, but I think I should stay with you. How are you going to get away?" She glanced down. "You don't even have both shoes."

"I'm aware. But I'm not going to try to get very far. I'm going to hide and wait for Lys—the king to get here."

"The king?" she exclaimed in a whisper. "Why is the king coming?"

"He's coming to find me and get me back." Best not to mention everything that would likely happen to their family.

"But why? Wait, get you back?" She shook her head. "I don't understand."

"I know. It's a long story, and I will tell you, I promise. But get yourself safe for now."

She hesitated, reluctance and that stubbornness all over her face, but she ultimately nodded. "All right. Be careful."

"You too."

After another brief embrace, Sascha watched as she slipped away through the trees, back toward the house, hoping she was able to get there unseen. Then he shook himself. He needed to move—they were sure to find him if he stayed here, so close to where he'd been held. He glanced around, taking a precious moment to orient himself. Sascha had played in these woods as a child and rambled through them as much as he was allowed when he got older, so he knew places to hide. But his siblings did as well. It didn't appear as if his sisters were involved in their parents' plotting, but would they reveal their old hiding spots if pressed? What about his brothers?

Sascha had thought he would be safe in one of those old hiding places until Lysander arrived, but now he wondered. What if his siblings divulged the locations, not realizing why they were being asked, and he was found? Sascha believed Lysander would come, but how long would it take him to learn where he was? Of course, his soldiers would arrive at some point soon even without Lysander—Lysander wouldn't call off his plans to apprehend the conspirators because Sascha had been taken, nor would Sascha expect him to. So, all he had to do was remain out of the hands of his abductors or his parents until either Lysander or his soldiers arrived.

Right. Easy.

Well, he was going to give it everything he had.

Deciding to avoid the spots he'd hidden or played with his siblings when they were children, he set off through the woods. He walked as quietly as he could, trying to avoid stepping on anything that would make noise. Or that would hurt his feet too much. Staying fairly close seemed to be a good idea—Sascha didn't want to miss the arrival of Lysander or his soldiers—even though everything in him screamed to run far away.

But if he did, how would he know when he'd been rescued?

It seemed more logical to stay near the house but out of sight. He paused and closed his eyes for moment—let him not be making the wrong choice. Carefully, as swiftly as he dared, he picked his way in a wide circle that would take him to the other side of the house, nearer the road where the woods were even thicker. He could only hope he could conceal himself there. He hadn't quite made it when a shout went up back the way he'd come. Sascha froze, a gasp sticking in his throat. Had they discovered he was gone? Had they found Inna? More shouts followed, and though he couldn't quite make out the words, he had to assume they'd noticed his escape. He could only hope Inna had made it back to the house unseen.

Sascha cursed silently, not letting the words loose as much as he wanted to. They probably knew he was gone, but they hadn't found him yet. He wished he knew where Lysander's soldiers were coming from. He would go straight toward them right now. With no better ideas, he continued circling around the house toward the road. Perhaps if someone was passing, he could beg a ride to...somewhere. His uncle's home wasn't too far in a carriage or cart. He had no money to pay, but... Sascha's hands went to his ears; he didn't want to give up the earrings Lysander had given him, but if he had to use them, he would. However, only his left hand found the shape of the earring. The other was gone. Pain and anger stabbed through Sascha. A silly thing to be upset about in the midst of his current predicament, but he couldn't help it. He wanted the earring back, and if it was lost forever due to the actions of his kidnappers, he would be furious.

More shouting from the woods behind him, and he froze, listening hard. He had to keep moving. Sascha pulled the small knife from his pocket and drew the blade from its sheath, as he began walking again. Everything he was doing was ridiculous —he had no real plan and couldn't imagine what help the dagger would be, but he couldn't stop.

A shout came from much closer. "He's there! I see him!"

Sascha ran.

CHAPTER 27

Lysander, Felix, and Galina had met up with the soldiers tasked with apprehending Sascha's parents—and the rest of his family, though nothing pointed to involvement by his sisters—and apprised them of the situation. Even though they weren't meant to raid the house yet, Lysander refused to wait. Sascha was in danger—might be harmed or moved elsewhere if they delayed, and he wasn't willing to risk it. If this went smoothly, their plan wouldn't be ruined. Lysander believed that, but he was ready to burn everything down if it got him Sascha back.

They swooped in on the place where Sascha had grown up from the air. The soldiers knew their orders and would vary little from them, except with regard to Sascha's presence. Finding Sascha was paramount to Lysander, his only purpose in being there—after which, he could mete out punishment to all who were responsible for what happened to him. The soldiers weren't to protect Lysander, as much as Alan expected them to —they were to do what they'd been sent here to do while keeping watch for Sascha.

Lysander and Felix landed at the edge of some woods

behind the house. Most of the contingent landed as well, surrounding the house, but some kept to the air, watching for anyone trying to escape. Galina slid from Felix's back quickly and gracefully, vigilant even as her feet touched the ground. She didn't have the dragon Talent, but her magic was powerful, and she would defend them while they changed back into their human forms. He and Felix wasted no time doing so.

After he pulled his magic back in and stood as a man near the trees, Galina glanced at him. "Where do we start, Your Majesty? Would they be holding Sascha in the house?"

Before they'd set out, she'd remarked quite politely that perhaps it would be safer if he stayed behind, or back at least. That letting the soldiers do their job, which certainly included retrieving Sascha, would be safest for the king. He hadn't faulted her for the suggestions, but he hadn't followed them either.

His soldiers had already entered the house and were fanning out to search the outbuildings as well, as those above flew in wide circles. The truth was Lysander had no idea where Sascha was likely to be. They were on their own here, but with the three of them to search and a force of soldiers rounding up everyone else, they would find him. The house seemed as good a place as any to start, and he was about to say so when a young woman stepped slowly out from behind a tree.

She was undeniably one of Sascha's sisters. The cast of her features reminded him of Sascha, though her hair was more auburn and her eyes a paler blue. She watched them warily as she came closer, but she didn't stop. Galina and Felix tensed at Lysander's sides.

Sascha's sister finally stopped several paces away. "Are you really the king? Sascha said you'd come."

He seized on her second statement. "You've seen Sascha. Where is he?"

She jumped at his sharp tone and again at some yelling from inside the house, but she rallied quickly. "He was locked in a cellar, but I helped him get out. He told me to go back to the house while he hid in the woods. But I heard shouting just before you came. I think they might have found him."

"Do you know where he went?" Could he trust her? She might be lying; she might be part of this plot, though they'd seen no indication Sascha of that. Sascha had always spoken fondly of his sisters, which didn't mean she was telling the truth, but they had no other clues to Sascha's whereabouts.

"No, but the shouts were in that direction." She pointed into the trees, around the side of the house.

"Then that's where we're going to start looking." Lysander took off in the direction she'd indicated at a run. A glance back showed him Galina two paces behind and Felix and Sascha's sister not far behind her. Lysander didn't know if Sascha's sister had decided to follow herself or if Felix had dragged her along, but he was glad—he wanted her close just in case.

Lysander listened as he ran, alert for anything to point him in the right direction. He'd seen from the air that the woods covered a large area on this side of the house, and he hated to rely on luck that they'd stumble upon Sascha. He considered calling out for Sascha, wondered if it would make the situation worse if Sascha's pursuers were catching up to him...and then decided it didn't matter. He needed to know where Sascha was. He stopped running abruptly, steadied Galina as she nearly crashed into him, and called out loudly, "Sascha! Sascha!"

"Are you sure that's a good idea?" came Felix's slightly breathless question from behind him.

"Do you have a better one?"

"No, I don't." Felix called for Sascha this time.

Lysander yelled Sascha's name louder, then stopped to think about what to do next.

"Lysander?" Lysander's heart leaped at the sound of Sascha's voice. He ran again, toward Sascha's call, vaguely aware of Felix, Galina, and Sascha's sister following.

"Sascha, where are you?" It was a ridiculous question, one Sascha couldn't answer in a helpful way. But Lysander needed to know he was going in the right direction, and Sascha's voice was his only guide.

"I'm— Where are you?"

If fear wasn't still gripping him, Lysander might have laughed. "In the middle of these woods. Keep talking to me."

But Sascha didn't call out again. Lysander pushed himself to run faster, as fast as he could through the trees. He yelled for Sascha again, Felix lending his voice as well, but Sascha didn't answer them. Then, a wordless shout came from ahead of them. Other voices followed, but Lysander couldn't make out the words. There was a pained yelp and cursing and another shout, and Lysander's heart stopped. Then he burst through the trees into a small clearing.

Sascha stood across the clearing from him, his back against the wide trunk of a tree. Three people were advancing on him, more slowly than Lysander would've thought given their numerical advantage. But then he caught sight of the small dagger in Sascha's hand and the blood on the arm of the left-most attacker. A fierce pride filled Lysander at the sight.

"Your Majesty?" Galina said.

He gave a sharp nod. She lifted a hand and one of Sascha's attackers, the one closest to him, jerked back as if snagged by huge invisible hand. The other two turned at their compatriot's shout and saw them. Lysander drew his blade and threw himself into the fight.

SASCHA GRIPPED the dagger in his right hand and pressed himself back against the tree as Lysander, Galina, and Felix neatly defeated his pursuers with a combination of magic and physical force. He wanted to help, but, though he had a knife, he didn't know how to use it—that he'd injured one of them was luck more than anything, and he didn't delude himself into thinking he would've remained uncaptured or alive much longer. Staying out of the way seemed the best help he could give at this point. Even Felix—who stayed to the periphery of the fight —had the dragon Talent and didn't hesitate to use fire where he thought it would do the most good.

But Sascha had managed to escape from his prison and keep himself alive until rescue arrived. He'd give himself some credit for that, and resolve to learn how to defend himself now that it appeared he would live to marry Lysander.

He hadn't doubted he would, not really. Not for long.

When the kidnappers were on the ground, Lysander strode across the clearing to Sascha. Sascha dropped the dagger and threw himself into Lysander's arms. Lysander responded immediately, pulling Sascha in, lifting him so his toes left the ground as he was pressed to Lysander's chest. He let out a long shuddering sigh and buried his face in Lysander's neck, breathing him in. His body went suddenly limp and heavy, and his head was spinning. All he could do was tighten his arms around Lysander's shoulders and hold on. Lysander didn't seem to mind. He was holding Sascha firmly with no indication he meant to let go any time soon, and Sascha was just fine with that plan.

"Are you hurt?" Lysander asked after a few moments.

Sascha shook his head. Scrapes and bruises and sore feet, but those seemed trivial compared to what almost happened. What came out of his mouth without his control was even more trivial. "I lost one of my earrings and a shoe."

Not the earring. Those earrings were not trivialities.

Lysander let out a chuckle and pressed a kiss to his hair. "I have them both. We found them back at the castle."

"They were going to kill me." The words came out of his mouth without his conscious choice as well, but they needed to be said.

Lysander went utterly still, his arms banded around Sascha's waist. "Were they?"

"We should've killed them," Felix said, and Sascha raised his head sharply to see him over Lysander's shoulder. Dressed in more utilitarian clothing than Sascha had ever seen him wear, Felix stood over one of the prone figures. Felix narrowed his eyes and shifted his weight, almost as if he wanted to level a hard kick at the man on the ground.

"Have you always been so bloodthirsty?" Sascha asked.

"You're my brother in all ways but blood," Felix replied fiercely. "I protect my family."

Warmth filled Sascha at Felix's words, and tears pricked at his eyes. His brothers by blood might not care one bit for him, but Sascha had Felix and that was enough...better than enough.

"That one is my brother by blood," Sascha said with a jerk of his head to the man at Felix's feet. Seeing him among his pursuers had been more of a shock than it should have been. "But he isn't family anymore. You are, Felix."

Emotion swirled in Felix's eyes, then he glared down at Grigoriy and kicked him.

"I protect my family too," Lysander said as he turned and set Sascha gently on his feet. He didn't let go of Sascha, though, for which he was grateful. Sascha couldn't find the energy to be ashamed of how shaky he was, and standing on his own was something he didn't want to try quite yet. "They'll face the consequences for their actions, but we'll see what information we can get from them first."

"I suggest we have some of the soldiers take them into custody until they're more able to give us that information, Your Majesty. I have them secured." Galina stood in the middle of the clearing, the three unconscious bodies surrounding her. She looked as calm and collected as she did in the comfort of the castle. Barely a hair was out of place. Sascha—who felt as grimy and disheveled as he surely looked—wondered how that was possible, after he'd seen her fight both physically and with magic, but it wasn't his most pressing question. As if Galina read it on his face, or assumed they would all want to know, she said, "Magical bindings. They can't move until I release them."

"Good," Lysander said decisively.

Galina volunteered to fetch a few soldiers, who were apparently there already. Lysander assumed they would be finished in house—in which case, Sascha assumed they'd be looking for their king—and free to take these additional prisoners. Sascha leaned into Lysander as they waited. He'd wanted Lysander all day, and he would take his support and perhaps give him comfort as well. Lysander never let go, and sometimes Sascha thought he felt a fine tremor go through him. He snuggled even closer.

Felix walked over to them, smothering a few still smoldering patches of grass as he did. When he reached Sascha and Lysander, he bent and picked up the dagger he'd given Sascha what felt like a lifetime ago. "You kept it with you."

Sascha accepted it back from him. "I promised I would. I need to learn how to use it properly."

"You gave him the knife?" Lysander turned an inquiring look on Felix.

He shrugged gracefully. "It seemed like a good idea."

Lysander sighed. "I suppose it was. We'll make sure you can defend yourself, but I never want you to have to again."

"Agreed," Sascha answered placidly. Then someone else caught his eye. "Inna?"

She stood across the clearing, awkwardly twisting her hands in her skirt as she watched them. In the waning light, he could see the smudges of dirt on her clothes and strands of hair straggling out of her braid.

"Are you all right?" she asked, her voice shaking.

"Yes." It was true, mostly. "Are you?"

"Of course." She glanced furtively at Lysander and Felix, but she gave Sascha a small smile and stilled her hands. "Why wouldn't I be?"

"Well, a lot has happened today."

"Most of it to you."

Sascha couldn't argue with that, but Inna certainly had quite a bit to come to terms with.

"Sascha? Is this your sister?" Lysander asked from beside him.

"Oh, yes, I'm sorry." He wanted to know how Inna had come to be here, but he also needed to introduce her to Lysander. "Lysander, may I present my sister Inna?"

Inna dropped into a graceful curtsy. They'd all been trained well, their parents ever hopeful of making advantageous matches for their daughters and Sascha. The clan was prestigious and well-placed, and they weren't too far removed from the titled branch, so perhaps they weren't dreaming when they schemed, but Sascha could only be resentful at what they'd traded him for. Nevertheless, Inna was prepared well enough for an unexpected encounter with the king.

But how much of today's events had been something they could've expected?

"And this is Prince Felix." Sascha was bungling the proper way introductions should be done, but he couldn't remember the proper way now, and Lysander and Felix didn't seem upset. "Inna helped me escape from where they were holding me."

"She helped us find you," Lysander said. "For which I'm grateful."

He sounded wary despite his words, but Sascha understood —his family was conspiring against Lysander and Ivria. He had no guarantee Inna wasn't involved.

"You didn't go back to the house." Sascha wasn't asking a question, but she answered anyway.

"I didn't have the chance. All these dragons arrived, and then the king was there..." She shrugged a bit.

"As long as you're all right." He wanted to go to her and hug her, but fatigue dragged at him. The distance across the clearing seemed much longer than it was, and Lysander's body was firm and strong against his. He didn't want to let go, wasn't certain Lysander would let him.

"I'm all right. I just... I'm sorry, Your Majesty, I just don't understand." She bit her lip, a habit their parents had been trying to break her of for years, and glanced from Grigoriy on the ground to Sascha again. "What's going on, Sascha? Why did all those dragons come? Why were you locked up? Why were Mother and Father going to let them..."

Inna couldn't seem to continue, and Sascha didn't mind— he didn't need the reminder their parents were happy to let him be killed.

"What were your parents going to let them do?" Lysander asked quietly, though his voice vibrated with something intense.

Sascha swallowed and closed his eyes for an instant before opening them and bracing himself. "They were going to let them kill me. They had no objection. I overheard them."

Lysander's silence had a deadly quality to it. It was Felix

who spoke, carefully, each word precise. "Are you positive we can't just kill them all now, Lysander?"

"I'm tempted, but you and I both know the value of information." Lysander took a long breath. "They won't go unpunished for long."

Felix nodded sharply. Sascha tried to dredge up some feeling for his parents, some desire to plead for their lives, but he couldn't find any, not after all they'd done to him and tried to do to Lysander. Inna had drawn back against a tree trunk and was twisting her hands again.

Lysander took note of the change. "If you had no part in their plotting, then you have nothing to fear."

"I don't know what their plotting was, Your Majesty. Sascha?" She appeared close to tears, but they never fell.

The sound of footfalls on the forest floor had Sascha pausing, the snapping of twigs and rustling signifying several people not trying to be quiet as they walked. Galina's voice rising above it indicated she was returning with the promised soldiers. He had no time to explain to Inna, if he would even be allowed to. "I'll tell you as soon as I can. I promise."

He glanced up at Lysander who nodded slightly, letting him know he hadn't lied to her. With all the planning, with everything Lysander and the others had done to find the traitors and expose their plot, Sascha would not be the one to ruin everything now.

"All right," Inna replied quietly. She likely would have pushed more if Lysander wasn't there.

Galina strode into the clearing with the soldiers at her back. There was some relief on the faces of the soldiers to see Lysander and Felix well and whole, and Sascha thought, perhaps, him as well. Though he couldn't imagine he was anywhere near as important to them as their king.

"What's the situation?" Lysander asked Galina as she continued closer to them while the soldiers began dealing with the people on the ground. Felix drifted closer as well to hear her answer. A glance showed Sascha that his sister remained where she was, trying to make herself unnoticeable by shrinking into a tree.

"Everything is well in hand at the house. The family is being held inside and will be transported shortly." Galina glanced at Sascha, as if to gauge his reaction to the news, but she continued with hardly a pause. "The few servants have been found as well. They're currently doing a search of the outbuildings on foot and flying over once more."

"Thank you, Galina. It's time for us to get back. I want to know the situation elsewhere. And I want to get Sascha home and make sure he's all right."

Sascha glanced up to find Lysander watching him, the intense look in his eyes showing Sascha which of those things was more important to him. Warmth suffused him. Lysander had come for him himself in the middle of something so important to Ivria, and he was still most concerned about Sascha's well-being even though he could see Sascha wasn't seriously hurt—he would probably have nightmares, but he'd worry about them later, worry too about everything catching up with him and how he would react. For now, he had to be strong. Lysander had to turn his attention to the critical things happening today. Sascha didn't resent the man he loved for his duty and wanted to make sure he knew it.

"I'm all right. Do what you need to do." He spoke quietly but tried to put as much assurance into his voice as possible.

"I will, but part of what I need to do is take care of you." Lysander lifted Sascha's hand to his lips and pressed a kiss to his knuckles.

Sascha could do nothing but nod under the intensity of

Lysander's gaze. It still surprised him sometimes, to be loved so much by such a man. By a king who would put him first.

"Good. Let's go." He gestured and they began filing out of the clearing, leaving the soldiers to handle the prisoners.

Inna gave Sascha a wide-eyed look but didn't protest when Felix nudged her along to walk behind Galina. Sascha stayed at Lysander's side, despite an urge to go to his sister.

"What's going to happen to her now?" he asked in a low voice.

"They all have to be questioned," Lysander replied, his voice gentle. "No one believes she's involved, but we need to make sure, and we need to learn what they know or we'll never find the extent of this."

"I know."

"Your sisters will be taken care of."

"I know." He did; he trusted Lysander to make certain of it. "Thank you."

"No need to thank me." Lysander raised Sascha's hand to his lips again for another kiss. "They're your family."

"Not all of them, not anymore."

"No, not all of them, and you aren't beholden to them anymore. They have no power over you. You have power now." He rubbed Sascha's hand as they walked, his thumb passing over the ring Sascha was grateful not to have lost during the tumult of the day.

The words and the reminder—likely not meant as such—of the ring he wore and what it meant nearly stopped Sascha in his tracks. Lysander had removed him from his parents' influence months ago and given him the ability to decide his own future. Sascha had taken the opportunity and decided that, whatever else he did, he wanted to stay with Lysander. But now, he wasn't King's Concubine anymore. He was the king's intended, his future consort. It was a role he would have to learn and one he intended to fulfill to the best of his abilities. But he'd only thought of his love for Lysander and the duties of the position he was taking on as his husband. He hadn't considered the power it gave him.

Sascha straightened his spine, the realization giving him the motivation despite his fatigue. He had no idea if he even wanted to see his parents again, but he refused for them or anyone else to see him looking so defeated and exhausted. He wasn't defeated. He'd won. He'd lived. And he was happy, with Lysander, with the future that stretched out before them.

CHAPTER 28

When they emerged from the trees, Sascha glanced around the area behind the house. It bustled with people. The king's soldiers looked to have the entire household outside, separating out the servants from the family. Would they all be taken from here to be questioned? Or were they only making certain the house was empty? Sascha would ask Lysander, but now was not the time.

Galina turned back to them. "I'll take Inna over to the rest of the family."

Lysander nodded and thanked her, but Inna turned away from the scene in the courtyard to search out Sascha, her eyes wide and confused and a little frightened. "Sascha? What's going on?"

Sascha squeezed Lysander's hand briefly, then went to his sister. "Our parents have been involved in a plot against the king."

She gasped, and her gaze darted to Lysander before flicking over her shoulder to their family.

He took her hands. "It's going to be all right. The soldiers need to question everyone, but just answer honestly."

"What's going to happen to us?"

"If you weren't involved, nothing. Lysander and I will make sure you're fine. Trust us. Go with them for now and answer their questions." He gathered her into a tight hug. "I promise I'll see you soon."

He caught Galina's eyes over Inna's shoulder. She nodded, and he took it as reassurance. Sascha drew back and stared into Inna's eyes, trying to will her to believe that all would be well for her. He very carefully hadn't mentioned what would happen to their parents or their brothers, if they too were involved.

"All right," Inna said quietly. "Soon?"

"As soon as possible." He gave her one more hug. "Tell the girls to be truthful as well, and I'll see you all soon."

Inna nodded and let Galina lead her away. Galina took her not to their parents but to their younger sisters, who were standing together separated by a small but significant distance from the rest of the family. Had the soldiers positioned them that way, or had the girls? Yelena and Roza immediately pulled Inna in close. He couldn't hear them, but he could imagine their words were expressions of concern and fear. He did hear his mother when she snapped out his sister's name and demanded to know where she'd been.

It was obvious Inna didn't know how to answer their mother even before her eyes sought him out across the court-yard. Unfortunately, his mother followed her gaze and saw him too. "Sascha! What are you doing there?"

Sascha could envision his appearance—bedraggled and dirty, scraped skin and tangled hair, missing a shoe and an earring—but he stood a fraction straighter. He was not perfectly turned out, but he was the king's soon-to-be consort, and he would act the part even when he didn't look it.

He stared at his mother, unwavering. "Why do you ask, Mother? Surprised I'm still alive?"

She flinched, and he took some perverse satisfaction in provoking the reaction. He'd done everything his parents had asked of him, fit himself into the role they'd expected of him his whole life. And they'd chosen to use him, not only to further their own interests but also to further a plot against the king. They hadn't even cared when they learned he was about to be murdered.

They weren't his family anymore.

Lysander was next to him, but he wasn't trying to stop Sascha from speaking. He would let Sascha say whatever he wanted to his mother, Sascha knew that. Knew also, from the tension in his body, that Lysander would jump to his defense the moment he needed it. Sascha leaned closer to him, because he wanted to feel that support. Lysander's hand came to rest low on his back, radiating warmth.

Sascha lifted his head a fraction more. When he spoke, he pitched his voice to carry clearly across the courtyard. "I know what you did, Mother. I know what you were plotting and how you used me. And I know you were going to let them kill me without a single regret."

Her face contorted with rage, the change so quick and stark Sascha had to work not to jump back. "Sascha, what did you do? You've ruined everything. You always were far too selfish."

Sascha had never been anything of the kind, though he'd been told he was often enough. He'd done all he could for his family, accepting the role they'd planned for him, never protesting. He considered interrupting his mother's rant to deny it, but what would it matter? She wouldn't listen to him. Sascha turned to Lysander. "Can we go home now?"

Lysander curled his arm more tightly around Sascha. "Yes, we can."

Before they could leave, Lysander had to speak with the leader of the squadron, though he did so impatiently and grudgingly. He wanted to bundle Sascha up and away, to take him home without another word, but Sascha's abduction had caused complications in the situation that needed to be dealt with, at least superficially, before they returned home.

And didn't Lysander like that Sascha thought of him and the castle as home, not this place?

He sent someone off to find a cloak or coat for Sascha while he spoke to the captain. His kidnappers hadn't spared a thought for his comfort, but Lysander wanted him adequately protected against the chill that would come with flying in the night air. Because they would fly home. He didn't want to stay here for the night or spend extra time on the road to return to Wyndward, for both their sakes.

Sascha stayed by his side, not even flinching at his parents' and brothers' constant outraged protests. When the noise turned into shocked exclamations, Lysander assumed they'd learned he would soon be marrying Sascha. At the edge of his vision, he could see them staring, but Lysander refused to give them his attention. The soldiers moved to quiet them quickly when they began to yell for Sascha, but to Lysander's utter shock, they argued with the soldiers and their demands for Sascha to go over there immediately became increasingly strident. A baby in the arms of a woman standing beside one of the brothers wailed, but it didn't stopped anyone from yelling. Sascha remained stoic at his side, but Lysander slid inexorably into fury.

How dare they? How dare they believe they had the right to demand a thing after all they'd done?

Lysander turned and roared, "Enough."

Across the courtyard, Sascha's parents and brothers went silent. The baby kept shrieking.

"You presume to speak in such a way in front of your king, to his betrothed?" But of course they would, since they thought nothing of working to undermine their king.

Sascha's hand came to rest on his arm before he could say anything else. He whispered, "Don't. They aren't worth even a moment of your attention. Leave them to the trouble they've brought upon themselves."

Lysander nodded sharply, though he continued to glare at them for a moment longer. They hadn't heard what Sascha said —did they believe he was interceding on their behalf with Lysander? If so, they would be unpleasantly surprised.

Felix came to his side, a cloak in his arms. Presumably, the soldier sent to find one had delivered it to him—or he'd taken custody of it in the middle of the chaos. Lysander accepted it from him with a quiet word of thanks. He shook it out and held it open for Sascha, who turned and allowed him to place it over his shoulders. Sascha fastened it himself as he faced Lysander once more. The cloak swallowed Sascha—it probably belonged to his father or one of his brothers, all taller and broader than Sascha was—but it was the correct weight to keep him warm in the air on the way back to the castle.

As Felix handed Sascha a pair of gloves, Lysander turned his attention back to the captain. "We're returning to Wyndward. We'll take your report upon your return."

"Yes, Your Majesty." The captain bowed and backed away before beginning to call out orders to his soldiers, making sure Lysander and Felix and the guards returning with them had a clear space to transform. Lysander wasted no time doing so. He pulled on his magic, letting it rise up to fill and transform him. When he opened his eyes again, his gaze was fixed on Sascha, now much farther below him. He bent his head down to meet Sascha's outstretched hand, letting him caress Lysander's jaw briefly.

"Time to go," Lysander told him, and Sascha nodded.

Lysander only gave the briefest part of his attention to Felix not far off, also transformed, and Galina getting herself settled on his back. Only enough to make certain they were ready to go. The rest of his focus was on Sascha. Lysander crouched, and the captain gave Sascha a hand up to help him onto Lysander's back. The man did not visibly react to Lysander's decision to carry Sascha himself. Lysander didn't care what anyone thought. Keeping Sascha close was necessary.

Once Sascha and Galina were securely seated, Lysander leaped into the night sky, using powerful legs to push off the stones of the courtyard. Felix followed a second later, along with their guards. In the air, Lysander turned unerringly for home. The guards fanned out around them, alert for threats. While he and Felix could defend themselves with fire and claws if necessary, Sascha was more vulnerable. Even Galina, with all her magic, could fall during a fight. Best that the guards were with them to watch for trouble. Lysander didn't expect it—at Wyndward, only Thalia and Alan knew he'd left, and Lysander trusted no one would learn of his absence or destination from them—but better safe.

They flew steadily, arrowing toward home. Night had fallen long ago, but the moon was full. Despite their fatigue, Lysander didn't want to stop and he thought the others agreed. Lysander wanted Sascha home and safe as quickly as possible, so they pressed on. When the castle came into view in the distance, something inside of him relaxed slightly.

Almost there. Almost home.

He landed lightly on the tower, leaving room for Felix to do the same beside him. The soldiers circled above them, still watching for danger. Lysander was more worried about danger inside, but he also trusted Alan to make their rooms as secure as possible. As if the thought had summoned him, Alan stepped out of the door into the castle with Thalia following. Sascha slid from Lysander's back and moved just far enough from him that he could transform. He let the magic flow through him, wanting to push it, to force it to work more quickly, but he made himself relax and it was mere seconds until he was standing as a man again. Even that felt too long.

Sascha moved back to his side once he finished, and Lysander put an arm around his waist, drawing him closer as they were joined by Thalia, Alan, Felix, and Galina. Pure relief filled Thalia's face.

"You found him." Thalia smiled brightly, though her eyes were weary. She pulled Sascha into a hug with no regard for Lysander's arm hold on him. "Are you all right, Sascha? Should I call for a healer?"

Sascha shook his head slightly when she pulled back. "I'm fine."

If Thalia's expression was anything to go by, she wasn't convinced, and Lysander wasn't entirely certain he believed Sascha either, but he'd check over every inch of him soon enough. "What's the news here?"

"All is going as planned," Alan said. "I've increased security on the royal apartments and have started quietly questioning the staff."

"It won't stay quiet," Felix put in.

"No, but it has to be done," Alan said firmly. "We need to make certain there are no other traitors here in the castle. I will question the steward again, but I'd like more information from the others we've taken into custody today first."

"Good work," Lysander told him. "We'll have more details as the reports from the squadrons come in." Lysander squeezed Sascha's waist gently, to reassure himself he was still there. "For now, I'm going to take Sascha inside and make sure he's all right."

"I'm fine," Sascha repeated.

"Indulge me."

Sascha studied him for a moment, then smiled fondly and nodded.

The others took Lysander's words for the dismissal they were. Alan and Galina bowed briefly and walked inside. Felix came to Lysander and Sascha and tugged Sascha into a tight hug. Felix whispered something into Sascha's ear that Lysander didn't catch, and Sascha nodded. Then Felix released Sascha and stepped back. He reached out and squeezed Lysander's arm briefly, but he didn't linger. Once Thalia had hugged Sascha again and bid them good night, they went inside together. If the voices filtering out from the stairs were anything to go by, they caught up to the others quickly.

Lysander took a long breath of the crisp night air, grateful for these people in his life he could trust implicitly, people he could lean on and rely on.

He looked at Sascha, who was staring up at the swath of stars in sky and shivering. "Let's go in."

Lysander needed to coddle Sascha, to cherish him and lavish love and care on him. He always did, but the urge was stronger tonight. Sascha needed to know he was safe and loved, that he was home. He'd been strong and brave and Lysander was so proud of him. Now he wanted to give him comfort.

They went directly into the bathing room. A steaming bath waited for them—Thalia most likely ordered the bath prepared when they were sighted approaching. More gratitude welled up in Lysander, for the consideration and for the confidence that he would find Sascha.

"Oh, that looks wonderful," Sascha sighed. He reached for the fastenings of the borrowed cloak, but Lysander brushed his hands away, taking over the task. The fond smile came to Sascha's lips again, and he didn't protest.

Lysander undressed him with care, removing each piece of clothing with gentle, caressing hands. He discarded the clothing in a heap on the floor, certain Sascha wouldn't want to even see it again—and doubting any of it would be fit to be worn again anyway. The single earring Sascha still wore, he carefully removed and stowed in his pocket with its mate. Sascha curled the fingers of the hand wearing his ring in, so Lysander left it where it was.

"In you go." He took Sascha's hand and helped him step into the large tub—whether Sascha needed the aid or not, the action soothed Lysander's protective instincts.

Sascha allowed himself to be steadied as he climbed into the tub. "Aren't you going to join me?"

Lysander returned his smile at the flirtatious words, glad beyond words Sascha was able to utter them. "Not this time, but I am going to help you get clean."

Sascha's smile quirked a bit. "I am generally able to wash myself."

"I'm aware. Let me take care of you." He leaned forward and kissed Sascha's lips lightly. When he drew back, Sascha nodded.

As Sascha settled into the water, Lysander rolled his sleeves up and knelt. The soap Sascha preferred, with its delicate floral scent, sat with a cloth in the dish beside the tub. Lysander took up both and proceeded to wash the dirt and sweat and fear of the day from Sascha's skin. Each pass he made with the cloth, he tried to imbue with all the love he had for Sascha, with how he wanted to cherish and protect him. Sascha relaxed into the water more and more, his eyes fluttering closed, a dreamy smile coming to his lips, as Lysander tended to him.

They didn't speak as Lysander bathed him and washed his hair and worked the tangles from the long red locks. They would speak—there was much they had to talk about and much Sascha would probably need to say after his parents' actions—but unless Sascha wanted to talk now, it could wait. Let Sascha be warm and comfortable and comforted before he had to dredge up his feelings and his pain.

When the water began to cool, Lysander urged Sascha up and out of the tub with a few quiet words and gentle guiding hands. He dried him with a soft towel and wrapped him in the velvet dressing gown left waiting for him. Lysander carefully drew Sascha close and kissed him softly, running his hands up and down Sascha's arms, dragging the soft velvet with him. Then he linked his fingers with Sascha's. "Let's get you to bed."

Sascha nodded and walked with him into their bedchamber. Lysander pulled back the blankets on the large bed and waited for Sascha to climb in, before smoothing the covers over him.

"Please tell me you're going to join me in here," Sascha said, with a smile just on the edge of mischief. Lysander's heart lifted seeing it.

"I am. As soon as I clean up." He dropped a kiss on Sascha's damp hair. "I'll only be a moment."

"You could be in bed with me now if you'd shared the bath," Sascha called after him as he returned to the bathing room. Lysander didn't answer. Mostly because Sascha was right.

He got himself out of his clothing and cleaned up quickly. Lysander's only concern at the moment was returning to the man he loved and continuing to give him whatever comfort he needed. Sascha didn't appear as shaken by his kidnapping as Lysander feared he would be. He might be hiding it or suppressing it. Or maybe he was fine, though Lysander couldn't imagine anyone would be. Whatever happened—if Sascha needed to fall apart, whatever Sascha needed—Lysander would be there.

Sascha was curled under the blankets when Lysander returned to the bedchamber. Did some tension bleed from his body when Lysander reappeared? He'd been taken from their own apartments; Lysander would have to make utterly sure nothing like it could ever happen again and he'd have to reassure Sascha of his safety until he believed it. Lysander wouldn't let anything happen to him ever again.

Lysander climbed into bed beside Sascha and wrapped his arms around him when he crowded close. "Do you want to tell me more of what happened?"

"Can it wait until morning?" Sascha looked up at him with large blue eyes. "Or do you need to know tonight so that you can..."

"No," he said when Sascha's voice trailed off. "We know who did this, and we have them. The details aren't important tonight if you don't want to talk about them."

Sascha nodded and rested his head against Lysander's shoulder, and they were both quiet for a while. Lysander breathed in the scent of Sascha's hair and let his own tension fade. "I was so scared when we realized you'd been taken." Some would say he shouldn't admit to fear, that in his position, he shouldn't ever divulge a weakness. Lysander thought such a thing was ridiculous, especially when the person he was telling was Sascha. Maybe he should've kept it to himself to avoid upsetting Sascha, but he had to trust him about that too. "Just terrified. They took you from right here where you should've been safe."

Sascha burrowed closer to Lysander and tightened his arms around him, but this time it was to comfort Lysander. "I was scared too, but I knew you'd find me. I knew you'd come for me. I just had to keep myself alive until you got there."

"So you ran off into the woods to hide with only a dagger to defend yourself." He couldn't help the smile despite the horror at the thought of it. His courageous Sascha.

"It seemed like a good idea at the time."

"It was." He drew Sascha up and kissed him. "I'm proud of you and so grateful. You're very brave."

"I'm not." Sascha shook his head before Lysander could argue. He threaded a hand into Lysander's hair. "Kiss me again, and make me forget about everything for a while. Everything but you."

"I can do that."

After, when they were tangled together, Sascha warm and heavy and relaxed where he lay on Lysander's chest, Lysander asked, "Are you all right?"

Perhaps he shouldn't have brought it up, after Sascha asked him to help him forget, but he had know after the abduction, after the revelation of just how far Sascha's family would go... Lysander had to know.

"No, I'm not," Sascha said quietly. "But I will be."

EPILOGUE

And Sascha would be. His kidnapping, his family's betrayal wouldn't break him. He wouldn't let it—the people he loved wouldn't let it.

But that didn't mean the following days weren't difficult.

Nightmares plagued his sleep. Of being trapped in that room, of being unable to escape, of not being rescued in time. The jeering faces of his kidnappers, his parents, his brothers. He woke in a cold sweat each time, sometimes with a scream on his lips. His breath came short and his hands shook and... Lysander was always there, holding him, murmuring words he didn't always comprehend but always felt the love and comfort in.

During the day, he startled at the smallest noise. He hadn't realized how bad it would be, knowing that he'd been taken from his home with no one the wiser. The place in the castle where he had been the most comfortable was now a source of fear and anxiety. Lysander and his family were there for him then too. He wasn't left alone in the days immediately following his rescue. If Lysander couldn't be with him, Felix or Thalia was and the children showered him with their love and attention. Lysander showed Sascha the escape tunnel used to take him out of Wyndward, and they watched together as it was bricked up. After a while, he began talking about what had happened, how he felt. And after a while, it started to get better.

Lysander held nothing back from Sascha when it came to the arrests and what they found out. Once, Lysander would have kept Sascha out of the meetings and away from the information—at first, he hadn't been trusted and then it just wasn't his place. But everything had changed. Sascha had both Lysander's trust and love, and they would be married. He would be King's Consort and he promised himself he would learn to fulfill that role, to be the best he could at it. That started by listening to everything Lysander told him, by attending every meeting he was invited to, by poring over the information they received. He didn't have the experience the others had, but he would learn.

The plan Lysander had set in motion went surprisingly smoothly, despite the deviation due to Sascha's kidnapping. The people taken into custody were being questioned methodically, by Alan or Galina or one of Alan's people, and that information was added to what they knew. Some—spouses or family members of conspirators like Sascha's sisters—were let go; others were held. Sascha tried not to think about what would follow for them, what the punishment for treason was, but he would stand by Lysander through it, just as steadfastly as Lysander supported him. Lysander was used to dealing with difficult things as king, but being king didn't make those things any less difficult or him any less of a flesh and blood man—and what he dealt with now was far beyond anything he'd had to in the past. Sascha had always tried to be a comfort to him, but the knowledge of Lysander's feelings for him, as much as his new status as the king's betrothed, gave him more security to stand at his side in public as well as private. Lysander wouldn't have to handle everything alone anymore, wouldn't have to worry about what anyone thought of him for leaning because he could always come to Sascha. Sascha would give Lysander all the strength he could, just as Lysander did for him.

What really worried them was that they hadn't caught everyone. Jannik's son was still missing; Triana was giving them all the information she knew that might help locate him, as well as everything about her husband's father. The more they questioned, the more they discovered, the more they wondered if there were others involved and unknown. But Ivria knew about the plot now, and the people were horrified and angry. The conspirators had been, by and large, nobility or in the upper ranks of the clans—it would probably be a long time before Lysander, Sascha, Felix, and Thalia would be able to trust that anyone who came to court was as loyal as they said they were, but the overwhelming support of the country went some way to reassuring them.

Lysander announced their betrothal two weeks after the kidnapping. It gave the kingdom something joyful after the revelation of treason, and an air of excitement grew as the wedding festivities drew closer. There were those who were skeptical of Lysander's decision to marry him. No one said anything to Sascha, but a few of the clan heads brought their misgivings to Lysander and Felix heard plenty—which continued to baffle Sascha. As Felix and Lysander were cousins and not estranged, how could people not realize anything said to or around Felix would make it back to Lysander? Felix, of course, did share everything he heard with Lysander and Sascha. Some complaints certainly stemmed from resentment that Lysander hadn't picked someone highly placed in the clan of one of the complainers. It had been anticipated that when he finally married he would pick someone from a prominent branch of the clans—and Lysander had anticipated resentment and jealousy.

The more serious problem with many of them was that Sascha's parents had committed treason, and though Lysander didn't show them any more mercy than he did other conspirators and though Sascha showed no feeling for them, people still talked and speculated and expressed their suspicions of Sascha. The whispers worried him, made him wonder if he was a liability to Lysander at a time when he needed to be strong, but before Sascha could get too twisted up over it, Florestan stepped in. While condemning his parents' actions, his uncle took in Sascha's sisters once they were, predictably, exonerated, and then adopted both them and Sascha, though he was legally an adult. Both by words and actions, Florestan loudly proclaimed his belief in their innocence. Lysander fumed at the aspersions leveled at Sascha by some, but he held back his angry reaction, agreeing with Felix and Florestan that the adoption made sense. It separated him from his parents and elevated him to a place many found more acceptable for the king's betrothed.

When word of the kidnapping filtered out, sympathy turned toward Sascha. He thought Felix might have directed that information the way he wanted it to go, but he didn't ask. It was enough that the talk about Sascha's suitability quieted. Sascha knew quite well Lysander would've married him anyway—and wouldn't have taken it kindly if Sascha had tried to tell him they shouldn't wed, which he was too selfish to do—but it eased Sascha's mind that the decision probably wouldn't hurt Lysander in a time that was already precarious.

Sometimes, he marveled that Lysander had fallen in love with him, that he wanted to marry him. He remembered himself not all that long ago in a carriage ready to meet an uncertain fate with a man who would've treated him nothing like Lysander did. And then he let those memories go, put them aside in favor of a much better present.

Because today was his wedding day.

Sascha had woken uncharacteristically early to Lysander's arm snug around his waist, his chest firmly pressed to Sascha's back. It was just perfect. Sascha would've been perfectly content to stay right there, listening to Lysander's steady breaths, wrapped in Lysander's warmth. But anticipation and anxiety about the day's ceremony fizzed in the back of his mind —he wanted everything to go as it was supposed to, so the beginning of their marriage would reflect well on both of them. The jitteriness drove him from the cozy bed.

He ended up in the sitting room at the window, gazing out at the clear blue sky over the sparkling water of the lake, the vibrant green of the trees and the summer flowers. There had been fairs and performances for days in town, the people celebrating the marriage of their king. The court was celebrating as well with a round of parties and entertainments. Romilly had returned yesterday, exhausted from the long journey—much of it done at night by wing to get them back to Ivria in time for the wedding. Sascha had pushed them into first a bath and then bed, letting them sleep through last night's party, knowing they needed the rest far more than anything else. Romilly would be at the wedding today as one of Sascha's attendants, their presence filling Sascha with joy and gratitude.

He'd done all he could in the planning and preparation for this day. He had to believe all would be well.

All felt well.

There would be challenges ahead, and he would have to be strong to be the consort Lysander needed and deserved. He didn't delude himself into thinking everything would be easy— they would likely be dealing with the repercussions of the treasonous conspiracy for quite a while. The thought of what lay ahead had anxiety rising inside him, but he wanted a life with Lysander. He couldn't walk away now anymore than he could when they first met, though for very different reasons. Sascha was where he needed to be.

The thought was steadying.

An arm slid around his waist and lips brushed his temple. Sascha smiled, then shivered as Lysander kissed him again, this time on the side of his neck, his closely trimmed beard tickling the sensitive skin there.

"Good morning," Lysander rumbled.

"Good morning, love."

"You're up early. Is everything all right?"

Sascha snuggled into Lysander's arms. "It is now."

ALSO BY ANTONIA AQUILANTE

About Antonia Aquilante

Antonia Aquilante is an author of LGBTQ fantasy romance and a copy editor/proofreader. She has been imagining characters and plots for as long as she can remember, and at the age of twelve, decided she would be a writer when she grew up. After many years and a few career detours, she returned to that original plan. Her stories have changed over the years, but one thing has remained consistent—they all end in happily ever after.

Find out more about Antonia:
www.antoniaaquilante.com